LUCAS

A PRESTON BROTHERS NOVEL

A More Than Series Spin-Off

For My Boys

PROLOGUE

LUCAS

THE BLOOD on my clothes is still damp, but the blood on my hands is not.

At some point between the hospital and this waiting cell at the police station, it managed to become nothing more than red flakes on my palms and fingers. I can feel it on my face, too, mixing with the tears now soaked into my skin. I wonder how the others in the cell see me—barely a man, huddled in the corner of the room, bloodstained tux, and a missing shoe—and I imagine, for a moment, the thoughts and stories that run through their minds.

Maybe I was in a wreck, drunk.

Maybe I was in a fight, drunk.

Maybe I tried to kill someone.

I try not to think about it for too long, the repercussions of my actions beyond my mental capacity. So I stare down at the floor in front of me, the sole of my single bloody shoe print leading to where I sit, like a road map to my demise, and I think about the only thing that makes sense.

I think about *her*.

And I wonder if I'll ever get the image, *the feel*, of her limp body in my arms out of my system.

SIXTEEN CLICKS.

Eight seconds.

That's how long it took me to realize I'd been in love with her for four years.

Eight, life-changing seconds.

It's also the exact length of time it took to lose her.

PAST | LOIS

"It's nice that your boss wanted to have us over," I murmured to my dad who was sitting next to me, hands on the steering wheel as we drove through a new town we were supposed to call home.

After the divorce, he'd wanted a fresh start, and that meant getting as far away from my mom as possible. If he was disappointed he only managed to get a job a mere four hours away, he never mentioned it. But he assured me it was a good job, one that paid well for a site foreman. And though the town was a lot smaller than where I'd spent my early years, he said it was a good place to live out the rest of my childhood until I eventually left him for greener pastures—college and such. Those were his words, not mine. Besides, I was only eleven at the time. Old enough to have an opinion, but still too young to care either way. "So what's your boss like? It's Tom, right?"

Dad nodded as he checked his side mirror before changing lanes. "He seems nice enough. He's tall. And his wife's tiny. Her name's Kathy."

My dad's one of those men who seemed like they never aged. Only he wasn't ever young looking. He'd always had a beard that was scattered with grays, always had dark circles around his eyes as if he was tired *all* the time. But what stood out the most is the way he always looked worried—as if the world was going to end and he was the only one in on the secret. When things got worse with Mom, the worry turned to stress, turned to fear, and slowly turned to acceptance. I think for him the acceptance was the worst part of all—knowing and *believing* that it was just him and me against the world. Then he got offered this job. I don't think I'd seen him smile since before *The Breaking Point*: when my mom threw a chair at his head.

He nudged my side with his elbow and smiled down at me. "Guess how many kids they have?" he asked.

I shrugged, pushing aside my thoughts. "How many?"

"Guess, Lo," he said, his voice filled with anticipation.

"I don't know. Four?"

"More."

"Five?"

He shook his head.

I sat higher in my seat, my eyes wide, and asked, "*Six?*"

He nodded, thank God. Any more and my eyes would've fallen out of my head. "Yep. Five boys and one girl. The girl's the oldest. And all their names start with L. See, *Lois*? You'll fit right in."

I looked down at my flip-flops, denim shorts and t-shirt that had a picture of a cat and the words *Look at meow. I'm getting pay purr.* "Maybe I should've worn a pretty dress or something. Tried to impress them, you know?"

It took a while for him to answer, and when he did, the words resonated so loudly that even now, six years later, I still hear them loud and clear. "You impress people with your mind. With your kind heart and humble attitude. And while you're a beautiful girl, your looks or the way you dress shouldn't be the reason people are impressed by you. And when you're older and boys start to notice you, I want you to remember that. Because if it's *only* your looks they're attracted to, then they're not the one for you, Lo. You can do better. You *will* do better."

That speech alone is reason enough as to why I'd chosen to move away with him instead of staying with my mother.

"Unless it's Justin Timberlake," I joked, trying to hide my true reaction to his words. "Then he can like me for my looks, right?"

Dad chuckled under his breath. "You can *totally* do better than Justin Timberlake."

"I think not!" I said seriously. *JT was no joke.*

He laughed, a sound so pure that at that moment I almost hated my mother for trying so hard to take that away from him. Yeah, I was young, but I wasn't blind. Or deaf. And though I'm sure I didn't know *everything* that went on with them, I knew enough.

I went back to thinking about Tom and Kathy and their army of children. "Dad…"—I looked at him sideways—"are you sure you want this job? These people might be in some weird sister-wife cult. You never know… one day you're working construction for him and the next you're asking people to drink the Kool-Aid."

He playfully rolled his eyes. "I should monitor your TV watching more. Enough true crime shows for you." He slowed the car to a stop. "I think we're here." Then he leaned over the steering wheel to look at the number on the mailbox. It was basically all you could see from the street. That, and a long gravel driveway surrounded by endless trees. "Yeah. This is it," he said to himself, turning the car to creep slowly between the open gates on either side of the driveway. "Wow…" he whispered, and *wow* it was.

It was as if time slowed when the Preston house came into view. Beautiful, white two-story house, dark shutters on the windows and a wraparound porch. There was also a detached garage with an apartment above, and the yard was kept, neat and trimmed to perfection. It was the kind of house you'd see in magazines. I guess we shouldn't have been surprised considering Tom Preston owned the largest construction company on this side of North Carolina, but still… I'd never seen anything so grand before. At least not in real life.

A smaller picket fence surrounded the house, probably to keep all their children within viewing distance on their hundred plus acres of property. Lake *not* included.

As we got closer, people started to appear from what seemed like everywhere. One. Two. Three… I stopped counting at four. *Four* had my breath catching and my fingers fidgeting with my top and the only thing that went through my mind was that I should've worn a pretty dress.

DAD WASN'T KIDDING when he said that his boss was tall. He was also wide. Not overweight, just large… and extremely intimidating, though I doubt he meant to be. He just had this deep voice that seemed to echo around him. Tom introduced my dad as Brian—his new foreman—and myself to his family while we stood in their front yard. There were a lot of names and a lot of head nods mumbled between those names. Honestly, though, the only names I caught were Kathy, his wife; Lucy, their daughter; and Lucas, aka Four.

He was the last to be introduced.

"Luke's the same age as you, Lois," his mother said. The sun beamed down on her, making her white dress pop and her dark hair glow. Kathy looked like an angel, and my chest tightened as I tried not to miss my mother. She added, "You'll be going to the same school and you'll be in the same class together once the summer's over."

"Isn't that great?" Dad said, nodding in my direction.

"Great," I repeated, pushing my glasses higher on my nose.

Lucas did the same thing with his black, thick-rimmed glasses. They suited his dark hair and bright blue eyes, and then he smiled, revealing the gap between his two front teeth, and *crap, he was cute.*

I was eleven and he was cute.

He was cute and he was looking *at me.*

"I'll introduce you to my friends so you have people to chill with," he said, shaking his baseball mitt from his hand. I watched it fall to the perfectly green grass beneath our feet, then looked up at him. He was still smiling. *Still cute.*

"Thank you." Swear, I'd never felt lamer in my entire life.

"I brought cookies," Dad said, lifting the store-bought plastic container in his hand. A sudden commotion occurred at his words. Lucy said, "I'm going to read," then flew up the porch steps, one of her brothers following after her. The twins, identical, went off in the other direction and started throwing a ball. Another of the brothers mumbled something under his breath and disappeared, and the phone rang. "I'll get it," Kathy said, excusing herself.

Tom motioned to his house. "I'll get started on the grill out back."

"Sounds great." Dad squeezed my shoulder and followed after him.

I started to go with him, but a hand landed on my arm, and I turned to Lucas who was smiling wider, *looking cuter.* "You want to see something cool?" he asked.

HE TOOK me to his secret hideout; somewhere far away from the picket fence, but not far enough that we couldn't see the house. Why he showed it to me when it was supposed to be a secret, I had no idea. But I didn't care. It was a space between two trees and an old blanket hung between the trunks, hidden beneath a bunch of leafy branches. "This *is* cool," I said.

"Just wait." He cleared the branches and pointed to a tin box in the corner of the space.

"What is it?"

"A secret stash," he whispered, looking around him. I did the same. Honestly, I had no idea what I was doing. Did I mention he was cute?

He got down on his knees, dirt flying up from the impact. "Come on," he said, waving a hand at me while picking up the box with the other.

11

I got down on my knees next to him, our arms touching while he lifted the lid. "Dammit!" he spat.

"What's wrong?"

"Logan," he said simply.

"Who?"

He sighed. "My brother."

I blinked.

"Okay. So it's Lucy, then me,"—he pointed to himself—"Lucas. And then there's Leo, Logan, and the twins, Lincoln and Liam."

"Oh." I nodded, trying to remember not just their names, but the order. "What about Logan?"

He shook his head as he pulled out a single Snickers bar. "He must've stolen the others. There's only one here." He held it out to me. "You have it."

I shook my head. "No, it's yours."

"But you're my guest. My *friend*."

Hiding my smile, I grabbed the chocolate from him, unwrapped it, broke it in half and pulled it apart. Then I handed him his half. "Friends share," I told him.

We ate in silence.

"My brother's so dumb," Lucas said after a while. "The only things in here were Snickers, and he's allergic to nuts."

A giggle burst out of me. "Then why would he take them?"

Lucas rolled his eyes. "Because he's *Logan*."

Later, I'd learn that the simple word *"Logan,"* said in the tone he'd used then, would be explanation enough in the Preston household.

His mother called for us a minute later, and Lucas stood quickly, wiping his chocolate-and-dirt-covered hands across his Superman logo t-shirt. Then he held his hand out for me. "Ready?"

I took Lucas's hand; the first boy I'd ever been nervous to hold hands with. He released it as soon as I was on my feet. "Race to the fence?" he asked.

After looking down at my clothes, I shrugged. "Okay."

"Ready?" He had the sprinter pose down, even back then.

I copied his stance and ignored the fact that he was in sneakers and I was in flip-flops. "Ready."

"Go!"

I won.

LUCAS PUFFED out a breath as he took the paper plate from his mom. "She left you in the dust, son," Kathy teased.

I giggled.

Lucas said, "That'll be the last time." And it was.

His mom laughed and ruffled his hair before handing me my plate. Then she looked between Lucas and me a long moment before she called out, "Tom! Brian! Come look at this!"

Lucas and I stayed side by side, catching our breaths as we waited for our dads to join us. They all stared at the two of us, Kathy's smile growing wider with every second. She pointed to Lucas's shirt. "Clark Kent," she said, then shifted her gaze to me. "And Lois *Lane*."

CHAPTER ONE

LUCAS

L ANEY!" *Knock knock.* "Laney, answer the door!" It's 1 AM, pitch black. "Yo, Laney!" I knock again, a little harder.

Light shines from beneath the door, and I shove my hands in my pockets and wait. Finally, the door opens and Laney appears, dressed in flannel pajamas, her black hair a mess. She squints as if trying to work out who's at her door... as if there'd be anyone else.

"Are you going to let me in? I've been waiting forever."

Turning slowly, she mumbles something under her breath, her feet sliding across the tiles of her basement bedroom.

I shrug off my jacket and throw it across the room to her couch. By the time I look back at her, she's sitting on the edge of her bed, rubbing her eyes. She moans in frustration before getting under her covers and saying, "How was the end-of-summer party?"

I strip out of my jeans and stand in my t-shirt and boxers. "Same old," I tell her, taking the spare blanket and pillow from the trunk by the foot of her bed. I create my usual spot on the couch while she waits for me to settle. She doesn't watch me, though sometimes I wish she would. Ego and all.

"Was Grace there?"

"Yep."

"And you couldn't go back to her place, or better yet, back to that amazing garage apartment at your own house that you have all to yourself?"

"You're grumpy." I wait for a response and when nothing comes, I add, "And you know I can't have girls over at the house."

"I'm sure you could sneak a girl in considering it's not even attached to the house." She motions with her hand for me to hurry up, so I smack the pillow a few times, get under the blanket and point to the lamp.

Once the room's filled with darkness, I say, "I don't bring girls home because it's Dad's rules and I respect that." I look over at her, but the only thing I can make out is the outline of her body. "Maybe I just miss hanging out with you." I shift to my side and try to get more comfortable, but it's cold in the room, and this couch isn't what it used to be. "Laney?"

"What?" she snaps. She's angry. She's so cute when she's angry.

"I'm cold."

"Suck it up, Princess Asshole."

"You're mean."

She sighs loudly as she shuffles around in her bed, and before she even offers, I'm on my feet, pillow in hand, walking toward her. "I'm the absolute opposite of mean, especially when it comes to you."

I allow myself to smile because I know she can't see me. Then I throw my pillow on her bed and climb under the covers with her. It's a game we play, over and over. A game I *always* win. I turn to my side and face her back. "Laney?"

"What?"

"I'm still cold. Can I cuggles?" Only with Laney would I ever use Lachlan's toddler talk. Not just because it's lame, but because she's the only one who understands it.

She huffs, annoyed, but still, she scoots back until her body's pressed against mine. I put one arm under her pillow and the other over her waist.

"You're freezing," she says, her tone clipped.

"Well, yeah, your room's an ice chest."

"You're the most cold-blooded person I know."

I laugh under my breath, pull her closer, use her body heat to warm me. "That's an unfair assumption. How many guys have you let hold you like this?"

She doesn't respond. In fact, she's silent for so long I start to second-guess my words. *Was that mean?* Maybe it was. Even if it *is* true. "Sorry," I say because I've been with enough girls to know that a single word can save any and all future drama.

"It's fine. I need to sleep and you need to shut up."

"Got it." I shift closer.

"Did you drink tonight?" she asks.

"Yep. Three light beers. 435 calories. I should be able to burn it off tomorrow morning. Ten miles… fifteen minutes, plus what I normally run."

She sighs. "Did you drive here?"

"If I drove, I'd have my keys, and if I had my keys, I would've let myself in and I wouldn't have been standing—"

"Sorry I asked," she cuts in.

"You're so snappy tonight. What's going on with you?"

She turns over and faces me, her eyes still closed. "I'm tired."

Reaching behind me, I switch on the lamp, knocking her glasses off the nightstand. After replacing them, I turn back to her. And I try to read her—the same way I've seen my sister's boyfriend do with her. "If something's going on, you'd tell me, right?

Her eyes flutter open. First one, then the other. The corner of her lips lift, and I know I've said the right thing. Her forehead meets my chest and her toes tickle mine. The smell of her shampoo hits my nostrils: coconuts, lime, and *Laney*.

I don't know how long we lie there, the lamp still on, my hand on her waist, her head on my chest before my stomach rumbles, slicing through the sound of our mixed breaths. She laughs once, her exhale warming me. "You hungry?" she asks, tilting her head back to look at me.

I'm not sure how much of me she can see without her glasses, but the contacts I'm wearing allow me to see all of her; the freckles across her nose, the scar below her right eyebrow, the fullness of her lips… I've tasted those lips. Accidentally, but it still counts. It was Christmas. We were fifteen. I went to kiss her cheek. She went to kiss mine. Our lips touched. She tasted like strawberries, and to this day I can't look or smell a strawberry without thinking of Laney's full lips.

"Luke?"

"Huh?" *Fuck, I'm a creep.*

"You want me to make you something?"

I swallow loudly and look at anywhere but her. "Is that okay?"

Laney throws the covers off both of us, then reaches over me to get her glasses. "I'm awake now anyway."

"YOU SHOULD MAKE your own sandwiches," she mumbles, cutting the bread in triangles as if I'm Lachlan. Her eyebrows are drawn. She's annoyed. She's cute when she's annoyed. She's cute always.

I swing my legs back and forth while I sit on the kitchen counter watching her. "Last time I did that, you almost puked at what I put in there."

She hands me the plate and moves to the fridge. "Pickles and peanut butter are not..." she trails off. "That's just gross, Luke." Opening the door, she asks, "Water or soda?"

"Water."

I catch the bottle she throws at my head, then freeze when I hear her front door open. "Is that your dad?"

She shrugs. "Probably."

I look at the clock on their microwave and with a mouthful of food, I ask, "It's 1:30 in the morning. Where's he been?"

Laney leans back on the counter next to me, her arms crossed. "On a date."

"Lois, is that you?" Brian calls out from the hallway.

She doesn't respond.

"I thought I heard voices." He peeks into the kitchen, a smile forming when he sees me. "Lucas," he says in greeting.

Before I can respond, Laney says to him, "Young man. Do you have any idea what time it is?"

Brian laughs.

I chuckle.

Then Laney says, "I've been up all night worried sick!" And I can no longer tell if she's kidding.

Brian rolls his eyes. "Sorry, *Mom*."

"You could have called," Laney says.

Her dad slips into the room. "I said I was sorry," he whines dramatically.

Laney giggles.

Oh, so she *is* kidding. Man, I suck at reading her.

Brian says, looking between us, "Let me guess how your night went. You"—he points to Laney—"stayed home and watched TV or knitted a scarf, and you"—his finger moves to me—"went drinking at a party and came knocking on my daughter's door."

I take a sip of the water and jump off the counter. "And you," I say, pointing to him, "went on a *date*?"

"I did," he says, lifting his chin.

"So..." I sway from side to side teasingly. "What's her name? What does she do?"

"Her name's Misty."

"Oh," I say through a chuckle. "Is she a stripper?"

Laney slaps the back of my head. "Luke!"

Brian laughs. "She's sure got the body of one."

"Dad!"

"What?!" Brian and I say at the same time. Then he adds, his eyebrows lifting, "She's a police officer. Handcuffs and all."

"Dad!" Laney shouts.

"Nice." I high-five him. Brian and I had gotten close over the years. Besides the family get-togethers and ball games, I guess he found it necessary to get to know the kid who was constantly knocking on their front door and asking to see his daughter. It's not a bad thing. At all. I like Brian and I hope to God he likes me. He has to, right? I mean, there's a reason he's permitting my knocking on Laney's door at all hours of the night and getting into bed with her. Well, the bed part he probably doesn't know about. We always make sure the couch looks slept in.

"Honey, why don't you ever go to these parties with Luke?" Brian asks her.

Laney shrugs and looks down at the floor. "It's not really my scene."

"Yeah, but if Luke's there then it—"

"He doesn't invite me," she cuts in.

"You would go?" I ask, my voice loud. *Too loud.*

Laney's eyes snap to mine. So do her dad's. Great. *The Sanders Stare.* There are very few things in life more terrifying than the Sanders Stare. I stutter, "It's just, I mean, it's not really... you're not—"

"I wouldn't go," Laney says, saving me.

"Why not?" Brian asks. "You're almost eighteen, Lo, and you barely leave the house."

Laney shrugs. "Just because you've gotten a social life in the past year, it doesn't mean *I* have to."

Brian rolls his eyes again. "You should be out there..." he says, throwing his hands in the air. "...making mistakes and falling in *like*. Not love. Not yet. But you should at least be dating."

I choke on the bite I'd just taken.

"I've dated," Laney says. She doesn't say it with pride or with snark. She says it so matter-of-factly that I know she's telling the truth and that thought alone has the food lodged somewhere between my throat and my stomach, and I thump at my chest, hoping to clear it.

"Who?" Brian asks, his eyes narrowed.

"*Who* is not important."

Brian steps closer to her. "Tell me."

Swallow. Water. Gasp for air.

Laney presses her lips tight, refusing to answer.

I look between the two because I just now realized there is one thing more terrifying than the Sanders Stare. It's the Sanders Stand-Off.

"I'm sorry," Brian concedes, stepping back. "I just worry you're missing out on life."

Laney points to me. "Because I don't want to be *him*?"

"Hey!" I look down at myself. "What's wrong with *me*?"

Brian points a finger between the two of us. "Why don't you two…"

"Dad, that's gross. It's *Luke*."

Ouch. "I'm right here!"

They both laugh. I don't know why. I don't find it funny.

"Goodnight, kids," Brian says, turning away and waving a hand in the air.

"Wait!" I square my shoulders. "What's wrong with *me*?"

CHAPTER TWO

LOIS

STUPID ALARM.

Every night he stays here, there's his stupid alarm.

4:45.

Every morning.

Stupid, *stupid* alarm.

"Luke, your alarm. Get up. Go!"

With his eyes still half closed, he reaches for his phone in my hand, switches the alarm off, then throws it across the room.

I stare at it, expecting it to grow legs and make its way back to us. Did I mention it was 4:45? "But…"

"But what?"

"Your run."

"No," he murmurs, digging his head in the pillow.

"No?"

"No."

"But you run every morning."

"Not today," he says, wrapping his arm around my waist and maneuvering me until I'm lying back down. "Let's sleep in."

"Sleep in?"

He moves closer. So close that when he says, "Leave it alone, Lane," I can feel his warm breath against my neck.

"Okay…?"

"Good."

Ten minutes later I'm wide awake, lying on my back, his hand flat on my stomach. I listen to him breathe, feel the goosebumps prick my skin, feel an overwhelming amount of emotions. It's not the first time we've been this close physically, but there's something different, something *off*. And there's this nagging in the back of my mind that's telling me this should be the last time. I *want* it to be the last time. Because having him here is too much, and at the same time, it's not enough. It won't ever be *enough*.

Without warning, his fingers start strumming against my skin. "Can't get back to sleep, huh?"

I shake my head, but refuse to look at him.

He removes his hand and untangles his legs from mine, and I exhale, relieved, hoping he'll leave. "Do I have sweats here?" he asks.

"Bottom drawer."

I sit up halfway and watch him move across the room—one hand in his hair, the other covering his parts. I'd be lying if I said the attraction to him wasn't physical because it plays a part. Unlike me, he'd changed *a lot* over the years. I was still Plain Lane, and he was no longer the cute boy I crushed on when we were eleven. He'd gotten rid of his glasses and opted for contacts the moment he joined the track team in sixth grade. In seventh grade, he got braces to fix the gap in his teeth. In eighth grade, he had a growth spurt and never really stopped. By the time tenth grade started, he'd dated more than his share of girls. Now, at seventeen, he topped out at 6'2" and showed off muscles in places I didn't know existed.

He was too much.

He wasn't enough.

"Don't forget your phone," I tell him, lying back down.

"I'm not leaving."

I glance over at him just in time to see him pull on a pair of his sweatpants. "You're not?"

"Unless you want me to," he says, eyes on mine.

After seconds of waiting and no response from me, he shakes his head, his gaze shifting to the floor. "I'm going to brush my teeth, and then we're going to talk because something's going on with you and we need to deal with it." He makes his way to the bathroom, and I follow behind. It's a routine we've done many times before; we stand in front of the mirror, brush our teeth, take turns to spit, pass each other the mouthwash, then I leave so he can do his business, and when he's done, I do mine.

He's back in bed when I get out, his gaze fixed on the bathroom door, waiting. "So?" he says.

I shrug. "So."

22

He pats the spot next to him, and reluctantly, I do as he suggests. I lie beneath the covers and wait for him to put his hands on me, somewhere, anywhere, it doesn't really matter. He opts for his fingers on my forehead, pushing away my bangs so he can look in my eyes. "What goes on, Lane?"

I shrug again, but there's a backlog of tears in my eyes and a lump in my throat and I know he can see it because his eyebrows bunch and he moves closer again, so his head's on my pillow. "Was it about the party last night? The whole class was invited and if I thought that you'd go—"

"It's not about the party."

"Then what?" His voice is soft, unmasking his concern. His gaze fixes on mine while mine searches his and I find *nothing*. Not a damn thing.

He licks his lips, his eyes narrowing even more. "Are you worried about school starting tomorrow? Because if you are, you don't need to be. It's only senior year. One year of our entire—"

"Why do you come here, Luke?" I cut in.

He rears back an inch. "In general or…"

"Why do you spend nights with me instead of going home or sleeping at one of your many girlfriends' houses?"

Luke pulls away and faces the ceiling. "Don't do that, Laney."

I lean up on my elbow and look down at him. "Do what?"

"Make me out to be something I'm not. Yeah, I've had a lot of girlfriends, but I've never been with more than one at a time and you know that."

I look away, the guilt quick to consume me because he's right.

He says, his voice low, "I come here because I like being around you. Because my own home doesn't feel like home unless you're there. Because I want to know what's going on in your life and I want to tell you what goes on in mine. Because you're there for me through every breakup, through all the shit that goes on with my family, through *everything*. And mostly, I come here because I *want* to." He inhales deeply. Exhales loudly. "Is this what it feels like to have someone you care about break up with you because if it is, I think I'm done with dating." He rubs his chest… right above his heart. "This feeling sucks."

There's power in his words that go directly through my ears and pierce my heart. But I remind myself that it's a lie. He doesn't care about me. If he did, he'd remember. "Luke…"

23

His gaze moves to mine, his eyes revealing his pain. I've only seen that look a few times. Once when we were twelve and he showed up at my house, soaking wet from the storm outside, and again when we were thirteen and he accidentally swung a baseball bat too far back and caused me to get three stitches under my right eyebrow. "Did I do something?" he asks, his voice hoarse.

I blink, push back the emotions, the tears. "No," I lie.

"Then what the hell's going on?"

I lie back down, my head landing on his already outstretched, waiting arm. And I think... I try to come up with a lie so that we can move past this. So that his actions, or lack of, from the past twenty-four hours don't define him or us or our entire friendship. And so I give him a half-truth because right now, it's all I can offer. "The summer's almost over and summers remind me of your mom and how great she was. And I miss her, I guess. I just..." I trail off, unable to finish with the lump lodged in my throat. *So maybe it was more than a half-truth.* Maybe it was all I needed to feel, needed to say. Maybe it was everything. "I *really* miss her."

"Why didn't you say something?" he whispers.

"Because she's *your* mom. I have no right to miss her."

He pulls me closer until I'm on my side and my head's resting on his chest. Then he kisses the top of my head and wraps both his arms around me. "She may be my mom but she loved you beyond words, *Lois Lane*. And next time you feel like this, tell me and we can miss her together."

PAST | LUCAS

"It looked like you got on well with Laney. You like her?" Mom asked, her hands and fingers working frantically on whatever knitting project she was working on while sitting on the couch opposite me. It had been more than a few hours since Lois and her dad had left, and the house was a rare kind of quiet. The twins were in bed, Logan was off being Logan, and Leo and Lucy were lost in their own fictional world, as always.

I feigned disinterest, kicked out my legs and got more comfortable on Dad's recliner. "Her name's Lois, not Laney."

Mom smiled. "Well, I think I'm going to call her Laney. I like it better. It suits her."

I scoffed. "You can't just go changing people's names, Ma."

"Why not, Bobby Jo?" she sang.

"Who the hell is Bobby Jo?"

She laughed under her breath. "You are now."

I laughed with her. "I think I prefer Lucas."

"You still didn't answer my question, Bobby Jo."

I ignored her use of my new name. "She's cool."

"And cute," Mom added.

I pretended to wipe my mouth with my forearm, hoping it would somehow hide my blush. "She's cool," I repeated.

"Mmm-hmm…" She tried to hide her smile, but I didn't need to see it to hear it. "I was thinking—"

"Uh-oh. This can't be good."

"Smartass." She grinned. "Brian mentioned that Laney would be staying home alone for a couple of days while he works, just until he can decide if she's old enough to stay on her own for that long a period. But if you don't mind, I thought I might invite her to spend the summer with us. It might be nice to have an extra hand around here."

"So you're using her for child labor?"

She laughed at that. "I didn't think of it that way. But I don't know. It'd be nice to have another girl around, and besides, I think we'd be good for each other. I just don't want your mom to cramp your style by asking your crush to come over."

"She's not my crush," I said. Way too loud. Way too obvious.

Mom didn't respond to that. Instead she said, "She kicked your ass in that race."

I lifted my chin. "Like I care."

"About what? Her spending the summer with us or her kicking your ass?"

"Neither."

Lies.

All lies.

I SET my alarm and woke up early the next morning. It was barely light out, and the twins weren't even up yet. Slowly, and as quietly as possible, I made my way downstairs and to the kitchen where I left a note for whoever would find it.

25

Gone for a run.
Won't leave our property.
Don't drink all the milk, <u>Logan</u>.
- Lucas.

And with that, I slipped on my sneakers by the front door, tied them extra tight, and I ran. I ran and I ran and I ran until my legs burned worse than my lungs and by the time I was back at the house, my t-shirt was covered in sweat and the rest of my family were all sitting around the kitchen table.

"Did you speak to Lois's dad?" I huffed out, taking my seat opposite Lucy.

"Good morning to you, too." Mom ruffled my sweaty hair and poured me the few drops of milk leftover in the carton.

I glared at Logan, who gave me a shit-eating grin. He was such a douche.

I pushed the glass of milk away and opted for water instead. "So, is she coming?" I asked Mom.

"Why so eager?" she teased.

"I want to race her again."

"Right. Well, it's early and Brian doesn't start work until tomorrow, but I'll call later today."

"Call now."

"Luke."

"Please?"

She looked at her watch. "I'll wait another hour, okay?"

"Fine."

"Luke and Laney, sitting in a tree…" Logan sang.

"Shut up!"

"Enough," Dad warned.

"May I please be excused?" Leo asked, already standing with his bowl and glass in his hand.

Dad nodded, and a moment later, Leo set the bowl in the sink and took his glass with him to wherever he was going. The twins—age four—spoke to each other in a language that was part English, part something they'd made up. Logan ate as if there was a competition to see who could eat the loudest and messiest. See? *Douche*.

Lucy was… *sigh*. Lucy was a mess, milk stains down her top from being too busy reading to concentrate on eating. She dropped her spoon an inch from the bowl and reached out in search of her

26

juice, knocking over a pile of napkins and salt and pepper shakers on the way. I rolled my eyes and picked up her glass and physically placed it in her hand.

Mom set a plate of bacon, eggs and toast in front of me, squeezing my shoulder as she did—a silent acknowledgment that she'd seen what I'd done and even though Lucy was too zoned out, *Mom* noticed and she appreciated it.

The thing about Lucy, though a little kooky, is that she's my *only* sister. *Our* only sister. And it was an unspoken oath between us Preston boys that we all look out for her. Even if it meant handing her a glass or moving a toy out of the way while she walked around the house, nose in a book, so that she wouldn't trip over it. Some of our friends called her a princess, and maybe they were right, and if that made my mother a queen, so be it. I'd seen the way Dad had treated the two women in the family—different to the boys—and growing up I knew it had to mean something, I just wasn't sure what. *Yet.*

I ate my breakfast slowly, so slowly it was almost a chore, and I kept my eye on the clock. Seconds ticked by, turned into minutes and by the time my body had finally stopped sweating, only fifteen minutes had passed. I sighed loudly, annoyed.

Mom must have noticed because she said, "If you're that desperate, you could call her yourself."

Logan chimed, "Who? You're giiirlfriend?"

"Shut. Up!"

"Lucas," Dad warned. Then added, "Shut up, Logan."

I stood up. "I'm going for a run."

"Again?" Mom sighed. "Luke, your stomach hasn't settled yet."

"I'll be okay."

"Wait five minutes."

I sat back down.

Each ticking of the second hand on the clock felt like torture. I didn't know why I wanted to run so bad. Why I felt it necessary to beat Lois in a race, but my eleven-year-old brain said that I absolutely *had* to. So as soon as five minutes passed, I shot to my feet and a few seconds later, I was out the door. I didn't run far. Our parents had set up boundaries on our land that we all had to stick to so that if anything happened, they wouldn't have to search far for us. But still, I ran to one border, then to the next, and the next, and the next, again and again, until the burning set in and man, I must've really wanted to impress her. I mean *beat* her.

27

Dad's car was gone when I got back to the house and Mom was sitting on the porch, cordless phone to her ear. "Sure, Brian, it's no problem at all."

I stopped in my tracks, my eyebrows raised as I tried to catch my breath. "What did he say?" I mouthed.

Mom raised a hand between us.

I stomped my foot. "What did he say?" I asked again.

"Okay, I'll see both you and *Lois Lane* tomorrow morning."

I pressed my lips together to hide my smile.

As soon as she hung up, she looked over at me and grinned from ear-to-ear, her eyes bright against the sun and her long dark hair flying with the wind. Up until I met Laney, I swear my mother was the prettiest woman I'd ever seen. Well, her and Mila Kunis. "So she's coming over tomorrow for a *date*," she teased. Again. "Oh my… Lucas Preston, what are you going to wear? Maybe that ugly sweater your aunt Leslee bought you for Christmas? Or maybe that hideous plaid suit she got you for your birthday. Maybe I'll just dig out that picture of you as a baby when you decided to go digging around your poopy diaper and eat—"

"Ma, stop!" I yelled, but I was laughing.

Because of all the qualities I love about my mother, being a smartass is one I miss most.

CHAPTER THREE

LUCAS

EVEN THOUGH LANEY told me what was going on, she still seemed distant, still *lost*, and I knew she wasn't giving me everything. I tried to get more out of her, but she kept changing the subject and after a while, I had no choice but to let it go. So we spent the rest of the morning talking about anything and everything other than her feelings. I was pretty good at reading most girls, but Laney... she was something else. The truth is I didn't make too much of an effort with other girls, but I wanted to with her. She was more than a fling, more than a random attempt to pass the time. She meant a lot to me... in fact, she meant the world.

"What are your plans for the rest of the day?" she asks, her head still in the crook of my arm.

"Well, it's Sunday, so family breakfast—which I'm dragging your ass to—and then..." I turn to my side so I can face her. "I was thinking of driving down to Charlotte. I hear there's this amazing craft store that—"

She sits up, her smile instant, and I know I've said the right thing. "Shut up!"

"I could use the company on the long drive."

Her eyes roll, but she's still smiling. God, her smile does something to me. "It's only an hour away."

"So... you're coming?"

"Why would you spend your last day of summer sitting bored in a craft store while I—"

"Because you're sad and—"

"Lucas..."

I take her hand and place a kiss on the center of her palm. A simple kiss. A *restrained* kiss. A kiss she has no idea drives me insane. "I don't like seeing you sad, Lane."

MOST PEOPLE HATE SUNDAYS. It's the day before the norm of the routine begins again. Work, school, whatever.

I'm not most people.

Up until a few months ago, Dad had hired a full-time nanny who lived in the garage apartment that's now mine. Dad let her go a few weeks after Leo got his license. The twins had a lot of weekend sports, and Lucy was at college, so between Leo, Dad and me, we were able to divide and conquer. Anyway, Virginia (the nanny) started Sunday family breakfasts—a way to reconnect us all so we knew what was going on with each other. Now we all cook breakfast together, even Logan. When Lucy is home from UNC, she attempts to do it all. My sister is a *horrible* cook, but we all grin and bear it because she's Lucy and we're her brothers and we love her. And, if not for her, we probably would've been separated years ago.

So, I like my family.

I like the one day a week that brings us all to the same room at the same time to do the same thing.

I like Sundays.

"Laney!" Lachlan practically bounces as he runs toward her, arms out waiting.

"What's up, Lachy?" Laney says, lifting him off the ground and spinning him around. "Jeez, you've gotten big!"

"I'm six!" he tells her.

"Really?" she says in mock surprise. "Another year and you'll have a beard like your daddy!" He giggles and runs away to continue setting the table.

"You're staying for breakfast I assume?" Dad asks her, kissing her on the cheek.

"If that's okay."

"Of course!" Over his shoulder, he says, "Lachlan, set up another place for Laney."

The greetings continue, one brother after another—high fives and hugs—everyone except Logan who's stuck doing the dishes. He's fifteen, and I guess in his mind he *has* to hate the world. Dad's completely set on the idea of Logan being the first Preston to end up in juvie or rehab. Not that Dad would ever tell him that. Laney doesn't seem fazed by his attitude, though, and slowly makes her way over to him. She nudges his hip with hers and says something too quiet for me to hear. Logan glances at her then drops a spoon back in the sink. He wipes his hand on a cloth before giving her a hug. It's quick, but it's real, and for Logan, it's a pretty big deal.

"What can I do?" I ask the room.

Laney's the first and loudest to speak, "You sit down. You've had, like, three hours sleep and a long day ahead. Relax." With a smile, she moves to Dad working over the stove and reaches up to grasp his shoulders and lead him to his chair at the head of the table. "You, too, Tom. You've worked hard this week."

"And me, too?" Logan asks, eyebrows raised.

Laney laughs. "You finish those dishes."

He groans but does as she says.

A moment later, Laney's moving around the kitchen as if she lives here, opening and closing cabinets, working on the stove, pouring Lachlan's infamous Coco Pops and Froot Loop mix into a bowl with milk, flipping pancakes and plating bacon. "Eat!" she orders, so they eat. I don't. Instead, I watch *her*. And I find myself smiling, though I don't really know why. She places a plate of Dad's regular Sunday breakfast in front of him and says, "Dad tells me the Baldwin development is ahead of schedule."

"Thank you," he tells her. "And yes, your dad managed to get two weeks ahead."

"Something about council permits, right?"

"Right," Dad confirms, but he's looking at me. He waits until Laney's at the other end of the table, sitting down with her own plate and talking to Leo about what he's currently reading, before leaning across Lachlan and toward me. His smile reaches his eyes. "It's like having your mother back."

PAST | LUCAS

My mom used to tell me that I loved numbers, that ever since I could count, I used the skill on everything. I mean, *everything*. How many peas were on my plate, the steps from the front door to the fence. Obviously, as I got older and my strides got longer, the steps lessened, but still, I counted. Then I learned how to tell time. I counted that, too. How many seconds it would take for Mom's morning coffee to brew, how many times droplets of water leaked from the kitchen tap right after being shut off. The number of clicks per minute, per second, Mom's knitting needles clicked together. Two per second, just in case you're wondering. So, it's no surprise when I raced Laney, I counted. The first race, I counted my steps. The second, I counted the time.

I won both races, just so we're clear.

She was also wearing flip-flops, which I'm sure didn't help. But if it was the reason I won, I wasn't going to mention it.

THE FIRST FEW days spent with Laney went by quickly. Mom called them play-dates. She also called us inseparable. Every morning I'd wake up early and run, come home, have breakfast, and wait. Laney's dad would drop her off, offer my mom money (to which she declined), then Laney and I would spend the day racing each other, the distance getting farther each time. On the fourth day, she wore sneakers. She still didn't win, but she was closer. No more than five strides behind me each time. The next day, while sitting out on the dock by the lake, our feet in the water, bodies sweating as we tried to catch our breaths, she asked why all we did was run. I didn't know what to say so I said nothing. Telling her that I was trying to impress her would've made me a loser, and if she had to ask *why* then it probably wasn't working.

She looked out beyond the lake and toward the horizon, kicking her feet beneath the water. "Next week, if I bring my swimsuit, can we go in?"

"Next week?" My eyes snapped to hers. "You not coming tomorrow?"

"It's the weekend. My dad's home."

"Oh." I was confused by the sudden ache in my chest. "So I won't see you all weekend?"

"My dad and I are going to the hardware store to pick out paint for my new room. He said I could have the whole finished basement to myself. It has its own bathroom. How cool is that?"

"It's cool," I said. I almost offered to help just to be around her more. But that would make me lame. And desperate. So I kept my mouth shut.

"Mom?"

"Yeah, sweetheart?"

I sat on the couch next to her. "I don't think Laney likes running," I told her.

"Well, yeah, I don't think many kids your age want to spend their summers chasing after a boy... even if he's as handsome as you."

I stayed silent, my mind lost in thought until she stopped knitting and turned to me. "Maybe you guys should do something she likes. What is she into?"

"I don't know." I shrugged. "I never asked."

"Well, maybe you should, and that way you can split your time with the activities."

I picked up a random magazine off the coffee table and pretended to flip through it. "She's painting her room with her dad this weekend. You think I should call them and offer to help?"

"You can't. Garray's coming over for the weekend. You're camping out back. Don't you remember?"

"Oh yeah." After everything that had happened throughout the week, I'd almost forgotten about Garray—my best friend since first grade. His parents couldn't decide between Gary and Gray, so they called him Garray. It was a dumb name, so much so that Logan called him *Dumb Name* to his face. Then everyone started calling him Dumb Name behind his back. Even Dad. Mom said it was mean, but I knew she thought it was funny. "I forgot about Dumb Name."

Mom smiled, but it was sad. "Besides, I think maybe you should give the two of them the weekend. They've been through a lot, and this move was a big change for them. They need to spend some quality time together."

My brow furrowed in confusion. "What do you mean they've been through a lot? Is Laney okay?"

"Oh, she's fine, Lucas."

After a beat, I asked, "Do you know what happened? Why is it just her and Brian? Did something happen to her mom? I mean, did she die or something?"

"No, sweetheart." Mom shook her head. "Some parents just don't end up together forever."

"But you and Dad will, right?"

Mom picked up her knitting needles, a wistfulness in her tone when she said, "Your dad and I are forever, Luke. Eternal. Like the rise and fall of the sun. I promise."

"Good. I'm glad her mom's not dead. I don't know what I'd do if something ever happened to you." I kissed her cheek and stood. "Besides, you're the best mom I've ever had."

"I bet you say that to all your moms."

IT WAS A SUNDAY NIGHT. I remember it clearly. Garray's parents had picked him up right after dinner, and Lucy and I were cleaning the larger dishes in the sink (her washing, me drying) when the home phone rang. Dad mumbled something about telemarketers while Logan walked past, pushed all the already dry dishes back into the sink water and shouted, "Lucy Goosey! Lucas Pukas! Logan Rules!"

"Logan!" Lucy and I yelled at the same time.

Dad picked him up, threw him over his shoulder and left the kitchen.

Mom entered, cordless phone in hand, palm covering the receiver. "It's for you," she said to me, then lowered her voice. "It's Laney."

I snatched the phone from her and started running to my room, ignoring Lucy's shouts about finishing up the dishes. Twelve steps on the staircase and fourteen (eleven-year-old) steps to my room later, I was shutting the door behind me and trying to catch my breath. Not because I was exhausted, but because I was nervous. Slowly, I raised the phone to my ear. "Hey," I said.

"Hey," she said back. "It's Laney."

I bit back a smile as I sat on the edge of my bed. "You calling yourself Laney, too?"

She giggled. "I figure you all do now, so I wasn't sure if you'd know it was me if I said it was Lois."

"I'd know." Even if she didn't introduce herself, I'd know. I'd recognize her voice anywhere.

"So how was your weekend?" she asked at the same time I said, "What color did you paint your room?"

"Green," she said.

"Pretty good," I answered.

34

Then we both laughed.

"I don't really know why I called," she murmured. "I guess I'm just used to seeing you every day and I miss you."

"You do?"

"Is that lame?"

My heart skipped a beat. "No. It was weird not having you here."

"Yeah… so…"

"So…"

She asked, "What did you do over the weekend?"

"My best friend, Garray, was here."

"Gray?"

"No."

"Gary?"

"No." I then went on to explain how he got his name. She cracked up at the part about my family calling him Dumb Name, even though she agreed it *was* a little mean.

"I'm sorry I made you run the whole time you were here," I admitted. "You probably hate me."

"I'm at your house every day, Luke. I don't expect you to give up what you normally do just because I'm there. If I didn't want to hang out with you, I wouldn't have done it."

"What would *you* like to do, I mean, besides going swimming in our lake? Is there something else? We can do it. I don't mind."

She thought about this for a while, the static in the phone and the usual background noise of my family the only sounds I could hear. "I like playgrounds," she finally said.

I laughed. I probably shouldn't have, but I did. "Aren't we a little old for playgrounds?"

"Name one time a playground hasn't been fun."

"True. There's one close by that Mom lets me and Lucy go to on our own."

"We could bring your brothers. I like them. Well, maybe not Logan. No offense… he's just so…"

"So *Logan*?"

We spent three hours on the phone that night—longer than I've ever spent on the phone with any other girl, but not as long as I'll spend with Laney in the future. I fell asleep with the phone to my ear—her light, quiet breaths lulling me to slumber, letting me know she'd done the same.

35

And so without meaning to, without wanting to, I started to fall in like with a girl who would become my best friend.

My confidant.

My courage...

...A girl who would later crush my heart and destroy me.

CHAPTER FOUR

LOIS

LUCAS'S DAD practically shoved us out the front door, thanking me for breakfast and telling me that I'd helped enough and the rest of them would finish the clean-up. I had my license, but I didn't have a car, so Luke did all the driving for us. He got his license the exact day he turned sixteen. His dad had taught him how to drive on their property from the time he was twelve. His dad taught me to drive the same way, too.

Luke didn't have a car at the beginning, so he drove the minivan whenever it was available. Then later, his dad gave him the keys to the oldest, most beaten-up truck they had in the company fleet. Lucy was given their mom's old car when she got her license. He'd also built her a cabin on the property her junior year so she could get some space away from all the boys. But, just like Lucas, she worked whatever available Saturdays they had doing jobs for their dad to "pay it off." Luke worked construction and Lucy did admin work in the office. When Lucy went off to college and didn't need her car anymore, she passed it down to Leo. Even though there was no monetary value to pay off, Leo (without being asked) still worked construction—the same amount of hours as Lucy—because he knew, like all the Preston kids, that it wasn't about money. It was about the principal. The thing I learned quickly about the Prestons is that while they had money, they didn't flaunt it or throw it around like it meant nothing. The kids weren't spoiled, and because of their dad, they knew the value of hard work.

"I gotta get gas," Lucas says, pulling into the gas station.

I reach into my purse. "I got it."

"Shut up," he mumbles, already halfway out of the truck. He fills the tank, and when he returns from paying, he hands me a

Snickers bar. Without thinking, I break it in half and give back his share.

The drive is easy—Lucas permitting me to connect my phone to his Bluetooth so I can play *my* music, which is Justin Timberlake's Justified album on repeat. He says he's not a fan, but I often catch his lips moving along with the lyrics.

Forgetting that all calls go through Lucas's car speakers, I don't hesitate to answer when Dad rings. "Hey, Dad," I say in greeting.

"Your mom called," he says, and Lucas's eyes snap to mine.

"When?" he mouths.

I can already feel the sweat forming on my brow because I recognize the tone in Dad's voice—the anger mixed with worry. "When did she call?" I ask Dad.

He doesn't answer me. Instead, his voice rises, the anger overpowering his worry, and I wonder how much he knows, how much she had told him even though I begged and pleaded for her to let me be the one to break the news. "Did you forget to mention that you had dinner with her last night?"

Luke slams on the brakes so fast I have to extend my arm to catch myself on the dash. I glare at him, but he's too focused on pulling the car over in the middle of a busy fricken highway of all places. "Luke!" I shout, trying to grab onto his arm as he steps out on the road.

"Lois, why didn't you tell me?" Dad barks.

"Dad, it's—"

"What happened? What did she have to say to you?" Okay, so she must not have told him the *why* we met up. Just the *how*. And as stupid as it sounds, I'm grateful to her for that. And gratitude, especially for her, isn't something that forms easily.

"Nothing," I rush out. "She was just nearby and asked to meet up. That's all. It's not a big deal, Dad. She just wanted to see how I was doing."

I give him lie.

After lie.

After lie.

Dad says my name. Just once. And I know him well enough to know it's because he has *too much* to say, too much insight into how my mother works. But he's built enough strength over the years to keep his thoughts to himself so I don't end up hating her as much as I know he does. *But it gets worse, Dad.*

"I have to go," I tell him, hanging up and opening the door so I can get to Luke. At least he's on the passenger's side now, away from the oncoming traffic of the highway. His arms are outstretched, hands resting on the hood, head lowered because he finally remembered. I try to touch him, to comfort him, but he steps back, his hands raised. "Don't," he says.

"Luke," I say with a sigh. "It's fine."

He shakes his head, refusing to meet my gaze. "It's not fine!" he shouts above the noise of the dozens of cars that seem to pass by. "I'm such an asshole, Laney. You told me about the dinner. You *asked* me to be there for you. You even specified a time to meet you at the diner and I—"

"Forgot," I finish for him.

He starts to pace, his strides long, toes of his sneakers kicking at the loose gravel beneath our feet. "You should *hate* me right now. *I* hate me right now."

I shrug.

I did hate him.

For the hour I spent sitting in an almost empty diner on a Saturday night waiting for him, I *hated* him. But I realize now that maybe my hate wasn't directed at him, my heart was just full of it and he wasn't around to redirect it.

"This is a deal-breaker, Lane." He stops two feet short of slamming into me. "I don't even know why you're standing here right now. With me. You should've shut the door in my face last night." His eyes search mine for a long time, and when I don't respond, he asks, his tone solemn, "What did she want?"

I offer another shrug, which apparently is the wrong answer because he's grasping his hair, kicking at his tire. It's not the tire's fault he was an ass. "I wanted to hate you," I yell. A car honks its horn, the volume rising and fading as it drives past us and to its destination. I wait for the sound to dwindle before adding, "I think for a moment, I actually did. And when you showed up last night, completely unaware of the hurt you caused, I wanted to be done with you… with this entire friendship."

"And you had every right to!" he yells.

"But—"

"But what? What could've possibly happened to make you change that?"

"You skipped your run!"

He steps closer. "What?"

"You never skip your morning run and you did! And you lay with me and held me for four hours because you knew something was wrong, you were just too stupid to know what!"

He shakes his head. "That doesn't excuse what I did, Laney!"

I want to push him. Shove him hard. Do something to physically hurt him because a part of me is still in that diner, waiting, wanting him there. But I've already forgiven him, so there's no point. "It doesn't matter," I tell him.

"Of course it does!" Now he just *wants* me to hate him, but I can't.

"You're my best friend, Luke, and you're standing here right now on the side of a highway telling me I should hate you while driving to a store an hour away. For *me*!"

"But—"

"It doesn't matter because you're human and you're flawed and you make mistakes." I step to him and hug him quickly, afraid he'll pull away again. But he doesn't. He just holds me back, his chest rising and falling harshly against mine. I look up at him, at his normally bright blue eyes now filled with guilt. "And when I felt like my own mom had turned her back on me, you gave me yours."

PAST | LOIS

Garray, aka Dumb Name, was an idiot. A moron. A pig.

This, I worked out, after spending five minutes with him and Luke. Why Luke was and is *still* friends with him is a mystery wrapped in an enigma covered with puzzles.

It was halfway through the summer when I first met him. His greeting words were: "Four-eyes dresses like a boy." So I left him and Luke to play out in the backyard and went inside the house.

Kathy was sitting at the kitchen table with the twins, crayons and paper sprawled all over the place. She looked up when she must've heard the back door open and smiled at me. "Dumb Name—I mean Garray,"—she corrected quickly—"already got to you, huh?"

"I think he must be an acquired taste," I mumbled.

She laughed loud and free and so contagious, even the twins joined in. Once settled, she said, "Is there something else you'd like to do, Laney? Maybe with me instead of the boys?"

I shrugged, feeling a little awkward. "I see you knitting sometimes. I wouldn't mind learning that."

"Oh, yeah?" She smiled, surprised. "Well, let's go." She left the twins at the table and moved to the living room where she sat down on the couch, patted the spot next to her. I sat while she reached into a basket between the couch and the recliner and pulled out two knitting needles and a ball of yarn. "It looks harder than it is," she told me, positioning the needles in my hands. Her touch was soft, as soft as her voice. "There are only two stitches. Knit and pearl. I'll show you knitting first." Her fingers guided mine as she spoke and even though I tried to focus on her words, on what she was showing me, I couldn't stop watching her. And I tried to remember the last time my mother sat down with me, talked to me the way Kathy was. The last time she showed interest in me at all. I couldn't remember, but it didn't stop me from missing her and wishing that she was more like Kathy.

I SPENT the rest of the summer between messing around with Luke and being taught by Kathy how to knit, crochet, cross-stitch, and scrapbook. To be honest, I enjoyed the time with Kathy the most—maybe because I enjoyed the activities, so much so that I begged Dad to let me get my own supplies, even though I knew we couldn't afford it. Or, maybe because Kathy was a mother-figure when I felt like I didn't have one. I hadn't spoken to my mother since I got in the car with Dad and drove away. If Dad had spoken to her, he didn't mention it. If he missed her, he didn't act on it. If he hurt, he didn't show it. So I made a choice early on that I wouldn't either. I spent a lot of days lying to him and lying to myself.

"Where's your head at, Laney?" Kathy asked, her fingers working the yarn as if it were an extension of her body.

I realized I'd been lost in my own head, thoughts of my mother invading my mind. There were tears in my eyes, tears I hadn't known were there. I wiped at them quickly, not wanting to show my weakness to the three boys sitting on the floor in front of us, PlayStation controllers in their hands. "Nothing," I whispered, looking down at my attempt at a scarf.

LUCAS

"Your hands have been in that position for over five minutes," she said, her voice low, her words meant only for me. But Lucas turned to me, his eyebrows furrowed in confusion.

"Owned you, noob!" Logan yelled, and just as quickly, Lucas turned back around and refocused on the video game.

"Laney." Kathy dropped her yarn on her lap and freed her hands. She turned to me and said, "You can always talk to me about anything. I know that it's just you and your dad here, so if things are going on... with yourself, or with your body, or anything else you feel like you can't talk about with him, I just want you to know I'm here."

I stared at her—at her sad eyes and her sad smile—and I could feel it in my heart that the words she'd spoken were sincere. The tears pooled again and this time, I let them free, along with the words that would haunt me for years. "I feel like I'm not good enough. My mom hasn't spoken to me in months... not since my dad and I left her. And now I sit here with you and I wonder why it's possible to feel more love from you than I felt from her, and I crave it, but I can't miss it because I never felt it. And I can't tell my dad because I don't want him to think that I regret the choice to be with him instead of her, because I don't. Not for a second." I wiped at my cheeks, looked down at my hands, and pushed through the giant lump in my throat. "So I wonder if I'm not good enough. If that's the reason why she can't seem to find time to pick up the phone and call me. I don't expect much from her, honestly, but I at least want to know she's thinking about me."

Silence filled the room... the video game now paused. I felt four pairs of eyes on me, watching, waiting, and the only sounds that broke the silence were my sniffles as I tried to keep it together.

By the time I found the courage to look up, I was met with Kathy's tear-stained face. But it wasn't her who spoke the words which would later define me. It was Luke. "I'm sorry, Laney," he said, his voice shaking. I refused to look at him, but I felt him stand, felt him come closer until he was sitting on the couch next to me, his hand reaching for mine. "I'm sorry that your mom makes you feel like that because you *are* good enough. For *me*. For *all of us*. And if she doesn't want you as family then it's her loss, because now— now you're a part of ours. Right, guys?"

"Right," Leo agreed, while Logan shouted, "Your mom's an ugly, smelly bitch."

42

He was eight.

CHAPTER FIVE

LUCAS

"YOU CAN GO NOW," Laney says, sitting back in the car, the engine idle. "You have time." She's looking between the seats and onto the road behind us. I'm looking at her. We should drive, but I can't. I don't want to pressure her to talk, but I can't leave until I know what's happening because I know it can't be good. Anything to do with her mother ends in her misery. Sometimes it lasts days, sometimes weeks. And I feel as though I need to plan my next move more than I need my next breath.

I comb my fingers through my hair, pleading words filtering in and out of my mind too fast, and I don't know what to say.

"Luke?"

I don't bother sparing her feelings. "What the fuck did she want? Why was she here?"

She blinks hard, probably trying to find a response that'll both satisfy me and keep my mind at peace. I don't want any of those things. I just want the truth. I raise my eyebrows, relentless. I'll sit here and I'll wait for however long it takes for her to speak. Seconds tick by, then she inhales deeply, her words rushed when she says, "When I was younger and my parents were still together, my dad set up a bank account for me." She's not looking at me. Not at my eyes, anyway. She's fixed on my t-shirt, at the faded Nike logo across the chest. "It was supposed to be a college fund." She swallows. Once. Twice. "For the past few years, we've been putting money in there and saving. I guess when Dad set it up, he thought the bank required both signatures to withdraw any money..." Her voice breaks and she looks up at me, her eyes wide, the shape and color of almonds.

I know where this is going, but I don't want to admit it as much as she doesn't want to say it, and so I say, hoping, *praying* she says yes, "So you need you and your dad to sign?" She shakes her head, and my chest tightens. I've heard enough of Laney's stories about her mom to know what she's capable of. The shakiness in my exhale reveals my fear. "This is bad, isn't it?" I mumble, moving closer to her.

We're supposed to have four more years. Ever since we visited Lucy and Cameron at UNC a couple of years ago, this was our dream. We were going to do it together. My athletic scholarship was a sure thing because I worked my ass off to get it. I pushed away other offers. I wanted UNC because Lane wanted it. Because we walked around campus, her hand on the crook of my elbow while she pointed out where she'd be sitting when she sipped her coffee. Or where she'd hide out at three in the morning trying to study because her crazy roommate she'd already named *Sasha* listened to death metal and dealt ecstasy from their messy, tiny dorm room. She stood at the exact spot where she said I'd one day pass out drunk, but not before sending her cryptic text messages to find me because I'd just beaten a state record in the hundred-meter sprint and had celebrated a little too hard with my teammates.

UNC was *our* dream.

Our future.

After clearing her throat, she tells me, "When Dad got back on his feet financially, he looked into the account and saw that it hadn't been touched, which to him meant that she probably forgot about it. And I guess she did. Until she wanted to switch banks. So when she went to close out all accounts, they must have mentioned my college fund and she—"

"No." I mentally block my ears. "Don't say it."

"She took all the money, Luke."

I blow out a breath, my cheeks puffing with the force of it. "And it's *all* gone?" I ask hesitantly.

"She used the money to pay for an in-ground pool in her house that my dad paid for, to be enjoyed by her new husband and *his* kids."

My fists ball, but I keep my anger in check. For her. "And she wanted to what? Rub it in your face?"

"Not mine," she says, her voice a whisper. "Dad's."

I pinch the bridge of my nose. "I hate her."

"Me too."

I reach over and cover her hand with mine. "So what does that mean?"

"I don't get to go to college."

"I fucking hate her," I repeat, my heart pounding.

She says, again, "Me too."

After moments of silence, I ask, "Are you going to tell your dad?"

"Eventually, yeah."

I'm holding her hand now, my fingers laced through hers, my grip tight.

She adds, staring down at our joined hands, "Dad's just so happy at the moment with Misty and everything, and I don't want to crush his spirit."

"And break his heart," I murmur.

"My mom's already done that."

My eyes meet hers, her frown causing my own.

"We'll still see each other, right?" she asks. "When you come home for holidays?"

"It won't be the same," I tell her.

She sighs. Then a slight smile breaks through. "I'm going to miss seeing your ugly face every day."

"Shut up. You love my face."

Her eyes roll. "Yeah, it's like looking into the sun."

"So beautiful it hurts?" I ask, unable to contain my smirk.

"Blindingly *painful*."

"You like me," I tease.

"I *tolerate* you," she retorts.

I inhale deeply, my smirk fading. There's a shift in the air—thick and overwhelming. "So we only have a year," I murmur. I lean in closer, so close my breath fogs her glasses. Her eyes drift shut the moment my lips find her temple.

She's too much.

She's everything.

"I'm sorry, Lane," I whisper. "About UNC. About your mom. I should've been there for you, just like you've always been there for me."

PAST | LOIS

I felt the sincerity in the Preston boys' declaration to be part of their family, and I carried that with me through the following months. I'd gotten even closer to Lucas and became friends with Leo and Logan because we attended the same school. I even *attempted* to make friends with Dumb Name so Luke didn't feel like he had to split his time between us.

When Kathy announced that she was pregnant (again), I was there, sitting between Luke and Leo on the couch with the rest of the Preston kids scattered around the living room. I squealed and wrapped my arms around Kathy and Tom.

Later that day, while Luke pushed me around the merry-go-round at the playground, he teased me about my reaction. "It's exciting!" I giggled. "Aren't you excited?"

"Not really," he said, using both hands to push the bars, his legs moving quicker, spinning me faster. "It's my fourth pregnancy announcement. Fifth baby. I was kind of expecting it." Then he jumped on while it was still moving and sat down next to me, his gaze on the sky, my gaze on him.

"Luke?"

"Yeah."

"Your parents must have a lot of—"

"Shut up!" he shouted, his hand quick to cover my mouth, muffling my final word.

I smiled against his palm, and he must've felt it because he smiled back. Then suddenly, he leaned forward, his lips puckered. He kissed the back of his hand—the hand covering *my mouth*. When he pulled back, his eyes were huge. He dropped his hand quickly and looked away. I touched my lips and wondered what it would feel like to have him kiss me. If it felt anything like I felt then, it was going to blow my mind. I lay on my back, looking up at the dull gray sky, and even though the merry-go-round had lost its momentum and was barely moving, my mind was spinning and the world had never seemed so bright.

When I got home, I hugged my dad like I'd never hugged him before. "What's this?" he asked, hands on my shoulders when I finally let him go.

"I just love you."

"Me?"

"And I love it here. Thank you for finding this place."

His beard shifted, revealing his smile. "So you're happy here?"

I nodded. "The happiest."

It was all true. Meeting the Prestons, spending time with Kathy, meeting *Lucas*, it changed my outlook, my life.

I felt worthy.

I finally felt like I was enough.

Especially when baby Lachlan was born and Kathy asked me to be his godmother. There was no official ceremony, but the title stood.

I remember sitting at my desk and writing a letter to my mom— a letter I would never send. It told her that I loved my life. That I loved my new home. That I loved my decision to leave with Dad. And that I was happy and I was *loved*.

Then one day, it all crumbled—my world, my heart—the moment Dad sat me down and told me Kathy had been diagnosed with cancer. I remember looking up at the ceiling, at the bright, white light hanging in the center of my room while my head spun, and spun, and spun some more. The walls closed in, the air thick in my lungs as I tried to wrap my mind around what it would mean. Not just for her, but for her seven children. And then I thought about Luke, about the boy who offered me friendship when I had no one and nothing. I stood quickly, my heart racing. "Lucas," I whispered.

"Lucas is fine, Lois."

"No." I shook my head. "I need to see him."

"You'll see him at school."

"No! I need to see him now, Dad!"

"Honey," he said, reaching out and taking my hand. I yanked it back and ran for the door. I kept running until my lungs burned, until my legs felt like jelly, all the way to the Preston house. Logan answered the door, his cheeks splotchy. I couldn't get a word out through the tiny spurts of breath I was struggling to get through, but I didn't need words. Logan fell into my arms, his sobs muffled by my hoodie. "It's okay," I whispered, stroking the back of his head. "It's going to be okay."

"Laney," Luke said from behind him, his eyes filled with tears even though it was clear he'd already shed so many of them.

Logan released me and Luke approached, his attempts to stifle his cries forcing my own. "I'm so sorry," I told him.

I don't know how long we stood in his doorway, his arms around my neck, mine around his waist, holding onto the only thing that felt right, that made sense, in an otherwise cruel and hurtful world. "I'm glad you're here, Laney."

"I'll *always* be here."

***

WINTER TURNED TO SPRING, spring turned to summer—a summer a complete contrast to the year before. But at the same time, it was identical. The previous summer, I said goodbye to my mom and, as strange as it sounds, I found a replacement.

That summer my dad said a single word that had me falling to my knees and sobbing in front of him: *Terminal.*

I wanted to run to Lucas, to hold him in my arms and never let him go. I wanted to curl up at the foot of his bed, keep him safe, tell him everything would be okay. That I would be there for him through it all. Dad was the only reason I didn't. "They need some space, Lo," he said. "They need to spend whatever time the have left as a family."

KATHERINE ELIZABETH PRESTON passed away September 25th.

Her funeral was five days later.

It seemed like the entire town mourned her death.

I can't really recall much of the actual funeral, my heavy heart and heavy tears preventing me from remembering most of it, but I remember Lucas. I remember the way he stood with Lucy on one side, Leo on the other, his head lowered, wearing a suit with a tie (crooked and tied completely wrong). I also remember feeling like I was a horrible person for thinking that he'd never looked as handsome as he did right then, at his mother's funeral, surrounded by nothing but heartache and fear.

I wanted to go to him. To all of them. But I didn't know what to say. What do you say to seven kids who've just lost their world?

"You should talk to Luke, sweetheart," Dad said, making our way up the Prestons' long driveway, along with many other cars, after the ceremony. "You're his best friend, and he needs you now more than ever."

I managed to find my voice for the first time that day. "What do I say to him?"

"You tell him the truth, Lo. That you're sorry. That you're there for him. That you always will be."

The words filtered through the knot in my throat and out of my mouth, "I'm scared, Dad. What if I say something wrong?"

"You won't, sweetheart. Just be you."

I FOUND Lucas in his secret hideout, his eyes glazed as he looked out on the lake. "Hey," I said, barely a whisper.

He didn't respond. Not verbally, and not in any other way. I sat on the ground next to him, forgetting the expensive black dress Dad had bought me because I didn't own anything suitable for a funeral. Minutes passed, neither saying a word, neither making a move to do so. My mind worked, trying to find words of comfort, of grace. "Don't," he said, breaking the silence.

"Don't what?"

"Don't say you're sorry. Or that you'll miss her. Or that she was an amazing person and the world is a lesser place because she's no longer part of it. Or that I'll be okay. That one day, I'll get over this. Or to remember her for everything she was, because I've heard it all. There's not a damn thing you can say to make it *okay*. Not now. Not ever." He didn't say it with malice, and I didn't take it that way. He was just… sad. So damn *sad*.

And *right*.

And I realized then that it wasn't as if Kathy had died suddenly—been in a car accident or any other form of accidental death. For months we knew this was coming. For months Lucas, along with all the other children, would've heard the same words over and over. It would do nothing to take away the pain. The hurt. The sadness he was so openly displaying. He was a twelve-year-old boy who was hurting, and the one person who could make it better had been taken away from him. He pulled his knees to his chest, his tie now undone, separated and hanging loosely around his neck. His hair was a mess, his eyes tired and teary.

The words came to me quickly, without thought—words I'd held onto and kept secret until that moment. "My dad's not my real dad," I told him. "I mean, not my biological dad. I don't know who *he* is. Dad married my mom when I was five and he's treated me

LUCAS

like his own ever since." I glanced at him quickly, but he was looking down at his lap. So I focused on the lake, at the ripple of water that seemed to mirror my emotions. "After they got married, Mom took a late shift at a tile factory. She would sleep in the mornings and be gone in the afternoons, so for a long time Dad was the only parent I had. I barely saw her. On weekends she'd be gone hours, sometimes days at a time, and we didn't know where. So Dad and I got closer while Mom chose to drift away. After a few years, I'd hear them arguing. A lot. I'd hear her yelling at him for not doing enough to support her, for breaking promises to her that he'd take care of us." I licked my lips, my mouth dry. "She didn't have the life she expected, but I'd never been so happy. And as the years went by, things got worse. The breaking point was when Mom came home late one night and Dad asked where she'd been. She picked up a chair from the kitchen table and threw it at him. He told her then and there that he wanted a divorce." I reached out for his hand, and he let me hold it. "I kind of just stood there frozen, my heart sinking because I was losing the only parent who cared about me." I blinked back the tears, knowing I had no right to carry them. Not that day. "A few months before I moved here... I stood in the driveway, watching him load up his car, leaving the house *he* owned, a house he offered to my mom and me... and I just stood there crying, not wanting to say goodbye. I couldn't let go of him when he hugged me... when he promised to keep in touch. I didn't want him to *keep in touch*. He was my dad, regardless of what my birth certificate said." After heaving in a breath, I found the courage to continue. "And I looked at my mom, pleading with my eyes to not let him go, and she just looked at me, not a single ounce of sorry or regret on her face, and said, 'Make your choice, Lois. Him or me.' So I got in his car and we drove away. For weeks we stayed in a hotel room, and she never once checked in on me. Sometimes I'd dream of seeing her waiting for me outside of school, just to let me know she was there, that I could go to her." I swallowed loudly, pushed through. "He gave up everything, the house, the car, all the money he had. And he never once looked at me the way she had— that I'd somehow ruined his life. So now we're here, and he's struggling to make ends meet because he wanted to keep the peace. And I know he did that for me so that I didn't have to deal with her. And I know you don't want to hear how great your mom was or any other generic speech you may have heard a million times, but your mom was the closest thing I've had to one, and I'd give up *my* mother if it meant that you could see yours just one more time."

He stared at me, his head slowly moving from side to side, his eyebrows drawn. "I don't know what I would've done without you." He kept his hand on mine, the other wiping at my unjustified tears. "*My* Lois Lane."

I hugged him so hard I swear I pushed all the air from his lungs. "*My* Clark Kent."

IT WAS a few weeks after the funeral—thunder and lightning and huge gusts of wind accompanied the rain, and I lay in bed—deathly afraid of storms. Justin Timberlake's *Cry Me a River* the soundtrack of my current life status.

The song suddenly stopped and the room filled with darkness. "Lois?" Dad shouted from upstairs.

"Yeah?"

"The storm must've cut off the power."

"I figured."

He made his way down the basement stairs and toward me, flashlight in hand. "You okay?"

"How long do you think it's going to be out for?" I asked.

"Why? You expecting to outweigh the rain with Timberlake's tears?"

I said nothing.

"That song's been playing for three days straight, Lo."

"I like the song."

"It's a little depressing."

There was a knock on the basement door which led to the backyard. The only one who would know to use it would be— "Lucas!" I shouted.

Dad opened the door.

Luke stood just outside, hair soaked, along with the rest of him. His arms were crossed, shivering against the cold. "I'm sorry for coming around so late, sir." He was in a white t-shirt and running shorts and nothing else. His teeth clanked together as he said, "Laney told me once she was scared of storms... I wanted to make sure she was okay."

"Does your dad know where you are, son?" Dad asked.

Luke shook his head, droplets of rain falling on his shoulder. "No, sir. My dad doesn't really know where *he* is most of the time." His gaze shifted to me standing behind my dad. I swallowed the knot in my throat, a million emotions hitting me. He looked so sad, so hopeless, so *young*. *Too young* to be feeling the way he did.

"Get inside," Dad said, breaking the silence and pulling on Luke's arm to get him out of the rain. "Did you run here?"

Luke held my stare. "Yes, sir."

I finally found my voice, my eyes glazed with tears. "Why are you here?" I breathed out.

He spoke, his voice hoarse. "I wanted to make sure you were okay."

I looked at him, disbelief washing through me. He stood there, his skin glistening and his eyes red and raw. "Lucas... Are *you* okay?"

He stared at me a long time. Then he let out a sob, so quiet I barely heard it. I stepped toward him, my hand going for his. "I hurt, Laney," he said, his voice cracking with emotion.

"Where?" I rushed out, searching his body for any sign of injury. After what felt like forever, and finding no blood or broken bones, I looked up at him, and I could instantly tell that the pain he spoke of wasn't physical. It was so much worse. I wrapped him in my arms, ignoring his wet clothes and my dry ones, and at that moment, we pretended the storm and the darkness drowned out his cries and devoured his pain. His chest rose and fell against mine, his grip on me getting tighter with each passing second. Then he exhaled a shaky breath, his mouth to my ear. "I hurt everywhere."

MY DAD MADE us hot chocolate, and we pretended like we didn't think we were too old for it. Lucas spoke while Dad and I listened. He told us about how his dad was suffering, lost, and trying to find the answers at the bottom of a bottle of whiskey. Luke had seen his dad passed out drunk more times than he'd seen him upright, and Lucy was the one holding it together. Her and the twins' baseball coach—some boy named Cameron who would later play a huge role in all their lives. The night before, Logan had gone missing. No one noticed until Luke checked in on everyone at around two in the morning. Logan was out in the freezing lake, his pajamas still on.

When Luke had found him, Logan simply said, "I wanted to feel *something*." They promised each other they would never tell Lucy because she had enough to worry about, and Luke gave Logan the clothes off his back and snuck him back into the house, up the stairs, toward baby Lachlan's room where Lucy and Leo were awake, attending to a fussing baby. The twins woke, too, and joined them in the nursery. All the kids cried. Together. Apart. But silent, not wanting to wake their dad.

IT WAS the first night Lucas ever spent in my house, in my bedroom, on the couch. It took him a few hours to fall asleep, and I watched as his chest rose and fell, his search for peace finally found in his sleep.

It was heartbreaking, breathtaking, and in a way, it was kind of beautiful.

Lucas Preston was beautiful.

CHAPTER SIX

LUCAS

LANE FOUND out about this craft store a few months ago via Reddit. Yes, apparently there's a Reddit page for *everything*. Even craft junkies like her. And, apparently, she traded one Saturday shift for three Sunday shifts at the small movie theater where she works so she could hop on a bus to check it out. When she told me that she'd been, I got *so* mad. I gave her this huge lecture about how girls like her shouldn't be traveling on buses by themselves. I yelled, told her she was naive and she should have told me she was going so I could've driven her. Then she started getting angry back because she's crazy. She said that my anger was unjustified and that I was overreacting. I told her she was an idiot. She said I was stupid. We froze each other out for three days. Those three days sucked. So I apologized—even though I didn't really know what I was sorry for—and told her she was right. *She wasn't.* If anything, she was stubborn and clueless. Still, I conceded. Like I said, those three days sucked. She forgave me quickly, then started on about how she was old enough to do what she wanted. It wasn't about her *want* to go visit the stupid store. It was about her safety. So I told her that, which then led to another argument. Another three days of suckage, and then, on the fourth day, she opened her locker and there—next to her psychology textbook—was half a Snickers bar.

So, I'm a sucker who hates fighting with his best friend.

She was still wrong.

I was right.

The end.

LUCAS

"THIS PLACE NEEDS some form of organization," I whisper, hovering behind her.

"It's kind of what makes it amazing, though," she says, half turning to me, her smile uncontainable. She steps over a random pile of who-knows-what. "All this yarn and thread and patterns everywhere."

"Is there something you're looking for in particular?" I ask. It's not that I'm in a rush to get out, but I'm hungry. And antsy. I skipped my run and now I have all this built-up adrenaline, and I don't know what to do with it.

She smiles up at me, and the adrenaline doubles.

I smile back. "You have a list, don't you?"

"It's only a small one. I promise," she says quickly, her hands on my chest as if she's trying to calm me. Now she's biting her lip, her full, strawberry-tasting bottom lip, and an image flashes into my mind with what I could do with all that built-up adrenaline. It includes her, her bed, and her lack of clothing.

Blink. Push out fantasies. Breathe.

I say, "Take your time. Honestly."

"You can sit over there," she tells me, removing her hands from me and pointing to a chair covered in yarn. *Put your hands back on me, Laney.* "Go on your phone or something. I won't be long."

"I left my phone on your bedroom floor."

"Oh."

"I'll help you find what you're looking for. What's your next project?"

She seems to hesitate. "A cross-stitch."

Without so much as a flinch, I say, already making my way to the right area, "So we need to find all the right colored threads, right?"

She nods.

Good. I can do that. It's time-consuming and mind-numbing and it'll take my thoughts away from her, her bed, her naked in her bed.

She told her dad she'd dated. *Oh, hey random thought I tried to forget about. Nice of you to sneak up on me like that.*

I place my hand between us, palm up. "List me."

We spend two and a half hours in the store without so much as a single complaint from me. Maybe because I still feel guilty about last night, or maybe because she's smiling and happy and no longer sad, because I wasn't lying when I said I didn't like seeing her sad.

58

Or... maybe because I can't stop thinking about her "dating" other guys. What does that even mean? She goes on dates, then they drop her off at home and she goes to her room and knits me gloves? Or does she go on a date, sneak the guy back to her room through the basement door and have wild monkey sex with them in the same bed I was just fantasizing about? *Wait!* Am I sleeping in another guy's sweat and leftover sex juice when I get into her bed at night? *What the fuck, Lane?!*

"Are you okay?" she asks, sneaking up behind me. *Sneaky Lane.* I don't like Sneaky Lane. Sneaky Lane sneaks guys into her room and does sneaky things to them. "You look lost."

I am lost, Lane—drowning in visions of you with faceless guys having over-the-top sex in positions I've only ever seen on the Internet. Obviously, I don't say that to her. That would make me insane. "I'm fine," I tell her. "Did you see anything else you like?"

She nods, her eyes bright. "And now that I'm not saving for college, I can buy *all the things!*"

I pout, and her hands go to my chest again. I should pout more often.

"We should finish up here and find somewhere to feed you. You look hungry."

I exhale loudly and place a hand on her waist, the other holding the basket filled with different colored threads. "I am hungry," I tell her, *just not for food.* I tighten my grip so I can pull her closer to me. Her arms are at her sides now, her tits pressed against my chest. She got them right after she turned fourteen. Her tits, not her arms. I remember because it was the summer I spent the most time in the lake. I was too embarrassed to show exactly how my body reacted to her body. Stupid uncontrollable body and stupid uncontrollable hormones.

"Where's the list?" she says, her voice hoarse. She clears her throat, repeats the question. Her cheeks are red. She's blushing. Fidgeting. Her eyes won't meet mine. Her body's reacting to my body. To the closeness. So... maybe not-so-stupid uncontrollable bodies. I like that she's blushing. That she hasn't pulled away. That she's bending over, giving me a clearer view of her tits as she picks up the list from the basket. She turns to face the wall of threads but doesn't move too far, her back's to my chest, my hand on her waist, the top of her head an inch below my chin. *Coconuts, lime, and Laney.* "What number are you up to?" she asks.

59

One, I almost say. It's not the answer she's looking for, but it's the only number in my head. I have *one year* left with Laney. *One year* to make her see me the way I see her.

One.

I'M HOLDING HER HAND.

I don't know how it happened, when it happened, but we're crossing the road toward a diner and we're holding hands, and not in the way I hold Lachlan's hand when we cross the road, but in the way I hold my girlfriend's hand. Because I have one of those... a girlfriend, not a hand. Grace has been my girlfriend for about six months, and she's the only girl I've ever stuck with through an entire summer. Grace is shorter than Lane, blonde, beautiful. She runs track, like me, and knows the demands and the self-control it takes to be where we are. She's also easy—not sexually, but that, too, I guess—but she's fun and we get along, which makes me an asshole for enjoying holding another girl's hand more than hers because like I said, she's my girlfriend.

"I'm still so full from breakfast," my non-girlfriend, hand-holding partner says. "I'm probably just going to get a salad."

I laugh out loud. "You? A salad? You'll be going straight to the back of the menu—dessert—and you'll probably order two different ones."

"Or not!" Laney exclaims, nose in the air. "I'm trying to watch my figure." She pats her stomach.

"Shut up. You have an amazing figure. Especially considering you do absolutely nothing to maintain it."

She stops in the middle of the road, causing an oncoming car to brake and swerve slightly. "You think I have an amazing figure?" she asks.

Girl's blind. Naive. And also completely unaware of her surroundings.

I pull on her hand and drag her off the road and onto the safety of the sidewalk while I wave an apology at the driver who's cursing at us. "You do. But I'd prefer it if you were alive." I open the diner door for her and she stops just inside, scanning the place for what I know is a corner booth, a table made for 4-6 instead of just the two of us because I know what she'll do the minute we sit down. She'll

60

dump the contents of the paper bag I'm holding and mark off all the items on the list to make sure we got everything she wanted. And she'll do it alone because she doesn't trust me, all because of that one time I read her handwritten 5 as an 8 and got the wrong colored threads and the store was closed the following day, a Sunday, and she couldn't finish her project on the weekend and swear, she acted as though I set her hair on fire.

We get a corner booth. She orders two desserts. I order a steak sandwich and loaded fries, and she hands me her phone as soon as the waitress leaves because she knows I need to work out how many calories I'm about to devour to calculate how many miles I need to run to burn it off. I type in her PIN number, the same code she uses for everything, a code I memorized from her bike lock when we were twelve. Then I glance up at her. She's too busy, focused on marking the items off the list, which gives me a little time to go through her phone and look for any interaction with guys she may have dated/had monkey sex with.

I go through her text messages first. An invasion of privacy? Maybe. A way to placate my insanity? Definitely.

The first three sets of messages are from who I'd expect. Me, her dad, her mom.

Then there are a bunch with numbers but no names linked to those numbers. *Are we still on for tonight?* one reads, dated last Saturday. What the fuck?

"Having trouble?" she asks.

I drop the phone, caught red-handed, even though she would've never known if it wasn't for my guilt-ridden overreaction. Her eyes narrow, her gaze dropping to the phone now on the table, a clear view of the message I'd just read.

She smiles.

That's good. At least she hasn't picked up the fork and threatened to stab me in the eyes. "Was that an accident, or are you curious about something and don't want to ask?" she says.

I push the phone aside. Stupid thing gave me away. "What do you mean?" I ask, feigning… I don't even know.

"You seemed to have a reaction to me telling my dad that I'd dated. I'm surprised you haven't brought it up yet." She says this so casually, like she's asking me about how many calories might be in the brownie she just ordered and not the copious amounts of sex she's having in *our* bed. Okay, it's not *ours*, but it may as well be. Now she's ticking off items on the list.

61

Tick.

Tick.

Tick.

My damn jaw is ticking with the visions blowing up my brain. *Stop having sex in our bed!* I clear my throat and lean back in my seat, one arm on the table, the other balled at my side. "How many guys have you dated, anyway?" Good question. Good start.

She shrugs. Casual Laney is as unpleasant as Sneaky Laney. "A few."

"A few?" I ask, leaning forward. "A few like, between three and five, or a few as in… there's a number but you've lost count?"

She smiles again.

She ticks. Again.

I wait.

She looks up at me. "Why does it matter?"

"Why keep it a secret?"

"You've never asked before."

I sigh. "Do I know any of them?"

"Again," she says, her smile spreading. "Why does it matter?"

"I do know them, don't I? Am I friends with any of them?"

Her coffee arrives the same time my water does. She waits until I take a sip before saying, "Dumb Name and I went out a few times."

I spit out my drink. "What?"

She's laughing, wiping at the list now splattered with my post-mouth water. Luckily, I missed her recently-purchased items. "We didn't want to tell you in case you were all excited about the prospect of your two best friends dating. Needless to say, it didn't work out."

"You're serious right now?" Why is my chest tight? Why is my fist tighter? I'm going to punch something. Not here. Not now. But I will. After I drop Laney off. Yeah. I'm going to drive to Dumb Name's house and punch him right in his dumb face.

Laney shrugs. "It was toward the end of freshman year. He came up to me after school all nervous and he said he always thought I was beautiful but I was always your girl, you know? But then you dated a bunch of girls that year so he figured it was just in his head—you and me—so he asked me out, and I don't know… for a moment, he made me feel beautiful, so I said yes and we went out a couple of times. He was my first kiss."

I can't speak, too busy stewing, replaying her words over and over.

She goes back to her list. Tick tick tick.

Then our food comes and we eat and she talks and I *barely* listen.

She pays for our food, makes another joke about not needing money for college anymore, and as she packs her stuff back into the paper bag, a girl approaches, around the same age as us. "Hi," she says, smiling brightly between the two of us. She kind of looks like Grace, the forgotten girlfriend, the girlfriend whose hands don't feel anywhere near as good as Laney's. Only the girl in front of us has brown hair, wider hips, bigger breasts than Grace. "Are you guys leaving?" she asks, reaching into her pocket.

Lane smiles.

I nod.

"Oh," says the unnamed girl. She reveals a piece of paper from her pocket and slides it across the table toward me. It has her name, *Kate*, and her phone number. She's grinning when I look back up at her, but I don't look at her long. Instead, I'm drawn to Lane, to her reaction. She's focused on packing up her things. *Too* focused. Like she's avoiding the situation completely.

"Um…" I look up at Kate, at her waiting expression. "I have a girlfriend."

"Oh," she says again, then focuses on Lane. "I'm sorry, I thought—" She covers her face, as if embarrassed. She's not, though. Any girl who has the confidence to approach a guy who's shown absolutely zero signs of noticing her can't possibly be embarrassed about getting turned down. "I thought she was your sister."

Lane finds her voice for the first time since Kate approached and uses it to say, "Oh, I'm not his girlfriend. Definitely more like his sister. It's cool."

You know that phrase… sticks and stones may break my bones, but words will never hurt me?

It's bullshit.

Words hurt.

Sticks and stones may break bones, but words dig and dig and dig deep into your heart until the hurt resonates, and your heart fails to remember the reason it beats in the first place. For a moment, almost for an entire day, Laney was that reason. Until those words: *Definitely more like his sister.*

I drive home in silence.

She sits in the passenger's seat. In silence.

I drop her off at her house. Still silent.

Then I drive to Dumb Name's house so I can punch him.

I don't.

I'm not really a punchy kind of guy, no matter how badly I want to be. Instead, I look him in the eye and I ask, "Why her?"

He says, knowing exactly what I'm talking about, "What does it matter? I wasn't the one for her. And besides, you're two years late. That's two years too long. What the fuck are you waiting for, Luke?"

CHAPTER SEVEN

LOIS

ALL BLOOD DRAINS from Dad's face.
He looks shocked.
Angry.
Furious.

We sit at the kitchen table while his new girlfriend, Misty, sits in the living room, a glass of wine in her hand. It's the first time I've met her and I wish I could've left a better first impression, but there's not a lot you can do when you've spent the last hour alone in your room, an endless stream of tears running down your face, leaking into a pillow, a pillow that smells like the boy that's caused your tears. I heard them come in, their voices loud, their laughter louder. Then Dad called my name, and I answered that I was here, so he asked for me to meet *his* Misty. He actually said, "Come meet *my* Misty." I loved that he called her his. *She* would love that he called her his. I loved that he sounded so happy. So, *so* happy. But I also knew that I had to tell him about Mom, and I knew I would be the reason why his happiness was short-lived, so I didn't bother wiping my tears, didn't bother hiding that I was going through some kind of emotional breakdown. I wanted the news to come from me, and it had to be soon because I didn't want to give Mom that victory. We've given her enough.

"I'm so sorry, Lois," Dad says, his voice breaking. "I should've been more diligent. I just…"

"You can't blame yourself for this, Dad."

"We saved for so long. You've worked so hard the past two summers for this."

"It is what it is. There are other colleges, financial aid. I can always go to community college or whatever."

"But UNC's your dream."

Because I wanted to be close to him. Because I didn't want to leave him alone. But in the past year, he's started dating again and he's on his feet and his social life has taken off and he doesn't *need* me around. "It is what it is," I repeat and come to a stand. "Go be with your girlfriend, Dad. Enjoy each other's company. You deserve it." I smile, but it's forced.

"Lois," he says. "How was your day with Luke?"

I shrug. "It was the same as always."

"You seem to be taking this college news pretty well. Did he say or do something to make you feel better about it all?"

I nod. "Yeah. He did." He made me realize that no matter where we were, how far away from home we were, things wouldn't change. So what if we had another four years together? It was only four years. After that, he'd go off and do his own thing, and I'd do mine, whatever that might be, and nothing would change. Three years ago, I had the same thought. We had four years of high school together. Maybe then he'd look at me differently. He'd look at me the way he looked at any one of his past girlfriends. Or the way he looked at the girl at the diner today. He'd see the wideness of my hips, the largeness of my breasts. He'd blush when I'd smile at him the way he did with her.

But he teased me all day. His hands, his words, his everything. He liked the attention I gave him, the way I'd blush when he jokingly flirted with me.

Because that's how we worked, Luke and me.

He was a tease.

And I was a joke.

LUCAS

I wanted to kiss her.

I've wanted to kiss her since the moment I saw her.

But we were eleven. It would've been weird.

Now I'm almost eighteen, and I've kissed enough girls to make up for all the pent-up angst that's built from not finding the courage to actually kiss the girl I *want* to kiss.

She told her dad that she'd dated. She'd never told me she dated, never even mentioned a date or a guy in passing. And it made me want to kiss her more. I didn't want to bring it up because

66

I knew she had other things going on, but I was curious. So I asked, and she answered, and her answer made me furious.

Curious and furious.

And rhymy, apparently.

"Watch!" Lachlan demands.

I push aside my thoughts of Laney and focus on my brother. "I see, bud. You're getting good at brushing your teeth on your own," I tell him through the reflection in the bathroom mirror.

He smiles wide, toothbrush in hand, a mixture of baby and adult teeth on full display. "I'm Thor years old!"

"You mean four?"

"No. Thor! Tongue to teeth, Luke. Thhh-or!"

With a laugh, I say, "Four is the number. Thor is the superhero. And you're six, dude."

"I know!" he laughs out, looking down at his hands holding up five fingers. "Six." Then he continues to brush his teeth. When he's done, he asks, "Do you think I'll live to be eleventy-three?"

"I've told you, eleventy-three isn't a number."

"Is so."

"Is not."

"Is so."

Sigh.

"Lucas, will you buy me a four hammer? I asked Dad. He says I have to do chores. But you'll just buy it for me because I'm your best friend, right?"

I shake my head. "If Dad says you have to do chores, then you have to do chores. And *you* are *not* my best friend. Laney is."

"And Dumb Name."

"Don't call Garray that."

"Why not?" he asks, stepping down from the stool we have set up so he can reach the taps at the sink. Clearly, he got his height from my mother. "Everyone else does."

"Because..." I drop to a squatting position and wait for him to climb onto my back. "Just because."

"Because why?"

When he settles, I stand up and piggyback him to the door. "Because I said so."

"Fine," he moans, switching off the light. "Laney's my tooth fairy."

"What?"

"Daddy said she's there to watch out for me and take care of me if no one else can."

I walk us to his room, a room filled with my trophies and medals and pictures of me running, pictures of us together. I drop him on his bed. "You mean your godmother? How in the world do you get godmother and tooth fairy confused? You goose!"

"I'm not Luce!" He cackles and squirms on his bed, shifting the blankets beneath him. "You ready for your one minute?" I ask.

He nods, still squirming. When Lachlan was a baby, he wouldn't sleep unless he was being held. Then as he got older and moved to a big boy bed, the only thing that changed was that only *I* was allowed in his bed. So every night at 7:00, I'd get in his bed with him and wait until he fell asleep. Sometimes, he wouldn't be able to sleep and after a long-ass time of lying there, wide awake, I'd attempt to leave. He'd cry. I'd tell him that I would only lie with him for *one minute*. He had no idea how long a minute was so it was more like five seconds. At some point, he started calling tuck-ins "one minute" and now it's stuck.

I fix his blankets and tell him to get under before joining him. "Can I cuggles you this time?" he asks.

I shift to my side and face him. "Sure."

His small arms wrap around my neck and pull me toward him so his forehead's touching mine. "Remember that time when you weren't here to cuggles and do my one minute?"

My eyes narrow, my mind searching. "When I was at track camp?"

He nods. "And New Jersey at the start of summer."

"How do you remember track camp? You were three."

"I remember things from when I was free."

"Three," I correct. "Tongue to teeth. Thhhh-ree."

"That's what I said!"

"Okay." I close my eyes, the exhaustion quick to consume me. I hadn't slept much last night, and I'd been out with Lane most of the day. I'm almost tempted to sleep in Lachy's bed with him, but the second I close my eyes, Laney fills my mind.

I wanted to kiss her.

When she told me she'd miss seeing me every day—I wanted to kiss her.

"Do you love Laney?" Lachlan asks.

The kid reads minds. "What?"

"Do you love her?"

"Yes," I tell him truthfully.

"Like Cam loves Lucy?"

I wanted to kiss her when we were in that store, my hand on her waist, her chest against mine. I wanted to dip my head, find her lips with mine and devour them the way I've only ever dreamed about.

"Luke!"

"What?"

"Do you love her like Cam loves Lucy?" he asks again, his blue eyes big and waiting.

"How do you think Cameron loves Lucy?"

"They sex," he says simply.

"What the f— What the hell did they teach you in school?"

"Do you and Laney sex?"

I get out of his bed and throw the blankets over his face. "Go to sleep."

"Do you?" he shouts, but I'm already rushing out of his room. "Do you and Laney sex?" he yells, louder this time.

Dad freezes at the top of the stairs. "Did he just say what I think he said?"

I nod. "I don't know where he got it from."

Surprisingly, Dad grins. "So, do you?"

"Do I what?" I ask, bouncing on my toes, anxious to leave.

"Do you and Laney have sex?" he asks, arms crossed, waiting for my response.

"I have a girlfriend!"

"Keep telling yourself that," Logan says, stepping out of his room.

I ask, "What's that supposed to mean?"

"You know what it means," he says, eyes narrowed.

Leo climbs the stairs, deciding to join in. "What's going on?"

"Luke and Laney are having sex," Dad says with a chuckle.

I sigh. "This is how rumors get started."

"They're not having sex," Leo mumbles, removing his t-shirt as he walks past me and moves to the bathroom.

"How do you know?" Logan asks, raising his chin.

Leo steps inside the bathroom and turns to face us all, one hand on the door, ready to close it. "Because Laney's smart and beautiful and way too good for Luke."

"What the *hell* is so wrong with me?" I whine.

"SEX!" Lachlan shouts.

I TRIED to get her off my mind, but the only thing I could think about was Laney.

One last year with Laney.

Sure, I'd see her on holidays, and I'd make sure to come home on weekends whenever possible, but it's not the same. I'd be gone, living a life where she wouldn't be around to call me out on my screw ups, and she'd move on and live every day without me. Fuck the fact that I wouldn't be able to crawl into her bed whenever I felt the need to be close to her, but I'm positive she'd fill those nights with date after date, guy after guy. All of them *not* me. That thought alone has my stomach doing somersaults and my heart beating wildly. I almost thump at my chest, mad and frustrated with myself, because I have *one year*. Just one year to make her want me the way I want her. She listened to me talk about girls, about my awkward-as-fuck fumbly first time, and she never mentioned anything. Not a damn word. And now I'm mad. At her. Because she should've said something, right?

Without thinking, I slip on my running shoes and head out. I have zero knowledge of the time. It was seven when I put Lachy to bed, but who the hell knows how long I've been in my apartment, pacing back and forth, trying to push thoughts of her out of my mind.

I'd felt closer to her today. Closer than I've ever felt. And not just physically. I feel like there's a giant clock hanging over me, counting down the days, hours, minutes, seconds until... I can't even process what happens when the final second ticks over.

Before I know it, I'm at a crossroads. A *literal* crossroads. I've spent day after day here—the only part of my routine run where I stop. I look left. Look right. Not for the cars, but for guidance. Right brings me past Laney's work, toward the school, and a couple more rights take me home.

Left?

Left brings me to *her*.

With two fingers on my pulse, I attempt to count the beats, but the numbers are blurred, my concentration drowning in thoughts and images of *her*.

She looked good today.

She smelled even better...

Fuck, I almost lost my mind.

I'm *still* losing my mind.

I take the 468 steps to her door.

I KNOCK ONCE.

Twice.

On the third time, I begin to panic, because seriously? What the fuck am I doing here? I turn to leave, but the door opens and my panic triples.

"How dumb am I? I tried calling you," she says, and I face her.

She's looking right at me, her hair damp and loose, cascading around her shoulders.

I blink.

"Your phone, right?"

She's not wearing pants.

Jesus shit.

She's wearing on oversized shirt—her dad's work one—and nothing else. Well, maybe something but I can't see it, and so I let my imagination take me away.

"Luke?" She waves a hand in my face. "Are you here for your phone?"

When I don't respond (too busy imagining what's beneath the clothes—or cloth... or whatever the singular for clothes is), she says, "How long have you been knocking? I was in the shower."

Goddammit. Now I have naked Laney in the shower in my head.

"Luke!"

Of all the things I can say, I choose to tell her, "My name's on your shirt."

"What?" she asks, looking down at her chest. Then she glances up, her eyes narrowed in confusion.

"*Preston* Construction," I say because apparently she needs help reading. "My name."

She shakes her head. "It's not *your* name."

"Is so."

"Is not."

"Is so."

She spins on her heels and walks farther into her room, leaving the door open for me to follow. Which I do. Because did I mention *she's not wearing pants!* Girl's got legs for days and doesn't even

71

know it—this I learned the summer we were fifteen, and she showed up at my house in a bikini top and cut offs and kept asking why I was walking behind her, looking down at her shoes. I wasn't looking at her shoes. Obviously.

She walks to her desk, hidden beneath the staircase leading to the rest of the house. "I think it's dead," she says, her back turned. I stand behind her, look over her shoulder, sniff her. God, she smells good. Her shoulders straighten, but she doesn't turn around. "Did you just sniff me?"

I ignore her question, move closer to her. Just an inch. My chest is touching her back, her bare legs skimming mine. And I ask her something that's been infiltrating my mind all damn day. "How far do you go on these dates?"

"What?" she breathes out. Her breaths are rapid, matching the rise and fall of her chest. *Boobs.* "Are you still going on about this?"

"I haven't stopped thinking about it," I tell her truthfully.

She's struggling to breathe now.

So am I.

She turns slowly. Oh, so slowly. I don't budge. Not a bit. Her dark eyes meet mine through her glasses. "Do you want to charge your phone?" she asks, her voice barely audible.

"Yes," I say, but neither of us makes a move to do so.

She stares.

I stare back.

Six seconds.

Eight heartbeats.

Her throat moves when she swallows. I zone in on the movement and lick my lips, wanting them there, kissing her, tasting her. "Do they touch you?" I murmur. Her gaze drops, and my hands are quick to move. One goes to her waist, the other to her chin. I make her look at me. "Do they?"

"Luke."

"Where do they touch you?"

"Who?"

"Any of them. All of them." Jealousy can make someone insane. I'm proof.

Her hands are on my chest. I like her hands on me. Anywhere. *Keep touching me, Laney.* She's fighting against herself. I see it in her eyes. In her fists, balled against me. She wants to push, but she wants me closer. *Choose to be closer, Laney.*

72

She pushes. "I hate when you do this."

"Do what?"

"Tease me."

I almost laugh. *Almost.* She has no fucking idea. "You think I'm teasing you? You're the one who answered the door without pants."

"I knew it was you," she whispers.

"Exactly."

She shakes her head, her arms extended, palms an inch from my skin. There's space between us. I don't want space. I want her.

One year.

Tick. Tock.

She says, "You didn't come here for your phone, did you?"

My lips twitch. Curve.

Hers do the same.

She leans back against her desk.

I lean into her.

Bye-bye, space.

I say, "I came here for you."

"Why?"

"Because I want to kiss you, Lane. Because I want to wipe the memory of every other asshole who's ever touched these lips." I skim my thumb across her bottom lip, and her eyes drift shut. Her lips part. My thumb's in her mouth now, against her tongue, her soft, wet tongue, and Jesus Christ, I've never been this fucking hard in my life and I've barely touched her.

My mouth waters.

My pulse pounds.

She sucks harder.

"Shit."

She releases my thumb and her hand curves around my nape, pulling me to her. Her legs spread, welcoming me. My mouth's on her neck, on her throat, right where I wanted to be. She arches her back, makes a sound that has my knees buckling, collapsing into her. She's warm between her legs and she's moving, searching, wanting. I finally, *finally,* go for the kiss. Her mouth's open when I get there, her tongue warmer on my own than it felt on my thumb, and she's grinding, grinding, moaning, moaning. And I'm falling, deep, deep, deep into her web, and swear, if she kisses every guy the way she's kissing me I'm going to find every one of them and kill them dead.

I want to rip her shirt open, devour her breasts. Move lower so I can devour her some more. But I take my time. I reach up, undo one button. Another. My mouth doesn't leave her. Her fingers are in my hair. Tugging. Pulling. She breaks the kiss. I miss her lips. Another button and I'm kissing her collarbone, listening to her make those sounds. *Those* damn sounds.

My body wants her.

My mind knows I *have* her.

Another button.

Then: "Luke, wait."

I freeze. Blink hard. Keep my mouth on her. I try to stay focused on her. On here. On now. And not where I want us to be in ten minutes. Each and every one of her exhales hits me like a punch to the gut, bringing me back to reality. She says, "I've forgiven you for a lot before, and if this is some weird territorial thing because you realized I've been with other guys, then you need to leave. Now. Before we do something we'll both regret and can't take back."

Each word is like rapid fire going off in my head. I try to stay calm. But it's been four seconds, eight heartbeats. *Thump thump thump.* "We were supposed to have college," I murmur, my mouth suddenly dry.

She isn't pushing me away. Not yet.

So I keep going. "I was supposed to have four more years to make you fall for me, Lane. For you to see me the way I see you and now... I'm not ready yet. I'm not good enough yet."

She tugs on my hair, makes me face her. She's looking at me, concern deep in her eyes. "What are you talking about, Luke?"

"I screw up," I admit. "A lot. I make stupid mistakes and forget important things, and as your friend, that's okay. But I can't be that if I want to be more, and we were supposed to have college, Lane, where I don't have to worry about raising my brothers and making sure they get to all their activities. And there won't be this pressure to train so I can break Cooper fucking Kennedy's stupid high school records and get to all-state. It'll just be me and you and I can focus on you so I don't fuck up and make mistakes and forget important things like you asking me to meet you after seeing your mom and I'm sorry. But I don't want to be sorry. I don't want to give you a reason where I *have* to be sorry. I want to be better." I shut my eyes tight and pinch the bridge of my nose because I can't believe I just said all that. To her. Spilled the truth I'd kept secret for so long. Girl

74

after girl, night after night, trying and failing at not thinking of her when I was with each one of them and now we were here: crossroads.

"Do you love me, Lucas?" she asks, and I can tell from the weakness of her voice that she's crying. I wonder how often I've made her cry without knowing. "And I don't mean like a friend or a sister. Do you love me and want to be with me and only me? Because I *need* to know that you do. You have to show me. Anything less and this will ruin everything."

I blow out a heavy breath and open my eyes to see her watching me, waiting. My response is instant. "I've loved you forever, Laney."

I GO SLOW WITH HER, take my time, worship her body the way she deserves. She writhes beneath me, around me. Her skin's light against mine, pale porcelain against sun-kissed tan, something I don't notice until we're tangled limbs on *our* bed. I spend a lot of time outside, running after my goals, after my brothers. She spends a lot of time inside… click click clicking with her knitting needles.

She giggles, makes a joke about it.

Then she comes once on my fingers.

Another time on my tongue.

She wants to do the same with me, but I know I won't last, and it'll be messy and "We'll have time for that later," I tell her. Besides, I want to be on top of her. Inside her.

She keeps condoms in a box under her bed. I don't ask why. I don't want to know. But I know she hasn't done this before. I feel it when I enter her for the first time. She whimpers, and I ask if she's okay. I kiss her neck, her jaw. I stroke her hair. She whimpers again, and I ask if she wants to stop. She doesn't. "It's perfect," she says.

It *is* perfect.

She is perfect.

Every inch of her is perfect.

I want the moment to last forever.

But it can't.

It's hard to control your body, your lust, your desire. Especially when it's connected to a girl you've been in love with before you had a grasp on what love was.

75

I pull back, kiss her once. Her fingers strum across my back. "It's okay," she whispers, then smiles. "We'll have time for more later."

SHE WATCHES me slip my boxers back on, her dark hair a mess against the white pillowcase. Her cheeks are flush, strands of her hair caught in the sweat on her brow. She's smiling, and I feel like a god that I caused that. I grab my phone off her desk and connect it to the charger on the nightstand. I sit on the edge of the bed and wait for it to switch back on so I can make sure I have my alarm set. I'll definitely need a run in the morning.

The bed shifts with her movements, and I turn to her, her fist wrapped around the blanket, covering her breasts so they're not revealed when she sits up to kiss my bare back. I like that she finds it necessary to hide parts of her even though I've already seen them up close. She's still shy. Still innocent. Still Laney.

I turn enough to kiss her forehead, taste the sweat. "You okay?" I ask again.

She shrugs, her chin on my shoulder. "I'm still a little sore."

"I'm sorry," I tell her.

"I'm not."

My phone powers back on and she lays back down, her fingers stroking my back. My phone vibrates, again and again, and my eyes narrow as I pick it up, still connected to the charger. My pulse begins to race because I have no idea how long I've been here, no means of contact, but if something were wrong at home, Laney would be the first person they'd think to call. The alerts for messages and missed calls aren't from home, though. It's worse. My breath halts and the world shifts from this dream, this fantasy, to a harsh reality where the naked girl in the bed is *not* the girl who's been calling all day, *not* my *girlfriend.*

"Is everything okay?" Laney asks.

And the only thing I can say is, "It's Grace."

Silence passes.

I don't count the seconds.

"Oh my God, Luke," she whispers, "What did we do?"

I turn to her, the girl I love, and I give her what she deserves. "You didn't do anything, Lane. This is all me."

"But—"

"But nothing, baby." I kiss her forehead and dress quickly. She watches, thumb trapped between her teeth, tears in her eyes, and I know she's hurting. She feels guilty, as if it's her fault this happened, but it's not. She didn't cheat. I did. I didn't even think of Grace—not once. I sit back on the bed and rest my hand on her leg. "Are we going to do this? You and me?"

She stares at me a moment, nods once, but she seems unsure.

"Then I have to take care of this. Tonight."

"Okay," she croaks, her gaze lowering.

"Lane, you know I'd love nothing more than to stay here with you, but I need to do this."

"I know," she says, but she doesn't. She's insecure, and I'm not surprised.

"Lane."

She looks up, meets my eyes.

"I love *you*."

CHAPTER EIGHT

LOIS

I EXPECTED Luke to call in the morning and offer me a ride, but then I realized it wasn't just our first day back at school; it was Leo's, too, and Logan's first day of high school. So he'd be busy making sure everyone was set, probably fighting with Logan to get him out of bed. I look for him in the hallways, in the cafeteria, but our paths never seem to cross. I figure he broke up with Grace last night and might not want to rub it in her face by openly seeking me out. Luke's an arrogant jock, but he has a heart of gold.

I SEND HIM A TEXT.
    Two.
    Three.
    He doesn't respond.
    I start to get giddy, wanting, needing to see him, because I spent all night tossing and turning and remembering what it felt like to have him on top of me, inside me, whispering words of *love*. He told me he loved me, more than once, and that has to mean something, right?

HE HAS track practice after school, so I go to the library and leave with enough time to meet him outside the locker rooms when he's done. I stand in the tunnel that joins the field to the locker rooms, and I wait amongst the captured wind flowing in and out. I become cold, because even though it's summer, the sun's not on me, it's out there on the field with Lucas. So I reach into my bag, pull out a sweater, and shrug it on. It covers my eyes, blinds me for a moment, and when I can see again, there's a guy standing in front of me—a guy I recognize but haven't seen for years. He hasn't changed much, though, same rich-kid haircut groomed to look perfectly messy, same dark eyes, same smirk that always makes him seem like he's thinking about things he shouldn't be thinking about. He should be at UNC, where he got in on the same scholarship that's been promised to Luke, not standing outside the locker rooms of his old high school. Cooper Kennedy was your typical, entitled bad boy. Luke, along with many others, thought he was a dick. But he was also Luke's competition our first/Cooper's last year here. Even though they were technically on the same team, track wasn't a team sport. And if Luke and I had heard the rumors, so had he. Luke was set to break his records, take his titles. And that meant they were enemies, on and off the field. "You're Lois, right?" Cooper asks. "Preston's friend?"

I nod.

"You're all grown up," he says. His eyes trail me from head to toe, and I don't know what he's looking at.

"And you're still the same," I tell him.

"Why so hostile?"

"I'm sorry," I say, and it's true. I don't know Cooper from shit on a stick. "I'm just waiting on someone."

"Preston?"

I nod.

"He was finishing cooldowns when I left, so he shouldn't be long."

"Thanks."

"No worries." He points down the tunnel toward the field. "There he is now."

Luke stands center of the tunnel, a silhouette against the bright backdrop. "Lane?" he asks.

"Babe! Wait up!" I recognize the voice. I couldn't not. The voice had been part of Luke's life for the past six months. Grace appears, ponytail swinging from side to side, another silhouette, and now she's holding his arm and Luke's letting her, and I can't see his face, or hers, because I'm blinded. By the sun. By the rage. By the overwhelming heartache. And it's as if all air, all life, leave me at once, and my shoulders drop and so does my gaze because I can't look at them and I feel

So.

Fucking.

Stupid.

"You okay?" Cooper says.

I pick up my bag, the pieces of my shattered heart, and I hate tunnels. There's no escape. One way leads me to the locker rooms, and the other way leads me to *them*.

So.

Fucking.

Stupid.

A hand curls around my elbow, Cooper's, and he says, his voice low, "I'm trying to work out which one of you is the woman scorned."

"Fuck off."

Footsteps get louder and louder, echoing off the stupid walls of the stupid tunnel, and I'm angry and terrified all at once. Cooper puts his arm around my shoulders and says, "I'll give you a ride home, okay?" And he leads me away, using his body as my barrier, and Luke says nothing as we pass him. Not a damn thing. I get in Cooper's tiny red sports car, a Porsche or a Lamborghini or some other obnoxious car his parents gifted him when he turned sixteen. Or maybe it's not the same car. Whatever.

"You want to talk about it?" he asks.

The last thing I want to do is talk about it.

He drives, and by the time I push aside the rage enough to look at the time, an entire hour has passed. "You've been driving for an hour?" I yell.

Cooper laughs. "Well, I asked where you lived and you didn't respond, so I've just been driving."

"You're an idiot."

He laughs again. "Okay. *I'm* the idiot."

"What are you even doing here?"

"I'm giving you a ride home."

"I don't mean here, in the car." I'm mad at him for existing. "I mean, why were you at the school?"

He shrugs. "Community service."

"Your parents' credit card bounced, so you held up a liquor store?"

"I like how you think you know me, *Lois Lane*."

"Don't call me that."

He changes gears, changes lanes. We're on a highway. He's taking me somewhere far away and he's going to kill me. *Well, at least I won't die a virgin.* He says, "So only guys who treat you like their personal fuck toy get to have nicknames for you?"

I scrunch my nose. "You're a pig."

"And you're mean."

I roll my eyes.

He smiles. "I feel like we got off on the wrong foot." He extends his hand. "I'm Cooper Kennedy. And you are?"

I reluctantly shake his hand. "Lois Sanders."

His smile widens. "The girl with the blue dress and bright red cowboy boots…"

"What are you talking about?"

"It was the dress you wore the first day of your freshman year."

"You're kidding…"

"My eyes don't lie, Lois Sanders." He winks. A little creepy. "So Lucas did a number on you, huh?"

I press my lips tight.

"And let me guess. You're feeling pretty damn stupid right now."

So.

Fucking.

Stupid.

PAST | LOIS

"So Cam and Lucy want to take us to the movies tomorrow night. Do you want to go?" Lucas asked, laying across my bed, baseball mitt in one hand, throwing a ball in the air with the other.

"Why?" I ask, turning away from my mirror on the dresser and facing him. Dad said I was too young to wear make-up even though high school started in a couple of days, so he bought me a pack of colored, flavored Lip-Smackers in the hopes we could find a happy medium. The strawberry one was red, made my lips pop and smelled nice, too.

Luke shrugged and rolled over onto his stomach. "I guess they want to celebrate us starting high school or something. If it's a money thing, I can cover you."

I smiled. I couldn't help it. "Like a date?"

"Pshh." He scoffed, then his features straightened. "I mean. It's not a *date*. My sister and her boyfriend will be there so…"

"Okay," I said, hiding my disappointment. "Only if you're paying, though, because I spent all my allowance on some new outfits."

"Oh yeah?" he asked, sitting up, his eyes narrowed. "What kind of outfits?"

"Just stuff more suitable for high school, you know? I can't walk around in slogan tees forever."

"I like your slogan tees," he said.

I smiled again and turned away from him, watching him watch me through the mirror. "You've changed," he stated, his tone very matter-of-fact.

"How?"

He shrugged. "I don't know."

"Good or bad?"

"I said I don't know."

And just like that, my smile faded.

I WORE a new outfit I'd been saving for school. It was a purple dress with black palm tree prints that went to just above my knees and boots that stopped just below them. I'd never owned boots before. At least not ones like those. And I sprayed on perfume my grandmother (on my dad's side) had sent me for my birthday. So even though Luke had said it wasn't a date, I treated it like one. I couldn't help it.

That was my first mistake.

WHEN THE DOORBELL rang at 7:30 PM on the dot, my heart began to race. Dad answered, and I heard them talking. Three voices. Dad, Cam, and Lucas.

They exchanged pleasantries as I made my way up the basement stairs and toward the front door. "Wow," Cameron said when I came into view.

I rubbed my palms on my dress and smiled at Dad who was smiling at me, the look in his eyes conveying, "my little girl's all grown up." And I was. At least, I felt like it.

Cameron whistled, low and slow. "Lane, you look—"

"Overdressed," Lucas cut in.

My dad's eyes snapped to his.

"Not in a bad way," Luke said, hands up in surrender. "I just mean... I feel underdressed is all."

I quickly forgave him for his earlier comment.

That was mistake number two.

LUKE WORE khaki shorts and a white polo. He looked nice, even if he didn't work at it.

"Be good, kids," Dad said as he closed the door behind us.

"I'm sorry about what I said. I didn't mean you were overdressed. It's just..." Luke paused as he opened the door of the minivan for me. "You're dressed like this is a date or something, and I told you it wasn't."

I dropped my gaze, revealed my disappointment.

Mistake number three.

I SAT in the last row of seats in the van, between the twins' booster seats, because I didn't want him sitting next to me. I was hurt. His words hurt, and I felt stupid. Pathetic.

He didn't speak on the way to the movie theater where I'd later find my first place of employment. He didn't glance in my direction. Not even when Lucy said, "You look so pretty, Lane. Doesn't she look nice, Luke?"

He shrugged, mumbled, "I guess," and kept looking out the window.

It was the first time I physically felt my heart sink. Felt it crack.

I wanted to cry but doing so in the car on the way to our non-date would make the *actual* non-date unbearable, so I kept it together. I should've faked sick and asked Cam to take me home. I didn't.

Mistake number four.

I PAID for my own ticket even though Luke offered.

I paid for my own snacks, too, just to reiterate to myself that it was *not* a date.

I wanted to sit on my own, or at least on the other side of Cameron and Lucy and away from him, but I thought that might be taking it too far. I didn't *hate* him. He told me how it was, but my own wants and fantasies turned it into something it wasn't.

Yep. Mistake number five.

I SAID I needed to use the bathroom and that I'd catch up with them. That way they could choose the seating arrangements, and yeah, I realized even then that I was overthinking everything, and as I stared at myself in the mirror, my eyes getting redder from my withheld tears, I realized how pathetic I was being. Hurt, but still, pathetic. I yanked a square of paper towel from the dispenser, ran it under warm water and removed what little "fake" make-up I wore, which was just grape flavored Lip-Smacker that turned my lips a light shade of purple to match the dress that was apparently too "overdressed."

When I got into the theater, Cameron waved at me even though the room was practically empty and the lights hadn't been dimmed yet. They were sitting in the middle of the last row. It was Cam on the left, Lucy next to him, empty seat, then Luke. I assumed the empty spot was for me. Luke stood when I approached so I could get past him and take my seat. I looked at my watch. We were ten minutes early. I had to sit in silence with the light on for ten whole minutes. A group of girls sat a few rows in front of us, their ages ranging from mine to Lucy's. They turned around often, giggled to each other, then whispered words I couldn't hear.

"Are you wearing perfume?" Luke asked.

I should've scrubbed the perfume off me when I was removing the purple from my stupid lips. "Yeah. My grandmother gave it to me. I don't really have anywhere else to wear it so…"

"It's nice," he said. "It suits you."

"It's not really me," I admitted, choking on a sob. I whispered, "This really isn't me at all. I look stupid."

He didn't respond for a long time, and I felt that twisting ache in my chest again. "I liked your slogan tees," he said. "And your crazy colored flip-flops."

I tilted my head back and looked up at the ceiling, all so my tears wouldn't fall.

He hated my outfit, and I hated that it bothered me so much.

Mistake number six.

THE GIRLS GIGGLED AGAIN.

"If they do that through the entire movie I'm going to take a rusty chainsaw to all their heads," Lucy snapped. "Why do they keep looking this way?"

"Leave it alone, babe," Cam said, trying to settle her. "If they do it while the movie's on, I'll talk to them."

"Sure," Lucy said. "You talk to them, babe, and if they so much as even try to hit on you, I'll stab them in the eye with this straw."

"You're very death-to-the-world today," Cam said.

Lucy giggled. "I'll strangle them with my Red Vines."

Cameron laughed. "Stone them to death with your Whoppers?"

Lucy said, "Shove my hot dog up their—"

"Okay, that's enough," Cam cut in just in time.

Another round of giggles.

"What do you bitches want?" Lucy shouted, her arm raised, hand full of popcorn.

Cameron grasped her wrist, stopping her.

One of the girls, brunette and beautiful, pointed to Luke. "Come here," she said, laughing with her friends.

Luke pointed to himself, his eyebrows raised. "Me?"

Five heads, hair perfectly straight, nodded at the same time.

Luke turned to me, and I faced him for the first time since he was at my door. "Do you mind?" he asked.

I swallowed the lump in my throat, shook my head, said, "Why would I mind?"

His eyes stayed on mine. He said nothing. I said nothing.

"Luke," Cam said behind me. There was something in the way he said Luke's name. It wasn't to get his attention. It almost sounded like a warning. Like that was his chance to speak to those girls and if he didn't do it then, he might never get to again.

"He has a name," said one of the giggling girls.

"Luke!" they cooed in unison.

I dropped my gaze, hid my emotions.

He left, only to return when the movie started.

I timed the release of my tears to match Lucy's sobs.

She cried over the movie.

I cried over my life.

And when the movie was over and Cam, Lucy and I waited for Lucas to stop talking to the girls just outside the building, his words "I'll call you," acting as the final stab wound to my chest, Lucy turned to me, her voice full of pity. "You really do look nice, Lane."

"Yeah?" I asked, looking down at the prettiest dress I owned. "Because I feel so fucking stupid."

CHAPTER NINE

LOIS

THERE SHOULD BE a limit to the amount of tears a person can shed within a certain amount of time. Or at least some kind of chart to verify the level of tears to the level of tragedy. For example, losing someone like Kathy Preston should equal infinite tears for an infinite amount of time. Being hurt by the spawn of Kathy Preston should equal, say, three sets of tears for three fuck-ups and then said spawn should be deleted from your life, your mind, for all of eternity.

But there is no chart.

Just tears.

IT'S 10:30 PM when the knock sounds on my door.

I answer, but I don't speak. I have nothing to say.

"Just hear me out," Luke asks. "She called me over thirty times yesterday, sent me a ton of messages. I went to see her last night to break up with her, and when I got there, she was crying. Her brother was in a car accident over in LA and her parents flew right there and she was alone and she needed me and I wasn't there. She kept crying, Lane, like non-stop, and I couldn't get a word in and I couldn't do that to her. But I will. I promise." He takes a breath. "You just need to give me time."

"Don't," I whisper.

"Don't what?"

"Don't break up with her."

"Laney, stop."

"Did you stay with her last night?" I ask, refusing to meet his gaze.

"Yes, but we didn't do anything. I swear. I've been trying to get away from her long enough so I could see you and explain it but with school and practice, I couldn't, and then you saw us and you saw *wrong*. You have to believe me." He pauses a beat. "You believe me, right? Because I want to be with *you*. And you know that. But I can't break up with her right now. I just can't."

"You need to leave." I start closing the door on him, but he stops me, his palm loud when it smacks against the timber. "Lane, please."

I finally look up at him, my tear-stained eyes meeting his sorry ones, and I'm sick of his sorry eyes. Sick of his sorry face.

I blink, let the tears fall, and I don't wipe them away because I want him to see what he's done to me. I clear my throat so my voice doesn't falter. I want him to hear my words, and I want them to be loud. To be clear. "You need to leave because I don't want you here. I don't want you standing at my door, apologizing, trying to make me understand why I can't be hurt by this because I am. I hurt. And I don't want to hurt. I want to go back to last night when you made me feel beautiful, when you made me feel loved and worthy of that love. When I gave you something I'd been holding on to that I can't take back, that I'd been saving… for *you*. And you can't be here because having you here is making me forget that feeling, and I don't want to forget. I want to pretend like that feeling lasted more than seventeen fucking hours, and I want to pretend like I don't hate you for it. Or hate you, *period*."

CHAPTER TEN

LUCAS

I TRY TO BE QUIET, but I'm crashing into walls, into chairs, into Dad's giant desk in his home office. I got home from Laney's and went straight to the garage apartment and drank every single drop of alcohol I'd kept hidden from my dad. But it still doesn't erase the image of Laney's tear-stained face from my mind.

I HAD it all planned out. I'd tell her the truth, no sugar-coating, because she deserved that much. I didn't say it to hurt her. I don't want to hurt her. I fucking love her. In my head, she'd forgive me, tell me she understood that I didn't have it in me to hurt someone I care about. And honestly, I did care about Grace. I just didn't love her. I love Laney. Always have. If the roles were reversed and something happened to Brian, I'd have spent the night with Laney. I probably would've spent the night with her anyway. I just wouldn't tell Grace about it. Grace doesn't know I sleep in Laney's bed. No one does. And maybe that's where I fucked up. Where my mistakes turned me into an asshole because in a way, Laney was my *secret*, hidden away from the eyes of my friends so they couldn't want her, have her. She was mine. *My secret pleasure.* She didn't forgive me, obviously. She gave me her own truths, laid out her pain in detail so someone as stupid as me could understand. Then she slammed the door in my face and switched off the outside light, the light she always kept on for me. I *should* have expected it. But I didn't. And I stood outside her door, in the dark, and I knew it was over.

She told me, warned me, if I didn't *show* her I loved her, I'd ruin everything.

I fuck up, Lane. I make mistakes. I told you. I warned you, too.

"WHAT THE HELL are you doing, son?"

I don't bother turning to my dad, too out of my mind to care. I keep going through his keys, one after the other, trying to find the one that'll unlock his liquor cabinet so I can keep drinking the pain away, so I can drown in it, just enough to get her words, her face, her hurt, out of my mind. "I hurt her," I murmur, fumbling with the keys.

"Who?" he says, his voice louder as he steps toward me. "Grace?"

Fuck Grace. "Laney. She hates me, and I hate me, and I can't get the hate out of me."

Dad's hand grasps my shoulder, pulls me back until I tip over and land on my ass. I want to cry, but I haven't cried since Mom died and I sure as hell won't show him, the strongest man I know, how weak I am.

He gently pries my fingers off his keys, finds the right one, and a moment later, he's pulling out a bottle of whiskey and two glasses.

"Sit," he says

"I *am* sitting."

He sighs. "On the chair, son. Sit."

"I'm fine," I murmur, standing up, eyes on his office door because Dad and I don't drink together. We don't even talk. Not like this. We make plans, set schedules. We don't *talk.*

"Sit," he says, and this time it's an order.

I take the seat on the other side of his desk, the one where his clients or his assistant sit when they have meetings in the office, and I'm nervous, afraid of what he's going to say because he just caught his seventeen-year-old son trying to break into his liquor cabinet at two in the morning and he *loves* Laney. They all do.

He stays standing when he pours the brown liquid into both glasses, then slides one across the desk toward me. "Did you drive home like this?"

"No," I tell him. "I've been drinking in the apartment."

"Good. This family's already experienced one death. We don't need another."

I say nothing.

"Lucas," he says. "What happened?"

I finally look up at him, across the desk, past his sleep pants, beyond his white t-shirt, above his dark beard and into his worried eyes. I didn't expect to see worry. Disappointment, anger, yes. But not worry. For seconds he stands there, eyes on mine and when I don't speak, his shoulders drop and so does he, right into the chair opposite me. He sips on his whiskey, our eyes locked.

"Where did you go earlier?"

"To see Lane."

"Where did you sleep last night?"

"At Grace's."

He nods, like he already knows where this is going.

I add, "After I went to see Lane."

He puts down his glass, then places both elbows on the table and leans in, waiting for me to continue.

I swallow. Nervous. "I told her I loved her."

"Grace?" he asks.

I shake my head.

His teeth show behind his smile, but it lasts only a second before his brow bunches and his lips purse. "But you spent the night with Grace?"

I inhale deeply, exhale slowly.

He's shaking his head now, side to side, slowly, slowly. "What did you do, Luke?"

I tell him everything, *everything*, my knees bouncing the entire time because *we don't talk*, and now we're talking, and I'm giving him reasons to hate me like she does.

"Maybe she'll forgive you," he says, as if it's that simple. "She always does."

"This is different, Dad." He knows it's different. I can tell by the way he lifts his hand, pours another drink for himself and eyes my untouched one.

"She's going through a lot right now, Luke. Her mother coming to see her—"

"You know about that?" I cut in.

He nods. "Brian told me today." Another sip. "I told him we could arrange a loan if it meant getting Lane to UNC."

My chest tightens. "You'd do that?"

His huge shoulders lift once. "Lane's like a daughter to me, and your mother loved her. We all do." His voice cracks and he clears his throat. My dad's not an emotional man but any thought, any mention of his wife can bring him to his knees. "I wasn't sure how you'd react to her mother being here, but my truck has a full tank in case you need it." He stands up and heads for the door, but he stops beside me, his hand on my shoulder. "Give Laney time. You're a good friend to her, Luke, and maybe that's all you can be, even if it's from a distance."

PAST | LUCAS

"It's not a big deal," Laney said, slamming her locker shut.

"It's your sixteenth birthday!"

"So?"

"So you have to do something!"

"With who, Luke? My eleventy-three friends? I have you and that's basically it."

"You have me and your dad and my family... so that's eleventy-seventy."

She giggled, handed me her books and started braiding her long black hair to the side. I watched, fascinated. She raised her eyebrows. "What?"

"Nothing." Then I blinked hard and cleared the fog in my mind she'd created. "Will you at least let me take you out to dinner or something?"

She whined, "It's really not a big deal."

"But I *want* to," I said, giving back her books.

She stopped in front of me, her books held against her chest. "Nothing fancy?"

"I promise."

"Okay."

"Good."

"Good."

She started to walk away, and I followed. She must've washed her hair the night before because I could smell her shampoo and was stupidly drawn to it. She stopped suddenly, causing me to almost slam into her. "What are you doing?" she asked, eyeing our surroundings. She pointed behind me. "Your class is that way."

———

"LUKE! You promised it wouldn't be fancy!" she whisper-yelled over the menu.

"It's not *that* fancy!" I said. *It was.* A few weeks earlier I asked Virginia, our nanny at the time, for the fanciest place I could take a girl and so there we were, sitting opposite each other in a booth made of red, shiny leather, smiling at each other, her in an olive green dress and me in a suit, sans tie. "Order whatever you want."

She shook her head, her smile spreading. She said, testing me, "I'm going to order the lobster."

"Do you even eat lobster?"

She laughed out loud, and I wanted to kiss her right then and there in the middle of the fanciest restaurant in town. "I've never had it, but I always see it in movies, you know? The lobster's the most expensive thing on the menu." She started flipping through the pages, her eyes scanning each item quickly. "It's ninety-eight dollars, Luke!" she whispered, her shoulders bouncing.

I leaned back in the seat, basking in everything Laney, and said, "Order it."

She dropped the menu, narrowed her eyes at me. "How can you even afford this?"

"I've worked a couple of shifts for Dad lately."

Her eyes widened. "For *this*?"

"Yeah, for this."

"No." She shook her head. "Let's just order a pizza and go back to my room or something. This is too much."

I called for the waiter and ordered the damn lobster.

Laney did *not* like lobster.

Neither did I, but I traded my steak for it and pretended like lobster was the greatest thing I'd ever tasted. I skipped dessert, she ordered two, and I sat and I watched as she told me about her new job at the movie theater and how she'd made sure her shifts didn't collide with my track meets, and I fell deeper and deeper. And when she was done, I pulled out the rectangular box that'd been burning a hole in my pocket and watched her eyes light up when I slid it across the table toward her. She looked so beautiful, hair braided to the side, lips red, eyes bright. She whispered my name, and I imagined our lives ten years from then when she'd whisper it again but in a different way. She opened the box and instantly covered her mouth. "It's stunning," she said, and I verbally agreed, but I wasn't talking about the gold bracelet in the box. I was talking about her. "Now I feel bad for getting you that heart rate monitor strap."

"That was a perfect present, Lane." My fingers shook when I clasped the bracelet to her wrist. I was nervous. Scared. Because for the past few weeks, I'd been counting down to that night, to the moment I'd tell her how I felt about her.

"Can you send a picture to my dad?" she asked, so I took out my phone, aimed the camera at her, focused on her smile, and sent the picture to Brian.

"I can't believe you got me this, Luke. It's too much," she said.

It wasn't enough.

She added, "I feel like we need to make a pact or something to remember this moment. Like, what if something happens over the next couple of years and we change and our lives change and we never get to celebrate birthdays together again? We barely see each other now with school and your practices and me working on weekends and... we should go to senior prom together!" She shouted the last part. "Yeah, Luke. We should do that!"

I smiled. "Okay."

"Yeah?"

"Of course."

She leaned back in her seat, watched the light glisten off of her new present.

I told her, "We have one more stop before I take you home."

MY FAMILY WANTED to see Laney on her birthday, so I drove us back to my house where a cake was waiting, along with sixteen candles. My dad had taken my brothers to the mall, handed them each twenty dollars and said to pick out something for her. She opened present after present, responding to each one equally, even the candle made to smell like vomit that Logan had gotten her, which I'm sure only cost a few bucks so he could pocket the rest. Lachlan gave her a hand-made card with a picture of her and me and him in the middle, and I know she wanted to cry. She didn't. But she held him for a long time and kept him on her lap when Dad announced that he had one more gift. I wasn't aware of the gift until he pulled it out of the hallway closet. It was a basket, *Mom's* basket, filled with all her craft items: knitting needles, yarn, thread. It used to live on the floor between Dad's recliner and the couch where Mom would sit and hadn't seen the light of day since my aunt Leslee decided it was time to pack up all of Mom's things.

Laney actually did cry when she saw it, the back of her hand covering her mouth as she fumbled through her words, "Are you sure?"…"But it's Kathy's!"…"I can't."…"I love it."…"Thank you, thank you, thank you."

And then we lit the candles, sang Happy Birthday, and I took more pictures of her blowing out the candles, holding her presents, smiling, smiling, smiling. We told everyone about dinner, about lobster, about our pact to go to senior prom together and that's when Lachlan started acting out, laying on his back and kicking the crap out of Logan for no reason. He was tired, it was hours past his bedtime, so I picked him up off the floor and said I'd do his "one-minute." He was out like a light after a few seconds in his bed, but I lay there for a while, trying to form words that would hopefully bring Laney and me closer. I couldn't just come out and say, *"I love you, Lane. Will you be my girlfriend?"* because, at the time, I thought it would suck. Now, looking back, it probably would've been enough. I closed my eyes, tried to think, but then the song *Wonderwall* by Oasis started playing from downstairs, and I sat up quickly, my heart in my throat. Us kids had grown up with the song constantly playing loudly from the kitchen when Mom would be preparing dinner. Some nights, Dad came home early from work, and they'd dance together, my mom standing on Dad's feet, to the song they danced to on their wedding day.

I was almost afraid to go downstairs, to see my dad, to see his reaction to the song. But when I landed on the seventh step down, just enough so I could see the living room from my spot, I saw the lights dim, the original record playing, and Laney in Dad's arms, dancing amongst her many gifts scattered around the floor. "She'll be all ready for you come senior prom," Dad called out to me. *Smiling.*

I sat on the stairs, watched them through the gaps of the staircase. The song played on, and my brothers and I sat in awe as we watched my best friend give my dad a reason to smile, and we took a moment to miss our mother and to appreciate Laney for every single thing she brought to the family.

I HELPED Laney carry all her presents to her room, where Brian was waiting for us. "How was your night?" he asked.

Laney hadn't stopped smiling. "I tried lobster!" she announced.

Brian laughed. "Did you like it?"

She scrunched her nose, dumped the presents on her bed. "Luke did, though," she said.

Brian eyed me and I gave him a face that showed I *really* didn't like lobster, but that it was just between us. *The men.* He smiled at me, but his expression changed when he faced Laney and asked, "Did your mother call you, honey?"

"No." She sat on the bed next to her dad. "But I didn't expect her to, so it's not a big deal." It *was* a big deal. Even if she didn't admit it, it was a *huge* deal.

Brain said, "She called me a few days ago, said she might not have a signal today, but she sent you something in the mail."

For the umpteenth time that day, Laney's eyes lit up. "She did?"

Brian reached into his pocket and pulled out a small box wrapped in purple and gold paper. "This is from her. It came in the mail yesterday, but she asked I give it to you on your birthday."

"Wow," Laney said with a sigh. She unwrapped it quickly, revealing a pair of diamond earrings. It made the bracelet I bought her look cheap. It wasn't. Trust me. "These are great," she said, but her reaction was less than when she opened my brothers' or when she opened mine, and I felt pride swell in my chest. She removed her green and purple dreamcatcher earrings and replaced them with the diamond ones. "How do they look?" she asked her dad.

"Beautiful," he said. "You look beautiful, Lo."

"Beautiful," I agreed.

"Should I call her?" she asked. "To thank her?"

"No," Brian said quickly. "It's late now, and I'm sure she has no signal otherwise she would've called."

"Right," said Lane.

Brian stood. "Well. I'm off to bed. Don't stay up too late. You have school tomorrow."

Laney nodded, stood, kissed her dad on the cheek. "Goodnight, Dad."

I said goodnight, too, and waited for him to leave. It was time, I thought, the night was almost over and I had something to say.

"You hungry?" she asked.

"Not really."

"I'm hungry." Then she marched up the stairs and I followed her to the kitchen. She opened the pantry and pulled out a bag of chips. She was upset. She snacked when she was upset, and we both knew the reason why, but she'd never say it out loud. I hadn't missed her checking her phone every few minutes while we were at dinner or earlier in the day at school or in the car. She was waiting for the phone call or even a simple text. She'd lied to her dad. She lied to *herself.*

Lane grabbed two sodas from the fridge and handed them to me, her way of asking me to stay a little while longer. Then she emptied the bag of chips into a bowl, held onto the bag as she walked to the trash, pressed her foot on the lever to lift the lid, and then froze in her spot.

"What is it?" I asked.

She didn't respond.

I walked over to her, watched her eyes quickly fill with tears. Then I looked in the trash, at the cause of the tears, at the discarded purple and gold wrapping paper.

"It's not a big deal," she whispered. *It was.*

She used my chest to muffle her cries, not wanting her dad to hear her. And I stood there, holding her, knowing it wasn't the right time to tell her how I felt. But then she looked up at me, her eyes red and raw. "Thank you, Luke."

"For what?" I asked.

"For being here. For being my friend."

Her *friend.*

I DIDN'T TELL her I loved her that night.

I couldn't.

I was her *friend.* Nothing more. Nothing less. And at the time, I was okay with it because I had other, more important, things to worry about.

Dad was in his office when I got home, sitting at his desk where I needed to be. "I need the computer," I told him.

"Where's your laptop?"

"I need *your* computer," I reiterated. I moved behind the desk, stood and hovered next to him.

"What's the urgency?"

I bounced on my toes, rage washing through me. "You keep all the resumes of your employees, right?"

"Yes."

"So you'd have Lane's old address from when Brian sent you his?"

"Yes, but—"

"I need it," I cut in.

"Lucas," Dad said, standing up so I could take his seat. "What's happening?"

My fingers worked frantically, opening and closing files, trying to find the right one. "And I'm going to need your truck tomorrow."

"Luke!" He shook my shoulders and made me look at him. "What the hell's going on?"

"I hate her," I bit out.

"Who? Lane?"

"No!" I shouted. "Her mother. I hate her stupid mother. She hasn't been around. She's *never* been around. And she forgot Laney's birthday. What kind of mother forgets their own daughter's sixteenth birthday?"

"Okay. Calm down," he said, taking his hands off of me. "What are you going to do, Luke? Drive there, knock on her door, and then what? What are you going to say?"

I find the file. Email it to myself. Map out the destination.

"Luke?"

"I don't know, okay? But she keeps hurting Lane, Dad. She keeps hurting her and making her sad and Lane just keeps taking hit after hit and she won't say or do anything about it. And I'm pissed and I hate her and I want her to know that."

Dad nodded slowly, his eyes tired. "Okay," he said, then unlocked a drawer on his desk that housed all the important things: birth certificates, wills, Mom's engagement ring. He placed the family emergency credit card on the desk in front of me. "The truck needs gas."

I LEFT EARLY SO I could be back early. I wouldn't be going to school and I wouldn't be telling Lane why, so I knew she'd be going to my house to check in on me. Her old house was four hours away, and it didn't give me much time to make any stops. I skipped my morning run, ate breakfast on the way.

Laney's old house was four times the size of the one she and Brian lived in now, and it just pissed me off more. Her dad had given up everything, including the house, in the divorce, and now they were scraping for pennies and Laney had to work to save for college just so her stupid mom could live *that* life.

I didn't bother knocking on the door. I kicked it. Over and over. "What the hell?" was her mom's response when she opened the door. The moment I saw her, I hated her more. She looked like Laney. Almost identical. Same dark hair. Same dark eyes. Same light skin. "Want to tell me why you're literally kicking down my door, kid?"

My heart pounded so fast I couldn't count the beats. With shaky hands, I reached into my pocket, pulled out my phone, and brought up the picture of Laney in the restaurant from the night before. I showed it to her. "I just thought you might want to see what your daughter looked like on her sixteenth birthday."

Her jaw dropped.

"It was yesterday, just in case you'd *completely* forgotten *everything* about her. She ordered lobster. She didn't like it. Then we went back to my house and my brothers gave her presents and we sang Happy Birthday and she had cake and danced with my dad to his wedding song with my mom. My mom's dead now, but she loved your daughter, more than you ever will, more than you ever *have*. And I'm kicking down your door because I'm imagining it's your face—" She gasped, but I kept going. "Quit making her cry. Quit hurting her. I hate seeing her sad and *I hate you*. It would be so easy for her to hate you, too, but she doesn't have it in her heart because her heart's beautiful. *She's* beautiful. And you're missing out on all that beauty because your heart's black and ugly and full of hate!"

I shoved the phone in my pocket and turned to leave. I was halfway to my car when she called out, "You her boyfriend or something?"

I froze, my feet glued to the ground. Then I shook my head, told her the truth. "I should be so lucky."

CHAPTER ELEVEN

LUCAS

I TAKE DAD'S ADVICE, give Laney time, give her space. I hate space, but I need it, too, because everyone's noticed my deterioration. My brothers see it, but they don't ask. Garray asks, but I don't tell. The worst, though, is Cooper fucking Kennedy. He pushes me, on and on—physically, mentally.

Rumor says he was caught having sex on campus with the daughter of a UNC member of faculty—the girl was underage. His parents threw their money around, managed to get the charges dropped, but the school needed to do something to save face. They handed the issue over to the athletic department, made them decide on Cooper's punishment. His penalty? A semester off the track team and going back to his old high school to help coach. Apparently, the UNC athletic department doesn't understand the meaning of irony. So now he's here, every Monday and Friday, and I'm his pet, his project, his *punishment*. Only he's the one doing the punishing.

LANEY DOESN'T TAKE my calls.

Doesn't respond to my texts.

Doesn't answer the door.

Doesn't even glance in my direction.

Not until September 25ᵗʰ, the anniversary of my mom's death.

The kids don't go to school on September 25ᵗʰ. We visit her grave. Lucy and Cameron drive down from campus and they join us, too. Cameron asks Lucy to marry him. I'm happy for them. Really, I am.

But not as happy as when I see the crocheted flower sitting on our doormat, a sign that Laney had been here, that she remembered. Of course, she remembered. *She's not me.*

The first year anniversary, the flower was yellow. The following year, it was orange. Every year since, it's been a different color. This year, it's green.

I pick up the flower and place it on the mantel, along with the others, right next to a framed picture of my mother. I congratulate Cam and Luce again, then go to my apartment, change from my suit and tie and into my running gear and I run. I run the same route twice before I find myself at the crossroads. I pause. Look left. Look right.

468 steps.

Knock knock.

I don't expect her to answer, but if she's in her room, I want her to hear the knock and I want her to know it's me. And I want her to know I appreciate her and that I'm sorry. For everything.

She does answer, her eyes red. She has the same look on her face that she did the last time I was here. Only I didn't cause these tears.

"Thank you," I tell her.

"You're welcome," she says.

Then she closes the door, dividing the space between us.

I hate space.

THE DAYS PASS, turn to weeks, my mind a fog with zero clarity.

It's 11:49 PM. I know, because I've been clutching my phone, watching the minutes tick down. In eleven minutes, I'll be eighteen years old.

Every year since Laney and I have owned cell phones, she calls at midnight, on the dot, and over exaggerates the singing of Happy Birthday.

Every year.

Midnight.

11:59, and my thumb hovers over the screen, waiting, hoping, praying.

At 12:01, I die inside.

"AND THE SCHOOL had such high hopes for you," Cooper says, sitting on the grass in front of me while he does his own set of cooldowns.

I take the bait. "What's that supposed to mean?"

"I mean the fall season starts in a couple of weeks, and you're not even close to your PB."

"I'll be fine."

"But that's the thing," he says, switching positions. "You're not fine. Track is a lonely fucking sport, dude, and only you can control your performance. If your head's a mess, it shows in every stride, every millisecond you're out there."

"It's true," Garray agrees, running a hand through his shaved, blond hair. "And it's worse for cross-country runners like me."

Cooper nods. "You want my advice, Preston?"

"Not even a little bit."

"You're wound up. Something's messing with your head and you need to get rid of it." He points to his left, toward the girls' track team. "Go fuck the brains out of your hot girlfriend. Grace, right?"

I shake my head, eyes narrowed at him. He knows I broke up with Grace the day after I tried to explain it all to Laney. The *entire* school knows.

He smirks. "Oh wait, you're not with her anymore, right? Maybe it's that chick from my college?" *Fuck him.* I'd made out with a girl when I visited Cam and Luce on campus to get away from this bullshit, and when she got me in her car, I couldn't fucking go through with it. I lied, told Lucy's friends that we'd screwed. What was I going to say? That I almost puked at the idea of being with anyone other than Lane?

"Roxy, right?" *Fuck Cooper Kennedy and fuck him for knowing so much.*

"Fuck off."

He laughs, motions toward the locker rooms. "Or does your problem have to do with her?"

I follow his gaze to Laney standing just outside the tunnel leading to the locker rooms, adjusting the straps of her backpack. She glances up, then down again. I'm on my feet before I have time to register *why* she's here, just glad she is. My heart pounds, thuds hard against my chest, and I quicken my steps, widen my strides until I'm standing in front of her.

"Hey," I say.

"Hey," she says back.

"You, um…" *Breathe, Luke.* "You waiting on me?"

"Actually…" She looks over my shoulder.

"Hey, Lois," Cooper shouts. He waits until he's standing next to me before saying, "I need to hit the showers so I'll be a few minutes."

"No problem," Laney says, and my insides turn to stone.

Cooper pats me on the shoulder before strutting down the tunnel because he's a dick, and she's moved on and *it's only been a few weeks, Laney.* I stare at her, my chest aching, while she stares down at the ground like her shoes are fascinating. "So you and Coop?" I choke on his name, poison on my tongue.

She looks up, her expression unreadable. *Do you even miss me, Laney?* "Your ex-girlfriend's coming. Does *she* know about Roxy?"

My shoulders tense, and fuck fuck fuck Cooper Kennedy. "Hey, Lois." Grace spits. "Here to ruin another relationship?"

Lane's eyes narrow at Grace. "No." She looks at me. "I'm here for Cooper."

———

I'VE NEVER YELLED at Lachlan before. I discipline him. Tell him what he's done wrong. Talk him through it the way I'd seen Mom do with the rest of us. I've never shouted at him. Called him names. But I did.

Two minutes ago he spilled his water on the kitchen table during Sunday breakfast, and I called him a shit and told him to go to his room.

The table went silent.

He went to his room.

Now the others are looking at me like I've lost my mind. *I have.* Because this morning I went for my run and turned left at the crossroads. Cooper's car was in her driveway. I can still feel the cold steel of her chain-link fence I used to hold myself up while I puked.

The twins stand, leave the room.

Logan says, "What the fuck, dude?"

"Go check on your brother," Dad tells him, his tone stern. And so Logan goes, leaving me with Leo and Dad and a room full of anger and regret.

"Is this about Lane and Cooper?" Leo asks.

"Leo," Dad warns. At least he's on my side. He *knows* what I'm going through.

"No!" Leo thumps his fist on the table, and my gaze snaps to him. "I'm sick of this. You've been moping around the house for weeks and it's bullshit. If you're pissed, be pissed, but don't be mad at her for finally seeing the light."

"Leo." Dad sighs, shaking his head. "That's enough."

But apparently, Leo doesn't think so. "She's had to sit around and watch you date girl after girl for three years now. Three years she's kept her mouth shut, waiting for you to see her, and so she got sick of waiting! So what? She's too good for you anyway!"

"Why do you keep saying that?" I ask, my back straight, my eyes on his.

"Because she is. You don't even know half the shit you've done to her because you're fucking blind, Lucas."

"Watch your language," Dad snaps.

My jaw ticks. "You don't know what you're talking about."

"Oh yeah?" Leo says, leaning forward, his eyes filled with rage. "When she was fifteen, she went through a jewelry-making phase. You remember that?"

"Yeah. So?"

"You remember when she set up a table at the craft market to sell them?"

Vaguely.

"You don't remember because you weren't there. She sold six things that day. One to Dad and one each to the rest of us. Lucy got six items of jewelry that Christmas. And the worst part is that she told you about it, reminded you of it so many times, and you promised her you'd be there. She had two chairs set up behind the table. One for her and one for you but you didn't show! You were here, in the lake, with Dumb Name and a bunch of girls and you forgot about her. And she probably didn't tell you how badly you hurt her or that it even happened at all because that's who she is, and *that's* why she's too good for you."

I look over at Dad hoping he shows some kind of sign that it isn't true, that it never happened. He nods, but he won't look at me. And I feel my heart sinking, anchored to the twisting knot in my gut.

Leo stands, his fists balled. "Suck it up and quit being an asshole to everyone around you." He leaves out the back door and calls out for the twins, probably making sure I haven't scarred them, too.

107

"They're just friends," Dad says.

"Leo and Lane?"

He shakes his head. "Lane and Cooper. Brian told me they're just friends. For now, anyway."

"I went to see her this morning when I was out on my run," I admit. "His car was in the driveway."

"He comes home on weekends now that he's coaching over at the high school. He doesn't like Lane walking home from work late on Saturday nights, so he lends her his car. That's all it is."

I swallow loudly, but the pain doesn't fade. "Eat up," he says. "You got a long day of making it up to Lachlan. The kid worships you, Luke. Don't give him a reason to change that."

I force a smile. "Logan's up there with him. Who knows? Maybe Lachy can have a new brother to look up to."

"Jesus Christ," Dad mumbles, rubbing his eyes. "Eat quick."

LOIS

Cooper doesn't know I have a door that leads directly to my room. He doesn't know what my room looks like. He doesn't even know what the inside of my house looks like. The closest he's gotten is where he is now, on my doorstep, knocking and waiting for me to answer.

I grab his keys off the coffee table and open the door. "Hey."

"Hey." He smiles brightly, his body glistening with sweat from the run over here. His parents' house is fifteen miles away in a secure, gated community, and for the past three weeks (since he found out I walk home from work at midnight) he's lent me his car so I don't have to walk. I tried to decline, numerous times, but he was adamant and I was frustrated, so I agreed. It wasn't the first time he showed that he genuinely cared about me. Especially considering he understood, without a doubt, that my vagina was pretty much its own secure, gated community.

"Thanks for lending me your car," I tell him, handing him the keys.

His gaze trails from my messy bed-hair to my flannel pajamas and down to my cotton socks. "Nice to see you got all dressed up for me."

I shove his shoulder. "Shut up."

After mocking hurt, he says, "Let me take you out to lunch. I'll even allow myself to be seen in public with you exactly as you are."

I let myself smile. "You're going to regret that." And I step in the house, slip on my shoes, shout, "Dad, I'm going out for lunch!"

Cooper doesn't bat an eyelid. "Is your dad home?" he asks, following me to his car.

"Yep."

"Can I meet him?"

I come to a halt and turn to him. "Why?"

He shrugs.

"It's not like we're dating, right?"

He walks past me to open my car door, his smirk on full display. "Yet."

———

COOPER IGNORES the looks from everyone when we walk into the busy Applebee's. Kids from school are here, probably nursing hangovers from the night before. Families sit, enjoying their meals, and then there's me, pajamas and sunglasses, and *I'm* embarrassed *for* him. "Let's go." I yank his arm, begging to leave.

"No." He pulls back, laughing as he does. "No regrets, Sanders."

Swear, *"No regrets"* is Cooper Kennedy's mission statement for his life.

After emotionally breaking down in his car the day after I was (as he puts it) "smashed and dashed" upon, he finally drove me home. We stayed in his car, sitting idle in my driveway, while I waited for the pain to fade. I didn't want to go in the house, in my room, where memories of Lucas would for sure invade me. So I sat, staring out the windshield until he broke the silence. "It might hurt less if you get it off your chest, you know?"

I didn't want to. Not with him. So he said, "Want to punch something?"

"Yes," I whispered.

"Is her name Grace?"

I shook my head. "It's not her fault."

"So... I'm guessing that technically, *she's* the woman scorned." He paused a beat. "So why are *you* so mad?"

I faced him, eyes thinned to slits. "I could punch *you*," I told him.

He smirked. "You could try."

109

I did try. His arm was nothing but muscle. And so he laughed, put his car in gear, and reversed out the driveway. For the second time that day, I thought he was taking me somewhere to kill me, and as dramatic as it sounds, I didn't have it in me to argue.

He took me to his house, past the guard at the gate, through the pristine, quiet streets of his neighborhood until his car was parked safely in his garage. He got out, opened my door, and said, "Let's go."

So off we went, through his enormous house, past the large kitchen, through the giant sliding doors, walked through the backyard, and into another building that housed his own personal gym.

"Take off your sweater," he said.

I scoffed.

He smirked. "We're about to get hot and sweaty."

"You're such a dick."

I started to leave but he grasped my arm, and when I turned to face him, he was holding a pair of boxing gloves. He pointed to the punching bag hanging in the corner of the room, strapped the gloves to my hands and said, "Better out than in."

I don't know how long he watched me hit a stupid bag, release my stupid tears, yell out stupid things, but when he stopped me, his arms around my entire body, I felt weak. Weak and *stupid*. I collapsed on the floor and looked up at him. He held my face in his hands, his thumbs wiping my cheeks, removing the sweat mixed with tears. He seemed sad, sorry for the pathetic girl he didn't know. His eyes searched mine as he said, "I'm sorry he hurt you, but hurting yourself isn't going to change that. You can't control what people do or how they treat you. You can only control how you react to it." He squatted in front of me, his fist out ready to bump. "No regrets, Sanders."

I inhaled deeply, let his words sink just as far, then I bumped his fist. "No regrets."

CHAPTER TWELVE

LUCAS

TODAY, we skipped Sunday breakfast. Because today, Brian's coming over so we can meet his new girlfriend. I'm sure Brian would have told Lane, asked her to join them and she will because she does everything her dad asks of her.

THERE'S a knock on my apartment door and for a moment, I think it's Lane. But Lane doesn't knock. She just walks in, comments on the state of my apartment and then starts washing dishes.

The knock sounds again.

"Yeah?" I call out.

"It's Leo."

I get up, open the door, sit back on the couch and stare at the blank television like I'd been doing all morning.

He plops down next to me, his scrawny frame a contrast to mine. "I love this episode," he jokes, but I don't find it funny. After a sigh, he says, "I owe you an apology for what I said last week."

"It's fine," I murmur.

Silence passes. He breaks it. "She misses you, Luke."

I face him, my heart in my throat. "She tell you that?"

He shakes his head, his eyes as sorry as I feel. "She didn't need to. We go to the same school, I see her around, talk to her sometimes. She's not the same. She never is when you guys fight like this."

"We're not fighting." I look back at the screen. "She hates me."

"How bad did you screw up?" he asks, and I can hear the frustration in his voice.

Outside, a car pulls up, doors slam, and Lachlan shouts, "Laney's here!"

LACHLAN SEEMS HAPPY, sitting at the picnic table out in the yard next to his godmother while she plates up his food. The sun's out, shining brightly on both our families, but my mood is dark, my conscience darker.

She said, "Hey, Luke," when she got here. Hasn't said a word since, at least not to me.

I sit opposite her, watch her smile, watch her laugh, watch her be a part of *my* family.

Dad says, "So Lane, how did you do with that piece you entered into that... that uh..."

"The clothing design contest?" Misty finishes.

I didn't know she'd started making clothes, but it's not surprising. She'd been saving for a sewing machine for a while. My ears perk, waiting for Laney's response. She smiles at Dad and pours ketchup on Lachlan's plate. "I got second prize."

I smile, I can't help it. She sees my reaction but doesn't have one of her own.

"That's great," Dad says.

"So, Luke," Brian jumps in. "First track meet next week. You ready?"

"Yes, sir."

"Well, I'm sure Lois will be there. She hasn't missed a single one," he says, his gaze on his daughter. "Right, Lo?"

Swear, if looks could kill, Laney just aimed a gun at Brian and pulled the damn trigger. And I hate this. I hate that it's up to our dads to fill the conversation about parts of our lives we know nothing about.

A PHONE RINGS, and everyone but Lachlan and the twins searches their pockets, their purses. "It's me," Laney says, raising her phone.

The ringing continues and Misty coos, "Say hi to Cooper."

Jealousy courses through me, spiking through every vein, every cell in my body. Not because it's Cooper on the phone but because Cooper should be *me*. It should be my name on the end of Misty's sentence, my name making *my* best friend's dad's girlfriend coo and bat her eyelids. It should be *me* she knows, not a guy who's only been in Lane's life for a few weeks.

Laney says, "He's picking up his car, so he's probably having trouble finding the keys. I'll only be a second."

I hate that she's smiling as she brings the phone to her ear, hate the way she says, "Hey Coop" like they've been friends since they were kids.

They haven't.

We have.

And I hate, most of all, that I was the one who ruined it.

Logan says, "Why don't you ask your boyfriend to join us?"

I hate Logan.

Laney looks up, first at Logan, then at Leo. Leo shrugs. *Since when did Leo make the decisions for her?*

"It's behind the frog statue by the front door," Laney says into the phone. "Yes, it is, just double check." … "There is *so* a frog there." … "A turtle?" … "Oh yeah. Maybe it is a turtle."

"Ask him to come over," Logan says again, shouting over her shoulder.

Laney looks to my dad, then to hers. Brian shrugs. "I wouldn't mind actually meeting the guy who's been taking up all your time."

Please no. Not here. Not in my own goddamn home. I keep my mouth shut and make Laney decide on how badly she wants to pierce my heart with her actions.

"I'm sure he's busy today," Laney says, speaking to her dad, but glancing at me. Her voice drops, along with her gaze. She says into the phone, "You don't have to, Coop."

Logan leans across the table, past Lachlan, knocking over his drink. He yells out our address, and everyone laughs like this is some kind of joke, and maybe it is, and maybe I'm the fucking punch line.

"Really?" Laney says, holding the phone between her ear and shoulder to wipe up the spilled water. "Okay, I'll see you soon."

Three minutes, fifty-eight seconds, and I hear the familiar sound of tires spinning on the loose gravel of my driveway. I don't look up when Dad gasps, whispers a "Holy hell," when he must see the car. "Cooper? As in Lance Kennedy's kid?"

Brian says, "I assumed, but I wasn't sure. I mean, I've never actually seen him before, just his shadow lurking near the front door."

"Dad," Lane whines, getting up from her seat.

By the time I've found the courage to look up, she's halfway across the yard and Cooper fucking Kennedy's leaning against his car, hands in his pockets.

"Who's that?" Lachlan asks.

Brian says, "That's Lois's friend."

Lachlan's eyebrows pinch. "Her boyfriend?"

"Maybe," Brian says, looking over at them. "We're not too sure on that yet."

Everyone at the table turns to the maybe-couple now walking toward us.

"But…" Lachlan tears his gaze away from them and focuses on me. "I thought *you* were her boyfriend."

Silence passes, all eyes on me and I don't know what to say, how to act.

I stand when they get to us, shake Cooper's hand, do my best to pretend like that act alone isn't destroying me.

"Hey, man," he says, all casual like, and Cooper Kennedy might just be the first person in my entire life I hate enough to punch.

Laney introduces my brothers, my dad, then Misty, and finally, Brian.

"It's nice to finally meet you, sir. I've been asking but Lois, you know…"

Brian smiles at him, shakes his hand, strong and firm. "She's a little on the stubborn side."

Lane says, "Lucy's the oldest and only sister. She and her fiancé, Cameron, are on their way so you'll meet them soon."

Cooper smiles down at her. "I know Cam and Luce. We were in the same class, remember?"

Lane's cheeks heat. "Oh yeah."

"Wait. You were in the same class as Luce?" Brian asks.

"Yes, sir."

"So that makes you how old?" he asks.

Cooper glances at Lane quickly. "I'll be twenty-one in a couple of months."

Brian nods, but I can see the concern behind his eyes, and I wonder if he, too, heard the rumors about why Cooper is actually here in the first place.

Lane tugs on Cooper's arm, asks Lachlan to scoot over so Cooper can sit between them.

Jay McLean

"You hungry?" Dad asks him.

"God yes, and this food smells amazing, Mr. Preston."

Dad loads up a plate for Cooper and he eats, and I watch Laney watch him, a smile on her face, and I die a little more.

Lachlan leans on his forearms, his head tilted, eyes narrowed at Cooper.

"What's up, little man?" Cooper asks him.

"You think you could shove that entire hot dog in your mouth?"

Cooper chuckles around a mouthful of food. He wipes his lips on a napkin and says, "I don't know. I've never tried it. Think I should?"

Lachlan nods, his eyes wide.

"The thing is... I'm still trying to impress your girl Lois, and I'm not sure doing that would help my cause. Maybe another time?"

"Promise?"

"Yeah, man. Of course," he tells Lachlan, then looks over at Lane. "This is cute," he says, tugging on the sleeve of her dress. "Did you make it?"

Lane smiles, looks down at her clothes and nods once, her cheeks red.

He leans closer, his mouth to her ear. "You look really nice."

She pushes him away, the way she's done with me so many times before. "Stop it."

"What?" he shrugs. "I missed you."

Lachlan taps Cooper's shoulder. "Are you her boyfriend?" he asks.

I shake my head, stare at the table.

Cooper laughs. "I'm trying, dude, but she's not budging. If you can give me any pointers, I'd really appreciate it."

I can't fucking take it. Being here, watching them, makes me physically sick. I stand, say, "I have to go," and then I run and run and I have no idea whether I'm running from them or from myself. The yards feel like miles, my strides like leaps, until I end up at the cemetery looking down at my mother's grave and asking her if she's as disappointed in me as I am in myself.

CHAPTER THIRTEEN

LOIS

I WASN'T sure I wanted Cooper there, and I didn't invite him on purpose. Hell, I didn't invite him at all. Logan did. So he showed up, charmed the crap out of everyone. Everyone but Luke. I get it. In a way, Luke's had to deal with Coop at school, at track practice, he shouldn't have to deal with him in his personal space. But if Luke's reaction was about *me* with Cooper, then that was something else. Something I shouldn't care about. Just like he didn't care about me.

"You could've told me I'd be walking into the Prestons' house," Cooper says, driving me to work after the disastrous lunch.

"You didn't really give me a chance... you were all,"—I lower my voice to mock his— *"I'm totally down if it means hanging with you."*

He laughs, stops the car at a red light. Then he turns to me, his eyes on mine. "When are you finally going to let me kiss you, Sanders?"

"Shut up." I shake my head, look up at the traffic lights, hoping for a green.

"I'm serious," he says.

"You don't want to kiss me, Cooper."

"I don't?"

"No."

"Why not?"

Come on, light. He settles my bouncing knee with his hand, and I choke on a gasp.

"Lo?"

"Is this your thing?" I blurt out.

"What are you talking about?"

"Hooking up with younger girls... is that like, your fetish or something?" Yeah, I'm not deaf, nor am I immune to the high school rumor mill.

He inhales deeply and removes his hand from my leg, places them both on the steering wheel as he takes off again. He keeps his gaze on the road. I keep mine on him. He blinks, his long, dark lashes fanning across his tanned cheeks. His wide chest rises, falls, but he doesn't speak. Not until we're in the parking lot at work. He puts the car in park and turns to me, his lips twisted. "So you heard that, huh?"

I nod. "It's not a big deal or anything. I just don't want—"

"She was fifteen," he cuts in. "But she didn't look it. I swear."

"You don't have to explain, Coop."

"No." Another breath. "I think I do. Or, at least I *want* to with you."

I swallow, nod for him to continue.

"Her name was Jodie. She was suspended for smoking weed at her private school, and I guess she got bored, thought it'd be fun to go to campus and pretend to be a student. You know, mess with her dad's head." He rubs his forehead, his face scrunched as if it actually physically pains him to tell me all this. "I noticed her in a couple of my lectures. She'd raise her hand, join in on the class. Then after one of them, she asked if I wanted to grab a coffee with her. We actually dated for a couple of weeks, went out a few times. One thing led to another and here I am."

"Is it true?" I croak out, "About your parents paying her off?"

He nods and looks away. "That part is true. My lawyers think that maybe she singled me out because she knew my parents had money."

"I'm sorry," I say truthfully. "That all of that happened to you and now you have to be back at your old high school and—"

"It's not so bad," he interrupts, smiling over at me. "I wouldn't have met *you* otherwise."

I look away because he's giving me *that* look. The same one Luke gave me right before—

"Lo?"

"Yeah?"

"You're going to be late for your shift."

I'm hot, burning flames under his scrutinizing gaze, and my emotions hit me. Hit me hard.

Guilt.

Shame.

Both things I should *not* be feeling.

"You can kiss me," I croak.

His smile is quick to consume him. Then he nods toward the building. "You better go."

"But…"

"Oh," he says, his grin growing. "You want me to kiss you *right now?*"

My stomach turns, my embarrassment flooding me. "No."

He chuckles. "Sanders, I didn't ask if I *could* kiss you. I asked when you would finally *let* me."

"Okay, I get it." I wave my hands between us. "I got my wires crossed." I open the car door, quickly get out and shut it after me.

"Lois!" he calls, window lowered. He leans over the center console, makes sure I can see him. "I'll pick you up after your shift. Take you to dinner." He winks… not so creepy anymore. "First-date kisses are always the best."

HE SHOWS up to my work ten minutes before my shift ends and sits inside the ticket booth with me as if he owns the place, and going by his car, his house, and the way his parents throw around their money, he probably *does* own it. When I'm done, he waits for me to clock out and then walks me to a black truck. "Where's your car?" I ask.

"In my garage."

"So… whose is this?"

"Eddie's."

"And Eddie is… a friend?"

"Our gardener."

"Of course you have a gardener."

He smiles. "I traded cars for the night, threw in a room at a hotel for him and his wife, too. Trust me, they're in for good times."

I get in my seat, buckle my belt, and wait for him to get in. "So why change cars?"

"Because I'm taking you out on a date."

"And you need a truck because…?"

He smiles. "Because this is where we're having said date."

I shake my head, clear the fog. "I'm so confused."

119

"I'll explain later."

He drives to a Mexican restaurant, orders a bunch of food to go, then drives back to his place, past the guard at the security gate and through the pristine, quiet streets of his neighborhood. We don't go to his house, though. Instead, he drives to the outskirts of his prestigious little community until we're parked in a spot that gives us a view of all the cookie-cutter mansions from a distance. And as I look at the houses, I feel my heart plummet because he's taken me on a date, a date far away from everyone who can judge him for being with someone like me.

I'm thirteen again. Sitting in a cinema next to a boy I'm crushing on who doesn't feel the same and I feel

So.

Fucking.

Stupid.

"You ready?" he asks, handing me a drink. He picks up the bag of food, steps out of the car, and I stay in my seat while I work out what would be worse: sitting with him through our "date" or calling him out on it. He opens my door, and I step out, take his hand as he leads me to the bed of the truck.

For a few minutes, he eats in silence, and I feel too sick to take a bite.

"Did something happen at work?" he finally asks.

I shake my head and face him. "What are we doing?" I ask him, my voice cracking with emotion.

"You don't like tacos?" His smile fades when I look up at him, *attempting* to hide my true feelings. "You're mad," he says, not a question, a presumption. He exhales loudly, puts his food down. "When I said I would take you to dinner, you expected something fancy, right?"

"I don't know." I shrug. "Is it..." I take a breath and then another, and I decide to be honest because history shows that keeping my feelings hidden, *secret*, only lead to disaster. "I feel like you're ashamed of me. Like you want to keep me to yourself... your dirty little secret."

"Never!" he says quickly. "That's not..." He rubs his eyes, his frustration evident. "Look, I've done fancy before, Lois. I was twelve the first time my dad made me suit up and sit through one of his pathetic business dinners in the most expensive restaurant in town. And I've sat through many more since. For me, those places

120

are nothing but lies and deception and no, it's not that you're my dirty little secret but yeah, I kind of do want to keep you to myself. Or, at least, I want to keep you separate from that. Because you've experienced enough lies and enough deception, and I don't want that for you. I really don't. But this is me, the *real* me." He waves his hand around us. "And if you're not into this then I can go home, change, and we can go somewhere else."

"That's not what I want," I tell him, my voice low, my shame high. "I'm sorry, I shouldn't have said anything."

"No, I'm glad you did. I want you to be honest with me because it makes it so much easier to be the same with you. Because I like you, Lo. Like, *really* like you. And I've taken a lot of girls to a lot of fancy places and it all ends the same way."

My nose scrunches in disgust.

He laughs. "But I've never done this before."

"Tacos in a truck?"

Smiling, he says, "I've never been comfortable enough to just be *me*. And I don't know… you being here right now—it kind of gives me a reason to like who I am, you know? If you like me, then I can't be that bad."

I return his smile. I can't help it. "You make me happy, Coop."

His grin widens, but mine falls. And then I ask him something I'd been wondering my entire shift. "How is this going to work? Us *dating?* Is it, like, an alter ego for you? You go to college during the week and be this other guy you speak of and come home on weekends and be with me? Are you…" I clear my throat. "Are you going to see other girls while you're there?"

He chuckles. "I figure it'll pretty much be the same way it is now. I call you every night, beg for you to speak to me. Lose myself in your voice during the week, then satisfy all my cravings on the weekends."

"Your *cravings?*" I giggle.

"I crave you, Sanders. I crave your company." He cups my cheek, his lips meeting my forehead. "And your laugh, your smile, your touch. I miss you when I can't be around you, and when I am here I want more of you. Just you. There *are* no other girls. And there won't be."

"Promise?" I whisper, my eyes drifting shut when his lips hover over mine.

"I could promise you the world, Sanders, but it doesn't mean anything unless you trust me. And you *have* to trust me. You have to realize that I'm not *him*."

I exhale, slowly, drink in his words. "Are you going to kiss me now?"

He pulls back, his grin promising. Then he releases me, picks up his food again. He stares ahead while I stare at him, at the movement of his jaw as he chews his food, his mind elsewhere. And I no longer feel guilty that I want him to kiss me. And *soon*.

"You always walk with your head lowered," he says out of nowhere.

"What?"

"Yeah." He nods, wipes his mouth on a napkin. Then he turns to me. "It's like you're afraid of the world seeing you. Or, maybe, you're afraid that they *do* see you."

I drop my gaze.

"You're a pretty exceptional girl, Sanders. It sucks you think the world doesn't see you that way."

"You can't assume to know that about me," I tell him.

"Oh yeah? You're doing it right now."

"Doing what?"

"Look up," he says.

So I lift my gaze, and I do as he says. There's nothing but acres and acres of empty land. "What am I looking at?" I ask him.

"The world. Untouched."

I sigh, look over at him.

He raises his eyebrows. "Don't you want to be the first to touch something? To reach out and grasp onto the world around you? You can't touch it if you can't *see* it."

A sob forms in my throat and I keep it there, his words replaying in my mind, over and over, because he's *right*. I've lived my life, almost eighteen years of it, but I've never really *lived*. Every hour, every action, every decision was made with Lucas in mind. I didn't go to parties, hoping he'd show up at my door, wanting to get in bed with me, praying he'd see me differently. But the four walls of my basement bedroom aren't enough anymore, and when I'm done with senior year, there's nothing waiting for me but those same four walls.

"Are you cold?" Cooper asks, and I realize I'm shivering. Whether it's from the temperature or my sudden fear about my future, I don't know.

Still, he moves to sit behind me, his legs on either side, his arms around my waist. He rests his chin on my shoulder, his thumb stroking my stomach. "I didn't say that stuff to hurt you," he says.

I crane my neck, look up at him. "I know."

Then his mouth descends, his lips finding mine. He kisses me softly, slowly, as if we have all the time in the world. And maybe we do. He pulls back, inhales loudly. "Holy shit," he whispers, then goes back to kissing me. My body heats against his, his tongue like torture, dancing with mine. I shift so I'm sitting across his lap, making it easier for both of us, and I kiss him back, give him a piece of my heart that not so long ago was broken. His hand lands on my leg, creeping higher, bringing my dress up with it. And without thinking, I spread my legs just enough so he can slide his hand to where I want him. He stops an inch away, rears back, his eyes hooded, filled with lust. "I should take you home," he says.

I choke on a gasp, trap his hand between my legs. "Why? Am I doing it wrong?"

"No." He chuckles, shakes his head. "It's just been a long time since I've made out with a girl for this long without... you know, going further... and I need to take you home so I can go home and take care of it."

I grasp his shirt, pull him back down to my mouth. Kiss him. Long and hard. "Or we could go somewhere and have *me* take care of it for you."

He swallows. Loud. "Yeah," he breathes out. "We could do that, too."

I jump off the truck, wait for him to do the same. We get in his car, drive to his house. He leads me to his room, where I walk with my head high, looking at the world, and I decide then and there, to start *living*.

CHAPTER FOURTEEN

LOIS

DATING COOPER IS EXACTLY like he said it would be—it's basically what we did pre-dating, only now he's seen the inside of my house *and* my bedroom. And other things, like me naked in my bedroom.

For the past two weeks, we've spent every spare second together when he's in town. Fridays I watch him coach the track team's practice, we go out for dinner, and then back to his house. Mondays come along, I watch him do the same thing, then we have dinner, and he drops me off at home, kisses me goodbye, and we don't see each other until the following Friday. We speak, though, every day, sometimes on the phone, sometimes through video chat.

He studies. A lot. He told me his parents agreed to his athletic scholarship on the basis that he keep up a 3.8 GPA and get a degree in business and marketing so he could one day join his dad and later take over the family business. What that business actually is, is a little sketchy to me—something about investments and finance and nest eggs and loopholes.

NOW, I'm standing just outside the tunnel at school, watching them do cooldowns. Cooper waves over at me, and I wave back. Lucas turns, sees me standing there. Then he stands, starts to leave. Cooper stands, too, yells something I can't make out. Luke shoves him. I gasp, stand taller. "What's your problem?" Cooper yells.

"You're my problem," Luke shouts, shoving him harder.

Garray gets between them but he's facing Luke, words filtering from his mouth faster than I can make out. Then he leaves. Garray, not Luke. Luke's too busy having a stand-off with Cooper.

Garray shakes his head as he walks toward me. "You need to do something about your boy."

"Who?" I look from him to Luke to Cooper. "Cooper?"

Without so much as slowing, he says, "Luke! He's lost his fucking mind!"

Cooper comes next, his eyes narrowed, anger flaring on his lips. He sighs when he gets to me, hands on hips.

"What the hell just happened?" I ask.

"It's fine, baby." He kisses my forehead. "I'll be out soon, okay?"

I nod, watch him go down the tunnel and when I turn back, Lucas is walking toward me. "What the hell was that?" I ask him, blocking his path so he has no choice but to talk to me.

He tries to step around me but I shift, my hands going to his chest to stop him. His shoulders tense, his lips pressed tight. "What, Laney?" he shouts, his voice echoing off the walls of the tunnel. "Your boyfriend gets a little of his treatment back and *now* you want to talk to me?"

I drop my gaze. "What's going on with you, Luke?" I ask, my tone soft.

He shoves my hands off him. "Leave it alone, Lane."

"Luke!" I look him in the eyes, hoping he sees my concern.

"You want to know what's happening? Fine!" He steps closer, towers over me, his eyes right on mine—eyes filled with rage. "Your boyfriend won't get off my back. He just keeps pushing and pushing until I've got no room to fucking move!" He sucks in a breath. "Leo's grades were suffering, so the school brought a specialist in and they told him he's dyslexic. All those books he walks around with? He can't even fucking read them! And last night..." He laughs, but not out of humor. "Last night the cops showed up on our doorstep with Logan, cuffed. He was smoking weed at the fucking playground. And the twins are being bullied at school, so much so that Liam's talking about killing himself! They're only twelve! They shouldn't be dealing with this shit." His voice breaks, his pain slicing through his words. "And now Lachlan's going around asking every woman he sees if they're his mom because his mom's dead, Laney. She's *dead*, and he doesn't understand that. And it'd be really fucking nice if his godmother was around to get him through that!"

I wrap my arms around him, tears in my eyes, because abandoning Luke served a purpose, but abandoning his brothers...

His hand settles on the back of my head, the other grasping the fabric of my top. His chest rises and falls against mine. He wipes his eyes on my shoulder, his pain causing my own. He whispers, his mouth to my ear, "And I miss my best friend, Laney. So much."

"WHERE'S YOUR HEAD AT, Sanders?" Cooper asks, watching me from his desk while I study on his bed.

I look up at him. "Hmm?"

"You've been on that same page for the past ten minutes."

"I have?"

"What's going on?"

I blow out a heavy breath. "Have you been giving Lucas a hard time at practice?"

He rolls his eyes. "This is about that kid?"

"That *kid* is the same age as me."

"That's not what I meant," he says, getting up and sitting on the bed with me. "I do give him a hard time," he admits.

"Why, Coop?"

He doesn't skip a beat. "Because he's good. Better than good. He's the best one out there. He may even be better than me, and he's been slacking lately—"

"He's got a lot going on," I cut in.

He sighs, looks at me like I'm stupid. "And that may be fine off the track but if he wants that UNC scholarship he has to do better. I'm not doing it to be an asshole because he was one to you. He races well when he's under pressure, when he feels like he's competing against an enemy. I'm doing it for *him*, Lo. No other reason."

"Okay," I concede. "I'm sorry. It's just really not like him to explode like he did today. He's always been so calm and—"

"I really don't care," he cuts in.

I rear back. "Excuse me?"

"I'm sorry. I just don't care about Lucas off the track, especially after what he did to you. And I'm not going to sit here and pretend like I do. I get you guys were friends, but he means nothing to me."

"Wow. That's a little harsh."

He shrugs. "Maybe it's a little too much honesty when you're used to lies."

I start to pack my books. "I'm going home."

"No." He stops me, his hand around my wrist. "I'm sorry, okay?" He leans in, kisses me once. "I'm just stressing and I'm taking it out on you."

"Is everything okay?"

"Not really." He shifts his gaze away from me and over to the desk where he'd been doing his own studying. "My classes are killing me, and doing this whole coaching thing and training but not being able to compete is getting under my skin." He faces me again, a sad smile pulling on his lips. "You're my saving grace, Sanders. I live for this time with you. Stay. Please?"

I nod, open my books again.

"No," he says. "Stay the night with me?"

I swallow, nervous, because even though we've had sex, we've never *slept* together. There's a knock on his door, saving me from answering. A man pokes his head in, a man I've only seen in the pictures hanging on the walls. He seems taller in person, or maybe it's just his presence. "I'm sorry," he says, looking between us. "I didn't know Cooper had company."

I stand, fix my clothes, make sure he knows nothing inappropriate is going on in his son's room. Then I walk toward him, my nerves on end, my hand out to shake. "Hi, Mr. Kennedy. I'm Lois Sanders. It's such a pleasure to meet you, sir."

Behind me, Cooper chuckles.

His dad shakes my hand. "Lance Kennedy," he says. "It's good to meet you, too, Ms. Sanders." His smile is tight as his gaze shifts to Cooper behind me. "Sanders," he murmurs. "She's not Brian Sanders' kid is she?"

I nod while Cooper says, "Yeah, Dad. She is."

"Right." Lance drops my hand, keeps his focus on Cooper. "Your mom and I are heading out to some charity dinner I knew nothing about until an hour ago. We'll be home late."

"Sure, Pops," Cooper replies.

His dad looks down his nose at me. "Goodbye, Ms. Sanders."

Once he's gone, Cooper cackles. "*It's such a pleasure to meet you, sir,*" he mocks.

I walk to his bed, pick up a pillow and throw it at his face. "Shut up."

He attempts to contain his laughter as he tugs on my tee, pulling me down until I'm lying on top of him. He shakes his head, eyes on me, smile *for* me. "You're so cute, all nervous and stuff."

128

"You said your parents were out of town."

He shrugs. "They were. I guess they're home now."

"I wish I'd met them properly."

"What was wrong with that meeting?" he asks.

"I panicked."

With a laugh, he says, "A little."

"Did you know he knew my dad? And *how* does he know my dad?"

Cooper shrugs again. "My dad invests in a lot of property. They may have worked together in the past. Who knows?" He moves his hand to my back, under my top, moving higher until his fingers find the clasp of my bra.

"Really?" I ask. "*Now?*"

He kisses my cheek, moves across my jaw toward my ear, his tongue like fire against my skin. He bares his teeth, tugs on my earlobe. "*Right now.*"

I want nothing more than to get lost with him, but he was right. My mind is elsewhere. I lean back, look him in the eyes. "I'll stay with you tonight but tomorrow, I need to do something."

"WHERE IS MY BRA?" I whisper-yell, panic swarming through me.

Cooper rolls around in his bed, using his pillow to muffle his laugh.

Two seconds ago, the front door slammed shut, meaning his parents were home, and we were in his bed... naked.

I stumble around his dark bedroom in nothing but my panties, searching for my clothes while he tries to calm himself down enough to switch on the lamp for me.

"How long were we...?"

"Were we what?" he asks.

I find my bra, slip it on while my face heats with embarrassment.

"You can't even say it, can you?"

"Doing... *it*."

"Having sex?!" he shouts.

"Cooper! They're going to hear you!"

He laughs again. "The sex part, probably about twenty minutes..." He smirks, his eyes drinking me in. "The foreplay, though, that lasted about an hour."

129

I slip on his t-shirt and get back into bed, doing my best to make my hair look presentable. Meanwhile, he's still naked, a smug smile across his smug, post-sex face. "They're home early, right?"

He shrugs and flops back on his pillow, the slight light from the lamp casting a shadow across his brow. "Cooper!" I shove him.

"What?" he asks lazily.

"Get dressed!"

He pats my head. "They're not coming up here. Don't worry."

I whisper, "How do you know?"

"Because they're too wasted to even remember I'm home."

More doors open and shut downstairs, heels clank, footsteps thump. Another slam of a door. "Next time you want to act like a whore do it at home, Vivian!" Lance yells.

My jaw drops, my eyes wide and on Cooper.

"See?" he says. "Wasted. They always do this. Go to some function, drink too much, come home, argue."

I hear his mother's voice for the first time. "I was just talking to him! You embarrassed me in front of all my friends!" she yells.

"I embarrassed you?!" Lance booms. "My associates and business partners were there! How does that make me look? Having my wife—"

"All I did was talk—"

A chair scrapes. Glass breaks.

"Shut up!" Lance shouts. "Just shut the fuck up!"

I grasp Cooper's arm, my breaths short, my pulse pounding in my ears.

"Come on," he whispers, getting out of bed and slipping on his boxers. He removes the covers off his bed and takes my hand. Then he leads me to his walk-in closet the size of my living room and sits on the floor, tugging my hand for me to join him. I sit in front of him, my legs crossed, mimicking his position. He takes the ends of the blanket and wraps it around both of us. "I used to do this when I was a kid," he says, his voice low, his forehead touching mine. "I used to be afraid, too, but then it happened so many times it became my version of normal. It'll stop soon," he says, kissing my cheek. "I promise."

It stops then and there, the new silence deafening. We get back into Cooper's bed, and a moment later, he's fast asleep, his breaths even. I stare at his face, at the distant calm on his features, and I wonder how it's possible he can sleep after what we just heard. *It became my version of normal*, he told me. I find myself frowning, an overwhelming sadness creeping in my chest, images of a smaller version of Cooper sitting alone in his closet, hands to his ears to avoid the anger around him. I kiss his lips, and his breaths falter, but he doesn't wake. Then I spend the next hour tossing and turning, trying to find the peace he so easily found. The house is eerily silent, and my mouth is dry, my throat thirsty. I get out of bed, slip on my pants, and make my way downstairs and toward the kitchen. The tiled floors are cold against my feet, the rooms are dark, the curtains drawn. I walk with my hands out, hoping not to bump into anything, or *anyone*, on my way to the kitchen. A sliver of light shines from beneath the kitchen door, and I stop in my tracks, place my ear against it. I listen for sounds, proof that someone's in there. When I hear nothing, I open the door and freeze in my spot, my gasp loud.

A woman, blonde and beautiful, one that stands proud next to Lance Kennedy in the pictures on the walls, sits at the kitchen counter, an ice pack to her left eye, dried blood on the corner of her lip. She glances up, shocked. "I didn't know…" she whispers.

A shiver runs up my spine. "I'm… um… I'm Cooper's."

She smiles, sits straighter. "You must be Lois."

I step closer. "Are you okay, Mrs. Kennedy?"

She shakes her head and removes the ice pack, revealing the onset of bruising. "I had a little too much to drink and stumbled, walked into the doorframe."

"Oh." I clasp my hands tighter. "I just came down to get a glass of water." I move closer again, careful, not wanting to startle her. My mind and my heart want to believe her, but my gut tells me it's a lie. She didn't walk into a doorframe. She walked into her husband's hand. I ignore my need for water and ask, "Do you need help?" I motion to her face. "Cleaning that up?"

"No." She shakes her head again, freeing strands of hair from her once-perfect bun. "I'm fine."

No, Mrs. Kennedy. You're not fine at all.

"Do you have a first-aid kit?"

She seems to concede, drops the ice pack on the counter. "Under the sink in the guest bathroom."

I find the kit and quickly make my way back to her. Then I sit in the stool next to her, wait for her to face me before getting the supplies. My hands shake as I dab at her lip with a wet cotton swab, removing the dried blood and the dark red lipstick now smudged

131

at the edges, seeping into the wrinkles around her lips. In her day, she would've been so beautiful. Right now, she looks tired, not just from age, but from life.

"Cooper's told me so much about you," she says, her voice low, as if she doesn't want to disturb the sleeping beast.

I pause, look into her eyes. Her concern mirrors mine. *I won't tell, Mrs. Kennedy.* "I hope they were all good things," I say.

"Oh, they were," she replies, her eyes bright. She's acting like we're meeting for lunch, not sitting in her kitchen late at night, her son's girlfriend cleaning up the cuts and bruises caused by her husband.

I play her game, pretend the same. "I'm glad."

She forces a smile. "After what happened last semester with that girl... he was so depressed, so dark, and ever since he met you, it's like he sees the sun again. Feels the heat and the joy it brings. You make him happy, Lois."

I find the cut on her lip, apply some ointment. Then I clear my throat, look down at her shaking hands. "He makes me happy, too."

I get up to grab us both glasses of water and hand her some aspirins from the first-aid kit. She holds them in her hands, somehow still smiling. "Lance told me you're Brian Sanders' daughter?"

After a nod, I ask, "How does Mr. Kennedy know my dad?"

"He doesn't know your dad so much as he knows Tom Preston."

"Oh?"

"They've got history, so to speak."

I stare at her, wanting more.

She downs the aspirin with her water, then says, "A while back they worked together on a massive development project." She fixes the loose strands of hair across her brow. "Lance had investors come through from all across the country, and there was a big meeting. Tom and my husband were supposed to head the meeting. Tom showed up... inebriated, and blew the deal."

"He was drunk?" I whisper.

She nods. "He'd just lost his wife..."

"Oh."

"Are you close with the Prestons?" she asks, patting the swelling formed under her eye.

132

I don't respond. Instead, I lower my voice, lean in closer. "Mrs. Kennedy… my dad's girlfriend is a police officer and—"

The kitchen door opens and we pull apart, our eyes snapping to the sound. Cooper stands just inside, his gaze shifting between his mother and me. "I was looking for you," he tells me, his jaw tense.

"I was thirsty," I respond.

He steps toward us, his hand out for me, but his words for his mom. "You okay?"

She nods, smiles at him like mothers are supposed to smile at their children. "I'm fine. Had a little too much to drink and well, you know the rest."

Cooper visibly swallows, plays her game, too. He takes my hand, helps me off the stool. Then he reaches out, his hand as shaky as hers as he cups her cheek, kisses her forehead like he does with me. "I love you, Ma."

She chokes on a sob, grasping his wrist. "I love you, too, son."

We go back to his room, back to his bed, where he holds me tight, his body curled into a ball as he lays his head on my shoulder.

"Lois?"

"Yeah?"

I expect him to tell me to ignore what I saw downstairs, to swear to secrecy, to apologize that I had to see it at all. But he looks up at me, his gaze searching mine. He exhales, his breath warm against my lips. "I'm falling so deeply in love with you."

My mouth opens, but he doesn't let me speak. Instead, his mouth covers mine, urgent and needy. Then he shifts until he's on top of me, his knees parting mine.

We don't make love.

He fucks me.

Hard and fast.

Because he's hurting.

And I'm hurting for him.

So I let him.

Because he's not the only one falling deep, deep, deeply in *love*.

CHAPTER FIFTEEN

LUCAS

"LANEY'S HERE!"

I startle awake. Rub my eyes. Metaphorically open my ears to see if I'd been dreaming.

"Laney's here! Laney's here! Laney's here!"

Nope.

Not a dream.

I throw the covers off me, get out of bed. I skipped my run this morning; my motivation lost somewhere amidst the chaos of my life. I go to the bathroom, pour half a tube of toothpaste in my mouth, then proceed to cough and splutter as I attempt to swallow it while I slip on some clothes and shoes. I open the apartment door just as Laney steps out of a black truck I'd never seen before. "Hey, rock star!" she shouts to Lachlan, currently flying down the porch steps to get to her.

I'm a lot calmer than he was when I descend from the apartment stairs and walk over to her.

"Hey, Lucas," she says.

I point to the truck. "Did you get a car?"

She shakes her head, her smile as warm as the morning sun. "It's Cooper's gardener's."

Shoving my hands in my pockets, I rock back on my heels. "Of course he has a gardener."

"That's exactly what I said," she laughs out, and that sound alone chips away at the cold, hard ice surrounding my heart.

"So what are you doing here?" I ask.

"I called your dad," she says, grimacing as if she's unsure she should be here. She's always welcome here. This is her home, too. "I was hoping to get some time in with the Preston boys."

"They'd like that." I say *they* when I mean *me.*

She shuffles her feet, her hands clasped in front of her. "I feel like I have to tell you something," she says.

"Okay...?"

"I kind of knew about Leo... I mean before you told me yesterday." It's the most she's said to me since *that* night, and I bask in her voice, in her words, one after the other, and I wish she were holding me like she did in the tunnel because her touch is like oil, and my pain is the water. She creates a divide when I could be drowning.

I clear my throat, come back to the conversation. "You did?"

"Well, when we were younger, he'd always walk around with a book and I noticed it was the same book for weeks, and when I asked him what he thought of it, he'd kind of just shut down. Then he told me he had trouble reading, and I tried to help him through it. Once a week we'd meet up at the playground and read. Obviously, I didn't help enough, and I'm sorry because I should've told you or your dad, he was just really embarrassed about it so..."

"So you were a good friend to him. You don't need to apologize" *My fingers itch to touch you, Lane.* "I'm sorry for dumping all that stuff on you yesterday. It was just—"

Leo steps out of the house then, the screen door slamming shut behind him, putting an end to my apology.

LANE AND LEO walk side by side, away from the house, away from me. They speak in hushed tones, sharing secrets and sorrow. And it dawns on me now why Leo had been so upfront about his feelings toward me, about how badly I treated her. Because he knew her. One-on-one. And he loves her, maybe even as much as I do.

THEY RETURN an hour later and it's Logan's turn. He doesn't get the same treatment. She yanks on his ear, physically drags him down the steps, and then she kicks his ass. Literally, *kicks his ass*. He jumps, surprised.

I laugh, not at all surprised.

Then I sit in the living room of the main house and pretend to watch TV—something I never do because the shows I want to watch are too mature for the boys who want to watch them with
136

me. But that's not why I'm here. I'm just waiting for the second hand to tick over until it's my turn with Laney. I want that time with her, one-on-one, so we can do something I've wanted to do for what feels like forever.

Talk.

I just want to talk to her, to go back to the way things were, and if all she wants to talk about is Cooper, I'll sit and I'll listen and I'll do my best not to show her that it's killing me to have to do that.

ANOTHER HOUR PASSES and Logan returns, his general angry, broody mood replaced with laughter because Laney has the power to find light in the darkest of days and the darkest of moods. "Can I borrow the minivan?" she asks my dad.

He hands her the keys, no questions.

She steps out of the house, calls out to the twins wrestling in the front yard. "Feel like kicking my ass at the batting cages?" she asks.

They immediately stop what they're doing, grab their gear, and get into the car with her.

Another hour.

Well, an hour and six minutes to be exact, and I have no idea what's happening on the television, I just know that there are two Preston boys left, and I'm one of them.

Dad comes marching down the stairs, Lachlan and an overnight bag in tow.

"You ready, bud?" she asks Lachlan, taking the bag from my dad.

"He gives you any trouble you just call and I'll be right over," Dad tells her.

"It'll be fine," Laney assure him.

I stand up, no longer able to pretend as if I care about who the hell "A" is on whatever show I'm watching. I've acted casual all day and left her to do her thing, but *when the hell is it my turn?* "Are you leaving?" I ask.

"I'm having a sleepover at Lane's!" Lachlan announces, his grin from ear-to-ear.

My heart plummets, lands on my feet, heavy with the weight of her choices.

She says, "I got someone to cover my shift so we could spend some godmother/son time together."

I manage to hide my disappointment, scruff Lachy's hair. "Have fun. Don't miss me too much."

I obviously suck at hiding my feelings because he frowns, looks over at Lane. "Can Lucas come, too?"

Lane's cheeks turn red while the air turns thick and suffocating.

"I can't," I tell him, saving Lane. "Dumb Name's throwing a party so…"

"Okay." He stands on his toes, his arms outstretched. He hugs my neck and whispers, "I'll spend time with you when I get back. I promise."

"Good," I say through a chuckle. Then I look at Laney but she's looking away, and so I hug my brother tighter, tell him what I planned on telling *her*. "I *need* my best friend."

IT'S 9:33 PM when my phone rings. "I'm so sorry to call. I know you said you had a party or something, but Lachlan's been in my bed since seven and he won't go to sleep. He keeps asking for one minute and I get into bed with him and cuggles him and everything but he won't shut down and he says it's not the same. He wants you to do his one minute."

There is no party, but I don't bother telling her that. "Do you want me to pick him up?"

"No," she says quickly. "I want him here. Is it okay if you come over? Just until he falls asleep. I'm sorry if I'm ruining your plans."

I had no plans, but again, I don't tell her that. "I'll be there soon."

I KNOCK on her front door because I don't know if I'm welcome to use her bedroom door anymore—if it's now reserved for the one and only Cooper Kennedy.

She seems surprised that it's me when she answers the door. "Why are you knocking here?"

I shrug, feeling stupid. "How's he doing?"

"He's wide awake, throwing pillows and jumping on the bed."

I cringe. "Sorry."

"It's fine."

I make my way down to her room while she follows behind. I take off my jacket, throw it on her couch. *Habit.*

138

"Pukas!" Lachlan shouts. "Are you here for one minute?"

"You know you're not allowed to jump on beds," I tell him.

He continues jumping. "Lane said I could."

I face Lane.

"I said he could do it once," she defends.

I grab Lachlan by the waist and effortlessly slam him down to the bed. He finds this hilarious. Using my sternest voice, I say, "Time to sleep."

"Yes, sir," he giggles, saluting me.

I slip off my shoes, get under the covers with him.

"I'll be back," Lane says, taking her phone from the nightstand and going upstairs.

"I like Lane's bed," Lachlan whispers through a yawn. "It's constable."

"Comfortable."

"Have you slept in Lane's bed?" he asks.

I really wish I wasn't in bed with my six-year-old brother while he forces the images and memories of the last time I was here into my mind.

"Luke? Have you?"

I nod.

He giggles. "Did you sex?"

My eyes widen. "What is with you and sex? Go. To. Sleep!"

"I can't," he whispers.

"Why not?"

He shrugs. "Can you sing the Prestons in the Bed song for me like Mommy used to do for you guys?"

I rear back, look him in the eyes. "How do you know about that song?"

"Laney told me. We talked about Mommy all day."

"Oh yeah?"

"Laney said Mommy was pretty."

"She was," I tell him, the slight ache in my chest building the longer I watch him.

He smiles wide. "As pretty as Laney?"

"No one is as pretty as Laney."

"Yeah," he says. "So can you sing it for me? Like she did for you?"

I clear my throat, ready my voice. I force a smile and whisper the song to him. "There were seven Prestons in the bed and the little one"—I point to him— "said, roll over, roll over, so they all rolled over and Lucy fell down."

He laughs under his breath, his eyes drifting shut.

"There were six Prestons in the bed and the little one said, roll over, roll over, so they all rolled over and Lucas fell down."

Even though he's fast asleep by the time I get to Logan, I finish the song until it's done. Then I get out of bed, listen to Lane upstairs on the phone, probably talking to Cooper. For the first time ever, I feel out of place. Being here doesn't feel like it used to. I don't know if I should leave or if I should stay to let her know I'm going to leave. I exhale loudly, try to calm my nerves. I start to pace, back and forth, round and round. Meanwhile, she's upstairs, laughing at whatever Cooper's saying to her. I freeze when I get to her desk, a desk full of memories I have to try to forget somehow. There's a familiar picture of us on there. Once upon a time it was in a frame and sat in the center of her bookshelf like a proud possession. The picture was taken by my mom the day we met, me in my dirty Superman shirt, her in her slogan tee. Her hair was shorter then, not as wavy as it is now. We both wore glasses, and my pathetically wide grin showed the giant gap between my two front teeth. Our arms are around each other as if we'd been friends for years, or maybe we just knew that we'd be friends for years to come.

I move papers out of the way so I can pick it up, but my fingers graze on a piece of cloth—one that she uses for her cross-stitches. I pick it up, and my eyes widen, my breath catches, my knees weaken. It's a replica of the picture of us, but it's incomplete, certain parts of us missing. Her smile is there, though, and my chest aches when I skim my thumb over it. And even though I can hear her footsteps on the stairs making her way down to me, I don't put it down. I don't move. *I can't.*

She's next to me now. *Coconuts, lime, and Laney.*

"I was working on it to give to you for your birthday but..." She doesn't finish her sentence. She doesn't need to.

"I should go," I whisper.

"Wait," she says, and I swallow my pride and face her. "Can we talk, maybe?"

I nod, though I'm terrified of what she has to say.

She points to the couch in her room—my old bed when I was strong enough to stay out of hers.

We sit.

"So..." I say.

"So..." she says back.

"Um..." I push back the puke. "How are you and Cooper?"

"Fine," she says quickly. "But I don't want to talk about him."

Good. Neither do I.

"I wanted to apologize to you."

"Me?" I ask. "For what?"

She looks away. First at one wall. Then another. Then she clenches and unclenches her fists, a sign of nerves. Her hands always need to be doing something, that's why she finds knitting so therapeutic.

I say, "You don't owe me anything, Lane."

"I do," she says, her voice quiet. She inhales loudly, exhales the same way. "I've always put you on a pedestal, Luke. I always thought you were a god amongst men, and I think, deep down, I expected you to act that way. And that wasn't fair to you. At all." Her lips tremble, and I inch closer, wanting to save her from her own thoughts. She sniffs once, tries to keep it together. "I've been in love with you since the moment I saw you, and as we got older I started seeing you *differently* and I don't know, I guess I just had this picture in mind of what it would be like to be with you in *that* way." She wipes at her eyes before her tears can be released, but I don't need to see them to know they exist, I can hear it in the shakiness of her voice, feel it in the breaking of my heart. I hate seeing her sad. I hate it even more when I cause it.

I let her speak, not interrupting, because I know it's important to her that she says what she needs to say and have me *hear* it. "In my mind, and in here,"—she covers her heart with her hand— "it's always been you, Lucas."

It's always been you, too, Laney.

"And in the end, I got what I wanted. And *my* expectations of you have nothing to do with who you are as a person or as a friend. That's all on me."

"Laney." I shake my head, my vision blurred by my own tears, my own thoughts. *I hate that you feel this, Laney.*

"And I'm sorry that I've been shutting you out the way I have, because it's not your fault." She looks over at Lachlan, sleeping peacefully in what was once *our* bed. "I should've been there for him." She sniffs again, wipes her eyes on the sleeve of her sweatshirt. "Besides, it was just sex, right?"

I drop my gaze, the ache in my chest intensified. Laney's never been an *"it was just sex"* kind of person. I was, and now I *made* her the same way. Either me or... "So you and Cooper?" I hate asking the question as much as I hate seeing the answer in her eyes. I lift the cross-stitch I'm still holding onto. "Can I have this?" I ask.

She offers me a half-hearted smile. "But I'm not done with us," she says.

I look into her eyes, memorize them. "Yeah, Lane. I think you are."

CHAPTER SIXTEEN

LOIS

THE TEXTS STARTED AT 5:30 this morning.
Single-letter messages.
The first was an H.
Then an A.
Followed by a P
P
Y
I was almost back to sleep when the next set came.
B
I
R
You get the rest.
All from Cooper.

THIS YEAR, my birthday landed on Wednesday, which is also Cooper's busiest day on campus. He couldn't be with me physically, but he sure let me know he was here in spirit.

I sit in my first class, half asleep because of the thoughtful (and relentless) texts all morning. Dumb Name walks toward me, a piece of paper in his hand. "From Luke's brother," he says, dropping it on my desk.

"Which one?"

"I don't know all their names," he huffs out. "The annoying one."

I unfold the note, smile when I see the stick-figure drawing of a girl holding balloons next to a cake the same size as the girl.

Dear Lamey,
Lunch.
Cafeteria.
Be there or be a fucking idiot.
I like your boobs,
- Logan.

There's a knock on the door and Mrs. Miles sighs, annoyed by the distraction, and opens the door. A man waits on the other side behind a giant bouquet of flowers. "Is there a Lois Sanders in here?" he asks.

I sink lower in my seat, listening to the *oohs* and *aahs* coming from my classmates. Mrs. Miles points me out, and the delivery man brings the flowers to me. "Lucky girl," he tells me. I've never really been a flowers kind of girl, so I can't say what they are. They smell good, though, and they're so big I have to stand to look for the card, even though I know who they're from.

"Thank you, young man." Mrs. Miles shoos him away.

"I'm not done," the man says. "Our customer wanted to make sure the other girls didn't feel left out." He then proceeds to hand a single red rose to all the girls in the class, including my teacher, while the class breaks out in whispers, Cooper's name on everyone's tongue. My cheeks burn with embarrassment, hating the attention.

"High school relationships aren't what they used to be," Mrs. Miles mumbles, trying to regain the attention of the class.

I find the card, read it.

Happy 18th Birthday to the most beautiful girl in the world.
I love you.
- Cooper.

"How are you even going to fit that in your locker?" Dumb Name asks. "Coop didn't think this one out, huh?"

"Who cares?" a random girl I've never spoken to rebuts. "Cooper Kennedy has money and he's not afraid to spend it."

Grace scoffs. "Lucas has money," she says, facing me and shooting daggers with her eyes. I slump in my seat, avoiding her glare.

"Yeah," Dumb Name agrees. "Luke has money, but Coop has *Fuck You* money."

"Garray!" Mrs. Miles says through a gasp.

144

"What does that even mean?" the random girl asks.

I'd smash my head against the desk, but the giant bunch of flowers is in my way.

Dumb Name says, "It means the Kennedys can say *Fuck You* to anyone, and their money makes it okay."

I WAVE Logan down when he enters the cafeteria. He smirks and strides toward me. Then he dumps his bag on the table and slumps down in his seat. "I heard you got a delivery this morning."

"You heard that, huh?"

He chuckles. "The whole school heard." His gaze shifts around me. "So where is it?"

"Mrs. Miles offered to keep it in her office until the end of the day."

He nods.

"So..." I start. "You wanted to see me?"

"I'm waiting on Leo."

"We're here," Leo says, walking up behind me. But he's not alone. He's dragging what seems to be an unsure Lucas with him. They move to the other side of the table where Leo forcefully makes Luke sit in the middle. Leo dumps his bag on the table, unzips it, then looks up at me. "Ready?" he asks, his grin wide.

I smile back, unable to contain it. "What did you guys do?"

Leo dramatically drops the paper plate on the table. "Ta-da!" he shouts.

My jaw drops, my eyes moving from the plate to each of the Preston boys in front of me. "Are these Virginia's brownies?"

Three heads nod in unison. All dark hair, all piercing blue eyes.

"You hunted down your old nanny to bake my favorite brownies?"

Logan shakes his head. "No. She's working down in Wilmington, so she emailed us the recipe."

I peel the Saran Wrap covering the brownies. "You *made* these?" I look at Lucas, hoping he's the one who answers. I'd made peace with the situation between us, but it seems like he's the one pulling away now, creating an ever-growing divide between us.

"Technically," Leo says, laughing at my reaction. "All *six* of us tried to make them. Dad had to take Lachy because he kept

145

throwing eggs. After the third failed batch, the twins gave up. So it was just us three left."

"We got it right on the fifth batch, but then Luke remembered you liked yours with walnuts, so we *had* to make those," Logan says, leaning forward and resting his elbows on the table. "Lane," he says seriously. "I could've died making these for you. Then what would you do? Because I know you *want* me, and you can't have me if I'm dead."

I pout, meet Lucas's eyes across the table. "This is really nice."

"I'm glad you think so," Leo says. "Dad was pissed when he saw the kitchen this morning."

Lucas chuckles, breaks our stare to glance at Leo. "Was he?" God, I miss his voice, his laugh, his smile. I miss being part of the Preston world.

"*So* mad," Leo says.

I pick up a brownie, inspect it. "It's perfect." I bring it to my mouth, but Logan stops me.

"We have to sing Happy Birthday first!"

"Don't you dare!" I hiss.

They all laugh. "Why not?" Leo asks.

"I'm trying to avoid any more attention."

I ATE four brownies for lunch and now I feel sick.

In my defense, they were *so* good.

"I tried to cut you off at two," Leo says, shaking his head as he watches me walk, my hand on my stomach, toward Mrs. Miles office after school.

"You just here to gloat?" I ask.

"I thought I'd give you a ride home so you didn't have to catch the bus with the botanical gardens in your arms."

"I appreciate it."

I knock on Mrs. Miles' door and she opens it, flowers in her hand. "Tell your boyfriend I said thank you for the rose."

"Sure thing," I tell her, taking them from her.

I shuffle through school, cheeks red, past everyone pointing and whispering. Leo has to open doors and walk with his hand on my back to lead me around because I can't see over or through or

146

around my present. We finally make it outside, and I feel like I can breathe again. Then he says, "Um. Lane?"

"Yeah?"

He takes the flowers from me, points to the parking lot. Specifically, Cooper and my dad in the parking lot standing next to a blue car with a giant red bow.

My stomach twists. "Oh no..."

"Happy birthday, baby!" Cooper shouts.

"You got me a car for my birthday?" I ask, moving toward him, a million different emotions rushing through me.

"Not just me," he says, hands up in surrender. He can read my expression: shock mixed with embarrassment mixed with a whole lot of *what the fuck?*

"Cooper came to me with the idea, and we worked out a budget that suited both of us," Dad says. "Cooper found the car online, and I got it checked out." His eyebrows pinch, concern deep in his eyes. "Do you not like it, sweetheart? Is it the color or—"

"No," I cut in, hugging him close. "It's perfect." But he can't afford to buy me a car, or half of one, or whatever, and Cooper has an endless stream of *Fuck You* money. I lean up on my toes, whisper in his ear, "Dad, you can't afford—"

He releases me, his eyes on mine. "It's fine, sweetheart." He glances at Cooper, then back to me. "It's a wonderful thing Cooper thought to do."

I turn to Coop. "Thank you." Then I hug him, too. "This is too much."

Cooper grins. "You deserve it, Lo."

"Hey, Brian," Leo says, standing behind me. "You got Lane a car?"

Dad smiles at him, pride in his eyes I haven't seen in a long time. Ever since I got my license, Dad had dreamed about buying me a car but he'd never been able to swing it, and with everything that went on with my mom and the college money, he'd given up hope. But now Cooper is here, and he'd given Dad the chance to do something he'd wanted for so long.

Leo sets my flowers on the roof of my new car while Dad tells him all about it. I step closer to Cooper, put my arms around his waist. "I can't believe you did this. And what are you even doing here? You're supposed to be in class."

He shrugs, kisses me once. Then his lips curl, his gaze lingering on mine. "To be fair, it was a selfish gift. Next semester, I'll be back

147

on the track team and I won't be able to come home as often. I was hoping maybe you'd come see me on campus?"

"I'd love that," I tell him honestly.

"So do you like it?"

I look at the car, the hood now lifted while Dad shows it off to Leo *and* Lucas. "I love it so much," I tell him. Not necessarily the car, or the fact that it's mine. I love what it means for my father.

"I'm taking you, your dad, and Misty out to dinner tonight," Cooper says. "And this time, we're doing *fancy*."

"Holy shit," Logan says, now standing next to Luke. "Is this yours, Lane?"

I face him. "All mine."

He laughs. "So much for avoiding attention."

COOPER TAKES us to the same fancy restaurant Luke took me to for my sixteenth birthday.

He orders the lobster.

We talk about my new car, about Coop at UNC, about the track team.

"What about you, Lane?" Misty asks.

"Me?" I ask, a mouthful of steak.

"Are you planning on going to college?"

I glance at Dad, realizing he hasn't told her.

"We had a little hiccup," Dad says, his gaze lowered in shame. But he's not the one who should be ashamed, and I hate that he feels that way.

So I clear my throat, stab at my steak as if it were my mother. "I wanted to go to UNC, too, but my mom stole my college fund."

Misty chokes halfway through sipping her wine while Cooper's eyes snap to me. I'm still stabbing away, pissed that my mom still has the power to make my dad feel like shit. "She just stole it?" Coop asks.

"It's fine," Dad says.

"No, it's not," I hiss.

"Not here, Lo."

Awkward silence passes while I try to regroup.

"You know," Cooper says, "both my parents are UNC alumni."

If he offers to pay for college—

148

He adds, "My mom's good friends with the dean of admission there, and I'm sure she'd be happy to meet you, direct you toward some scholarships."

I say, "I don't have the grades for a scholarship."

"Maybe not, but there are a ton of them out there and not all of them are academic based. There are some for single-income families," Coop says, pointing to my dad. "There are some ridiculous ones, too, like if your birthday falls on a certain date. They're not much. I mean, a single scholarship won't get you all the way through four years, but if you get enough of the smaller ones, it might help."

"Lo's a senior and it's halfway through the first semester now," Dad tells him, "Isn't it too late?"

Cooper shrugs. "It can't hurt to ask, right?"

***

I SKIP DESSERT, a surprise to everyone at the table. But seriously, those four brownies are *still* playing havoc on my stomach.

"I have one more gift," Dad says, reaching into his breast pocket. He pulls out a square velvet box and I gasp, cover my mouth.

"Dad, you've already given me so much. I can't take that."

"It's not from me," he says, sliding it across the table. He reaches into another pocket, reveals an envelope. "Tom wanted me to give it to you."

Cooper goes rigid beside me. "Tom Preston?"

Dad nods at him, looks at me. "Lois?" he says, and I tear me gaze away from the box and up at him. "It's from Kathy, sweetheart. She left it in her will for when you turned eighteen."

My hands shake as I pick up the box, lift the lid. It's a gold necklace, a simple key charm attached to it. On the inside of the lid, there's a note in Kathy's handwriting:

Lois Lane,
It will make more sense when you read my letter.

I choke on a sob, pick up the envelope. "Excuse me," I whisper, standing up and taking the box and the letter with me. "I need to uh—"

"It's okay," Dad cuts in. "Go."

I run to the bathroom, close the lid on a toilet seat, and sit, my knees bouncing, my hands shaking. I try to contain my sobs, but it's hard. *So hard.*

When I finally work up the courage, I tear open the envelope, pull out the letter.

Dear Lois Lane,
Happy birthday, sweetheart. It saddens me that I won't be there to see you grow up, to see the kind of woman you've turned into. As silly as it sounds, I hope you haven't forgotten about me. I hope that deep down, I'm still in your heart because you'll always be in mine. I didn't know you very long, but I feel like I knew you well. You brought so much laughter and joy to my family, and I'm forever grateful for that summer you spent with us.
I wanted to give you something that my mother gave to me when I turned eighteen. Don't worry, Lucy gets my engagement ring and everything else.
It's a key to your world, Laney, and I want to tell you the same things my mother told me when I was your age, just in case yours isn't around to pass on a similar message.

Love hard, love fierce, but love <u>right</u>.
Be careful with your heart, guard it, and if you feel the need to be reckless, make sure <u>you</u> are the one making that choice.
See the world, the good, the bad, the ugly.
Learn. Never stop learning, Laney.
And lastly, take your time, but don't waste it. Trust me on that one.

You now hold the key to <u>your</u> world. You choose which doors to lock, which to open. You choose who to let in and who to keep out. But do me a favor? Don't shut out too many people. You're too good, too precious to be kept hidden.

In case I don't get a chance to tell you before I pass away, I want you to know now that I love you, sweet girl. And I hope that you and Lucas are still in touch, still friends—maybe more?
If not, I hope one day you find it in your heart to forgive him his mistakes. He's learning, Laney. Always learning.

- Kathy.

CHAPTER SEVENTEEN

LUCAS

A S SOON AS my phone rings, I know it's Laney. And for the first time in a long time, I don't know how to feel about it.

"I don't really know why I called," Laney says, her voice weak.

I frown, looking down at the bottle of beer in my hand. "Where are you right now?"

The silence stretches the space between us. She sniffs, exhales. "Remember that restaurant you took me to for my sixteenth birthday?"

"Yeah."

"I'm in the bathroom, sitting on a closed toilet seat, crying."

Leaning forward, I place the beer on the coffee table. Then I move back on the couch, tilt my head up and stare up at the ceiling. And even though I know the answer, still, I ask, "Why are you crying?"

"Did you know?" she whispers.

I close my eyes, let the effects of the alcohol kick in. "Dad told me a few days ago." I hear her breaths through the phone, short and sharp, piercing my chest with each intake. "Do you like it?"

"It's so beautiful, Lucas," she whispers.

I swallow, thick, my own emotions threatening to escape. We've never spent a birthday apart. Until now. Maybe that's why I'm sitting in my dark apartment, drinking alone. "Then it's fitting you have it."

"There was a letter, too."

"I know."

"Did you read it?"

The sadness in her voice turns my insides to dust. "No. I didn't read it."

She sniffs again, and I imagine her in a beautiful dress, sitting in the bathroom, her hair braided to the side, her eyes filled with tears—tears she doesn't want to release, so she looks up at the ceiling, just like I am, in the hopes that gravity's on her side. She says, her voice hoarse, "Sometimes I imagine hearing the knock on my bedroom door late at night as if you're on the other side waiting for me to answer. And I know it's not real and that you're not there, but I'd gotten so used to it and..." Her breaths are shaky, her voice even shakier. "What happened to us, Lucas? You were my *best friend*."

I sit up. "I still want to be that, Lane."

"You don't act like it."

"Losing you..." I can't even begin to describe what I feel. I tug at my hair, hoping the physical pain will outweigh the emotional one. "I'd give *anything* to be that again."

I hear her shift, hear her breaths even. "I have to go. Cooper's waiting." Then she hangs up, and I look over at the empty beers scattered on my coffee table. I don't count the bottles, the calories, the number of miles it'll take to burn off. Because numbers stop having meaning when there's no end in sight.

I DON'T KNOW how long I sit on the couch, the sole invitee to my own pity party. Someone knocks on my door and I try to make out the time on the microwave, but it's too far away and I took out my contacts a while ago. The knock sounds again, and this time, I force myself to stand. I don't bother putting on a t-shirt as I shuffle my feet to the door.

Seeing Laney on the other side has me instantly tensing. I stopped drinking after she hung up—when I realized that alcohol didn't help take away the pain and frustration of not being the one to celebrate with her. "Hey," I say, standing straighter.

She's exactly how I pictured her to be: a simple black dress that hugs every inch, every curve, her hair in a side braid, loose strands falling around her beautiful face. She watches me from the corner of her eye before pushing on the door wider and searching my apartment. "You've been drinking?" she asks.

"A little. I'm not drunk, though."

"Oh."

"Not that I'm not happy to see you, but what are you doing here? Aren't you supposed to be at a fancy dinner with your fancy boyfriend and your fancy new car?" If she can hear the pain in my words, she doesn't show it.

With a shrug, she says, "We've spent every birthday together since we were eleven and..." She reaches into her pocket, pulls out the velvet box Dad had offered to show me. I declined. I didn't want to know.

"Do you think you could..." She holds the box closer to me and blinks, her huge brown eyes right on mine. "It just... it would feel wrong if anyone else did it."

I *want* to say no, tell her that she shouldn't be here and close the door on her and somehow try to forget everything we were. But instead, I open the door wider so she can step inside, and switch on the light so I can see what I'm doing. She turns, faces the now-closed door. I stand only inches behind her while she collects her hair, lifts it so I have access to her neck and I stop breathing, memories of her skin on my lips flooding me.

What are you doing here, Laney?

I try to hide the shakiness of my fingers when I clasp the gold chain around her neck. "All done," I say, but it's barely audible, and so I clear my throat. Repeat the words. She releases her hair but doesn't turn to me. Instead, she looks down at the necklace, the charm now clasped in her hand.

I count.

Five seconds.

Six heartbeats.

When is it going to end, Laney?

"Do you remember the day before we started high school?" she asks, her voice as weak as it was on the phone.

It's a random question, but I run with it, pretend like her being here isn't destroying me. "You mean that time I practically begged Cameron to take us to the movies?"

She turns slowly, looks up at me, her eyebrows drawn.

I force a smile, go back to the day I'd spent many years trying to forget. "I got changed four times before we left to pick you up."

She looks so confused. So sweet. So Laney. "But you said it wasn't a date..."

"Well yeah..." I rub the back of my neck, look away to hide my embarrassment. "I didn't want our first date to be with my sister and her boyfriend, so I asked him to take us so I could see him in

153

action." I shake my head, chuckle under my breath. "I was so dumb. I kept telling you it wasn't a date until you understood, and when we picked you up..." I push back the pain of that day and force myself to continue. "You had on a purple dress and boots, and you wore your hair as it is now." I step closer, reach up and tug on her braid. "God, Laney, you looked so beautiful. You literally stole my breath. But I knew it wasn't for me because you *knew* it wasn't a date, so I figured you were into Cameron and trying to impress him."

Her hands meet my bare chest, and I look up at her, startled. "Luke..."

"What?"

She shakes her head, her eyes wild. "That wasn't for Cameron!" she whisper-yells.

"But you knew it wasn't date!" I whisper back, just as confused as she is. "Right?"

"Says the guy who changed outfits *four* times!"

I shrug, unable to hold back my smile. It's like having *Old Laney* back. I like *Old Laney*. "It's not like it matters," I say, one hand on the door behind her, the other grasping her wrist. Her hands are still on my bare chest, warm and soothing. "You ignored me the entire time."

"I did not!" she says, her nose in the air.

"You totally did!" Somehow, I manage to laugh. "You didn't even sit next to me in the car and you wouldn't let me buy your ticket or your food, and then you disappeared for what felt like forever before the movie even started."

"I was upset," she whispers, her gaze lowered. She tries to remove her hands, but I keep one there, wanting her to touch me, to tease me, even if she has no idea she's doing it.

I wonder if she can feel my heart beating wildly beneath her fingers. "Why were you upset?"

"Because... because..." she stammers.

I take a risk, move closer until the heat of her body radiates against mine. "Because why?"

She shakes her head again, working through her confusion. "But you got that girl's number..."

"Laney." I press into her now, trapping her between me and the door. In the back of my mind, I know it's wrong. I can't have her; she doesn't belong to me. But fuck, I want her. I wait for her to look at me before saying, "I *asked* you. I looked you right in the eyes and asked if you'd mind and I wanted so badly for you to say *yes*. For you to tell me that you didn't want me with another girl because you wanted me for yourself." I look down at our bodies pressed together, and my voice drops to a whisper, "Do you know how disappointed I was when you told me you didn't care?"

Her mouth opens. Closes. Opens again. "But…"

I lean in, my mouth an inch from her shoulder. "But what?"

"You said you'd call her."

I release her wrist and as soon as she drops her hand, I link my fingers with hers, wanting to touch her, to hold her hand, to make her see things from my perspective. "I never called her." I pull back, watch her eyes—see the confusion turn to clarity.

"I remember that day *so* differently," she mumbles.

I take a chance I should've taken back then, wet my lips, kiss her neck. "I meant what I said, Laney. I've loved you forever."

"Don't do that," she whispers. "We can't make the same mistakes again." Then she pushes me away. "I have to go. Cooper's waiting."

I bite back my disappointment, my frustration, my *anger*. "Then why are you here, Lane?"

She doesn't respond, she simply turns and walks out my door.

Why were you here, Lane?

I find myself smiling.

Because she's loved you forever, too, idiot.

THE NEXT DAY, I wait for her in the parking lot with a Snickers bar. "Friends," I say.

"Friends?" she asks.

I shrug. "For now."

CHAPTER EIGHTEEN

LUCAS

L OVING LANEY from a distance is hard, but not as hard as hoping to one day *loathe* her. That's impossible.

Between Tuesday to Thursday, I treat her as mine. It's as destructive as it is healing, but I don't know any other way to deal with the feelings I have for her.

I wait for her in the parking lot in the mornings, walk her from her locker to her car in the afternoons. I eat lunch with her, show up late to her work when no one is around just to get that extra time in. We don't discuss what happened with us. We *definitely* don't discuss Cooper. We dance around in circles, over and over, around and around. She plays the game as well as I do. When Cooper is around, I smile, nod, do everything he says, and I pretend like I'm not in love with his girlfriend. She waits by the tunnel for him after practice, every practice, and I smile and nod at her, too. But that's all I do because upsetting her relationship with Cooper means upsetting her, and that's the last thing I want. And so I creepily lurk in the shadows of her life (not *literally*) and wait for my turn. She doesn't realize any of this, of course, because she's so naive, so innocent, so Laney.

COOPER HEADS for the locker room a minute before I do. "Hey, Luke!" Lane smiles brightly at me from her usual spot.

"Hey." I glance toward the locker room, let her know I'm aware of her situation. *Sly.* Then I lower my voice, keep our secrets hidden. "You're still coming to Luce's wedding tomorrow, right?" Okay, I don't know if her possibly spending the day with *me* is a secret, but I pretend like it is. It's more fun that way.

She nods. Her volume matching mine when she says, "I can't believe they're getting married so soon."

"It's Cam and Luce. There's no point waiting with them."

But I'll wait, Laney. I'll wait forever for you.

WE'VE HAD a lot of functions on our property before. Birthday parties, company picnics, but never a wedding. When Luce would talk my ears off about it after I talked her ears off about everything going on with Lane, I couldn't really picture what she had in mind. The moment I got Lachlan dressed and stepped out of the house, I knew her vision had become a reality. A section of our land is scattered in white... white chairs, white tents, white fairy lights. It's as beautiful as she was in our mom's wedding dress, walking down the aisle toward her forever. I don't think there was a dry eye in the house when they said their vows. Romance and love and promises of eternity can do that to people. Even Dad.

Laney wiped at her tears the entire time, and I expected nothing less. She'd been around, watched from a distance as Cam and Lucy made love look easy. It wasn't as easy as she thinks, but I let her believe in the fantasy.

At the reception, she sits with her dad and Misty. Cooper wasn't invited. It was at my request, but Cam and Luce had no problem fulfilling it. They didn't like Cooper either, and considering they went through their entire school lives with him, there was probably a good reason for it.

I TAP LANE'S SHOULDER. "Come on. Lachy's about to break out his dance moves. Trust me, you don't want to miss it."

She takes my offered hand, walks with me to the dance floor.

"Watch me!" Lachlan yells, and he moves to the center of the circle and attempts what I guess is break-dancing, but really, he's just rolling around on the floor. Still, my brothers and I pretend like it's the greatest thing in the world, our hands in the air, our shouts of "Woah" and "Yeah" spurring him on.

Next to me, Laney laughs.

"The sprinkler," Logan yells. "Do the sprinkler!"

158

So Lachlan stands, does the sprinkler dance.

I throw my arm around Laney's shoulders, dip my head, speak close to her ear so she can hear me over the music. "You having fun?"

She tilts her head back, smiles up at me. "I am." Then she motions over to where Cam and Lucy are sitting with their friends. "It was such an amazing ceremony, and Lucy looks so beautiful."

"She's the second most beautiful girl here," I tell her. And it's the truth. When I saw her get out of her car, my stomach did that stupid twisty thing. It shouldn't be fair that one person can hold that much enchantment, that much grace. It took Leo shoving me and practically forcing me to trip over a pile of chairs for me to tear my gaze away from her. "You can look, but don't touch," he warned.

I *was* just looking.

Laney coos, fanning herself dramatically. "And Cameron…"

I tense.

She smirks. "He's so dreamy," she sings, teasing me about my assumptions all those years ago.

"Shut up." I shove her away jokingly. "I totally thought you were into him, okay?"

Her smile falters, her hands going to her purse to fish out her phone.

"I have to go. Cooper's waiting," she tells me.

I rear back, my lips pressed tight. "Really? You can't even stay for my speech?"

She looks as disappointed as I feel. "I wasn't sure how long the ceremony would go for, and I told him I'd be there an hour ago."

I sigh. "All right, Cinderella. Let me walk you to your carriage."

"YOU COLD?" I ask her, walking under the twilight sky toward the temporary parking lot.

She rubs her hands on her arms. "A little."

I shrug out of my jacket and gently place it on her shoulders. "You really do look beautiful tonight, Lane."

"Stop it," she murmurs, backhanding my stomach. It's like having Old Laney back.

I fake hurt, but she doesn't. She grasps her hand, her eyes wide. "Have you been hitting the gym?" she asks.

159

"I have," I say. "Under *your* boyfriend's advice, actually. He suggested I need more power in my start, so…"

With a smile, she says, "I'm glad you guys are getting along so well."

"You know what they say, right? Keep your friends close, your enemies closer…"

"Lucas," she warns.

I nudge her side. "I'm kidding." For forty-six long ass seconds, we walk in silence. Then I say, "Not that it matters, but I just wanted you to know that I won't be around for a few days."

"Really? Why?"

"I'm going to hit up Vegas with Lucy and her friends—kind of like their honeymoon."

She stops walking. "Vegas?"

"Yeah."

"Does your dad know?"

"No," I say through a chuckle. "He thinks I'm visiting Jason in Jersey."

She chews on her lip, looks down at her feet. "Vegas, huh? It's like stripper capital, right?"

"I don't know. I'm not really going for the strippers." I laugh.

She looks back up at me, her brow knitted. "Then why *are* you going?"

"I just need to get away for a while, clear my head."

"Is something going on? Are you okay?"

No, I'm not okay. I'm in love with you, Laney. And you're in love with someone else. "I'm all good. Don't worry about me."

She starts walking again, slower than before. "So are you nervous about your speech?"

"Not really."

"Have you got it planned out?"

I chuckle when she pats down my jacket, searching for the written speech. "I don't have it written out if that's what you're looking for."

She stops searching and pouts up at me. Yeah. I *love* Old Laney. "I'm sad I'm going to miss it. What are you going to say?"

"I don't know." We get to her boyfriend-bought car, and I lean against it. "It'll be easy, though, I'll just speak from my heart."

She copies my position, our sides touching. "You should practice on me," she says. "What better person is there to trust to tell you if it sucks than your *best friend*."

I hide my smile, look down at the ground. Then I clear my throat, shove my hands in my pockets to keep me from touching her. "I guess I'm just going to talk about a boy—a *kid*, really—who fell in love with a girl at an age and a time when love felt bigger than the world around them. How he was her strength when she needed it, her voice when she didn't have one. I'll say something about the way he looks at her as if there's no one and nothing else out there that could possibly hold his attention as much as she can..." I chance a peek in her direction, wondering if she can hear it in my words—that I'm speaking from *my* heart. But she's looking down at her shoes, her breaths shaky. I add, "He's always loved her, way before he realized that she loved him back. But I could see it in the way he looked at her. He hoped that one day she'd see him the way he saw her. And he *saw* her, Lane. I mean, Cameron—he was always able to *read* her—to see her in ways she didn't see herself. He knew what she wanted, what she needed, and she never had to say a word. And I think, ultimately, that's what true love is, you know? To want to be someone's hero when they're faced with villains. To want to be the one who saves them. To be their *Wonderwall*." I choke on a sob, visions of Laney dancing with my dad in our living room filling my mind. I clear my throat again. "And I'll end it by saying that I wish, more than anything, that I can one day be the man he is."

Silence fills the space between us, while the laughter of the wedding party brings everyone else together. "Wow," she whispers, sniffing once. "That didn't suck at all."

"You think?" I ask, stepping in front of her.

Her smile contradicts the sadness in her eyes. "I should go."

"I know." I swallow the pain of her pulling away. "Cooper's waiting." I reach around, open her door for her. She starts to get in but stops when I say her name. "Cooper might not be too thrilled with you showing up wearing my jacket," I tell her.

"Right." She quickly removes my jacket, hands it back to me.

I step back, watch her start the engine, hands on the steering wheel, getting ready to pull away, and I question myself. Wonder if this is worth the searing ache in my heart.

"Lucas," she says, her eyes meeting mine. "You already *are* that man. You just need to find a girl who's going to make you want to prove that." Then she drives away, farther and farther. More and more *space*.

LOIS

I pull over on the side of the road just outside the Preston property and I cry. I cry and I cry and I cry some more, and I don't know why I cry but I can't get Lucas's words out of my mind, out of my system. I shouldn't have shown up to his house the night of my birthday because now everything is blurred. The friendship, the feelings, the *lines*.

I settle my breaths, settle the beating of my heart and try to focus my vision, but like everything else, it, too, is blurred.

My phone rings, and I shut my eyes tight, knowing who it is. He'd been calling relentlessly for the past hour but I'd been selfish, enjoying the feeling of being part of the Prestons' world again.

I clear my eyes, re-apply the little makeup I wear, force myself to smile and start the journey to his house. The security guard lets me through the gates, through the pristine streets, and onto the Kennedys' driveway, and I can't help but feel the shift of emotions when I stare up at the mansion, my skin crawling. Because *I don't belong here*.

The front door's unlocked so I let myself in, just like Cooper had suggested I do in one of the many texts he'd sent me. The house is dark, eerily silent, and fear runs up my spine, creeping deep in my chest. Ever since the night I met his mother after she "walked into the doorframe," I've been afraid of what's concealed by the walls of this home. It feels like walking into a haunted house during Halloween, monsters and secrets lurking in every corner.

"Cooper?" I call out.

He doesn't respond, so I make my way up the stairs and toward his room. He's here, sitting on the edge of the bed, in the dark, a bottle of bourbon in his hand.

"What are you doing, Coop?"

He doesn't lift his head when he asks, "Did you have fun?"

I swallow, afraid. I've never seen Cooper like this, but there's something in his tone that stops me from going to him. I stand by the door, my heart in my throat, my hands behind me. "Yeah," I tell him. "It was a beautiful wedding."

He faces me now, the light outside barely exposing the anger in his eyes. "You said you'd be here an hour ago," he says. But I don't hear him. I hear his father.

"I um…" I look down at the floor, unable to make eye contact. "I lost track of time. I'm sorry."

He stands, his shadow reaching me before he does. "Are you into him?" he whispers, his body an inch from mine.

"Who? Cameron?"

I flinch when his hand slams on the wall beside me. "Lucas! Did you fuck him?"

"No!" I shout, looking up at him. "God, no!"

He punches the wall and I shut my eyes, press my lips tight, do everything I can to stop the tears because I fear the tears will make it worse. "I have to go." I push him out of the way so I can turn for the door but he grasps my wrist, twists until the pain causes me to yelp.

He drops my hand as soon he hears it. "Fuck," he whispers, switching on the light. His eyes are wide when I turn back to him, his face pale. "Lois…" He shakes his head, his breaths rushed. "I would never…" Then he grasps his hair, the anger in his eyes replaced with shock. Guilt slams into me, forcing a sob to escape. He's so desperate, so defeated, and it's my fault. I should've answered his calls, his pleas for some form of clarity. He sits on the bed and breaks down, his shoulders shaking with his withheld emotions. He says, "I'm so sorry, baby. I don't know…" I can barely make out the words through his pain, and so I go to him, ignore my aching wrist and kneel in front of him. He looks up when I settle my hands on his legs. "I would never hurt you, Lois. You know I wouldn't. You *know*, baby, you've *seen*—" He chokes on a breath, cutting him off, and I scoot closer, take his face in my hands. He grasps my wrist, gentle and *safe*, and he kisses it a thousand times over while his eyes meet mine, his distress palpable. "It doesn't make sense. Why…?" He trails off, looks away.

"Why what?" I ask, my hand on his cheek, forcing him to face me.

"If nothing's going on with you guys, then why didn't you ask me to come with you?"

My guilt forces my heart to stop, but his phone rings, saving me from responding. He doesn't go to answer it. He just stares at it flashing and vibrating on his nightstand.

"Are you going to answer it?"

"It's just my dad. I was supposed to be at an important dinner meeting with him, but I couldn't..." His jaw tenses. The phone stops ringing. "I couldn't fake caring enough. Not tonight." He looks back at me the same time his phone starts again.

"Is he going to be mad?" I ask.

"It's my dad, Lo. He skips angry and goes straight to..." His throat bobs with his swallow. Then he stands, his hands gentle on both my wrists. "You need to get out of here before he gets home."

The fear rises again, doubles. Not for me, but for him. "I'm not leaving you."

The ringing stops, but a text alert comes through, and he stands, releases me. He picks up the phone, reads the message. "It's my mom," he says. "They'll be home in ten minutes." His eyes lock on mine. "You need to go. *Now!*"

I stand so fast my head spins. "I'm not going anywhere!"

He covers the distance between us, places his hand on the small of my back and his lips on my forehead. "I'll call you later. I'll be fine," he assures me.

His words do nothing for the panic that kicks in, along with the painful reality that *I* caused him to act like this. My lies and my ignoring him at the wedding caused his reaction and... *I love* him. I love him and I don't want anything to happen to him. Not like it did with his mother. "Let's go," I tell him, taking his hand to force him to come with me.

He doesn't budge. "Go where, Lo?"

"Anywhere!" I turn to him, plead with my eyes. "Please, Cooper. Let's just go anywhere but here. I don't want you here tonight. I want you with me. And I want you safe."

His sighs, and I question how many times he's felt the same fear I'm feeling, how many times he's watched the clock, waiting for the moment the door opens and his demons haunt him. How many times he's locked himself in that closet, alone and afraid, and so I wrap my arms around him, refusing to leave his side.

"I need to stay, Lo. There are consequences to my actions, and I need to face them like a man." *How old he was when his father first gave him that speech?* He sees the concern in my eyes, forces a smile to comfort *me*. "It's okay, baby. You don't need to save me."

"But I do," I rush out, wiping at my tears. "Because that's what true love is, right? To want to save the person you're with?"

164

WE GET in my car and drive to an ATM where he takes out some cash, and then we drive some more until we find a hotel two hours away. He pays with the cash he took out, mumbling something about his dad not being able to find him that way. And just like with what happened to his mother, we don't speak about what could've happened to him. Because with me, his secret is safe, and with me, so is *he*.

WE SPEND two nights at the hotel, and when Monday morning comes, I leave for school, and he leaves with the promise of seeing me later in the afternoon. He does see me... but with only one eye, the other forced shut, puffy, black and bruised. He tells everyone he took a basketball to the face during a pick-up game on campus. But I know the truth. We both do. Because he didn't go back to campus. He went home to face his demons... like a *man*.

CHAPTER NINETEEN

LUCAS

I CHOKE on whatever the cafeteria lady passes as food and look up at Laney, my eyes wide. "Say that again?"

"Have you ever had a threesome?" Her tone is nonchalant, but the red in her cheeks gives her away. Laney's a blusher, always has been.

Leaning forward, I glance around us, make sure I'm not dreaming because of all the things that I've imagined coming out of Lois Sanders' mouth (and trust me, I've imagined *a lot* of things), the word "threesome" is not one of them. "Is Cooper, like, pressuring you to—"

"No!" She throws a plastic fork at my head, hitting me square on the cheek and thankfully distracting me from my images of her and that asshole. "It's just..." She leans closer, lowers her voice. "The other day we were in my room and—"

"Stop!"

"—and this girl sent him a picture of her making out with another girl."

I put on my best friend persona and act like I'm okay with the conversation. "And what did he say about it?"

She shrugs. "Not a lot. Just that it was a girl he'd hooked up with once and she wanted to know if he was interested in doing it again with another girl added to the mix. He wrote back right away, in front of me so I could see."

"What did he write back?"

"That he wasn't interested and he was with someone so to stop messaging him."

"And you believe him?"

"I mean..." She leans closer again. "If he wanted to lie, he could've told me something else, right? Like the person must've sent it to the wrong number. But his story seems legit so..."

"Did you argue about it?"

"No. He said it so, like, matter-of-fact, that I couldn't even come up with an argument."

"Do you trust him?"

"I don't know." I can see by the way she lowers her gaze, bites down on her bottom lip that she's lying. She doesn't trust him but she *wants* to and that's eating at her, clawing away at her thoughts, and I get it. Picturing the one you love with someone else can twist your insides to shreds.

And she *thinks* she loves him, and I *know* I love her, and so I tell her what she wants to hear: "He's with you all the time, Lane."

"Yeah, on weekends. But what happens during the week when I'm not around?"

I shrug. "It's college."

"That's what he said!" *Great, the last thing I want is for me and Cooper to think alike.* She adds, "But what does that mean?"

I'm already sick of the conversation, sick of talking about him. "Can we talk about something else?"

She rolls her eyes. "Like what?"

"What are you doing for winter break?"

"I don't know," she shrugs. "My dad's going to Savannah to meet Misty's family and Coop's home so he'll probably just hang at my house."

"New Year's?"

"No idea. Why?"

"Dad's taking the twins and Lachlan on some fishing slash bonding trip and Logan's been banished to my aunt Leslee's, so Leo and I are going to have a few people over to the apartment. It'll be low key. We're not really down for anything big this year. But you're welcome to come."

She scrunches her nose. "Remember the first time we did New Year's together?"

"You mean that time we hid out and spied on Luce and Cam and their friends? And Dumb Name thought it was a great idea to steal a bottle of vodka from them?"

She holds her stomach and groans. "Don't remind me."

"You puked so much that night."

"In my defense, it was my first time drinking and we were thirteen!"

"You kept asking for God to take you away for all your sins."

"Shut up!" Then her eyes widen and her face pales, and I follow her gaze across the room to Cooper walking toward us. He smiles at her, glares at me. As soon as he gets to us, he leans down, and before she has time to decline, he practically sucks her entire face into his sloppy, gaping mouth, putting on a show for the entire cafeteria.

I look away, bile high in my throat, an indent of his foot now in my gut. He sits next to her, his arm around her shoulder while she wipes his drool from her mouth. "What are you doing here?" she asks.

It's Friday, which means he's here for practice, but he's not normally this early. At least not that I know of. Or does she mean *here* in the cafeteria where the high schoolers hang out and not in the teachers' lounge or wherever the fuck it is coaches go on their lunch breaks. It doesn't seem to matter what she means because he faces her, eyes narrowed, "Why? Did I interrupt your little rendezvous?" He raises an eyebrow, his attempt at intimidation. "Are you not happy to see me?"

Laney glances at me, then at Cooper, and I don't think she's taken a breath since she saw him. "I am, it's just—"

"What did I interrupt?" He cuts in, points to me. "Were you guys planning on what time Dawson here was going to climb through your window tonight?"

I lean back, unfazed at his attempt to intimidate me, and if he cared enough about his *girlfriend*, he'd realize I'm not the one affected by his bullshit. *She* is. I smirk, right in his face, and fuck I wish I could punch him. "I use her door and I don't need to be invited."

"Luke!" Laney gasps, covers her entire face.

"I cut out early," he says to her, "wanted to see you. I miss you."

She lowers her hand, smiles at him. Swear, it's like he puts all his bullshit in a blender and feeds it to her with a *Fuck You* money, platinum, handcrafted spoon.

And it's hard, so hard, to keep my irritation in check. But I do. I say, "I was just telling Laney—"

"Her name's Lois. Who the fuck gave her that name, anyway? It's dumb."

169

Her hand lowers under the table, probably to his leg, and she whispers his name. She doesn't *gasp* like she did when I threw shit his direction, but hey... she *loves* him. And love is fucking blind. She doesn't go on to tell him the details of her nickname, that *my* mom gave it to her and how much she (apparently) *loved* my mom because it obviously doesn't compare to how much she loves him. Now I'm being mean. And stupid. And I know she loved my mom and that was a really shitty thing to think. I force a smile, let Laney know it's okay that she doesn't want to tell him, and say, "I was just telling *Lois* that I was having a few people over for New Year's." My fake kindness even goes as far as to say, "You're both welcome to come." And the bile's in my throat again.

"We can't," Cooper says, picking at the food on Laney's plate. "My buddies and I rented out a houseboat for the night."

"You know *Lois* gets sea sick, right?"

He hates me. I can tell by the tick in his jaw. He hates that I know more about his girlfriend, and I'm smirking at him because I *don't* hate him. It wouldn't surprise me if he stood up right now, in the middle of a packed cafeteria, and asked Laney to get a ruler while we both whip out our dicks for her to measure. She doesn't need a ruler. I've seen Cooper in the shower. I'd win. And when that didn't satisfy him, he'd challenge me to a pissing contest and I'd win again. But Cooper's dumb because it's not about either of those things. It's about who loves Laney more. And I'd win that, too. Every single time. Because I know she gets sea sick and I know that when she gets sick (even with lady cramps) she likes to have her back rubbed. And I know exactly where to rub it. I'm *still* smirking, and it takes him eleven seconds to start shrinking. *Fuck you, Cooper Kennedy.*

I win.

Lane grasps his arm, forces him to break our staring competition.

I win.

She asks him, "You want to get out of here? I have nothing important for the rest of the day."

She leaves with him, but not before he gives me another one of those pathetic attempts at intimidation. They walk out of the cafeteria with his hand on her ass and he thinks he's won, but I had that ass first. So...

I win.

COOPER GIVES me hell during practice and I expected nothing less, so I came prepared and got Garray in on the joke, too. "Yes Sir, Drill Sergeant, Sir!" is our new response to *everything*. God, I love that look in Cooper's eyes—the one that says he'd give absolutely anything to be able to sucker punch me in front of everyone but— and this is the best part—this is his "community service" and he's a "figure of authority" and Garray and I are nothing but cocky high school kids under his watch. It's glorious, really, to see his anger rise and rise and rise some more. It earns Garray and me an afternoon detention each from Coach Anderman, our *real* coach, and we pretend like we care until we turn our backs on him and snicker to ourselves like we're fucking eight, not eighteen. "Totally worth it," Garray says, bumping my fist because he's my best friend and he's on my side, the side Laney should be on. We walk toward the locker rooms and he keeps walking while I stop in front of Laney. She's always here, always waiting for her beloved. Her glare instantly wipes the smirk off my face. She sneers, "What the fuck is wrong with you?"

I wipe the sweat off my face with the bottom of my tee and shrug. "It was just a joke, Lane. Christ."

She steps closer, her tone somewhere between a whisper and a growl. "You think this is a game, Lucas, and it's not." *Wait, is she about to cry?* "He was already on edge after that shit you pulled at lunch, and you keep pushing his buttons!" She pokes a finger into my chest, over and over, harder and harder. *Buttons.* "You've gone out of your way to piss him off, to make him angry, and it's all well and good for you because you're not the one who has to deal with him. I am!" Then she storms off, her feet heavy, stomp, stomp, stomping on my heart.

I throw my arms out and shout, late to retort, "If your boyfriend has a problem with me, I'm right fucking here!"

She turns swiftly, wipes at her eyes. "That's not how it works, Luke! Grow the fuck up!" And she *runs* away this time. More distance, more space and even though I could close the gap, catch up to her, I'd still *know* that my actions caused my fate, and somewhere along the way, *I lost you, Laney.*

CHAPTER TWENTY

LUCAS

I T'S 11:49 again.
Different month.
Different day.

A few of my friends are here, Dumb Name included, but there are more of Leo's friends than mine. We're drunk. Well, they are. I'm beyond it. I've spent the past few days thinking about her and wondering how she is. Where she is. She hasn't replied to a single text and every time I call, her phone is switched off. But, Cooper is home and Cooper despises me and she *loves* Cooper and maybe she even loves Cooper enough to despise me the same way.

I don't normally sit around at my own parties grasping my phone like a baby with their blanky, but it's called a "security blanket" for a reason, right? I should give up on her like I should give up on my phone, but my phone is what connects me to her, and it's *my* security blanket.

It's not as if I expect her to call, but I *want* her to. And maybe that's why Garray's grabbing my shoulder and telling me to, "Let it go, dude," while he points across the room to a girl who came with *his* girl—a girl I've never seen before, a girl who's looking at me with *fuck me* eyes, most likely because she was promised by Garray and his girl that I would, in fact, fuck her.

11:50 and New Girl has ten minutes to convince me that fucking her won't fuck over my chances with a girl who's in love with a guy who despises me.

"She's probably fucking Cooper right now, and you're sitting here like a junkie waiting for his next hit. Let. It. Go."

Dumb Name's right.

But still, I do nothing. Just sit. Watch the seconds tick by.

11:55 and New Girl sits down next to me. "Rad party," she coos.

In which decade was "rad" still a word people used? Pretty sure it was pre-Laney and I was walking around in a red eye mask, red knee pads and a red cape Mom made me so I could pretend to be Raphael. Ninja Turtles didn't even wear capes, but my mom was *that* awesome.

I smile, look at her properly for the first time. She's not as hot as Garray's girl and nowhere near as hot as Laney, but she'll do because I need to *let it go.* I casually rest my arm on the back of the couch and lean in close. "Who's your favorite ninja turtle?" I ask her.

When Laney had asked me the same question, I told her it was Raphael. Then she had asked why, and I'd said that I think, deep down, I wanted to be him. He was the bad boy, the black sheep of the brotherhood. Laney had laughed, said that *Logan* was more suitable to be Raph. I'd agreed, but I hadn't said that I was most *like* him. I'd said I wanted to *be* him. Some days I wanted to not care about anything, to not have the responsibility of being the oldest brother weighing on my shoulders. "You're more like Leonardo. The leader. The one they all look to for help," she'd said.

"Umm..." New Girl purses her lips, looks up at the ceiling, contemplates like I've just asked her the most complicated question in the world. "Michelangelo," she finally says.

It's 11:57.

"Michelangelo?" I ask. "Why?"

She giggles. "Because pizza?"

Laney's favorite turtle was Donatello. "Because he's so smart without being obnoxious about it, you know? He doesn't make the others feel dumb for not getting it. And he's stealth but not just in combat. In life. It's like he's invisible until the world needs to see him." Fuck, she was amazing. I could've had amazing. Instead, I'm stuck with *pizza.*

11:58 and some asshole turns on the TV so we can all sit around and watch the clock tick down together.

"You want to go to your room or something?" New Girl asks. Her hand's on my leg and I didn't ask for it or want it there, but when my eyes meet hers, I see the desperation. She came to a party at a stranger's house with her friend who's with a guy that has a friend who (they all thought) would be willing to fuck her brains out and she came because she wants me to fuck her, to erase the memory of some guy that's been haunting her dreams, her thoughts, day and night and *I get it, New Girl*. I really do.

"What's your name?" I ask.

"Sandy." Sandy / *Sanders*. Close enough. Because that's who I'll be thinking of when I'm deep inside her. Oh, the irony of it all. "So?" She blinks.

I sigh. "You not even going to ask what my name is?"

"I know your name. I just don't really care." Sandy is *rad*.

11:59, someone taps my shoulder and I look up to see Leo standing above us, phone in one hand, girl in the other. "It's Laney."

My apartment is too loud, too many people, too many drinks, and so I take the phone from him and I go out the front door, down the steps, and into the living room of the main house where it's dark and it's quiet and it's still 11:59 when I bring the phone to my ear and whisper, "Donatello?"

It's not as quiet where she is, but she still hears what I say and she laughs.

You get it, Lane. You're not pizza.

"That was random," she says.

"How's the houseboat going?"

"I'm in bed in a room on the lowest level, in the dark, and I've puked four times and haven't had a single thing to drink."

I lean back on the couch and stare up at the ceiling, waiting for my heart to settle while I hear the countdown begin. From my apartment and through the phone, people shout ten, nine, eight... we ignore the counting, my favorite pasttime, and when the fireworks begin to explode somewhere in the distance, she says, "How's your night going?"

I ask, "Is Cooper there? Is he taking care of you?"

She sighs, and I wait, not giving her a response to her question because it matters as much as my name does for New Girl. "He's up on the deck," she says. "Is that what it's called? A deck? I don't know. He's with his friends... I don't know them. But they're there, and he's there, and..."

"And so you thought you'd call me because you're lonely and you want to at least be with someone when the clock strikes midnight?" I'm too drunk to even contemplate how that comes out, but I hear her shift as if she's rolling around in bed, and she's sick, *sea sick*, and I told Cooper that, but it didn't matter to him because *she* doesn't matter to him like she matters to me.

"It's not like that, Luke."

It finally occurs to me that I'm holding on to two phones and she didn't call mine, so I ask, "Why did you call Leo's phone?"

She shifts again. "Cooper made me block your number."

"*Made* you?"

"It's not like that," she says again.

I should've been Raphael, the bad boy, the black sheep. Maybe then she would've forgiven me like she hands out forgiveness to that asshole. "So what's it like then? Explain it to me."

"He just… he sees you as a threat. That's all. Have you been trying to get hold of me? Did you need me for something?"

"No." I sit up, look down at my phone. 12:02 and the bastard hasn't even checked in on her. "I just needed you, Laney, and you're drifting, far and deep into this guy's web."

"I feel sick," she murmurs, and my anger fades.

"Did you take any pills for it?"

"Yeah. They help some. But I'm here all night and—" It's suddenly silent on her end.

"Who are you talking to?" Cooper asks, his tone as dark as the room I'm sitting in.

I sit up, alert. But the call cuts off and I stare into the darkness, promise myself I won't call back because I don't want to make things worse—whatever that means—and so I sit and I stew over my feelings, my hurt, until I force myself to my feet. I don't go back to my apartment, to my party, to New Girl. Instead, I climb the stairs to Lachlan's room and I get into his bed. "Just one minute…" I whisper.

12:48 and a text comes through on Leo's phone: *Raphael was a rebel. Some even called him a lost cause. But you're not lost, Lucas. In fact, most days I fear you're still the center of my universe.*

CHAPTER TWENTY-ONE

LUCAS

S CHOOL STARTS AGAIN, new year, new semester, new hope. Cooper's back at UNC, his penalty for fornicating with underage girls now over. Small price to pay for such huge fuck-ups but that's what money means to the Kennedys. A tool, a simple way to navigate through life in the hopes of sheltering members of their family from the harsh, bright lights of reality.

I WATCH from a distance as Laney steps out of her car in baggy sweatpants and an even baggier sweatshirt, and I wonder if she hasn't managed to go home and find clothes that actually fit her or if her boyfriend has "made" her start dressing in *his* clothes to warn off any threats, aka me.

We hadn't spoken since her phone call New Year's Eve, and I didn't even think to try. I'm blocked, from her phone and from her life, and maybe it's like the night she came to visit me on her eighteenth birthday and we talked about our first Non-Date. I question whether we see things differently. If we *always* have. Last year, I dated a girl—Bethany—who made an off-handed joke about Laney being a loner because she spent her free period on her own just outside the library, knitting. I ended the relationship the next day, and when Laney asked about the breakup, I told her Bethany had bad breath and kissing her was like licking the inside of a trash can. I knew I could lie and be as crass as I wanted because I knew Laney would never repeat what I said to anyone. She's always been a key holder to all my secrets. But now *she's* dating a guy who treats me and our friendship like shit, and she makes excuses for him. "*It's not like that, Luke.*" And when I asked her to convince me otherwise, she couldn't even come up with a decent lie. And then she texted me, almost an entire hour later, with the most cryptic fucking lie of all. Bullshit, I'm the center of her fucking universe. And bullshit she put me on a pedestal, because if that's fucking true then to her, Cooper is up in the clouds.

SHE DOESN'T EVEN LOOK up at me when she walks past, her head lowered, books held close to her chest. She looks different. Her glasses, I realize. Hers are black, and these are bright purple and three years old. Her script's changed twice since she wore those and they look odd on her now, because just like her eyesight, she's changed, too.

And to think I was actually nervous about seeing her today. I stood in front of my mirror and planned out what I would say to her. It started off with the standard stuff. "Hi, how are you?"…"Did you have a good break?" Even though I knew how she spent her Christmas (at her house with Cooper while her dad was in Savannah with Misty's family), I'd ask her about that, too. "How did you hold up after New Year's Eve?" was another one. And then I'd be done with the bullshit banter and ask, "What the fuck is wrong with you?" Then I'd go on a tirade about Cooper fucking Kennedy and how I don't think he's good enough for her and *"Why the hell are you even with him, Laney?"*

But no.

She didn't see me standing here, waiting for her, wanting to expose her bullshit relationship.

She didn't see me at all.

And when she enters the school, the door closing behind her, blocking me from her presence, it all becomes clear—maybe she never truly saw me at all.

IT'S BEEN three days and eight hours since she *didn't* see me, but she's seeing me now, stepping out of my truck and looking up at my apartment stairs where she sits, waiting for me to come home from school. How she managed to get here before me, I have no idea. Maybe she wasn't at school. I didn't see her, but then again, I stopped looking for her. Didn't you hear? I'm blocked.

My phone alerts me to a text, and I pause, make her wait, and read the message.

It's Sandy from your NYE party. My friend gave me your number. I wanted to see if you wanted to get together sometime. Maybe grab a bite to eat?

I reply: *Tonight? What are you craving?*

I hope it's cock because it's been a long time since I've been with Laney, and I haven't been with anyone since. It would feel like eating a frozen meal after a gourmet steak.

She writes back: *Pizza.*

Fuck irony in the ass.

"Lucas?" Laney's standing now, watching me from above, her eyes squinted because her stupid purple glasses are too weak to make her see clearly. Or maybe *she's* too weak. Maybe Cooper's fucked with her head so much she can't even see straight.

I ask, "What are you doing here?"

"I was waiting for you," she says. She shuffles on her feet, and I get it because I felt the same way in her room. She doesn't know if she belongs here and the truth is, maybe she doesn't. I don't want her on my steps, near my house, near *me*. I'm blocked, remember? But by the time I make my way up each step (twelve), she's looking at me with those eyes, and swear it, *those eyes* hold a secret power that can bring me to my knees. "Are you busy tonight?" she asks, and she's looking at my phone like she knows all my secrets. *She does.*

I want to tell her that I have a date with a girl I fucked on New Year's Eve, but I can't lie to her. Not when she has *those* eyes. "I can cancel."

"Feel like hanging out?" she asks. "Like old times."

Old times is a phrase that shouldn't exist in an eighteen year old's vocabulary because we haven't lived enough to have "old times." I tell her that as I open the door, and she laughs. Her laugh to my ears is what money is to the Kennedys—a tool used to manipulate reality. I know this. I *feel* this. But I'm as weak as her vision, and I concede, keep the door open for her to enter.

I shoot off a text to Sandy: *Something came up. Sorry.*

Lane's already in my kitchen washing the dishes piled high in the sink, like *old times.*

SMALL TALK SHOULDN'T SEEM like small talk when you're with a friend. It should just be conversation, but my mind is buzzing, trying to come up with "small talk" and there are birds outside and they're loud, too loud, and I can't think. She finishes the dishes, turns to me. She's wearing clothes that actually fit her, a little too well, skinny jeans and a loose (but not baggy) sweater, and I ask, "What happened to your other glasses?"

She shrugs. "It was time for a new pair."

Why is she lying to me? "They look like the same pair you had a few years ago."

Her eyes widen, her cheeks redden. Deer meet headlights. "They are. I mean, the same frames, not the lenses, though."

I press my lips tight and make a show of looking anywhere but at her because it's awkward as fuck and seriously, small talk can blow me.

She's going through the kitchen cabinets, and I don't know what she's looking for. If it's *the good old days,* she can forget it. She won't find them here. She pulls out a bag of Doritos and salsa and goes to the fridge for the cheese. She's making nachos because she's desperate to find the *old times,* and I'm desperate to know what the hell she's doing here. "How are things, like, with your brothers and stuff?" Lane asks. "How's it all going?"

I don't respond.

"My dad said that Logan got a slap on the wrist...?"

"Yeah. We're lucky, your dad's girlfriend vouched for him."

She faces me, her lips curved. "Misty's good like that," she says.

Okay, so maybe her being here isn't so much awkward as it is terrifying. She wants to go back to the way things were, and yeah, I want that, too. A little too much. But she has the power to take it away, to *block* me, and then what? *What happens to me, Laney?*

It takes two minutes for her to make the nachos and bring the bowl over to the couch along with two glasses of water. We sit on the couch, share the nachos (fuck yeah, nachos!), and she says, "I was thinking about the twins."

"Oh yeah?"

"It's because people are jealous. That's why they bully them the way they do."

"You think?"

She nods. "Think about it. I can't ever recall them picking up a sport or an activity and not being great at it. And they're great because they always have someone to practice with or compete against. Kids can be bitter and vindictive little assholes." There's a hint of anger in her tone, and it makes me smile. "You like this batch?" she asks, pointing to the bowl of nachos.

"They're good."

"Good is the enemy of great, Lucas," she sings.

I give her a cheesy grin. "They're *great!*"

She laughs, and my reality shifts, just an inch. And just like that, small talk turns to conversation. We finish the nachos, and she sets the bowl on the coffee table and sits sideways on the couch, her legs up, knees bent, toes poking my leg. "So, I have some news."

I take her feet, settle them on my lap and turn to her, my arm resting on the top of the couch. *Old times* is good times. *Great* times. "What's your news?"

"There's a slight chance I'll still be able to go to UNC."

My heart races. "How? Did your mom—"

"No!" She shakes her head and scoffs. "Fuck that bitch." I'll give Cooper this—he's boosted Lane's confidence because before him, she'd never say anything like that. She'd make bullshit excuses for her mom until one day she started to believe them.

"So what happened?" I ask.

She sits higher, shoulders straight. Then she goes on to tell me about Cooper's mom's friend who's the dean of admission at UNC and how they had a meeting over winter break and now she's looking into a bunch of scholarships. "It probably won't happen this year. I might have to take a year off or go to community college for the first year, but she thinks it's very doable," Lane says, her eyes bright.

"But if you skip a year, that means that you're going to miss Cooper's senior year."

She looks at me like I'm stupid. "I'm no Felicity and Cooper is definitely no Ben Covington."

I blink.

She giggles. "Never mind. The point is that Sue—"

"The dean of admissions?"

"Yeah. She says that to heighten my chances I need to add more school activities—show school spirit and all that, and I've literally done *nothing* so I'm trying to cram it all into one semester and so I signed up for the spring play."

"You?" I ask, incredulous. "On stage?"

"God no." She nudges my leg with her heel. "I'm designing and making the costumes."

"That's good," I tell her.

"Good or great?"

"Great, Lane. It's great."

"And we have someone to design the sets but..."

Uh oh. "But what?"

Her words are rushed as if she already knows my answer. "We don't have anyone to build them, and I know you can do it, Luke, it—"

"No!"

"But you'd be so *great* at it."

I sigh, knowing I'm about to disappoint her. "Lane, we're three days into the semester, and it's senior year, and I have track meets and practice and—"

"And it'll be the last thing we get to do together," she says, and I'm listening again.

"How much time and how closely do we,"—I point between us—"work together?"

"Is that a yes?"

Those goddamn eyes.

She practically leaps into my arms and onto my lap and she doesn't need a verbal response because she knows me. "This is going to be *great*, Luke. You'll see!"

———

SHE HAS dinner with my family—*old times*—and Dad forces her to spend the night because Brian's still in Savannah with Misty, and Dad doesn't like the idea of her being in her house alone. I didn't know she was alone, or I'd have offered her my bed. I would've even gone as far as not sleeping in it with her. She agrees, eagerly. At 7:00, I do my one minute with Lachlan and head back to the apartment where she's waiting for me. I sit on the floor between the couch and the coffee table and do my homework while she sprawls out on the couch and watches a movie. At 10:30, she's fast asleep. At 10:48, I stop watching her sleep and get a blanket to cover her. Then I go to my room and send my sister a text:

Lucas: *Do you know what a Felicity and a Ben are?*
Lucy: *OMGOMGOMGOMG. YES!!!! Why?*

182

Lucas: Who are they?

Lucy: Who are they to YOU?!

Lucas: Laney and I were talking about UNC, and she said she was no Felicity and Cooper was no Ben.

Lucy: Well, duh. Cooper is more like her Noel (but an asshole version of him) or maybe even that artsy guy she had that fling with. Dude! YOU are her Ben Covington. Seriously.

Lucas: I'm so fucking lost.

Lucy: There's this amazing thing called Google. Use it.

Lucy: PS - If Cooper isn't her Ben, it's a good thing, bro.

AT 2 AM and after numerous Google searches that would make any hacker assume I'm a (female) mildly obsessed, romance-drama circa late '90s TV junkie, I find out that Ben Covington was kind of a dick (me), but he loved Felicity (Lane), he just didn't know what to do with that love (Me! Me! Me!)

CHAPTER TWENTY-TWO

LUCAS

THE DAY after Laney's visit, I tell Dad about the spring play and about not really having time for it but agreeing only because it meant spending time with Laney. "It's like I'm a dog, and she's just thrown me a bone," I tell him.

He says, "You can't teach an old dog new tricks." Which is completely irrelevant, as are his next eleventy-three life-lesson analogies all related to dogs. Then he goes on to tell me about Rusty, the German Shepard he had growing up. When he's done, I just stare at him. "Sorry," he says, "Kind of went off on a tangent there, huh?"

"Just a tad."

"So what are you going to do?" he asks.

I rub the back of my neck, already feeling the stress from the added workload that hasn't even started yet.

"I have an idea," he tells me. "It'll be good. Trust me."

His idea isn't just good. It's *great*. Brilliant, even.

He makes my brothers do it, too. School spirit and all. (Rah rah rah!)

I do my part, get Dumb Name in on it, too. "Just think of the girls, Garray. They change into costumes right there in the open. Some even show their tits!" *They don't.*

Leo's up for it because Angela, a sophomore and his current conquest, got the lead.

And Logan... Well, he has no fucking choice. Dad still has him on probation for his joyous time with a joint.

It's been three weeks now and Garray, Leo and I have found a rhythm and we work well together. Logan's fucking useless until you get a paintbrush in his hand and give him direct instructions.

"Logan, do something, bruh!" Garray says. He spent the winter break visiting his grandparents in California, and now he calls everyone "bruh." It's so fucking cringeworthy, but you can't tell him that.

I give Logan a brush, tell him to paint the particle board I just cut to size the reddest red he can find. He does it, no questions. But he chuckles, mumbles to himself the entire time. "Dude," he tells me. "This is so fucking therapeutic and shit." ... *Okay?*

The next day, I have a conversation with Coach Anderman about Logan, and he gives me a cup. "Tell him to piss in it and bring it back to me. I'll take care of it."

I make Logan piss in the cup.

It comes back positive for marijuana.

"It's so fucking therapeutic and shit, bruh," Garray mocks when I tell Logan the results. Logan throws a swing at him. Garray ducks it. Leo laughs. I sigh.

The truth is, I don't really care if Logan smokes weed. I personally don't do it because being clean is a requirement to be on the track team, and track is my ticket to UNC. As long as he's not breaking the rules at home and burning down the house, it doesn't bother me. It bothers Dad, though, and his reasoning is justifiable. Dad had been on the wrong end of addiction with alcohol when Mom passed away, and so he thinks it might run in the family. Addiction is scary because it's unsteady, uncontrollable, and has the potential to damage everything in its path. I tell Lane all this while she sketches out a costume for Juliet (our school is big on Shakespeare) as we sit outside for lunch. "You know what you should do?" she says, looking up at me, her eyes bright against the spring sun. "Come over for dinner tonight. Misty's cooking. Talk to her about it. She might know a way to help." She looks back down at her sketchpad and smiles at her work and I stare and I stare and I wonder if maybe Logan's good, *great* even, and I'm the one who needs help because *I'm addicted to* you, *Laney.*

I go to dinner and Misty says she'll drag Logan's ass down to one of the volunteer counseling sessions she does for drug addiction, and the people there will scare the weed right out of his system. She's also going to talk to my dad, ask permission to collect a sample of Logan's piss every day for twenty-one days.

Dad agrees.

Logan gets *so* mad.

186

By the final day, his urine is crystal clean.

Yay, teamwork!

Between building shit for the set, track meets, training, family, I barely have time to breathe, but you know what? Laney was right. I *am* great at it, and Laney and I *do* get to spend a lot of time together.

Old times have become *now* times and small talk is purely conversation. Even when it comes to Cooper. "You heading to UNC this weekend or is Cooper coming home?" I ask, sitting opposite her, our legs crossed, making flowers out of tissue paper and wire. Hers look like they belong in a museum. Mine look like dog shit. Meanwhile, Leo, Logan and Garray attempt to piece together the set for the infamous balcony scene.

"I'm not sure," she mumbles, looking at the time.

I look at the time, too. It's 4:48 on a Thursday afternoon and my crew, she, and I are the only ones left in the drama room. Miss Lepsitch, the drama teacher, should be here, too. But she's probably sucking face with Coach Anderman in a broom closet somewhere. "Are you waiting for him to call?" I push.

She shrugs, focuses on the flower that's already done. She doesn't really talk much about him anymore, at least not to me, and whether that's a conscious decision she's made or the hype of him has worn off, I'm not sure.

"You guys are still together, right?" I try, digging for more information.

"Yeah," she says quickly. "We're still together. It's just hard... you know..." She glances up at me, searches for a reaction. She won't see anything. No anger. No spite. Hell, it took Ben and Felicity what literally felt like an eternity to finally get their shit together. Four seasons and one abrupt ending and I still don't have closure. But I did learn that my best tactic was to wait. And so waiting is what I'm doing. Plus, my mom was a big believer in fate. If it was meant to be, it would happen. Eventually.

"Are you missing him?" I ask.

She clears her throat, looks up at me, her eyes glazed.

Shit. "Did I say something?"

Her head moves, side to side, slowly, slowly. "There's so much I want to tell you," she breathes. "But it's..."

I shuffle closer, place my hands on her knees. "It's what, Lane?"

Her throat bobs with her swallow and she looks away. "It's..."

I hear footsteps approaching, but I'm too focused, too *addicted* to turn to the sound. "Lane?" I push, squeezing her knees.

"Lois?" *Fuck you, Cooper Kennedy.*

Her eyes are huge, her breath caught in her throat while Cooper stands above me like an angry giant, clenching and unclenching his fists. "Get your hands off my girlfriend, Preston."

Laney pushes my hands away. "I didn't know... you didn't say..." She stumbles to her feet and stands between Cooper and me, her hands on his chest, protecting *me*. "Let's go, Coop."

I don't need her fucking protection and I stand, my chest out, shoulders square and look down on him. "We're just *friends*, asshole!"

"You touch all your friends like that?" he spits, his words echoing through the room.

The guys hear his bullshit and come running. Leo gets between us. "Leave it alone, man," he says to me, his tone calm. He should be *Leonardo*, the ninja turtle. The smart, tranquil, leader of the brotherhood.

"What the fuck's going on?" Garray snaps.

Lane tugs on Cooper's arm, forcing him toward the door. They're almost out when Logan shouts, his hands cupped around his mouth, "Pedophile alert!"

I WAIT three hours and forty-six minutes to text Lane from Leo's phone.

Leo: *I'm sorry about what Logan said. He was out of line. Are we still on to finish up the set tomorrow afternoon? -CK*

That's what our friendship has become, sneaking in text messages and signing off in code (CK = Clark Kent) to settle her boyfriend's jealousy and keep the peace with them.

It takes her nine minutes to respond.

Lane: *It's okay. It's not your fault. It's mine. I shouldn't have let Lucas touch me like that. I know that now. I'll see you tomorrow at 3 PM. Great job, today! Thanks for everything, Leo.*

I give Leo back his phone and don't bother with a reply, because *what the fuck, Lane?*

She doesn't show the next day.

She doesn't call, doesn't text, doesn't email.

She's not at school Monday, so I make contact with her.

Leo: *You sick or something? Need me to come around? - CK.*

Lane: *No.*

Lane: *I'm not home.*

Lane: *I won't be at school for a couple of days, but I'm okay. Thanks for checking in, Leo.*

IT'S NOT JUST a couple of days she's off school. It's an entire week. I call Brian, ask how she is and he tells me that she got a horrible flu when she was at UNC over the weekend. She's *so* sick that she can't even come home. She's holed up in his dorm room but it's *fine*, he tells me, because *Cooper's* there and he's *taking care* of her. I wonder if Brian knows about New Year's Eve and the houseboat and Cooper's lack of taking care of her then—one night. How the hell has he taken care of her for an entire week?

If I didn't have to finish these stupid sets and compete in a race and take the twins to basketball and then Lachlan to a birthday party and hand deliver Logan's now-weekly piss cup to Misty at the police station, my ass would be in my truck, driving to UNC, punching Cooper in the face (fuck, I want to do that *so* bad) and throwing Laney over my shoulder to take her home. She'd sit in my apartment and I'd take care of her. Soup, meds and back rubs. I'd nurse her back to health and she'd call me her hero and she'd dump Cooper and then we'd have sex on the bed where I put the final nail in the coffin of bringing her back to life. Shit. I'm Dad with a dog story and there was my tangent.

But, I *do* have to do all those things, and I can't even call her to see how she is because that fucker still has me blocked.

MONDAY ROLLS AROUND, opening night, and everyone involved in the play, including Miss Lepsitch, is going out of their ever-loving minds because *the costumes! Where the fuck are the costumes?* I begin to panic as much as everyone else because now I feel like I'm part of this insanity called The Spring Play, and dammit, I worked hard for it. In the afternoon, Leo tries calling Lane. Garray tries calling Lane. Even *I* try calling Lane—it doesn't even ring. Logan sits on a makeshift throne made for King Capulet, or Sir Capulet, or whatever the fuck Juliet's dad was, and says, "You know, maybe

189

Cooper's one of those crazy cats who's, like, stupid obsessed with our little Laney, and he's got her hidden in a dungeon or something. She probably loves him because of that... what's it called? You know that thing..." He clicks his fingers while my brain throbs. "When the captured fall for their captor?"

"Stockholm syndrome," Leo tells him.

"Bruh," Garray says.

"Or you know," Logan continues, and I wish he'd shut the fuck up. "Maybe he's that fucking in love with her he killed her and then himself, like this here,"—he raises a finger, spins it in circles— "Romero and Juliet."

Leo says, "*Romeo* and Juliet, dickwad. Smoke another joint."

"Can't." Logan jumps off the chair. "Hot Cop Lady is all up in my shit thanks to Luke."

Swear my brain literally explodes and for some fucked-up reason, I actually believe (for a second) that Logan is onto something. I mean, Cooper's not a fucking nutjob, right? He's just your standard self-entitled dick.

"Costumes are here!" Miss Lepsitch shouts, and I practically sprint over to her.

"Where's Lane?"

"Who?"

There are people everywhere now, trying to find their costumes amongst the pile in her arms.

"Lois! Where's Lois?"

"She just dropped these off. She's gone back home. She must *really* not be feeling well."

I tell the boys I'm out and put Leo in charge, then waste nineteen seconds arguing with Dumb Name about why *he's* not in charge simply because he was born a couple of years earlier.

Luckily, Logan butts in. "Get over it, pindick. Let Luke find his Juliet."

I make my escape while they go toe-to-toe, and I get in my car and I think about Laney and think about who would actually win if Logan and Dumb Name got in a fist fight. Dumb Name's tall, scrawny but lean. But Logan carries enough unjustified anger to set off security gates at an airport. Cameron told me once that emotion *always* wins when it comes down to a fight. Always. So yeah, I'd probably put my money on Logan.

I park in Lane's driveway and go right to the basement door. The outside light isn't on, but I don't expect it to be because I haven't knocked on it since September 25ᵗʰ.

There's no answer, so I move to the front door. Again, no answer. I creep around the house looking through all the windows, but there doesn't seem to be anyone home. Laney's car's here, but Brian's isn't. Maybe he took her to the hospital or something. Maybe it was more than just a horrible flu. I call Brian. He says he's at Misty's getting ready to see the play. He doesn't know where Laney is. She's not answering her phone.

Fuck.

I picture Laney in a dungeon.

I picture Laney dead in a dungeon with dead Cooper next to her.

Dad calls me, tells me he's on his way to the play with the younger boys and that I should come home because Laney isn't in a dungeon. She's not dead. She's sitting on my apartment stairs.

I'M out of breath when I get to her and it's not because I'm unfit, it's because I was worried. I pick her up off the stairs and hold her and hold her, and she winces in pain because *she's sick, you idiot.*

"What's with you?" she asks when I put her back down.

"Dungeons and Stockholm and Romero."

Her eyes widen. "What?!"

I take a calming breath. "Logan."

She raises her hand between us. "Say no more."

The second we're in my apartment, she looks over at the empty kitchen sink. "No dishes?"

I shake my head. "No dishes." Then I take her hand, lead her over to the couch. "Sit," I order.

She sits.

I go to the kitchen, take out the canned chicken soup, pour it into a pot and switch on the stove. Then I get a microwavable heating pad from my room and throw it in the microwave, wait for one minute, take it out, stir the pot, go to Lane, and place the heating pad on her back where I know she likes to be rubbed. "What are you doing, Luke?" she asks.

I shrug. "You're sick."

"And you're sweet," she says.

191

Okay, here's a story that's going to take you on a *real* tangent.

One time, in tenth grade, I dated a senior named Rachelle. Rachelle was the head cheerleader, the hottest girl in school (excluding Laney, of course) and she was interested in *me!* Logan overheard me having a conversation with Dad asking for some shifts so I could buy Rachelle some fucking bag she kept showing me. Logan shouted that I was pussy-whipped. Lachlan was in the room, and *pussy-whipped* is not something you say around a four year old because four year olds ask a lot of questions, like "What does pussy-whipped mean?"

Logan left the room, leaving Dad and me to answer because *fuck Logan*. Anyway, Dad explained that pussy-whipped meant that you didn't like cats and you whipped them. So now, almost three years later, Lachlan makes it his mission to make sure I'm *never* around cats. The point of this story? I'm pussy-whipped by Lane, and she's not even *my* girlfriend. Because the truth is I'd planned all of this—not the *how* it happened or the *way* it happened, but I planned on her being in my apartment and me taking care of her. Proof: the soup that's currently heating on my stove.

I get the soup, put it in a bowl, watch her eat the soup. After she puts the empty bowl down on the coffee table, she says, "You know why I always do your dishes when I walk in?"

She was gone a week, and I missed her voice and her hair and her eyes and her coconuts, lime and *Laney*. "Why?"

"Because I never know what to do when I walk in here, so I do the dishes and you either sit on the couch and turn on the TV or you sit on the floor and do your homework, and once you're settled, I follow your lead."

"Really?" I ask.

She smiles. "Really."

"And what would happen if I went to my bedroom and stripped naked?" *Too far, dickhead.* But then she gives me a sound that shifts reality, and I know she's good, and I'm good, and we're *great*.

I pull her feet on my lap and notice what she's wearing for the first time. Baggy sweatpants and an oversized hoodie and it's not even cold outside. "How long were you waiting for me and did you walk here?"

"Not long and yes, why?"

"Because you're all bundled up like it's the middle of January. Are you cold? You want me to turn the heat up?"

192

She pokes my leg with her feet, and I start rubbing them through her socks and seriously, cats, hide from me. *Whip whip whip.*

I don't even want to tell you the effects I have from the sounds she makes when I start massaging her feet, because truth? It's a little embarrassing, and now her head's tilted back on the arm of the couch, and her eyes are closed, and her chest are breasts, and they're moving, and she murmurs, "I have to tell you something."

"Okay."

"I broke up with Cooper."

CHAPTER TWENTY-THREE

LUCAS

GIRLS AND GUYS are so different. Girls say things like: "We loved each other, but we didn't *like* each other, or maybe it was the other way around."

Guys say: "We were both kind of over it, you know?"

And I'd never been on this end of a breakup story, one being told by a girl, and I kind of wish that Lucy had dated more when she was younger so I could've eavesdropped on her conversations and been prepared for this. As it turns out, Lane was the one who broke up with Cooper, yet she's the one crying on my shoulder while he's probably balls deep in angry rebound sex. "I know it sounds dumb," she says, sniffling into my shirt. "It's just he's the first real boyfriend I've ever had, and he'd become such a huge part of my life and now… now he's gone."

The conversation's been going for thirty-eight minutes, and swear it's like reeling in a fish. You throw the line, they bite, then slowly, gently, you have to pull in the line, and sometimes they fight, move away, and you can't rush so you keep going, slowly, gently. She keeps making up excuses, and the excuses turn to regrets, and the regrets turn to reasons to go back to him and slowly, gently, with my words, I reel her back in.

She says he was controlling, and I agree. She says he was unpredictable, and I agree (even though I have no idea what she means), but she also says that he was there for her at a time when she felt like no one else was, and I (reluctantly) agree.

"I never really thought that I had confidence issues, you know?" she says, staring ahead. "He had this way of making me see things differently. Or just, making me *see* in general. And I think I needed that. After what happened with you and me—"

"Laney," I say through a sigh, cutting her off.

She turns to me. "No, it's okay. I can talk about it now… and I think we *should* talk about it. Don't you?"

I didn't think her being here, her saying "I broke up with Cooper" would lead to this; her and me talking about *my* regrets. "I never meant to hurt you," I tell her. "When I left you that night, I had every intention of coming back to you. Of spending…" *the rest of my life with you…* "the night with you. And then…"

"I know." She laughs once. "I think I had so much invested in that one night. It was stupid."

"Ouch."

"No. What we did wasn't stupid. I didn't mean that. I meant I had so much invested in you and me and *that* was stupid."

Still ouch. "And now?"

"Now what?"

"How do you feel about you and me?"

She smiles, drops her gaze. "I feel like I just got out of a *really* complicated relationship so…"

"So… I'll wait?"

"Lucas," she whispers, her smile getting wider.

I ask, "When did you actually break up with him?"

Her shoulders hunch, mind searching. "I haven't been completely honest… with a lot of people."

"What does that mean?"

"I haven't been sick," she admits. "I've just been… gone."

"What does *gone* mean? And answer my question."

"Promise you won't be mad?"

I nod once.

"I broke up with him the night after he showed up at school. Cooper drove us to his dorm while I spent the entire ride preparing what I was going to say and how I was going to say it—break up with him, I mean—and we got to his room, and I did and said everything I prepared in the car, and I was going to call you, ask you to pick me up, but he refused to let me leave."

"Refused how?"

"Just stood by the door, you know? I was going to wait for him to fall asleep and sneak out of there, but Cooper doesn't sleep—"

"He doesn't *sleep*? Like, ever?"

Her head moves from side to side, but her eyes stay locked on mine. "Ever since he's been back on the team, he's started taking

196

these ADHD meds, and now and then he crashes, and crashes hard, but he doesn't actually *sleep*, you know?"

"He has ADHD?" I ask. We're both sitting up now, facing each other.

"No! That's the thing. He doesn't. But he buys them off some guy on campus and he pops them like candy along with all these other meds and it keeps him awake and alert for days on end so he can keep up with his classes and his training and his dad's bullshit business agenda and his dad's bullshit in general."

I don't care enough to keep talking about Cooper, so I ask, "Where the fuck have you been, Lane?"

She sighs, takes a sip of her water. "I managed to escape—"

"Escape?!" *Christ, maybe Logan was onto something.*

"You know what I mean! The next morning, he went to meet the guy for some anti-anxiety drugs, and I left, but I didn't have a car, so I caught a bus to Charlotte and by the time I got there I was exhausted, and Cooper had been calling like crazy and I knew if I went home he'd find me and want to *talk* some more so I got a hotel room for the night and I've been there since."

My eyes are so wide I can feel them stretching my face. "You've been there for more than a week?"

She nods.

"But your dad said you were sick."

Another sigh. "I asked Cooper to tell him that, and we both kept up the front. I told Coop I was visiting my mom—he doesn't know about her. Not like you do."

I WIN. Just saying.

She adds, "I just haven't been ready to face Cooper or my dad or you, and I needed the time. You understand, right?"

Not really. "Yeah, Laney, I understand."

And with the explanations done, she goes back to crying, and I do my best to let her go through her emotions on her own, no matter how hard it is not to shake her and tell her that her tears are wasteful and that guy was a fucking dick.

AN HOUR LATER, Leo and Logan visit the apartment and tell us how opening night went. The rundown goes like this:

Logan punched Garray.

Leo got the girl's number.

LUCAS

Juliet said, "Romeo, Romeo, wherefore art thou, Romeo?" and Lachlan shouted, "Sexing!" and the entire theater laughed and laughed and laughed.

But Laney doesn't. She smiles, but there's no reality-shifting sound and the guys see it and they make an excuse to leave, and Laney goes to wash the pot and the ladle and the bowl used for her soup I'd made when she wasn't even sick. "I'm sorry you missed it," she says when I step behind her.

"I don't care. I'd rather be with you." I shut off the water and dry her hands with a cloth, leave the dirty dishes in the sink. I keep one hand around hers, the other reaching up to cup the side of her face. She flinches, probably afraid I'll make a move now that she's single, but I'm not a dick, and I don't want to be her angry rebound fuck.

I want to be her everything.

"You look tired," I tell her, and she does.

She whispers, another sob forming in her throat, "I'm *so* tired, Lucas. Of everything."

I lead her to my bed, move the covers to the side and wait for her to get in. "You want one minute?" I ask, and she frowns, removes her glasses and puts them on the nightstand.

She settles on the pillow, her eyes drifting shut. "Luke?"

"Yeah?"

"How do you get over it, you know, move on?"

"I'm the wrong person to ask that question," I say, shaking my head.

"But you've dated a lot of girls before, so… how?" She looks so desperate, so in need of closure.

I hate asking the question as much as I hate already knowing the answer. "Did you love Cooper?"

She doesn't miss a beat. "Yes."

"Then I can't give you the answers you need, Lane. I may have been with a lot of girls, but I didn't *love* any of them." I look away. "I mean, there was *one*,"—*You*—"and that lasted all of one night."

Her gasp is soft, but still, I hear it. "And that one girl?" she asks. "How did you get over that?"

"As soon as it happens, I'll let you know."

198

CHAPTER TWENTY-FOUR

LUCAS

THE NEXT MORNING, I run my regular route. Twice. I don't stop at the crossroads because the crossroads won't lead me to her. It took her just over three minutes to fall fast asleep last night, and I watched her for a few minutes more. Then I thought about doing something really stupid: going through her phone. I didn't, of course. But I wanted to. Because the entire time she sat with me, told me about the breakup, I could tell she was holding back. I just didn't know what. But I trust her, believe in her, *in us*, and I know—in time—she'll let me in.

LANE'S still sleeping when I get home and because of my extra route, I don't have time to make her breakfast like I wanted to. I sit on the edge of the bed and shake her. She flinches awake and gasps for air, her eyes wide.

"Hey," I try to soothe. "It's okay. It's just me. Were you having a nightmare or something?"

It takes her a few minutes to settle her breathing, gain focus, and when she does, her eyes meet mine. "Hi."

"Hi."

She shakes her head. "I'm sorry, I think… yeah. I must've been dreaming."

"I ran a few extra miles this morning, so I'm running late. I'm going to hit the shower and then go to the house, make sure the boys are up and ready. Are you going to school today or you still need more time?"

"No," she says, her voice hoarse from sleep. "I should go. I've missed enough."

"All right." I kiss her forehead. "I'll take you home so you can get what you need." Then I head to the bathroom.

"Luke?" she calls. "Thank you. You're a good friend."

THE KITCHEN IS A MAD HOUSE. Lachlan's spilled milk all over the table trying to pour his own cereal. He's crying, wailing, and Linc and Liam are pointing, laughing, doing nothing to help him. Logan's literally sleeping through his alarm. Obnoxiously loud gangsta rap fills his room, a room that reeks of stale socks, Cheetos and fifteen-year-old boy. The walls shake, the water in the eleventy-three plastic bottles scattered throughout his room ripple, and I pick one up, remove the lid. Then I pour the content all over his face. He sits up, gasps for air, spits and splatters and wipes his eyes. "You're such a fucking jerk."

"Get up. Get ready. We leave in fifteen."

"Okay!"

Then I go to Lachlan's room, pick out his clothes and run downstairs. "Linc, clean up the milk. Liam, help dress Lachlan." They whine, but they do as I ask, and Lachlan won't stop crying over the spilled milk, and he's trying to eat, but the milk's seeping out of his mouth and going back to the cereal bowl and Liam's getting frustrated with him and "Where's Leo?" I ask Linc.

"He's at an early session with the private tutor."

Fuck. I forgot about that, which means I have to take the minivan and drive everyone to school. I run back upstairs, open Logan's door, catch him masturbating under the covers. "You got two minutes, jerk-off."

"You said I had fifteen!"

I silence the music. "Change of plans."

I start to leave when he yells out, "I'm going to have blue balls all day."

Lachlan shouts from the bottom of the stairs, his pants wrapped around his neck, "What's blue balls?"

"Logan's joining the field hockey team," I tell him, walking past him just as the front door opens. Laney's holding a protein shake in one hand, my school bag in the other. "I wasn't sure if you had time for breakfast. Leo's car's gone. Are you on your own?"

I take the protein shake, thank her, and tell her where Leo is.

200

Logan thumps down the stairs. "I think I have a test first period so we can't be late. Oh, hey Laney," he murmurs. Then he smirks at me, goes back to her. "I was just thinking about you."

I smack the back of his head and tell Lane, "We're running so late."

Lane's eyes widen. Then she claps once. "We can do this! Lachy, come here, baby." I down the shake while she starts to dress him, talks to Logan, "Since you have the body of a girl, you think I could borrow some clothes?"

Logan rolls his eyes but starts up the stairs to his room, and Laney and I shout at the same time, "*Clean* clothes!"

I chuckle, and she says, "I don't really need anything from home so we can skip that."

I nod, then, "Crap. Laundry." I go through the house, find the dirty clothes and put on the wash while Lincoln finishes the kitchen clean-up and Liam loads the dishwasher and Logan helps Lachlan pack his bag and then Laney appears in Logan's jeans that somehow fit snug on her hips and legs, and a gray, long sleeve top underneath *my* old baseball jersey from middle school. I look at Logan. He shrugs. "You said *clean*. It was all I had."

WE PILE INTO THE MINIVAN, one by one, and after making sure Lachlan's buckled in right, I speed to Miss Anita's house—an old lady who lives a block from the elementary school and watches a group of kids. When it's time, she walks them all to the school. Then I drive the twins to their school, and finally, I get to the high school and quickly find a place to park. Logan jumps out before I've even stopped the car completely, and once he's gone, I take a moment, take a breath.

"Can I do anything to help?" Laney asks, and I almost forgot she was sitting next to me. I look from her worried eyes down to the jersey she's wearing. I smile, tease, "My name's on your shirt."

"It's not *your* name."

"Is so."

Her lips curve. Then she says, "Why wasn't your dad home this morning?"

Surprised by her question, I tell her, "Because Dad gets to work at five, does all the prep and paperwork before the phone starts ringing. Then he normally gets done by one, and he picks up the boys and does all their afternoon activities. It's a good compromise."

After a moment, her gaze drops, she says, "I already knew that, didn't I?"

"Yeah, I'm pretty sure you came up with the plan."

"I'm sorry, Luke, my mind's a little lost right now." She sighs, adds, "You're the glue, Lucas. Without you, that family would fall apart."

I look out the windshield, grip the wheel tight. "Sometimes I wish Dad didn't get rid of Virginia. When I go off to college, it'll just be Leo in charge and..." I trail off.

"And Logan."

"Yeah, but he *barely* counts now."

"Maybe you should tell your dad that."

I force a smile and motion to the school. "We better go, we're going to be late."

THE SCHOOL PLAY runs for another two nights, which means our afternoons and evenings are spent at the school theater. I trust Leo enough to handle any set mishaps that may occur, but being here means being with Laney, and I wouldn't give that up for anything. I stand beside her as she watches the play from the side of the stage, her eyes lost in wonder. "It looks so different," she whispers. "With the lights and the audience and the set and the—"

"Costumes," I cut in. "It's the costumes that bring it all together."

She smiles at that. "I did pretty good, huh?"

"No, Lane. You did *great*."

Her features soften as she continues to watch the play; Romeo's hiding in the bushes, watching Juliet on the balcony and he says, "But soft, what light through yonder window breaks? It is the east, and Juliet is the sun."

"I have absolutely no idea what they're saying," I whisper to her.

She glances at me quickly, then goes back to the play, her hand squeezing the key pendant on the necklace my mom left her. "He's describing Juliet, saying that she is the sun. That she can bring light to darkness, that the stars in the sky pale in comparison, that her

202

eyes..." She sniffs back a sob. "He's just talking about love, Lucas. About deep, irreversible love..."

In freshman year, Laney tried to start a knitting club that would meet at lunch one day a week and knit and talk about knitting. She was so excited about it, she posted flyers throughout the school. One time, she saw a bunch of girls making fun of the flyer and ripping it off the wall. In her bedroom that night, she told me she didn't care, but she did. And when no one showed up to her club, she tried so hard not to let it affect her. She kept telling me it was fine, but the cries and the tears were there, just under the surface. She'd hold her breath, not risking that they might force their way out of her. I told her I'd get us soda and went upstairs to her kitchen. When I came back down, she was sitting in her bed, looking ahead, tears streaking down her cheeks. There were no cries, no other sounds that matched those tears. Just tears. I gave her the soda and she wiped her cheeks, said thanks, and continued to stare ahead with silent tears.

That's how Laney spent the rest of the play, with silent tears and silent cries.

***

WE DON'T TALK about what happened even though she knows I watched her cry, and when the play's over, I take her home. Her house is quiet, dark, and the only car in the driveway is hers. She looks to the house, then back to me. "Dad must be at Misty's," she says, then sighs. "I've never slept at the house by myself before."

"But your dad's been staying at Misty's for a while, right? And during winter break..."

"Yeah, but Cooper..." *But Cooper's not around, and I am, Lane.*

Her phone vibrates in her pocket for the third time since we got in the car and she ignores it, just like the other times. She says, "I hate to ask—"

"Do you want me to stay with you?"

She shakes her head. "Can you just come in while I get my things and maybe I can stay at yours again? I'll sleep on the couch this time, and I'll get up early and help in the morning and do your laundry and—"

"Laney, you don't have to do that. You know my house is your house. It always will be."

I SIT on her bed while she shuffles around her room, filling a bag with more than enough clothes for just one night. She gathers stuff for school, her laptop, her toiletries, and I watch, confused, and her phone vibrates again, and again she ignores it, and I finally ask, "If there were something going on, you'd tell me, right?"

Her hands freeze midway through zipping up her bag. She looks up, meets my gaze. "I just don't want to be alone right now, Lucas. That's all."

I INSIST she takes the bed and this time, I don't wait for her to fall asleep. I don't watch her. Instead, I lie on the couch, count the seconds, minutes, hours, and I listen to her cry. It doesn't matter that I want to go to her, that I want to wrap my arms around her and comfort her, because it isn't about me, or *us*. If there even is an *us* anymore.

CHAPTER TWENTY-FIVE

LUCAS

SAME PLAY, different day. Garray slaps my shoulder backstage and whispers, "Is it true, bruh?"

"Is what true?" I ask, watching Lane fix the hem on Lady Capulet's dress.

"About Cooper and The Lo-meister?"

I face him. "The what?"

"Cooper and Lois. Did they break up?"

"Rumors are flying, dude," Logan says, standing next to him.

"What rumors?"

"She cheated on him," Leo joins in. "With *you.*"

"That's fucking bullshit!" I almost shout, earning me a round of hushes plus a confused glare from Laney. I lower my voice, add, "It's not true."

Garray says, "But you're driving her to and from school?"

"Yeah, so?"

"That's because she's slept in Luke's bed the past two nights," Logan says.

I shake my head at him.

"So what's the game plan, bruh?"

"There is no game plan," I tell them. "She *literally* just broke up with Cooper so..."

"So fucking what?" Logan whispers.

I look to Leo, hoping for a way out of the conversation, but he just shrugs. "It doesn't really matter. Come August you're not going to be around anyway."

IN THE CAR after the play, Lane tells me that her dad called, said he's at home and wants to see her. He misses her, of course, and those many phone calls she's been dodging? She says they're all from him. And here I thought Cooper was a creep who couldn't let go. But then maybe not such a creep because after dropping her at her house and making sure she gets in okay, I go straight to my apartment, jump into bed, and sniff the pillow she'd slept on. I do this for *way* too long, but I'd probably do it for longer if Leo wasn't knocking on my door. "Laney's on the phone," he says, eyeing me sideways, like he *knows* what I've been doing.

I take the phone from him, mute it. "Why is she calling your phone?"

"It's Lane," he says, shrugging. "She probably doesn't know how to unblock your number."

I unmute the phone, speak into it, "My number still blocked?"

"Can you come over," she rushes out. "Please?"

I BREAK every traffic violation getting to Lane's, which in our town is speeding and ignoring one yield sign. She opens the basement door before I get a chance to knock and I can tell she's mad and I take a step back in case I'm the one she's mad at, but I haven't done anything wrong. I mean, I've done a lot of things wrong and the majority have to do with her, but nothing recently. *I think.*

"Cooper went to see my dad today!" she whisper-yells.

I whisper, too, "Why are we whispering?"

"Because my dad's upstairs and I don't want him to hear, idiot!" Oh yay, *Old Laney!*

"Okay." I take her by the shoulders, and she flinches at the touch. "Calm down," I say, moving her to the bed. "Sit."

She sits.

I say, "I need a moment to wrap my head around what's happening right now because when you called, I thought something *really* bad was happening."

I take the phone from her hand, unblock my number while she says, "This *is* really bad. Did you hear what I said?"

"My moment's not over yet!"

She rolls her eyes, crosses her arms. She's frustrated. She's so cute when she's frustrated. "Now?"

206

"Fine." I give her back her phone.

"Cooper went to see my dad today—"

"We've covered this."

"—And he offered him a job."

"What?" Now I need to sit down. I sit on the couch opposite her bed and ask again, "What?"

"Cooper's starting his own construction company. Dad said that Cooper told him that his dad approved the business plan because they were wasting money using third-party companies, so soon, there's going to be a Kennedy Construction and he wants *my* dad to oversee *everything*. He offered him double his current wage and a $25,000 transfer payment."

"What the fuck is a transfer payment?"

"I don't know." She throws her hands in the air. "I guess to transfer from one job to another."

"What did your dad say? Did he say yes?"

"He said he'd think about it but, Luke... that transfer payment is a year's tuition at UNC, and that's all Dad can think about right now. He wants to take it. For *me*."

I drop my head in my hands, finally understanding her frustration. "He can't take it, Lane. Anything to do with the Kennedys is bad news."

"I *know* that. And I tried to tell *him* that. I even told him that I broke up with Cooper—"

"He didn't know?"

"No!" This entire conversation is whispered which makes it so much harder to communicate. "He asked when we broke up, and I said Monday when I got home because I didn't want him to know about spending all that time in a hotel in Charlotte."

"And what did he say?"

She sighs. "He said that I was cruel for breaking up with him after he spent the week taking care of me."

"You have to tell him, Lane."

"I can't."

"So he's going to take the job?"

"I don't know," she whines. "I can't believe this. I'm finally free of him, and he still finds ways to dig his claws into my life."

"What do you mean '*free of him*'?"

"Nothing." She shakes her head. "I'm just emotional."

"Maybe he's bluffing?"

"How?"

I get up, sit next to her on the bed. "What if he's making it all up? Like, maybe there is *no* business?"

She scoffs. "I wouldn't put it past him."

I get out my phone, call Lucy.

"What are you doing?" Lane asks the same time Lucy answers.

"Did I wake you?" I ask Lucy.

"It's 11:30, Luke, I have an early class. What do you want?"

It's 11:30! Holy shit, I must've been sniffing my pillow for longer than I thought. "When you were working admin at Dad's, you had to look up companies on some business register, right? Do you still have access to it?"

"What the fuck is this?"

"I need you to do me a favor."

"Right now?"

"Please, Luce."

She moans and not like, in an annoyed way, in a...

"Holy shit, are you guys having sex right now?"

"Cam will be done in two minutes. I'll call you back."

I drop the phone. "Fucking gross."

Laney's laughing now, silent but pure.

"It's not funny."

She flops on her back, holding her ribs from laughing so hard. I lean over her, take in all her features. I miss her smile, her laugh. *Her.* I reach up, run a finger across her forehead, move her bangs away from her eyes. I miss *those eyes.* "I miss your eyes, your smile." And without meaning to, I'm running my thumb across her full lips and licking my own and *I want to kiss you, Laney.*

"Luke," she whispers, her smile fading. "We can't."

"Why not? Are you planning on getting back together with Cooper?"

"No."

"Then why?"

Her gaze falls between us. "It has to be different," she says, and I have no idea what that means. "And it's too soon."

"It's too soon" = Throwing a dog a bone.

I ask, "So a month from now, would you consider going out with me?"

Her smile's back. It's small, but it's there. "Define *going out*?"

"A date?"

"One date?"

"Ten. Twenty. Fifty. A hundred! Whatever it takes."

"In a month's time?" she asks, and she's the fish and I'm reeling her in and I don't even care that I just heard my sister having sex because, in some fucked up way, it brought us to this.

"I can wait a month," I tell her.

"I doubt it."

"Watch me," I announce. "I'm the fucking Felicity of waiting, and you're my Ben Covington."

Her eyes go wide, her smile wider. "Did you just *Felicity* me?"

I nod, chuckle. "I'm that good, Lois Lane."

My phone rings and I blindly answer it, forgetting who it is and what they're calling about because Laney's still looking at me, smiling at me. Then Lucy says, out of breath, "What am I searching for, cockblocker?"

"Kennedy Construction."

"Not that Cooper asshole?"

"Yep."

I hear her typing the same time Laney reaches up, combs her fingers through my hair, and I close my eyes. She shifts beneath me until her mouth is to my ear. "I miss you," she whispers, and Lucy says, "Don't say that, Luke. It's *so* creepy."

I stifle my laugh and Laney does the same, falling onto her back again.

"Yeah, it's here," Lucy says. "Registered business as of... four days ago."

"Shit."

"Why the urgency on this?"

I come up with a lie. "I just heard the rumors and wasn't sure if it was true. I'm worried about them running Dad's business to the ground."

Lucy scoffs. "They can try, but Dad's been at this for a long time, and he's built a ton of great relationships with loyal clients. Also, the entire world hates that family... besides Lane of course, but Cooper has that charming, hot, older, bad boy thing going for—"

"They broke up," I cut in.

She squeals. "So what's the game plan?"

I smile down at Laney. "No game plan. I'm just going to do it right next time."

"There's a next time? Shit. I have to go, Cameron's asking for thirds."

"Thirds?"

Lucy's voice softens. "Well, he thinks because my chances of getting pregnant are so low, the more sex we have, the better our chances."

Lane's brow knits, her eyes questioning.

"Makes sense," I say. "Enjoy."

As soon as I hang up, Lane asks, "Lucy can't get pregnant?"

I nod.

She sits up, forcing me to do the same. "What happened?"

I try to hide my hurt by looking away because it's painful to think about Cameron and Lucy and what all they went through. Plus, I've never spoken openly about it before. "Remember last summer, when I went to New Jersey? Lucy was there and something happened and I found her bleeding out on the bathroom floor."

"Oh my God," Lane whispers.

"They rushed her to the hospital and long story short, she had to have an ovary removed and they told her it'd be difficult for her to get pregnant."

"That's so tough for her and Cameron to go through so young."

"Yeah," I say. "They separated for a while. It was hard on all of us."

"They broke up? Why didn't you say something?"

I shrug. "Because it wasn't my story to tell and I wasn't sure if Lucy wanted people knowing, but now you know."

She pouts. "That's so sad."

I inhale deeply, go back to the problem at hand. "What the hell are we going to do about your dad?"

"I don't know," she murmurs.

"Lucy said something about loyalty. You think that's going to come up when your dad makes a decision?"

She shakes her head. "I really wish it would, Luke. But that extra salary alone plus the twenty-five grand, that's my entire four-year college tuition and that's all he can think about. He still feels so guilty about it all."

"I hate your mom," I say.

"Me too."

"I should talk to Dad. See what he has to say."

She nods. "I want to be there when you do it."

I look back at her, smirk. "You want me to stay with you tonight?"

210

"See? You already suck at waiting."

I DON'T STAY the night. Instead, I go home and I fall asleep sniffing my pillow. Whatever. Felicity was a creep, too.

CHAPTER TWENTY-SIX

LOIS

A ND I THINK, *ultimately, that's what true love is, you know? To want to be someone's hero when they're faced with villains. To want to be the one who saves them. To be their Wonderwall."*

Lucas's words replay in my mind, over and over, and I think about the way he looked at me last night, the way his eyes met mine. Is that what he saw? Someone who *needs* a hero, *needs* saving? Because Cooper saw me as that, and we confused his need to be those things as *love*, and I fell for him—hard and fast—and it got me here. And as much as I don't want to admit it, I'm making the same mistakes again, only this time with Lucas. Lucas—who's standing a few yards in front of me, his back turned, looking out over the school parking lot. His hair's in need of a cut and his hands are in his pockets, his triceps on display. He'd changed over the past few months, physically and otherwise. His body had gotten harder, his demeanor the opposite.

I sneak up behind him, kick the back of his shoe and he turns swiftly, his eyes narrowed. Then he smiles. "Sneaky Lane," he says. "Sneaky Lane does sneaky things with... never mind. I didn't see your car pull in."

I joke, "You stalking me, Preston?"

We begin walking together, two of my steps for every one of his. He says, ignoring my comment, "Seriously, where's your car?"

"In my driveway. I caught the bus."

"Why? Something happen to it? I can check it out after school if you want."

"What do you know about cars?"

He laughs. "Not a lot, but knowing you, you probably left your lights on and drained the battery."

I nudge his side, and he feigns hurt. "There's nothing wrong with the car," I tell him as he opens the door to the school for me. "I just feel weird driving it."

"Why?"

"Because Cooper."

"Because he got it for you?"

I nod.

"That's dumb," he says, and he has *no* idea.

I stop at my locker and turn to him. "I'm sure I'll get over it, it's just..." *I don't know what it is.*

"Don't catch the bus anymore. I'll pick you up, okay?"

"There's nothing wrong with the bus."

"And there's nothing wrong with my truck, either."

"Fine."

"Good!"

We're twelve years old again.

I open my locker, get my books for first period, and he says, "Did you speak to your dad any more about the whole Cooper thing?"

I close my locker, hold the books to my chest. "Nah. He was gone by the time I got up."

"I called Dad this morning, said we needed to talk to him. You free after school?"

"Yep."

"Okay... Well, I'll see you then."

"Okay," I say, but he doesn't make a move to leave, and his locker's on the other end of the hall. "I should get to class."

"Yeah," he says, but he still doesn't budge.

"Bye, Luke."

"Bye, Lane."

I wait for him to leave and when he doesn't, I walk around him and toward my class. When I glance over my shoulder, he's *still* following me, looking down at my shoes. I stop abruptly, turn to him. "Luke?"

"Yeah?"

I point behind him. "Your locker's that way."

214

AFTER SCHOOL, in the Preston house, Luke and I wait for his dad *in* the office. It may not seem like a big deal that we're *in* Tom's office, but it is for me. I've walked past the room many a time and sometimes the door's even been open and I've looked inside, but it's been seven years since I first stepped foot in this house and I've never actually been *in* Tom's office. It feels so forbidden, so grand, so—"What's with your face, Lane?"

I side-eye Luke. "I've never been in here before," I whisper, checking the door to make sure Tom isn't coming. "I feel like I've been called to the principal's office." I use my jeans to wipe the sweat off my palms. "Doesn't it feel like that to you?"

Luke shakes his head, looks at me like I'm stupid. "We normally get our punishments in the kitchen or living room so..."

"Wow... yeah... that's true," I whisper absentmindedly.

"I was kidding, Lane. What's going on with you?"

"I don't know." I sigh. "I think I'm nervous to tell your dad. What if he ends up hating me? I mean, let's be real, this is all about Cooper getting back with me."

"*With* you or *at* you?" Lucas says, and now *he* looks nervous.

Tom enters the room, saving me from responding, and he sits his big frame in his big leather chair behind his big desk and smiles just as big at us. "Hey kids, what's up?"

I'm about to ruin everything you've worked so hard to build, that's "what's up."

"The Kennedys are starting their own construction company in town," Luke says, as if it's that simple, as if that's all there is to the story.

Tom's eyebrows shoot up, and he looks from Luke to me. I look down at my hands. "I know this," he says. "But how do you and why did you feel the urgency to tell me?"

"You're not worried?" Luke asks.

"Should I be?"

"Sir Tom," I start, and Luke chuckles.

"Sir Tom? Really?"

"Shut up."

"Lane," Tom says, "What's wrong?"

"Cooper—my ex—"

"Your *ex?*" he asks. "I wasn't aware..."

I force a smile. "Cooper offered my dad a job."

"Right." Tom nods. "And let me guess, he threw in a bunch of perks?"

"Yes, sir."

Luke laughs. "What? No *Sir* Tom?"

I kick his leg.

Tom sighs. "You know what the good thing about our town is, kids? And I say *kids* because that's what you *are*, and you really shouldn't be worrying about this stuff. The good thing about our town is that everyone knows everyone's business, and people like to *talk* about that business. I've known about this since the company was created five days ago."

"And you're not worried?" I ask.

"No."

"How can you be so confident?"

Tom looks from me to Lucas and back again. Then he leans forward, lowers his voice. I find myself leaning into the conversation. "Because I had Wendy in the office call Lance Kennedy, make out like she was from the newspaper and asked for an interview about his new venture into the construction trade and you know what Lance said? He said, '*What construction trade?*'"

"So Lance doesn't know?" I mumble.

Luke says, "So he lied to your dad?"

Tom leans back in his chair, gets more comfortable. "I spoke to Brian today, we had a good laugh about it. He didn't mention anything about Cooper offering him a job."

I sigh. "Maybe I made this a bigger deal than it is."

Tom chuckles. "I love you both. Really, I do. But you're only this young once, and you've both been through so much in your eighteen years. And Lucas, you carry more responsibilities than most your age. But this—worrying about me and the business—it's something I never want either of you to have to be burdened with. Do me a solid? Let loose now and then, enjoy life, get into a little trouble, y'know?"

Luke smiles. "Yes, sir."

"Good," Tom says. "Now that that's out of the way, what time's your meet next weekend?"

"What meet?" I ask him. I have all of Luke's track meets scheduled in my phone, and there's no meet next weekend. "I don't know about a meet."

"It's not a school one," Luke assures and then eyes his dad, shakes his head, just slightly.

"What meet?" I ask again.

216

Tom doesn't take Luke's hint. "It's an independent meet in Charlotte. Not school related."

"I want to go!" I say.

Tom says, "He'll probably beat his PB. He's so close."

I look at Luke. "You are?" I hate that I don't know this about him. Up until this school year, I'd been to all his meets and knew all his times and now... "I didn't know."

"It's cool," Luke says. "But this meet—I mean, I'll be competing in under 21s so I won't be competing *against* Cooper, but he'll probably be there so..."

Oh. "Oh."

Luke's gaze drops, and I feel his disappointment before I see it take over his body.

"So what?" I say, and I'm already preparing the excuses in my head. "I still want to go."

Luke shrugs. "We'll see," he says. He knows me too well.

"I got to pick up Lachlan and take him to the store," Tom says. "Lane, you staying for dinner? It's LTT night!"

"What's LTT?" I ask, looking between father and son.

"Lachlan's Tasty Tacos!" Tom says.

I cringe. "That sounds scary."

Tom chuckles. "It's pancakes."

"Folded," Luke adds.

"Because tacos," Tom says.

"Right." I nod.

"And I take him to the store to select and buy his filling."

"Candy," Luke says.

My eyes light up. "Pancakes filled with candy?"

Tom says, "But the best part is the hit or miss salsa."

Luke faces me. "Lachlan gets a bunch of candy and blends it together to make the sauce. As the name states, it's very hit or miss."

Tom's standing now, pocketing his phone, keys, and wallet. "It's dessert for dinner, Laney. Right up your alley."

"And Luke actually eats this?" I ask Tom.

"He gets this twitch in his left eye and his hands shake and he breaks out in a sweat."

"Probably pre-calculating the calories," I say with a giggle.

"He has one bite and then runs for two hours afterward."

Luke shakes his head. "I don't like LTT night," he murmurs, and I laugh, tell them that as much I'd *love* to stay for LTT night, I can't.

I have to work. Luke gives me a ride home so I can get ready, and I walk to work for my 4 PM shift. At 9 PM, an hour before my shift ends, Luke shows up with a Ziploc bag in his hand. "Lachlan didn't want you missing out on his tasty tacos." He slides it across the small opening of the ticket booth. The pancake's still warm as if he'd *just* made it, and I'm almost positive that Lachlan has nothing to do with this. "And I thought I'd give you a ride home."

"That's really nice, Luke." And it feels strange saying those words—as if I'm trying hard to be super, uber, extra polite, and I don't know why. "But my shift doesn't end for another hour."

"Oh."

"Yeah…"

"But you always finish at nine on Thursdays."

"New roster. Sorry."

"I'll come back then," he says quickly.

"Or you could stay," I say, just as fast. Truthfully, I could use the company. "You can hang out with me in here. It's quiet." I lift my psychology textbook. "I'm just catching up on homework."

Within seconds, he's opening the side door and joining me in a small room made for one, not two, and now we're close, too close, and it's terrifying in all the best possible ways. He gets out his phone, takes a picture of the noticeboard on the wall. "What are you doing?" I ask.

"Getting your new roster. I don't want you walking anywhere."

"Okay, *Cooper*," I say, and soon as his name leaves my mouth, I mentally cut off my tongue. Stupid. *So stupid.*

Luke's eyes drift shut, his shoulders tense.

"Sorry," I whisper. "I don't know why I said that." I try to find something to do so we can move on, and fast. I open the bag and pull out the pancake taco and a note falls out with it:

29 days, Lois Lane.

I find my voice, croak out his name and glance up at him. He looks from the note to me, his eyes searching. Then he leans against the wall, his shoulders slumped. "I get that you might feel pressured—with what's going on between us—and I know you're still at that stage where you probably have a ton of mixed feelings, but I don't, Lane. I want to be with you. More than anything. And I'm willing to wait until you're ready. But if there's any chance that you're still in love with him, or that you're going to get back together with him without even giving me a chance, then I'd rather know now. Save myself the disappointment."

"You're right," I say, and his gaze drops. "I do have a ton of mixed feelings, but none of them have to do with Cooper. They don't even have to do with you. It's all about me and whether or not I'm strong enough to go through it all again. As far as getting back with Cooper, that's never going to happen. Ever."

"Are you sure?"

"I'm positive."

A customer approaches then, asks Luke for two tickets to the latest Marvel movie even though I'm the one sitting behind the desk. "Sure." Luke steps forward and presses random buttons on the register. I cringe, and Luke says, "That'll be fifteen dollars, sir."

The man looks at the admission sign, looks at Luke. "It should be twelve."

"Sorry. My math is bad."

The customer points to the register. "Isn't that what that's for?"

Luke glares at him, presses more random buttons until the cash drawer flies open, hits Luke in the junk. I giggle. I can't help it. The man gives him fifteen dollars, tells him to keep the change. *He earned it.* Then I offer Luke my chair, and he sits, rests his head on my stomach. I stroke his hair, his ego. "Better?" I ask.

He shakes his head. "Not for another twenty-nine days."

CHAPTER TWENTY-SEVEN

LUCAS

OVER THE NEXT WEEK, I spend more time with Laney than I did the entire time she was dating Cooper. I drive us to and from school, and when I'm available, I drive her to work. But I always pick her up, and I always show up an hour early. I don't make excuses as to why I'm there, and she doesn't ask, simply opens the side door for me. I now know how to work the register. When I drop her home, I walk her to the door. She doesn't invite me in, and I don't ask. But the question is there, hanging in the air, another one of our little games, and one day (soon) I'll win. I always win. And so it's been a week of conversation, a week of building back what we once had, a week of touching and teasing and mentally counting down the days. Today, it's twenty-two.

LANEY RETURNS to the booth with a bucket of popcorn and hands it to me. "You've got that look," she says.

I take the popcorn, sniff it. "What look?"

"No butter, no salt," she says, "and that hungry I'm-going-to-eat-your-face look."

"Your face isn't what I'd be eating should it come down to that," I tell her.

"Lucas!" she gasps.

I sell two tickets to the couple who own the comic book/sex toy shop. The husband winks. The wife says, "We have body paint in all flavors."

They leave, and Laney's still staring at me with wide eyes and an even wider mouth and I look away. *The things I plan to do with that mouth.*

She sits in a chair in the corner of the booth, and I stand behind the register, our regular routine. She says, "That meet in Charlotte this weekend—you really think Cooper's going to be there?"

I throw a handful of popcorn at her.

"Luke!" she squeals, already getting the brush and dustpan. *Not working here is fun.*

"Why do you care if he's going? Do you *want* to see him?"

"It depends."

I turn to her. "On what exactly?"

She scoops up the popcorn, empties the dustpan in the trash. "On whether or not you can lend me $800..."

I switch the ticket booth sign to closed and shut the curtains. "You owe Cooper money or something?"

"No," she says, sitting back down, her hands empty. "I want to pay his share of the car, and I don't have enough. I tried to get a credit card, but it won't be here in time. I'll pay you back as soon as I get it."

"The car was a gift, Lane."

"And if it came from my dad alone, I'd appreciate it, but you don't know Coop. There's an ulterior motive for everything. I just don't know what it is yet," she says.

"Okay." I nod. "I'll front you the cash, but don't pay me back with a fucking credit card. The interest rates on those things are ridiculously high. Just pay me back whenever. If you need more, it's no problem." I hate talking about Cooper, and I hate the sudden awkwardness it brings, especially in such a tight space. I look at the time. 9:15. I should leave, drive, clear my head, come back when it's time. "I'll be back at ten," I tell her.

"Where are you going?"

"I forgot a thing... for my dad."

"Okay."

I leave, come back at 10:02, and the first thing she says is, "What got into you?"

I sigh, hands on the wheel. "I just don't like talking about Cooper, okay? And you can't be pissed that I get mad when you bring him up."

She doesn't respond, and we spend the drive to her house in silence. I get out, walk her to the basement door. "I'm sorry," she says, unlocking the door and turning to me. "I just thought..." She trails off, looks away.

222

"Thought what?"

Her eyes meet mine. "I thought I could talk to you about this, that you, out of everyone, would understand how important it is for me to cut ties with him once and for all so I can move on... especially considering *you're* the one I plan on moving on with."

I'm such a fucking dick. I step forward, one hand on her waist, the other in her hair, pulling her to me. Then I lean against the doorframe, one foot in her room. "You want me to stay?" I ask.

She says, "Yes," and my heart skips a beat. But then she adds, "But you shouldn't." She kisses my cheek, guides me back outside. "Twenty-two days," she tells me.

TWENTY-TWO DAYS turns to twenty-one turns to twenty, which is also the day of the track meet in Charlotte. I have to leave by 5 AM to get there by 6 for registration. At 4:45, while I'm packing my gear, my regular alarm goes off at the same time there's a knock on my door. Laney's on the other side, her hair a mess, her eyes half closed, and I don't even bother hiding my surprise. She'd already given me her share of the cash she wanted me to hand over to Cooper, as well as specific instructions: "Tell him it's for the car. That's all you have to say. Nothing more. Nothing less. I mean it, Luke. Nothing *more!*"

I open the door wider. "4:45 looks good on you, Sanders."

"Fuck you and coffee," she mumbles.

"Counter."

She pushes me out of the way and shuffles to the kitchen, and I go back to packing. "What are you doing here?"

"Coffee."

I look up at her. "You ran out of coffee?"

"Coffee first. Talk later."

"Right."

I finish packing, drop my bag by the door.

4:53. I need to get going, and she needs to tell me what's going on.

"Lane?" I slip on my shoes by the door. "What are you doing here?" I ask again. I should probably explain why nothing is making sense. Laney does *not* do well this early in the morning. That's an understatement. She doesn't even know how to function. Last time I had a meet she had to get up this early for, I picked her up, and she had on two different pairs of shoes, her arm through

223

the neck hole of her top and her jeans were inside out. After I helped her dress properly (the top half anyway—I left her to work out the whole jeans problem later) we got in the car, and she slept the entire drive, her head against the window and drool streaking down her chin. I found a parking spot, grabbed Wet Ones from the glove box I kept for Lachlan. I cleaned her up, helped her walk to the stands and wrapped her up in a blanket I brought specifically for that purpose. It took forever for me to register for the event, and when I got back to her, she was asleep. It wasn't until the first starter pistol that she shot up and realized where she was. She sent me a text right away.

Omg!
Did I miss it?
I fell asleep!
Did you win?

I was sitting right next to her. She jumped when she realized. Then she looked down at her lap, at her inside-out jeans. She covered her face. I told her she could fix it under the blanket. She told me it wasn't just that—she'd also forgotten to put on underwear. Then I *really* fucking regretted not helping her with that earlier.

NOW, she grabs a thermos from the top cabinet. She pours her coffee, then she walks past me, through the door, down the stairs and stands by my truck.

"You're coming with me?" I call out, still in my apartment.

She sips the coffee. Shivers. "Hurry up! We're going to be late!"

LANEY DOWNS the entire thermos (the equivalent of four cups of coffee) in less than five minutes, so it's no real surprise that halfway through the drive, she's dancing in my truck with Justin Timberlake blasting. "I love Justin Timberlake!" she shouts, winding down her window, causing her cheeks to redden, her hair to whip around. She looks over at me, displays her perfect teeth behind her perfect smile created by her perfect lips, and I want to punch Justin Timberlake in his perfect face.

I lower the volume, move on to her *other* love that isn't me. "You want to hit up that craft store while we're there?"

She stops dancing immediately, her eyes wide and on mine. "Don't tease, Luke."

"I'm not," I say. "My heats and final should be done by midday so we'll have time. Maybe grab food, too?"

She pouts. "I have to be at work by four, so we'll see."

WE GET TO THE TRACK, and I line up to register while Lane sits in the stands, a blanket around her shoulders, yarn and knitting needles ready. Garray cuts in line to get to me. He hushes the people behind me by saying, "Chill, bruhs, I'm just here for the tits." Then a few minute later, he laughs in their faces when he gives out his name, gets his number. "If you break your PB," he tells me, following me around like a sick puppy, "party at my house. My parents are… I don't know where, but they're sure as fuck not home."

"Cool," I tell him, but I'm distracted by Lane, her hands frozen, her gaze locked on the red Porsche pulling into the lot.

"Is she here for you?" he asks.

I point to the Porsche. "Or him. I'm not sure."

"You can't worry about that shit today. You're here on a mission. Focus." And he's right, of course, and focusing on Cooper is going to ruin that.

THERE ARE three heats in the Under 21s' hundred-meter sprint; each heat is an elimination round. I plan on flying through all of them, winning the final. I've done my research on the other competitors, and it's a given. But I'm not here to win or to compete against them. I'm here to compete against myself. Beating my PB will bring me one step closer to beating Cooper Kennedy's record. That's what I want. What I need. And I only have three more official races until the season's over, which is why I'm here. In a nonofficial school event that clocks official times.

I SIT NEXT TO LANE, wait until it's time to start warming up. "You think you could ask Garray to sit with me when you can't?" she asks, looking toward the end of the registration line where Cooper stands, watching her, me, *us*.

"Garray's running cross-country, so he'll be on the track a while," I tell her. "You want me to give him the money now, get it out of the way?"

"No," she says quickly. "He'll want to talk, and I don't want to—not yet. Not until you're done. This is your day." She turns to me, smiles. "How are you feeling? Confident? Scared? You're going to kill it. I can feel it."

"Yeah?" I ask, looking over at Cooper again. "You think he's going to give you a hard time?"

She cups my face, forces me to get lost in *those eyes*. "I don't want you worrying about him, okay? I want you to worry about you and about that PB and about where you're going to take me in twenty days."

I smile, I can't help it. I hold her wrists; *Keep touching me, Lane*, and say, "I have it all planned out." And it's true. I do.

"Can I do anything?"

I push my luck. "You could always give me an advance on that first-date kiss."

She rolls her eyes—*instinct*, but then bites down on her lip— *contemplation*. Then slowly, oh so slowly, she leans forward, presses her lips to mine.

Two seconds.

Zero heartbeats.

"Did it help?" she asks.

"You have no idea."

DAD SHOWS up with Lachy and the twins right before the first heat starts. They sit with Lane, and Lane points me out, and Dad smiles and waves. Lachlan gives me a thumbs up, and I return it while the twins check out the program. I win the race. I win another short, light kiss from Lane.

LOGAN AND LEO arrive just before the second heat. I didn't know they were coming but I'm happy they did, and I win that race, too.

226

They cheer from the stands—my brothers, my dad, my kind-of-now-but-definitely-soon-to-be girlfriend—all making me proud to be a Preston. I earn another kiss from Lane. When we actually do start dating, I'm going to ask for backpay on all my previous winnings. One kiss (or blowjob, whatever) for each win throughout my entire high school life.

I WIN THE THIRD HEAT, beat my PB. I don't need to see the clock to know I've done it; my body's already told me. So instead of looking at the screen, I look over at my family. Lane's the first to stand, her hand to her mouth. She says something to my dad, and he hollers, jumps, scares everyone around him and swear, this feeling, this *high*, is greater than sex, pre-Laney, of course.

"Close, but not close enough," Cooper says, cocky smirk and cocky face and cocky hair and cocky words, and I look up at Lane, see her hugging Lachlan and pointing to the screen showing my times, and I look at Cooper and realization smacks me in the face. This is *it* for him. His life is defined by what he does on this track. And me? My life is sitting in the stands, watching me, cheering me on.

I face Cooper, return his smirk.

One second.

Two.

"It was never about you, dude. Not with me." I motion to Lane sitting in the stands with *my* family. "And *definitely* not with her."

He shoves my chest, and I fall back a step, laugh at him. "That record's mine." It's a promise. A declaration. An oath.

I WIN THE FINAL, but I don't break Cooper's record. Not today. But I have three more races, and will, determination and *anger* are on my side. And like Cameron told me, emotion *always* wins.

I COLLECT MY TROPHIES, give them to Lachlan like I always do, and then spend the next hour in the craft store following Laney around like Garray did with me earlier—like a sick puppy and holy shit, there *are* a lot of analogies to do with dogs.

When we're done, Laney and I meet up with my family at the same diner we went to the first time we came here together. Lane orders the same two desserts, and I order almost everything on the menu because I'm fucking starving and the hour walking around aimlessly at the store nearly killed me, not that I'd tell her that.

Halfway through the meal, Laney grabs my arm, her eyes wide. "We forgot to give Cooper the money!"

"What money?" Dad asks.

I explain about the car situation, leave out the part about lending her some cash.

"Just give me the cash and I'll write a check," he says. "I'll send it to Lucy and she can give it to him. Unless..." He looks at Lane. "Did you want to hand it to him in person?"

Lane's quick to shake her head. "Not at all."

I take out my phone. Message Lucy.

Luke: Favor?

Lucy: Name it.

Luke: Dad's going to send you a check. Can you find Cooper on campus and give it to him?

Lucy: I'll have Cam do it. I can't even look at that guy without wanting to throw a brick at his face.

228

CHAPTER TWENTY-EIGHT

LUCAS

IT'S BEEN a long time since I've been to a party that didn't include cakes, cars and clowns (Lachlan's friends' birthdays), and so I feel a little out of place with the drinking and the shouting and the dry humping in dark corners. Garray said it was going to be small, mellow, chill. It's the opposite of all those things, and it takes me forever to find him sitting in his hot tub with a bunch of girls from the track team. "The man of the hour!" he shouts, and I have no idea who the people are that cheer for me, but I thank them anyway.

"I thought you said it was going to be small? Just the team."

"It was," he yells over the music. "I invited the team. They invited everyone else. Who fucking cares, bruh." He throws his arms out. "Enjoy it!"

I try to enjoy it. Honestly, I do. But sometime between last summer and now, this scene became no longer *my* scene, and I'd rather be sitting with Lane in the ticket booth *not* being paid to serve customers. I grab a beer from the cooler next to the hot tub and spend the next forty-three minutes wandering around, making awkward small talk. Then I find my way back out to Garray, still in the hot tub, making out with a girl I've never seen before. Or maybe I have, I don't know, I stopped paying attention a long time ago. I wait for him to take a break so I can tell him I'm leaving. He doesn't. I grab another beer, and I'll wait another ten minutes before I leave, with or without Garray's knowledge. I turn swiftly, bump my chin on the top of someone's head. "Oomph," she huffs.

"Sorry," I say, but all I can smell is coconuts and lime, and I look down at a sea of dark hair and "Laney?"

She looks up, adjusts her glasses. "I was going to do that whole arms-around-you-cover-your-eyes-guess-who thing, and it was supposed to be cute." She rubs her head, looks up at me with her nose scrunched, and she doesn't realize that without even trying, she's the fucking cutest girl here with her tight black jeans, torn at the front, her tight gray top and leather jacket, and I want to fold her up, put her in my pocket and keep her for myself.

"Aren't you supposed to be at work?"

"I got someone to cover my shift. I wanted to celebrate with you." She looks around. "I thought this was supposed to be small."

I hook my finger in her belt loop and pull until she stumbles forward, her eyes wide. I love her like this—her body pressed into mine and her breaths shallow. I dip my head, speak into her ear. "It can be small... it can just be you and me and a bottle of whatever you want. This house has five rooms, and those rooms have locks."

She steps back, bites her bottom lip, and fuck, I want to do the same. She says, "Anything but vodka." And I'm taking her hand, taking a bottle of whiskey from the cooler and taking her upstairs and into the first available room. It reeks of beer and sex and it's not at all romantic, but this isn't a date, and really, it's a Dumb Name party so it's to be expected. Still, I open a window, strip the bed, and sit in the middle. After a moment, Laney follows my lead. I uncap the bottle, hand it to her. "You trying to get me wasted, Preston?"

Yes. "No."

She takes a sip, passes it back. I decline.

"You not drinking with me?" she asks. Another sip.

"Someone needs to be sober to hold your hair when you puke."

She spits out the drink, liquid leaking out of her mouth, and I laugh, wipe it away with the sleeve of my sweatshirt. "You're a hot mess already."

Garray walks into the room—I forgot to lock the door—like he owns the place (whatever), and as soon as he sees Laney, he picks her up in a bear hug, giving zero fucks that he's dripping wet, and she's bone dry (for now), and she offers the world *that sound.* That reality-shifting, heart-stopping sound. She reaches for me, and I pull them apart, and now I'm wet because she's holding onto me.

Garray looks between us, finishes on Lane. "Who's the better kisser? Me or him?"

"Fuck off," I snap.

Now Grace is here with two of her friends, and the room is way too fucking small for this. "What's up, homewrecker?" she says to Lane. Then throws her drink in Lane's face.

I move Laney behind me, get in Grace's face. "What the fuck?"

"You need to leave," Garray tells her. "Now!"

Grace doesn't move, so Garray takes her by the shoulders, spins her around, forces her out of the room. "She'll be out of the house in two minutes," he assures.

I turn to Lane, her lips pursed, cheeks red. I say, "Sorry."

She uses my sweatshirt to wipe her face. "What the hell, Luke?"

"I have no idea. I haven't spoken to her since we broke up."

"And what *exactly* did you tell her when you broke up with her?" she asks, her breaths heavy, her anger spiking.

I lift my chin. "The truth."

"Which is?"

"That I was into you!"

Her eyes widen, her jaw drops, and then she sighs. "Well, I can't be mad at you now."

"Good. I don't want you to be."

She flops down on the bed, takes the bottle, and drinks way more than she should. "Do you feel different?"

"About?"

"About your new PB. I'm so proud of you. You've worked so hard, and it's all paying off."

My smile forms when hers does. "I still have to beat Coop—"

She covers my mouth with her hand. "Let's not talk about him. Not tonight. Not ever again."

Slowly, I pull her hand away. "What do you want to talk about?"

Her grin widens. "How hot you look tonight."

"Are you hitting on me, Sanders?"

She takes another long swig, her eyes staying on mine. She nods.

I smirk.

Game on, Laney.

AN HOUR LATER, I'm hauling her ass into a cab and telling the driver her address. While I didn't even get to start my second beer, she's slurring her words. Drunk Laney is Fun Laney. "Do you like?" she asks, throwing her feet over my legs. "The bootsh. Like?"

231

"Is she going to puke in my cab?" the driver asks, watching us in the rearview mirror.

Probably. "Nah, she's good." I squeeze her thighs, and she giggles into my arm. "She's a tough one."

"I am tough!" Laney announces. "Sticks and stones and fists and bones, right?"

I pat her crazy head and swear it, she *purrs*, moves closer to me. I don't count the seconds, the minutes it takes to get to her house because whatever it is, it's not long enough. I pay the cab driver when he gets us to Lane's sans puke (yay) and I get her into her room, take off her "bootsh," wait for her to dress in the bathroom and get her into her bed, safe and sound. I sit on the edge of the bed, look and smile down at her. Then I trace a finger across her forehead, move her bangs away from her eyes—eyes that drift shut at my touch. Her head lolls to the side and she sighs, licks her lips. "I love it when you do that," she whispers.

"Yeah?"

"It's as if you *have* to see me." Her eyes meet mine. "Sometimes when you look at me..." She grasps my wrist, places my hand over her heart. "Do you feel it?" she asks, and I close my eyes, focus on the touch.

Five seconds.

Eight heartbeats.

"You make my heart race, Lucas."

My eyes snap open. "Go on a date with me, Lane?"

"But—"

"But nothing. Don't you think we've waited long enough?"

"Yeah," she whispers. "I do."

"Tuesday?"

She nods. "Tuesday."

I kiss her forehead. "You need anything before I go?

She sits up. "Don't you want to stay?"

"Of course I *want* to stay." *But I don't trust myself with you, Lane.* "But I shouldn't."

"Yeah, you should," she says, nodding, her eyes wild. "You should also take off your t-shirt."

I chuckle. "I can't."

"Why?" she whines. "Besides, it's like, one in the morning. You have to get up in less than four hours, and by the time you walk home it'll be, like, 6 AM."

232

"It'll be ten minutes from now."

"But I *want* you to stay with me." She pouts, turns into a kid begging for candy. "Please?"

"Fine, but I'm not touching you."

"Good. I don't want you to touch me." She giggles, flops back down on the bed. "But you have to be shirtless."

"Lane," I warn, slipping off my shoes and removing my belt.

She watches me strip down to my boxers, her bottom lip caught between her teeth and her eyes hazy, from the alcohol or lust—I'm not sure, but I'm not willing to risk it, to regret it.

I get into bed, as far away from her as possible because the slightest touch could set me off. But she doesn't get the hint, she moves closer, her head on my chest, her breath warming my skin. Her hand flattens on my stomach, moves lower. Lower. "Lane," I warn again.

She kisses my jaw, and I can't catch my breath, and she says, "I said I didn't want you touching me. I didn't say anything about not wanting to touch *you*." Her fingers move, trace the outline of my stomach muscles and I clench my fists at my sides, try not to get hard, but I don't have control of my body, and my boxers are starting to feel really fucking tight. She kisses her way up my jaw to my ear. "I always get so turned on when I watch you race."

"Oh my God," I groan. "We shouldn't—"

"Are you hard?" she cuts in and her hand skims my erection, answering her question. "You want me to take care of it?"

Fuck, yes. "No." I grasp her wrist, stop her from moving. Then I shake my head, laugh at myself. "I can't believe I'm saying this."

"What?" she asks, the hurt in her voice unmistakable.

"As much as I want this, want *you*, I can't do it like this. When we do it again, I want to have earned it. I want it to mean everything. I don't want us to walk away with any regrets. From now on, I'm going to do it *right*."

CHAPTER TWENTY-NINE

LUCAS

TUESDAY COMES, my stomach in knots, and I'm a fucking wreck—more than the thirteen-year-old version of me pre-non-first-date with Laney. But there's so much more on the line now than there was then, and it needs to be perfect. *I* need to be perfect. She deserves nothing less.

I TEXT Leo when I get in my truck, tell him I'm on my way to get Lane.

He responds: *All systems go, Captain.*

I knock on the front door instead of her bedroom. Brian answers, his arms crossed. "First official date..." he says. "Come in, son." He opens the door wider, motions to the couch. I sit. "Lo, your date's here!" he calls out.

Brian eyes me up and down. "I should probably do the whole setting-the-rules-for-dating-my-daughter thing, huh?"

"Um..." I look around for Lane, but she's nowhere, and why the hell am I scared of a man who's told me he lets his girlfriend use her handcuffs on him? "If you feel like you need to."

"10 PM curfew," he says, and Lane's never had a curfew, at least not with me. He adds, "No drinking. No smoking. No sex."

I choke on my saliva.

He gets me water.

I down the entire glass.

He keeps going, "No touching below the waist. In fact, no touching at all. Not even to hold hands. No looking at her, even in her direction."

"Brian..."

"It's Sir to you, kid."

"Dad!" Thank fuck for Laney. "He's kidding," she says, and I stand up, turn to her and...

"Wow," I breathe out. She's wearing a long sleeve dress that reaches the floor, hides her skin but shows off her curves. "You look—"

"If you say overdressed I'm going to punch you."

"—ridiculously hot."

Brian clears his throat. "I think you mean *beautiful*, right?"

"Yes, *sir, Sir Sanders, sir.*"

Brian pats my back. "You need condoms? I buy 'em in bulk so I can spare a few."

"Dad!"

"YOUR DAD SEEMS REALLY HAPPY."

"It's the Misty mystique," she says, almost proudly. "He's so love-sick. It's sweet."

I settle a hand on her leg and start the drive back up to my house. When we enter the gates, she asks, "Did you forget something?"

"No. This is where we're having our date."

"Oh. Maybe I am overdressed."

"You're not overdressed. Are you disappointed?"

"Not at all."

I drive us past my apartment, past the main house, and she sits higher, looks around. "We going to the cabin?"

"No."

"Then where are we going?"

I stop the car, face her. "Hi," I say.

She smiles, her lips a light shade of red. "Hi."

"You really do look nice." I lean forward, run my nose along her neck. "And you smell incredible." It's true. She does. I noticed it the moment I was close enough to sniff her.

"It's the same perfume I wore on our first non-date," she tells me, and I already knew that. I spent an entire day in the perfume section at the mall trying to find the same one. I didn't. But I could never get the scent out of my mind. "So where are we going?" she asks again.

I pull back, hands on the wheel, and we start moving again. "It's a surprise."

We drive for another two minutes and thirty-eight seconds until Lachlan comes into view, jumping up and down holding a cardboard sign in the shape of an arrow that reads *Valet*. "They're here!" he shouts. "They're here! They're here!"

"What's going on?" Laney asks, her eyes as wide as her smile and I turn the car left, toward the lake, toward Logan standing in a bright green suit.

I stop the car next to him, and he opens Lane's door, helps her out of the truck. "Good evening, Madam. Fuck, you look hot."

"Quit it," I say, handing him the keys.

"Where's my tip?" he asks at the same time Leo says, standing in a suit behind a makeshift host stand we stole from the props department in the drama room, "Table for two?"

Lane grasps my arm to her chest, giggling with excitement. "What is happening right now?" She doesn't realize that this is just the beginning, that I'd been planning this for longer than I'd like to admit.

"This way," Leo says, taking two sheets of paper (menus) and leading us through the woods, toward the lake, the dock.

"Oh my God," Lane whispers, her feet glued to the ground. She looks out over the lake, and I look at her. I find myself smiling, watching her take in the view of the fairy lights hanging above the dock, a single table and two chairs set up at the end, all items leftover from Lucy's wedding. My brothers and I had spent the entire afternoon since we got home from school setting it up. Luckily, it's a calm evening, no wind, no rain. Just the onset of the dipping of the sun behind the horizon making *those eyes* a fiery orange. "Lucas, this is…"

"What our first date should've been a long time ago."

"Please to follow me," Leo says, his Italian accent *horrid*.

Lane laughs, finds her feet, and we follow him to the table. I pull out her seat and look down her cleavage (I'm a gentleman *and* a dude), then I take my spot opposite her.

"Here's to you, your meals for the evening, signora," Leo says, setting the menu in front of her. I should've paid him extra to wear a fake mustache and a fedora. As soon as he leaves, Laney takes my hand resting on the table. "Luke, this is all too much."

It's not enough. "Have you seen the menu?"

Her eyes drop to the menu, then she gasps, and I've never been more in love with her than I am at this moment, with the sun setting, her dark hair in that braid I love. She's *here*. *With* me. *For* me. Finally. And then she laughs and this time, reality doesn't shift. Doesn't change. Because reality is perfect. She's perfect. *We're going to be perfect, Laney. You'll see.*

"This is from Pino's?" she asks. *Her favorite dishes from her favorite restaurant because I'm* that *good.* "But Pino's doesn't do take out. How did you…" She looks at me, makes me feel like a god.

I shrug. "I worked on the head chef's remodel over the summer. I called in a favor."

She offers a smile. So shy, so sweet, so Laney.

The twins walk up the dock, matching suits, a food tray each. "No!" Laney says through a giggle. "How much did you have to pay them to do this?"

I shake my head. "You don't want to know."

"Luke!" She shows me her hands. "I'm, like, shaking with excitement right now!"

WE EAT THE FOOD, and she makes *those sounds,* and I chuckle. When she asks what's funny, I tell her, "I just wish I was the one causing you to make those sounds."

She doesn't skip a beat. "Me, too."

I choke on my food.

"What?" she says, shrugging. *Casual Laney.* "Don't think I forgot about Saturday night. You left me all frustrated and I had to, you know, take care of it myself."

"Oh my God." I cover my face, try to ignore the stirring in my pants. I should walk around to her side, bend her over the table and take her right here. Right now. And I'll show her… she'll never be able to get off on her own again.

"Dessert," Linc and Liam say in sync.

I jump in my seat. *When the fuck did they get here?*

Laney laughs at me, and I shake my head, glare at her. "You're bad," I mouth.

She waits for the boys to leave. "I can be bad," she says, and I fucking *love* Dirty Laney.

238

AFTER THE *PHENOMENAL* DINNER—her words, not mine—I drive us to the movies, help her out of the truck, and hold her hand to the ticket booth I've spent many unpaid hours "working."

"Two please, Evan," I tell the kid behind the counter, pushing over my cash through the window. By now, I know almost everyone Lane works with, and they know me.

He pushes my cash back. "Employees get in for free."

"I'm not an employee."

He points to Lane. "But she is."

I sigh. "Look, this is kind of a do-over date because I messed up the first time we did this, and she paid for her ticket when I should've paid—"

"That's kind of a dick move," Evan tells me.

Laney chimes in, "Technically, it *wasn't* a date."

"Still." Evan shrugs. "I didn't make you pay for your ticket on *our* first date."

"Seriously?" I look between the two of them.

Lane rolls her eyes, puts her hand on my chest because she *knows* I'm two seconds away from opening that side door and—

"We got in for free, Evan," she says. "No one paid."

I grunt. "Just take my money, dude."

He takes my money, keeps the change for himself.

The same thing happens at the food counter. The *exact* same thing. Zane, the kid working the counter, also refuses to take my money, *also* makes a comment about him dating Lane and *what the fuck, Lane?*

"YOU'RE MAD?" Lane whispers, sitting next to me in the empty theater, previews rolling.

I cross my arms. "So what if I am?"

"Luke, you can't be mad that I've dated. I can be at school and spit in any direction, and it'll land on some girl you've *screwed*. Not just dated."

"I just don't like the idea of you being with someone else."

"Seriously?"

"Yes."

"You're an idiot."

"What?"

"You're an idiot," she repeats.

"That's real nice, Lane."

She leans closer; her whispered words slice the air, slice my heart. "I've had to sit around for years watching you date girl after girl after goddamn girl. I've listened to you talk about them, talk about *having sex* with them. And not once have I ever shown you how upsetting it was for me. I had to put up with it for years! You can deal with it for one night!" She rears back, but she doesn't get far. I take her face in my hands and I kiss her, claim her, and I hate when she's right and I'm wrong and she's everything and I'm nothing. I swipe my tongue across hers, not wanting my frustration to show in the kiss, and I go slowly, gently, until I feel her relax beneath my touch, and her hands go to my hair and she's kissing away the anger, the pain, and it's been so long, too long, since we've kissed like this and I must've forced myself to forget what it felt like to be kissed by her because she's everything that's perfect in the world. The lights dim, and the movie plays and we pull apart, laugh quietly. We watch the movie with my arm around her and her hand on my stomach, and it's perfect, like it should've been years ago.

I TAKE HER HOME AFTERWARD, walk her to the front door. She's blushing when she turns to me, and I take both her hands in mine.

"I had a really good time, Luke." She moves our hands behind her back, leans up on her toes, kisses me once. "I like this," she says. "It's nice. You and me. *Us.*"

Say it, Luke. Tell her you love her. I swallow, nervous.

She says, "I think I'm going to drive myself to school in the morning."

"Why?"

She motions to her car. "Because it's just a car. It doesn't mean anything. *Cooper* doesn't mean anything. Not anymore."

I GET HOME, get into bed, and immediately shove my hands down my shorts. But then my phone rings and Laney's name flashes on the screen and I force myself to wait. What's another few minutes?

"Hey," she says. "Remember that first week I spent with you, and then on Sunday night, I called and we spoke on the phone for hours?"

240

I take my hand out of my shorts. "I remember."

"I guess I'm just missing you already. Lame, right?"

"No. I miss you, too."

"Did you, um..." She takes a breath. "It kind of seemed like you wanted to say something when you walked me to the door, but you held off."

"Yeah," I admit, sighing. "I did."

"What did you want to say?"

I run a hand through my hair, stare up at the ceiling. "You know what I wanted to say."

She's quiet a beat. Then: "Why didn't you say it?"

"I don't know," I mumble. "I guess it felt wrong to say it, but it definitely feels right to *live* it."

CHAPTER THIRTY

LUCAS

FOR THE NEXT couple of weeks, Laney and I date... without the actual dating part. We sneak in a kiss now and then, a boob grab sporadically, but besides that we don't have a lot of spare time. With me practicing four days a week instead of three and her working every possible shift she can get to earn the money she so adamantly needs to pay back, it doesn't leave room for much else. Now Dad's gone on a business trip for a week, leaving Leo and me in charge which means I'm sleeping in the main house and I'm starting to lose my damn mind.

My family responsibilities had always been a problem with my previous girlfriends; I didn't spend enough time with them, I didn't take them on enough dates, I didn't answer every single phone call every five minutes and why the hell did I have to be home at seven, on the dot, every night? They didn't understand. But Laney does. "Maybe I should stay here for the week while your dad's gone. Help out when I can?"

"You're sweet," I tell her, leaning on the kitchen counter flipping through one of Mom's old recipe books for something I can make for Lachlan's bake sale *tomorrow*. "But I don't want you sleeping in the apartment by yourself, and I don't think Dad would let you sleep in here. Do we have cocoa powder?"

She checks the pantry. "Nope. What are you looking for?"

"Lachy's got a bake sale, and I need to make twenty-five of something."

"You're going to *bake*?"

"I'm going to try," I say, flip, flip, flipping the pages. "And I need to do it soon because I have so much homework to do and I need to help Logan with his and make sure he does his piss cup and oh! Maybe you can bring the cup to Misty if she's staying at your house, it saves me a trip."

Her nose scrunches.

"Yeah. I didn't think that one through."

"Where's Leo?"

"Basketball practice with the twins."

"Okay," she says, "I'm not going to touch a cup with Logan's urine in it, but how about *I* do the baking, you do your homework, and when the cookies are in the oven, I'll help Logan with his?"

"Cookies?"

"They're quick and easy and"—she closes the recipe book—"I don't need a recipe and you already have all the ingredients."

"Really?" I ask, my shoulders suddenly rid of the weight they'd been carrying. "Are you sure?"

"I'm positive."

I hug her tight, squeeze her boob.

TWENTY MINUTES later I'm at the kitchen table drowning in textbooks and websites, and Lane's got the cookies in the oven. Logan walks in through the back door (God knows where he's been) and sniffs the air. "What the hell is that? It's like heaven in my nostrils."

"Cookies," Lane tells him. "And you can have one as soon as you finish your homework. Go get your books."

"No," he says.

She puts her hand on her waist, raises an eyebrow. Intimidating Laney is fucking hot.

Logan rolls his eyes, looks at me as he passes. "I liked her better when you weren't dipping your cock in her."

I stick my foot out, he trips over it, lands on his side. "Watch your fucking mouth."

"Fucking mouth!" Lachlan yells. Seriously, *where the hell do all these people come from?*

Lane kneels in front of him. "Don't repeat what people say," she says.

"Don't repeat what people say." He giggles.

"Cheeky boy." She ruffles his hair. "Can you go up to your room and build me a skyscraper with your Legos?"

244

"Yes, ma'am!" And he's off, and Logan's up, and Laney's checking on the cookies, and I say, "You're going to be a great mom someday."

She smiles. "Well, I have your mom to thank for that."

It hurts my heart to know that she didn't have that, that the little time she spent with my mom is all she has for guidance. "Hey, did your mom contact you on your birthday?"

She laughs once, bitter. "Did you expect her to?"

I shrug. "I was hoping."

Her head tilts to the side and she watches me a moment, then she takes the chair next to mine. "We're basically strangers now, and I think it's been like that ever since I left but I didn't want to admit it. Sometimes I think about her, you know? And I wonder if she does the same with me. I get this romantic notion in my head that one day she'll appear out of nowhere and realize she misses me. It's so pathetic."

"It's not," I say quickly, settling my hand on her knee. "She's still around, so it's always a possibility. With my mom, it was like… one night I fell asleep, and the next morning she was gone."

"I'm sorry, Luke," she says. And I know she is.

"I have this fear," I tell her, and I don't know if I should, but I do. "That one day, I'm going to wake up and you won't be here. You'll be gone, just like she was. And I know it sounds stupid but losing her… you saw what that did to me. You were there. And if anything ever happened to my brothers or to *you*…"

"Stop," she whispers, holding my head in her hands. "Nothing's going to happen."

I tilt my head, kiss her palm. "You know how I feel about you, right?"

"I know." She smiles. "Me too."

ONCE EVERYONE'S DOWN for the night, I call Dad from my old bedroom. I catch him up on what's been going on, assure him that everything's okay. He asks about the bake sale, and I tell him Lane took care of it.

"Is she staying at the house while I'm gone?" he asks.

"No. I know the rules."

He chuckles. "I figured you'd know that the rules don't apply to Lane."

"What do you mean?"

"The boys see her as a constant around the house. If it's going to help to have her around she can stay with you."

"But—"

"Only if you want her to."

"It would help *so* much."

"I trust you, Luke, and I trust her. Just don't give me a reason to regret that."

"Okay."

"And if Logan has something to say—if he thinks my decision is setting some sort of precedent, just get him to pee in a cup every hour. My orders."

I laugh. "Okay."

"I love you, son, and thank you."

"Love you, too, Dad."

The words are so simple, so rehearsed, and yet I can't even say it to the girl who holds my heart.

I text Lane, tell her the news.

She sends me back a ton of emojis insinuating hand jobs and blowjobs and wild monkey sex. I write back: *With my brothers in the house?*

She replies: *Gross. But cuggles?*

All damn night, baby!

I'D LOVE to say that cuggling Laney is amazing, but I wouldn't fucking know because some seven-year-old germ keeps crawling into bed with us at night and my girlfriend keeps letting him. Five nights she's spent with us, and all five nights there have been three in the bed and the little one said, "I'm in the middle!" But really, I shouldn't complain because having her around helps a lot. I don't think the house has ever been this clean and organized, and we're eating more than just pizza and take out, and the twins ask her if she can move in permanently. Brian and Misty have checked in twice, probably hoping we haven't killed her or scarred her for life, but I wasn't kidding when I told her she'd be a good mother. The one problem would be getting her up in the mornings. The only thing that works now is a reach-over-Lachy vicious boob grab and even then, it still takes her three coffees to function as a human.

246

NOW, we're sitting on the dock, *alone*, for some much-deserved peace and quiet. I'm lying on my back and she's resting on her elbow, leaning over me. She strokes my jaw, pouts down at me, waits for my anger to fade. That kid Evan from her work has been texting her, asking what's up. Last night, I went to pick her up and he was in *my* booth with her.

"You're being ridiculous, Luke!"

"Just tell me how far you guys went and I'll stop," I grumble, arms crossed.

Smiling, she says, "Trying not to laugh when you're like this is like trying to keep it together when a toddler yells, 'Fuck' in the middle of a busy store."

Next to us, our textbooks sit, open but forgotten. "It's not funny, Lane." I gently push her hand away. "You're so secretive about it all. I don't like Secretive Laney!"

After a sigh, she settles her head on my shoulder. "We didn't even kiss, and just so you know, I hadn't done anything but kiss with any other guy before you."

"Not even a handy?"

"Oh my God." She giggles. "No."

"Dad's coming home tonight, so maybe I can have one of those," I try to joke.

She sits up again, looks down at me. "Not if you keep talking about guys touching me."

"I didn't say anything about guys touching you. I said *you* touching them! Did he touch you? I'll kill 'em dead, babe."

"Luke, stop."

"Did they? Just a little tit tap?"

"Enough!"

I almost ask her about how far she went with Cooper, but I already know the answer and it's making me want to jump in the lake and drown myself.

"Are you hungry?" she asks. "You always get cranky when you're hungry."

I cross my arms again. "A little," I admit, then tug on her shirt for her to lie down with me again. She's closer now, her arm and leg over me, her fingers tapping on my chest. I shift her so she's on top of me, my legs spread, hers between them.

247

She says, her forearms on my chest and her fingertips stroking my jaw, "Do you know how many times I dreamed about this?"

"About what?"

"Laying here with you. This close. Having you touch me the way you are, being able to look at you and not fear getting caught." She dips her head, kisses me once. "Being able to kiss you."

"Same," I admit. "Sometimes I'd see Cam and Luce out here and imagine it was us."

Her lips twitch, curve up at the corners. "Really?"

I nod. "Really." Then I look around, make sure we're alone. "You want to fool around a little?"

Her eyes roll, but her smile spreads. "I guess."

Making out with Laney is equivalent to having sex with any other girl. Swear it. I'm hard before her mouth meets mine and I wish we weren't out here, in the open, because I know we're not getting much further but the kissing alone drives us both insane. She moves to straddle me, her hips jerking back and forth, rubbing against me in all the right ways. She whispers my name, her mouth still on mine, and I reach up the front of her shirt and cup her breasts. Her movements change, thrusting and grinding, and I decide here and now to make her come because I've been craving *those* sounds. She bites down on my lip, and I know she's close so I grab her ass, lift my hips higher so—"Are you sexing?" Lachlan shouts, and Lane rolls off me so fast she almost falls off the dock and into the water.

I sit up, scan our surroundings, and see Lachlan hiding behind a tree. "What the hell are you doing?" I shout, my cock aching in my jeans. "You know you're not allowed to be this close to the lake on your own! Who's meant to be watching you?"

He breaks out in a giggle and Laney's on her feet, picking up our books.

I don't get up yet, not really ready to have the conversation with Lachlan about what the bulge is in the front of my pants.

"Who's watching you, bud?" Lane coos.

Girls have it easy. They can be turned on, come in their pants and no one knows. I've got the Leaning Tower of Pisa poking my zipper.

Lachy walks toward us, a bunch of sticks in his hand. "Linc and Liam," he tells us.

"Well, where the fuck are they?" I snap.

248

Lane gasps. "Luke!"

Lachy laughs. "Luke said fuck."

"Don't say that word, buddy," Lane tells him.

I adjust myself and get up, hoping it's not too obvious. "We're not done," I tell Lane, walking past her to get to Lachlan. "Where are they?" I ask him.

He shrugs. "In the house."

"And you just left?"

"They're fighting. Linc's got a baseball bat and he's shouting at Liam."

I take his hand. "Come on."

WE HEAR Linc yelling before we get to the inner fence. "Tell me!" he shouts, "I'll kill 'em."

I meet Lane's panicked eyes and we dash for the house, Lachlan in tow.

Linc's pacing the living room, baseball bat over his shoulder while Liam... *"Holy shit.* What happened?" I sit on the couch next to him. There's blood on his lip, a gash above his eye. His elbows are grazed, his glasses crooked. I glare up at Linc. "What did you do?"

"It wasn't me!" he shouts.

Lane's on the other side of Liam now, her touch gentle as she checks over his face. "Are you okay?"

Liam presses his lips tight, shaking his head and refusing to answer.

My heart pounds, fear choking me.

"Tell me!" Linc yells.

"What the hell happened?" I boom, hearing Dad in my tone.

Linc stops pacing just long enough to say, "I had detention after school and Liam had to get Lachlan and I came home and he was like this."

"It happened before I got Lachlan," Liam croaks, his words rushed, his eyes darting between Lane and me. "Lachlan didn't see anything. I swear."

"It's okay," Laney says, hugging him to her.

I inhale deeply, exhale slowly, try to think of the right thing to do.

"Was it Benny and his boys?" Linc yells. "Swear, I'm going to kill them all."

"Stop it!" Liam cries.

Laney holds him tighter.

"That Benny Watson kid?" I ask.

Linc nods. "He called Liam a fag at school today."

"I'm not a fag!"

Linc sighs, his tone calmer when he says. "I *know* you're not, but even if you are, who cares." This is the dynamic of the twins. Even though they both get bullied, Liam has it worse because of his glasses and braces, and no matter how many times I tell him it'll pass—that I've been there—he gets defensive and Lincoln gets angry, set on war.

"Did Benny do this?" I ask, tone clipped. Watching your little brother break down and not being able to do anything about it is fucking crushing. Liam's sobs fill the room and Lincoln looks to me for answers—answers I don't have.

"I'm going to kill him," Linc grinds out.

"No, you won't," I snap. "I'll take care of it."

"Don't tell Dad," Liam cries.

I say, "I think we have to, dude."

"You know what I think?" Laney says. She rears back, holds Liam's face in her hands. "I think you look a lot like Luke when he was your age. Glasses, braces, everything. And I crushed so hard on him back then. You're so handsome, and you're just going to get better looking as the years go on." She glances at me, and I smile. I can't help it. "Screw those guys, Liam. They're just jealous of how *great* you are."

Liam sniffs. "You know what would make me feel better?" he mumbles.

"What?" she asks.

Then he moves in and fucking *kisses* her. And I'm not talking a peck on the lips, I'm talking full make out, sloppy twelve-year-old tongue and everything. Lane's eyes widen, but then she laughs, his mouth covering hers and she lets him go on... until he grabs her boob, and *I've* had enough. I pull him away by his shirt while silent shock fills the room. Then Liam chuckles and Linc bursts out laughing. Liam gets up and his twin follows after him. They cackle all the way to the back door. "I can't believe you did that!" Linc says.

Liam laughs.

"What do her boobs feel like?" Linc asks.

I groan.

"Like melons?" he pushes.

Liam laughs harder as he opens the back door. "Like peaches!"

I look over at Lane, raise an eyebrow. "What the hell was that?"

She shrugs, giggles. "At least he's better now," she says, straightening her clothes. "You did good, Luke." Then she moves toward me, her lips puckered, and my nose scrunches, disgusted.

"Can you, like, gargle some mouthwash? I can't kiss you when you've got traces of my brother in your mouth."

She laughs but complies, and I sit on the couch and stare at the ceiling, wondering how the hell I'm going to handle this. She returns, her smile from ear-to-ear, and sits across my lap. "This good?" She kisses me, her minty lips reminding me of what we started. I adjust us so we're lying on the couch, on our sides, and I return her kiss with more passion, more power. And I realize that her baggage might be her exes, but mine is my family. Hers are gone, but mine is forever. "Thank you," I tell her between kisses.

"For what?"

"For being here and making everything okay again."

She kisses me harder, her hands going between us, her fingers playing with my belt while mine sneak under the band of her jeans, and I get lost in the moment, in Laney. Until Lachlan cries, "Who's supposed to be watching me?"

"Dammit," I moan. I look up to see Lachlan standing beside us, his hand stuck in a fucking vase.

"It hurts," he sobs.

Sighing, I sit up, moving Laney to the side so I can see his hand. "How did you even do this?"

"It hurts!" he screams. "It's going purple, Lucas! Fix it!"

It is going purple and my fear is back and I'm on my knees trying to pull his hand out. It won't budge, so I panic some more and start smashing it against the coffee table, but the vase is plastic and Lachlan's crying louder, and I'm shouting louder for him to stop crying and now his hand's turning blue and "How did this happen?" I yell. Smash, smash, smash on the table.

"Here," Laney says, hand on my shoulder. She pushes me away, and I fall back on my heels, watch her pour baby oil into the vase and all over Lachlan's arm and then *pop*. His hand releases and she scruffs his hair and tells him to wash his hands, but he's rubbing the oil all over his clothes instead.

I look up, breathe, ask, "Where did you get the oil?"

She doesn't have time to answer before the door opens, and Logan steps in. "What are you doing with my baby oil?"

"Logan!" Leo screams, marching in after him.

Logan walks across the living room toward the kitchen, Leo on his heels. "It's not my fault she's into me, man."

"Look at me when I'm talking to you!" Leo yells.

Logan spins, rolls his eyes.

"What now?" I ask.

Leo glares at Logan, speaks to me. "I caught Logan making out with my girlfriend."

"What?" Lane shrieks.

"So what? She's hot!" Logan says.

Leo punches him square in the face, and a moment later, Lachlan's tiny, oily fist gets me in the jaw.

"Enough! Everyone in the minivan! Now!" Lane shouts, and when Lane shouts, we *all* listen.

We pile into the minivan, one by one, and once we're all seated, she asks, "What do you boys want for dinner?"

Six voices shout out five different meals (the twins choose the same), and she notes them all down in her phone. Then she drives us to the grocery store and dumps a bunch of stuff in the cart while we all follow silently behind her because when Laney gets like this, we know she means business. She makes me pay for the groceries and then we head home. As soon as I'm done unpacking the bags, she says, "You need to go!"

"Go where?"

"You have the parent-teacher interview with Lachlan."

"Shit."

"Shit shit shit!" Lachlan shouts.

<hr />

LACHLAN'S TEACHER—a woman in her mid-forties with bright red, frizzy hair—seems disappointed that it's me at the interview and not Dad. I tell her Dad's away on business, and she gets that look in her eyes—worry—as if she should be calling CPS to check in on us. I look over at Lachlan, make sure there are no bruises or scratches or general *boy* injuries, but he's clean. If it weren't for the stains on his shirt and if he didn't smell like he'd been bathing in baby oil, I'd have nothing to worry about.

I give her my most charming smile, compliment her hair, and she grins. Moves on. She says that Lachlan's doing well, but he loses focus. A lot. He also finds it necessary to interrupt the class by standing up and singing inappropriate songs. "The other day, he told the kids in his class to..." Her voice lowers when she adds, *"eat his booty like groceries."*

I stifle my laugh.

She sighs. "Maybe I should make another appointment with your father?"

"I'm sorry," I say, straightening my features. "Could he be like..."—I push my luck—"one of those kids who's exceptionally gifted and the class work is just too easy for him?"

"No."

"It could be—"

"No."

"But he's—"

"No, Lucas. Lachlan's not *exceptionally gifted*. I think you should find him an activity to focus on. Maybe start something this summer."

"Like what? Baseball?"

"Baseball sounds great. It'll give him the opportunity to play with kids his age instead of all his older brothers. Also, I'd recommend that you boys watch your language around him. We've had several parents complain that Lachlan's the one teaching their kids swear words."

Lachlan stands, shoves his finger in his teacher's face. "That's bullshit, lady!"

BY THE TIME I get home, Dad's here and they're all seated at the kitchen table, waiting, five different meals set out in front of them.

"Sit," she tells me, so I do. Dad's eyes meet mine, and he motions to Liam's damaged face. I jerk my head once. *Not now.* Laney picks up a bowl filled with a bunch of folded paper and says, "You will all select one piece of paper from this bowl. This bowl has each of your names in it. You will go in age order, starting with your Dad, and you will say one thing you love about the person on that paper. Understood?"

"Yes, ma'am," my brothers say.

"Good. Eat." She marches toward me, kisses my cheek. "I'll be in your apartment."

I SPEND two hours with my family at the kitchen table. We don't grab the names from the bowl, we don't talk about the things we love about each other. Instead, we spend that time talking about the things we love about Laney. And I carry their love, along with my own, as I climb the steps to my apartment, my heart full.

She's sitting on the couch watching TV when I open the door. "How did it go?" she asks, not looking up.

"It was... eye-opening." I move behind the couch, shift her hair off her shoulder and kiss her neck. "Meet me in the bedroom?"

When she gets into bed, the first and only thing I do is *cuggles* her.

She falls asleep almost instantly, not used to living off of such little sleep.

I spend the next eighteen minutes watching her sleep and after realizing what I'm doing, I try to convince myself that I'm not a creep. That it's completely normal to be doing what I'm doing because she *is* my girlfriend and I *do* love her. I want to shout it from the rooftops... but I'm not *that* creepy, and I'm also a little afraid of heights. And where did that expression come from anyway? In what world is the area small enough that a message from a rooftop could be heard? Was there no wind around to carry the dude's voice? Fuck, I need sleep. And I also need to claim Lane (because it's the 1950s and women are property, apparently). So I do our generation's version of rooftops and dame claims; I make us Facebook official.

Take that, Cooper Kennedy.

I pull her closer to me, a smile on my face, until I remember the day we had and the shit Liam's going through. I scan my brain, try to think of ways to fix it, but I come up blank. And so I do the only thing I know to do; I contact the one person I look up to for guidance when it comes to dealing with my brothers: Cameron, our brother-in-law.

CHAPTER THIRTY-ONE

LUCAS

CAMERON SITS in a recliner as if he's The Godfather, chewing on a fake cigar with a smirk on his lips. We're in Lucy's cabin with Cam's friends "Big Logan" and Jake while Lucy and Lane are in the apartment.

AS SOON AS I told Cameron what was going on with Liam and Linc, he promised to come home for the weekend and bring some reinforcements. They'd already planned out everything by the time I meet them on Friday night.

Jake says, his Australian accent thick, "We need to discuss possible roadblocks."

Logan nods. "Women."

Cam grunts and keeps his same tone when he says, "I'll take care of the wife." Then he points to me.

"Um…" I look between them. *Crazy assholes.* "Lane's working, so she won't be a problem. Also, you guys are fucking weird."

Jake chuckles.

Logan rubs his hands together. "Middle School Mayhem, motherfuckers!"

THE PLAN IS SIMPLE, really, and besides me walking the streets to pick up dog shit in the middle of the night, my brother Logan pissing into a different type of cup, and Cameron fucking with the chains on Benny Watson's bike during his little league baseball game, my brothers and I stay out of the *actual* mayhem. It's too obvious if people see us; six Preston punks plus our brother-in-law? Yeah, we're kind of hard to miss. But we all wanted to be here to see it go down, so we watch from behind the tinted windows of the minivan. "Here he comes!" Linc whispers, and we all scoot to one side of the van, press our noses to the windows.

"How far do you think he can get?" Logan asks Cam.

"Not far."

"This is bad," Liam says. "You guys, maybe we shouldn't do this."

"Shut up!" Linc snaps. "He called you a fag and beat the crap out of you. This is nothing compared."

"What's a fag?" Lachlan asks.

Logan groans. "I told you we shouldn't have brought him."

Lachlan repeats the question.

Leo says, "It's a guy who likes other guys."

"Why is that bad?" Lachlan questions.

"It's not," I tell him. "Come here." I rear back so he can sit in front of me and see what's going on. Then I point to Benny Watson. "See that kid getting on the bike?"

He nods.

"He wasn't very nice to Liam. He hurt him."

"Inside or outside?"

"Both," I tell him. "And you remember Cam and Lucy's friends Jake and Big Logan?"

He nods again.

"They're here to help him understand why it's wrong to hurt people."

Benny starts to pedal, and it takes less than three seconds for the bike to lock up. The little punk flies over the handlebars and falls on all fours, and I almost feel sorry for him. But then I look over at Liam and the damage on his face and arms and that feeling fades real quick. My brothers stifle their laughs while they watch part two of Middle School Mayhem come to fruition. Big Logan and Jake rush toward him, perfect in their display of fake concern. Cam puts his phone on speaker, connected to Jake's phone so we can hear what they're saying. "You okay, mate?" Jake asks. He and Big Logan squat in front of Benny, a hand on each of his shoulders.

"That was rough, dude," Logan says, his voice dripping with worry.

Benny looks up at them, tears in his eyes, and I wonder what Liam was like when he was copping a fucking beating from this asshole.

"Here." Jake slips a backpack off his shoulders and unzips it. "You look like you're about to pass out. You need to eat something." He pulls out the gourmet dog shit/peanut butter sandwich I crafted and hands it over to Benny. "You'll feel better," Jake pushes.

Benny takes a bite, munches a few times before spitting it out and cursing. The minivan erupts with laughter while Jake shakes his head, his brow bunched. "What's wrong, little man?"

Benny's still splattering everywhere, his tongue out, trying to get the taste of shit off his tongue. "What the hell is that?"

Jake shrugs. "Peanut butter and vegemite. Sorry, man. Must be an acquired taste." He takes the Logan-piss-filled drink bottle from the backpack. "You want to wash it down with something?"

Without a thought, Benny takes the bottle from him, tilts his head back, lifts the bottle, and squeezes. As soon as the liquid hits his tongue, his eyes squeeze shut, and he coughs and spurts everywhere.

Dying. We're fucking dying in the minivan, watching it all go down, and Benny tries to stand, but Jake keeps him in place. Benny's nothing but flailing arms and legs. "What the fuck?!" he shouts.

Big Logan says, "Ur-ine a lot of trouble here, kid."

Jake chuckles.

"Who the fuck are you?" Benny screams.

"We're delivering a message from Liam and Lincoln," Jake says. "You fuck with the Prestons, you fuck with their friends. You so much as look in their direction, you'll be eating more than dog shit and piss. You got it?"

I'd put money that Benny's pissing his pants right now. "Y-y-yes, sir."

They smile brightly at him and help him to his feet. "Have a fantastic day!" Big Logan exaggerates. "*Asshole.*"

Middle School Mayhem is *great.*

LATER IN THE afternoon while I walk to my truck, Cam calls out, running up to me.

257

"What's up?" I ask.

"We need to talk."

"I have to pick Laney up from work."

"It's quick," he says. "You know that check you sent us to give Cooper?"

"Yeah?"

"I can't find him on campus."

"What do you mean you can't *find* him?"

He shrugs. "He hasn't been in his dorm for days, and I asked Jake to ask around… jocks, you know, they stick together."

"And?"

"And Jake says no one on the track team's seen him for a while. He's missed training the last couple days. That jerk's AWOL."

I KEEP this information from Lane when I pick her up from work which I don't feel *too* bad about. It's not like she's asked, and come to think of it, her phone hasn't been blowing up the way it used to. At least not when I'm around.

I tell her about what happened today, the shit sandwich and piss bottle, and she's sad she missed out on it. I thought she'd be disappointed in the way we chose to retaliate, and I tell her that. She shakes her head, says, "You know, I followed that little punk home from school one day so I could see where he lives and speak to his parents. His dad's just as vile and pathetic as he is."

We go to her house to pick up her sewing machine to go with all the other crafting supplies she keeps in *our* little apartment where we *still* haven't had sex because we're taking it slow, doing it *right*. And then we go back home where we save dinner by "helping" Lucy in the kitchen, which means taking over without Lucy realizing it. After we eat, I help Lachlan with his bath and his bedtime and his one minute, and Lucy invites us to hang out at the cabin. Lane says she wants to shower, so she does that while I wait in the living room. Then her phone rings, and I know I shouldn't look, shouldn't answer. But I do look, and I see Cooper's name flash on the screen, and I *do* answer because I want to know what the hell he *still* wants and where the hell he is.

I don't speak when the call connects, just listen to him breathe. "Lois?" he says, and I keep quiet. "Why haven't you answered any of my calls, baby?" *Baby?* Seriously? At least I know she's not talking to him, listening to his blended, spoon-fed bullshit. "I need to see you. Just once. Please, Lo." He exhales into the phone while I hold my breath, waiting for more. "Please, baby." And I've had enough and I hang up because he's nothing but poison in her veins, and the sooner he's out of her system, the better off she'll be. I go through her phone, through the missed calls and messages. If he's been messaging her, she's been deleting them because there isn't a single one there. But there are a *lot* of missed calls from him. Too many to count. She's probably tried to delete that evidence, too, but she doesn't know how to because she's one of the few in our generation who can survive without an iPhone glued to her hand. I delete the call just made, the one that shows I picked up, and when she gets out of the bathroom, her hair still wet, I pretend like nothing happened. Because really, nothing *did* happen.

<hr>

AT THE CABIN, I tell Cameron about the interview with Lachlan's teacher and how she recommended Lachlan get into some form of organized sport. "I was looking into getting him on a baseball team during the summer league, but they're all full. But, the league's still accepting new teams…"

He eyes me sideways. "So what? You want to start a whole new team?"

"Not just me. *You and me,* and I thought the twins could help assist, you know, give them something to do during the break? We can throw in a few bucks, get the company to sponsor them, get some uniforms. It's not too late."

He thinks about this a moment. "You know, if we do that it'll be a bunch of Lachlan's friends, and you've met Lachlan's friends, right?"

I chuckle. "We could name the team The Misfits."

Cameron says he's in and that it'll be good times. Then somehow, the conversation switches to the senior prom. Lane smiles at me from across the room, and I wonder if she remembers the pact we made on her sixteenth birthday; that regardless of who we were to each other, we'd go together. I don't think either of us would've imagined that we'd be where we are, her practically living in my apartment and making plans for our future while subconsciously dodging the fact that come August, I'll be two and a half hours away and she has no real idea what she'll be doing.

259

"Tickets go on sale next Monday," Lucy says, and how she knows this stuff about a school she left three years ago, I have no idea. She must see the question in my eyes, because she laughs. "I still get the high school newsletter emailed to me." She looks at Laney. "Are you excited about it?"

Laney nods once, her gaze distant, and I know she, too, is lost in the memory of fancy restaurants and lobster and bracelets and *Wonderwalls*.

CHAPTER THIRTY-TWO

LOIS

I SIT in my car on the Prestons' driveway looking between the main house and Lucas's apartment, and I have no idea how I got here. The sky is dark, the stars bright, and I've never *felt* so much silence. I wipe at my eyes when the porch light comes on, look at the clock. It's 4:30 AM. Tom's leaving for work. *Shit.* I had no concept of time, no idea how long I've been sitting here. I try to scoot down in my seat, hoping he'll assume I'm just spending the night with Luke. My heart pounds, the tears come again. *Knock knock* on my window. "Lane?"

I wind down the window, do my best to smile.

"Why are you sitting in your car?" he asks, concern dripping in his words. He looks at the apartment. "Does Luke know you're here?"

"No, sir." I shake my head. "I finished work late last night and I didn't want to go home and I just started driving, ended up here, and I know Luke's got so much going on with his meet this weekend and I didn't want to wake him, so I've just been here…" A sob creeps up my throat, forces its way out of me. "I'm sorry. I'm just going to go."

"No, sweetheart. Come inside. You shouldn't be driving right now."

I nod, gather my stuff, gather *myself.*

THE HOUSE IS EERILY SILENT, and I tell Tom that as I follow him to the kitchen. He switches on the coffee pot, turns to me. "It's peaceful, huh? But it's also kind of lonely when you're used to the general mayhem." He points to a chair at the kitchen table, and I take a seat, listen to the clock ticking, the tap leaking, the coffee pouring.

"I'm sorry. You were on your way to work and I..."

He sets a cup of coffee in front of me, sips on his as he sits in his usual chair at the head of the table. He covers my hand with his, says, "I don't live to work, Lane. I work to live, and my life is my family. That includes you, so talk to me."

There's so much I want to say. So much I wish I could tell him. I almost do. *Almost.* But then he squeezes my hand, looks at me the way Kathy did when I told her about my mom, and I can't do that to him. The truth would destroy him.

I wipe my eyes, try to settle my emotions, give him a small part of the reason why I've been sitting in his driveway the entire night. "When Luke goes to UNC in August, will you need help with the boys? Maybe I could move into the apartment and—"

"Are you asking for a job?"

"I don't have any plans after graduation. I just thought, if you need it..."

He leans back in his chair, rubs his beard. "Luke mentioned something about you getting scholarships."

"Cooper was my link to all that so..." I trail off, shrug.

"Have you and Lucas spoken about what you both want to happen when he goes to college?"

I drop my gaze, feel the warmth of the mug seep through my palms, my fingertips. "I don't expect Luke to—" The front door opens, cutting me off.

Luke rushes into the kitchen, his eyes wide when he sees me. "I saw your car in the driveway," he says. "What's going on? Are you okay?"

"Yeah." I nod. "I'm fine."

Tom stands, kisses the top of my head. "Talk to him, sweetheart."

"Talk to me about what?"

LUKE LEANS on the kitchen counter in his apartment while I sit on the stool on the other side. For the past ten minutes, he's been patiently watching me stare at my coffee, waiting for me to form my thoughts into words, but nothing's coming and *I need time, Lucas.* "You should go for your run."

"No."

"Why?"

"*Why?* Because my girlfriend's at my house and she didn't even tell me she was here. Instead, she's talking to my dad and telling him things she should be telling me, and it's clear she's been crying. So no, babe, I'm not going for a run. I'm not leaving your side."

The truth forms on the tip of my tongue, but my fear pushes it away. "I was just asking him about a job."

"A job?"

I nod.

"Lane, I don't need that money. My mom left me some for when I turned eighteen and—"

"It's not about the money."

He's silent a moment. Then: "Have you even slept?"

"No."

He sighs. "Can you please look at me?"

I swallow, thick, and work up the courage to face him.

"Is it about us? Are you not happy with us?"

The desperation in his voice shatters me. "No. I'm happy." *I hate this.* "*So* happy. But I think that's part of the problem. That happiness can't last forever."

"You're not even letting it begin."

"In a couple months, you'll be gone. And I don't expect you to stay with me when you leave."

His hand slams on the counter. "What the fuck, Lane!" he shouts, his voice echoing off the walls. "It's like you're trying to find reasons to end this! If you don't want me, just say that!"

I jump in my seat, cover my ears. "Don't yell at me!"

He's quick to get to me, his arms around my head. "I'm sorry," he says, stroking my hair. "I didn't mean to lose it like that."

I grasp onto his shirt, sob into his chest. "I don't know what I'm doing, Luke," I cry, looking up at him. "You have so much going for you and you're so determined, and your goals and dreams are *this* close to becoming real, and I'm *so* lost."

"Laney…" he whispers.

I push him away. "And you're going to college and going to live this amazing life and I'll be here, doing *nothing*."

LUCAS

Those eyes give me everything. You could line up a thousand pairs of eyes, and I'd be able to tell you which were Laney's. I could even tell you exactly what she's feeling when I'm looking into them. If she's turned on, angry, confused, elated, *lying*.

There's more to what she's telling me, I know that much. But after seeing her reaction when I yelled, I don't want to push her. I want to heal her. And so I take her hand, lead her to the couch. "What did Dad tell you when you told him all this?"

She wipes her cheeks, looks down at her lap. "He told me to speak to you."

"He's a smart man," I say.

She sniffs once.

"When my parents graduated from UNC, Dad didn't know what he wanted to do. He just knew he wanted to marry my mom. So they got married, and he got a job working construction and for the first couple years, they saved every penny they could. They bought their first property when they were twenty-four. It was this shitty, tiny apartment just outside Raleigh. But they took the knowledge he'd learned through work, fixed it up, and by the time they were twenty-five, they'd flipped their first property, turned a profit. My parents took that profit, did it again and again. Then mom got pregnant with Luce."

Her smile is a slow build, a beautiful image.

"Eventually, they settled into a house—not this one, but it was bigger than the apartments they were flipping. My mom came from money, and my grandfather was the one who invested in Preston Construction after I was born. They moved here, got a fresh start."

She nods, *those eyes* confused. "Why are you telling me this?"

"Because for years, it's been something I've wanted to do."

"Okay?"

I shift her until she's sitting sideways on my lap, and I keep her close, stroke her leg. "Lane, Dad and I found this well-priced, two-bedroom apartment that's falling apart. It's in Chapel Hill, just outside UNC. My dad's in negotiations with the sellers, and if we get it, I want to spend the summer fixing it up, and I want us *both* to live there."

Now *those eyes* are wide, surprised *and* elated. "Are you serious?"

"I know that you might be confused about what you're going to do next year, but I'm not. When I say that I've been thinking about this for years, I mean *all* of it, babe. Ever since you said you wanted to go to UNC, I've been planning this. Even if we weren't together, I still wanted us to be *together*." I remove her glasses, wipe her tears with my thumb. "You've been such a huge part of my life, and I didn't want college to change that. I know that might sound selfish, and it is, but I didn't want to let you go. And now... I hate sleeping in a bed without you in it. I hate waking up and not having you next to me. I'm *in* this, Lane, and I'm *crazy* in love with you."

Her mouth meets mine, her lips salty with her tears. "I love you so much, Luke."

"So quit questioning it. Let's just be in love."

"Okay," she whispers, a smile tugging on her lips. She stands up, takes my hand and leads me to the bedroom. She closes the door behind us, making the room as dark as it is outside. Her hand skims my arm, over my shoulder, until she's pulling me down by my neck, her lips finding mine in the darkness. I savor her touch, her kiss, and then she's moving again, until I'm lying on the bed and she's on top of me, straddling my hips, and I know what she wants, I want it just as bad. She removes my t-shirt, kisses down my neck to my collarbone. "This is my favorite part of you," she says. "Whenever you run, the sweat builds here, turns me on so bad."

My hips jerk up, pushing into her. "I want a light on," I tell her. "I want to see you."

She shifts, and I sit up with her, help her take off her jacket, her top. Then she takes my hand, places it over the bare skin of her chest, just over her heart. "You don't need to see, baby. You just need to *feel*."

I nuzzle her neck, kiss the skin right below her ear and she whispers my name. I try to respond, but all that comes out is a groan. Her nose nudges my chin and I blindly cup her face, and a moment later, her soft, wet lips are on mine. I close my eyes and bring her hips closer. She moans, her lips parting, and I taste her tongue, touch her bare back. I lie back down, flip us over until she's on her back and my hand is on her stomach. A few inches lower and I'll be where I want to be.

She runs her fingers through my hair while I lower my hands to the band of her jeans, sliding a finger side to side. She squirms beneath me, her fingers clenching, tugging my hair, pulling me away from her neck. She kisses me again, soft and slow, and then

265

hard and fast, driving me insane with want, with need. Then she grasps my wrist, guides my hand so I'm moving lower while she unzips her fly. Now I'm under her jeans, above her panties. She's so hot down here, and I tap my fingers against her. She whispers, "Don't tease me, baby."

I'm quick to move the fabric aside and slide a finger inside her. "The way you touch me," she says. "I wish I could erase all other touch, feel nothing but you."

There's something almost magical about getting naked and exploring a person's body with your hands and mouth and sense alone without being able to see the person. Fingers tap and tease and you feel every curve, every dip. Hear every gasp, egging you on to keep doing what you're doing, tasting and swirling and flicking and sucking, and she squirms and she gasps and she moans and she cries out in pleasure, her thighs pressed against my ears, convulsing with her orgasm, and if that's magical, then her mouth around my cock is beyond a fucking miracle because I've never had an out-of-body experience until now. I close my eyes, let her take me to the edge and then pause. Tease. Edge. Pause. Tease. And I'd love to tell you how long this goes for, but I couldn't even count to ten if you paid me.

"Lane," I warn. "I need to come, baby."

She slides up my body, lithe and fucking perfect, her nipples grazing my chest. She kisses me like she was born to do nothing else, and when we finally break apart, gasping for air, she says, "Be gentle with me." I don't ask why, just reach into the drawer on my nightstand and pull out a condom while she sits up. We apply it together, in the dark, and it's the most erotic thing in the world, having both our hands on my dick preparing for what's to come. I kiss between her breasts, my arms around her waist while she shifts into position, her hand going between us to guide me in and *holy fucking shit, we're SEXING!*

I have to see her. *Need to.* I reach for the lamp, but she's quick to take my hands and link our fingers, pressing them into the pillow beside my head. She's moving me in and out of her, and I was wrong. She wasn't made to kiss me. She was made for *this*. To be on top of me, straddling me, and she collapses slightly, her weight on her elbows and *those sounds, those sounds,* and I try to think of something else that'll stop me from coming, and the only thing that comes to mind is World of Warcraft. Her hair brushes against my face while I lean forward, find her nipple with my mouth and she moans out a "Fuck" while I do everything I can not to break my hands free from her grasp and grip her waist and pound into her... *"Be gentle with me."* So I let her do her thing but she's not gentle herself, and I'm so close.

"I'm so close," she pants. "So close." And she's moving, faster and faster, deeper and deeper and *WorldOfWarcraftWorldOfWarcraftWorldOfWarcraft.*

"Shit shit shit," she breathes.

WORLDOFFUCKINGWARCRAFT!

"Oh my god!"

I sense the exact moment her orgasm hits her, and I finally allow myself the same pleasure. Then she collapses on top of me, her entire body soaked with sweat. A few seconds later, she breaks out in a giggle and rolls off of me. "Why did you shout *World of Warcraft?"*

My entire body bursts into flames. "Shut up! I did not!"

"You totally did," she manages to say through her laughing fit.

My feet are heavy, legs wobbly when I sit on the edge of the bed and "clean up." I warn her that I'm going to switch the lamp on so her eyes can adjust and when the light's on, I turn to her. The blanket's pulled up to her nose and her hair is a mess, strands caught on the sweat on her brow, and she's flushed, not from embarrassment but exertion. I kiss the top of her head. "You're kind of amazing, you know?"

She smiles, sweet and innocent and a complete contrast to how she was a few minutes ago.

"Are you okay?" I ask.

"I'm good."

"Good is the enemy of great," I throw back at her.

Her smile widens. "I'm beyond great, Lucas. I'm in love."

CHAPTER THIRTY-THREE

LUCAS

WE RIDE to senior prom in a limo paid for by Dad and chosen by me. It was the best one the company had: fancy leather seats, sunroof, DVD player, etc. I'd picked it out because I'd planned on taking Laney on a little cruise beforehand (aka sex in a limo), but Leo and Logan are with us because—get this—they're dating twins! Not only twins but seniors. They go from fighting over one girl to dating two who are fucking identical. Needless to say, the sex in the limo became unachievable. That, and the fact that Laney was late to get ready because she's head of the prom decorating committee and had to be there until the last possible second to make sure everything was perfect. I tried telling her that no one pays attention to the decorations, that people go, some loser/winner spikes the punch, you dance to maybe two songs, then you bail to the after-party.

"But it's my *first* and *last* dance, and I want to make sure it's perfect," she said, and she said it in such a way that I felt like an asshole for not caring about the decorations and that I'd been to every single dance, each with a different date, but honestly? I would've taken Laney to all of them had I thought I was good enough. Still, guilt is a dangerous emotion. It causes you to do stupid things like stay up until 2:30 AM with your girlfriend swiping at an iPad looking through eleventy-three million different versions of the same fucking centerpieces. But I love her. *Really*, I do. I love her so much I even spent hours at the mall with her making sure my tie matched the *exact* shade of her dress. Periwinkle, by the way, is the color of her dress. I'd never even heard the word *periwinkle* before but she swears it's a thing, and on her, *periwinkle* is more than a shade, more than a dress. It's a statement. One that says, "*Hey, boys, look at what I've been hiding all *these years!*" and I already want to punch every single guy who realizes what they've been missing.

"Do you know who's going to be prom queen and king?" one of the twins asks Lane. Her name's Kristen or Kirsten and no, I didn't get the names confused, I got *them* confused because yes, their names are Kristen *and* Kirsten, and as much as I'd like to make my opinion known on how silly I think it is when parents give their kids matching names, I can't. Because:

Lucy
Lucas
Leo
Logan
Lincoln
Liam
Lachlan

THE DANCE IS HELD at a ballroom attached to a hotel, the same ballroom all dances are held because small-town living is *rad*. By the time we get there, Garray's already been kicked out for being drunk.

He whistles when Laney steps out of the limo, fucks her with his eyes. "Lucas, bruh, who's this hot piece of ass?" As if he doesn't know. As if he wasn't the first one to lock lips with her.

Laney rolls her eyes, physically drags me away and up the seven steps toward the dance. We hand our tickets over to Miss Lepsitch at the door and then enter a winter wonderland. I knew what the theme was, of course, and I'd seen the room before, but now, with the lights and the music and the people and the dancing and, "Wow, Babe. You nailed it."

She smiles wide, her cheeks lifting her glasses from her nose. "You think?"

"Trust me. I've been to plenty of these, remember? This is the best one yet."

"Good," she says, "I wanted to go off with a *bang*."

270

WHEN MY MOM WAS ALIVE, music was a constant in the house. Anything from jazz to hip hop, rock to reggae. She'd listen to old records and whatever was on the radio, and when a song came on that she loved, she'd pick up the nearest child and dance with them. I was ten years old the last time she made me dance. The song was *Charlene* by Anthony Hamilton, one of her favorites. She smiled down at me, her eyes tired, and placed one of my hands on her waist, the other in hers. She swayed us from side to side, the music taking her on a journey I knew nothing about. Halfway through the song, I was sick of holding her hand, sick of two-stepping around the room. I told her dancing was lame. She shook her head. "One day, Lucas, you're going to fall in love with a girl, like your father fell in love with me, and you'll understand."

"Understand what?" I asked.

"That it's not about the dance. It's about moving, as one, with a person whose heart beats to the same rhythm as yours. It's about *love*, about *life*."

I never really understood what she meant. Not until I had Laney in my arms, her head on my chest, her heart in my hands. One song ends and another starts, and it's perfect. *Wonderwall* by Oasis fills the room, and she smiles, and her smile makes me do the same. "Do you know what this song is?" I ask.

"It's the one your dad and I danced to on my sixteenth birthday."

"It's also my parents' wedding song."

Her eyes go wide, her gasp soft.

We don't speak for the rest of the song, just move together. As one.

"You ever feel like this is as good as it gets?" she says, looking up at me with *those eyes.*

I give her a memory, a secret. "You know, I still remember the exact moment I fell in love with you. I mean, I always thought that I loved you, but I wasn't sure what that love meant." I kiss her once and go on, "We were fifteen, it was a Saturday, and I'd just come second in a race. I was in the worst mood even though you spent the majority of that morning trying to cheer me up. I sat on the couch in your room, and you were on your bed, your legs crossed, knitting gloves for Lachlan. They were special gloves—"

"The ones with the removable tip on the pointer finger so he could still play games on your iPad," she remembers out loud.

271

I bite my lip, nod once. "You looked up at something on the television and laughed, and I remember staring at you, thinking that you had the power to change my mood with a single sound. Your laugh."

"Luke," she breathes, tears threatening to fall.

"You went back to knitting... sixteen clicks of your needles, eight seconds, and my heart flipped. And I just *knew*. I knew I'd fallen in love for the first time. For the *last* time."

I taste her tears on her lips when she kisses me, her arms around my neck, holding me tight. But then she pulls away, and when I open my eyes, I see it's not by choice. Cooper Kennedy is here, and his hand is on her shoulder, and he looks like fucking death—as if he hasn't slept for days, and going by what Laney's told me, he probably hasn't. He's shaking, *twitching*. "Lo, I need to talk to you. Just one minute, please."

I separate them, step in front of her. "What the hell are you doing? Get out!" But he doesn't see me; his scattered gaze is on Laney.

"Please, Lo," he fucking *begs*, his hands clasped in front of him.

Lane steps beside me. "What do you want?"

"I need to talk to you."

"About what?"

Cooper looks around. "Not here."

My rage boils, bursts. "Fuck off!"

"Fuck you!" he shouts, then looks at Lane. "I just want one goddamn minute! After everything we were, you can't even give me that?"

He's fucking insane if he thinks I'm going to let Laney go anywhere with him. "You need to leave!"

"Luke." Lane's hand is on my arm, forcing me to face her. "I'll be back in—"

"No, Lane!"

"Please." *Those eyes, those eyes*, they ruin me.

I look away. "Fine. Go."

She blows out a breath, looks between us. To me, she says, "Please don't leave." As if I would. I let her go, and I stand in the middle of the dance floor, my hands in my pockets, watching my girl leave with another guy.

HE ASKED for one minute with her.

It's now been two.

Three...

And on the eighteenth second of the third minute, *Bang! Bang! Bang! Bang!*

YOU SEE it on the news. Read about it on the Internet. But you never think it'll happen to you.

School shootings don't happen in *our* town.

In *our* school.

Everyone runs, everyone searches.

And all I can think is *LaneyLeoLogan.*

I start shouting their names, shoving people out of the way.

"LaneyLeoLogan!"

Everyone's screaming, crying.

There's no fucking protocol for this.

My eyes dart everywhere all at once, my pulse thumps in my ears.

"LaneyLeoLogan!"

It's a sea of people rushing out the door, teachers screaming, shouting to stay calm.

There is no calm.

Not here.

Not now.

I run one direction, then another, back again.

Always looking.

"LaneyLeoLogan!"

Someone shoves me from behind, their scream ringing in my ears.

"Lucas!" Leo shouts, running toward me.

I check his body, head to toe, head to toe. "Are you okay? Are you hurt?"

He shoves my hands away. "I'm okay. Where's Logan?"

"I don't know!" I shout. *"LaneyLogan! LaneyLogan! LaneyLogan!"*

People run again, back *into* the room, into me. "Lucas!" Logan cries, and I exhale, relieved. He falls to the floor, gets trampled. I run to him, shove everyone out of the way, and pull him toward me. "Leo!" he cries, hugging his brother.

His tears are fat, falling fast. He's so fucking scared.

This shouldn't be happening.

"What's going on?" He's crying so hard I can barely make out the words, not because he's high, but because he's fucking *fifteen*. He shouldn't be experiencing this.

None of us should.

"Are you okay?" Leo yells. "Are you hurt?"

Logan shakes his head.

"Laney!" I'm on my toes, searching the sea of scared bodies. I look to my brothers, fear squeezing my throat shut. "Where the fuck is Laney?"

People line the back wall, sitting, hugging, crying.

I search for *periwinkle*, search for Laney. "Laney!"

"Preston! Get against the wall!" Coach Anderman yells. "Now!"

I turn to Leo. "Take Logan and go!"

"No!"

"I'm not fucking around, Leo. Go!"

"Luke!" someone shouts, but it's not the voice I want to hear. Garray charges toward me, his body slamming into mine. He grasps my shoulders, gets in my vision.

"Laney!" I roar.

"Luke!" He's pushing me back, his body blocking me. "Laney..." he huffs.

I can no longer see, blinded by fear. "Where the fuck is she?"

He wipes his eyes against his arm. "She's outside, Luke... you shouldn't go out—"

I push him away and run for the door.

Two seconds.

Seven steps.

My heart stops.

I drop to my knees.

"Laney!"

There's no more periwinkle purple, just crimson red.

Blood everywhere.

Those eyes, those eyes, they ruin me.

I pick her up off the ground.

Blood everywhere.

Her legs, her torso, her mouth.

Blood everywhere.

"No! Laney! Please please please."

She coughs blood.

Once.

Twice.

I hear, "I'm sorry, Lo! I didn't want this. I love you. Fuck!"

Crimson red behind my eyes.

Rage.

Murder.

Cooper's pacing the sidewalk, his hands behind his head, gun still in his grasp.

I don't know how it happens.

How I rush toward him.

How I knock him to the ground.

Rage.

How I punch his face, over and over.

Kick him, over and over.

Murder.

Garray grips my arms, pulling me back.

Cooper doesn't move.

Not an inch.

I run back to Laney.

Sweet, naive, innocent Laney.

I drop to my knees again. "Lane!"

Blood bubbles from her lips, tears form in her eyes. A single word: "Help."

I pick up her hand, search for a pulse.

One second.

Two.

Three.

Four.

Five.

Six.

Seven.

Eight.

Those eyes, those eyes.

Are *gone.*

CHAPTER THIRTY-FOUR

LUCAS

IN SEVEN MINUTES, we went from moving, as one, under snowflakes made of silk and twinkling lights and disco balls to *hanging on*, as one, lost in a sea of red and blue lights.

In the back of the ambulance, I hold her hand, I plead, I bargain for her life—for her to stay with me.

I'm told to move, to let some guy in a uniform holding a needle do his job, and so I sit in the corner and I cower and I beg and I break down. Cry.

The driver speaks into the radio, says he has a "female, eighteen to twenty, multiple GSWs, pulse weak, eta: six minutes."

Six fucking minutes.

It's too long, we're going too slow, and there's *blood everywhere, blood everywhere*, on my hands, on my face, on my tux, on my shirt, on my periwinkle tie to go with her crimson red dress, and the uniformed guy is in my face, his voice the only calm in an ocean of riptides. "Talk to her. Keep her with us, son."

I stand, hunched, my body not made to fit in such small spaces, and I take Laney's hand and I choke. I look up at the man meant to save lives, and I ask, "What do I say?"

He answers, "Give her a reason to stay."

So I look down at her face, a face I've loved before *love* had a meaning, and I ignore the blood trickling from her mouth, down her cheek, to her neck. I tell her, "You stepped out of your dad's car in your denim shorts and bright red flip-flops and t-shirt with a picture of a cat that said *Look at meow. I'm getting pay purr.*" I wipe my eyes with my bloodstained hands and blink through the pain. "I thought it was hilarious, but I didn't want to laugh because I didn't want you to think I was laughing *at* you. When Mom introduced us all, you stood there and looked around and I could see you counting the kids in your head. I was counting, too. Counting down the seconds until Mom said my name and when you looked at me, you just stopped. You stopped counting the kids, and I stopped counting the time and I wanted to know everything about you." I push through a sob cracking my open heart. "Our eyes locked and I think, in a way, they've never left. It's been years, Laney, and I've never stopped looking at you, looking *to* you, and I don't want to stop. Not now. Not ever. And I need to see your eyes and I need to hear your laugh and I *need* you. I *need* to love you. And I need to love you *right*."

IT TAKES seven minutes to get to the hospital. Not *six*. I go from twinkling lights and disco balls to a sea of red and blue to sterile, bright white, waiting room lights. They don't allow me to go farther, and I save what fight I have left for Laney's life, not for those who are trying to *save her life*. I sit by the huge swinging doors they rushed her through and grasp my hair. It's so quiet now. *Wonderwall* changed to gunshots changed to screams changed to sirens, and now I'm here and it's *too* fucking quiet. Another gurney comes through the doors and it's suddenly loud and it's Cooper fucking Kennedy and I stand and I kick at the fucking gurney like I kicked at his head. I lose my shoe, but I don't do any damage and he's rushed behind the swinging doors, his life treated as if its value holds the same as Laney's. It doesn't. And then *Brian*.

He's wild, frantic, just like I am on the inside. On the outside, I *try* to stay calm. For him. "What happened, Luke?"

I stand.

I puke.

On his clothes.

On mine.

Blood everywhere.

Puke everywhere.

And then I lean against the wall and I cry and I puke and I cry some more.

Leo and Logan are next and they try to pull me away from my tears and my vomit and try to force me to sit on the chairs, but I choose the floor while Brian paces. Questions.

My brothers don't ask questions.

278

Brian makes a phone call.

My dad arrives. Lucy, Cameron, and my other brothers in tow.

Lachlan's in his pajamas, dinosaurs shaped like numbers, and he looks at the blood and the puke and he ignores them both and sits down next to me, his tiny hand on my knee and his head on my shoulder and I cry. Then he says, "I thought it was you." And *he* cries.

I cry.

Brian cries.

Lucy cries.

The quiet that was *too* quiet is now too *loud* because a woman just entered, wailing for her son. "Where's my son? Cooper?" She gets ushered through the doors I'm forbidden from entering, and my heart throbs and my head throbs and everything throbs and *it hurts*. It hurts so fucking much, and I cry harder and Lachlan cries harder. I hold him tight, tell him, "It's okay." It's not. No one knows what's happening. Brian's asking questions *no one* has answers to. And then blue and red lights from outside filter into the room and two cops march in, their footsteps heavy, their focus on me and I know why they're here. I've been waiting. They say my name, and I slip on the puke and the blood as I come to a stand the same time Lachlan screams my name. The larger of the cops reveals a set of handcuffs and I shake my head, look down at Lachlan and like Laney's eyes, *his tears, his tears,* they *ruin* me.

"Please," I whisper. I cry some more. "I'll go wherever you need, but *please* don't cuff me in front of my brothers."

They hear my plea, give me grace, and I walk with my head down to the backseat of the police cruiser, ignoring the cries and questions from my family.

MISTY'S at the police station, in uniform, on duty. She stands just inside the door as if she *knows*, as if she's been waiting for me. "Lucas," she says, her voice hoarse. Then she looks at the two officers who escorted me in here, cuffs on. "I'll do the processing."

It's all a blur.

She speaks, but I barely hear her.

"Assault."

"Remand."

"Court."

"Bail."

"Hearing."

These are all words she says and words I don't care about.

She asks to take my prints. I let her. I have no choice.

She asks to take my statement.

I tell her I can't. Not now.

She understands.

I look down at her desk, at the scattered paperwork and half-filled coffee cup. She'd recently been promoted to senior deputy, I remember Lane telling me. There's a framed picture of her and Brian and a smaller one of her and Lane stuck to the edge of her computer monitor. I stare at the picture, at the *life* in Lane's eyes, and I force myself to breathe. I don't have control of my body, of my emotions. I'm dull, weak, and waiting. The tears well again and the puke rises, but I manage to keep it down. "Have you heard anything?" I ask.

She clears her throat, scoots closer, starts to uncuff me. "Four gunshot wounds. Three to her legs. One to her abdomen. The paramedics on the scene said she was lucky to be alive when they got there. She'd lost a lot of blood." Misty chokes on a sob but maintains her professionalism. "Lois is strong. She'll fight this. She has you to come back to."

"Where is she now?"

"They're operating on her. It could be hours until we hear anything."

I rub my wrists, now free of the handcuffs. "And Cooper?" I ask.

Rage.

Murder.

She sighs. "He'll be fine, Luke. He'll *survive*."

Finally, my eyes lock on hers. "Do you believe in fate, Misty?"

She forces a smile but doesn't give me an answer.

"My mother believed so boldly in *fate*, and if this is my fate, I'll wear it. But this *can't* be Lane's fate because the world isn't ready to lose her." I glance back at the picture of Lane. "Then again, the world wasn't ready to lose my mom, either.

THE BLOOD on my clothes is still damp, but the blood on my hands is not.

280

At some point between the hospital and this waiting cell at the police station, it managed to become nothing more than red flakes on my palms and fingers. I can feel it on my face, too, mixing with the tears now soaked into my skin. I wonder how the others in the cell see me—barely a man, huddled in the corner of the room, bloodstained tux, and a missing shoe—and I imagine, for a moment, the thoughts and stories that run through their minds.

Maybe I was in a wreck, drunk.

Maybe I was in a fight, drunk.

Maybe I tried to kill someone.

I try not to think about it for too long, the repercussions of my actions beyond my mental capacity. So I stare down at the floor in front of me, the sole of my single bloody shoe print leading to where I sit, like a road map to my demise, and I think about the only thing that makes sense.

I think about *her*.

And I wonder if I'll ever get the image, *the feel*, of her limp body in my arms out of my system.

SIXTEEN CLICKS.

Eight seconds.

That's how long it took me to realize I'd been in love with her for four years.

Eight, life-changing seconds.

It's also the exact length of time it took to lose her.

CHAPTER THIRTY-FIVE

LUCAS

LUCY WAS three when I was born. I was the same age when Mom gave birth to Leo. A year after him, she had Logan. To say she had her hands full is an understatement. By the time Logan came around, Lucy was six and already at school so it was just the boys at home. To stop me from running around destroying everything in my path, Mom would pick me up and place me in Leo's crib. I'd grip onto the bars and watch through the gaps as Mom changed their diapers, got them dressed. When Leo was all clean, she'd put him in with me, and I'd find ways to make him laugh. Then Mom would bring us Logan, and she'd say, every time, "Be gentle, boys. He's just a baby."

Fifteen years later, I'm behind a different set of bars, but I'm doing the same thing: watching them.

A few seconds ago, I heard Leo yell, "Misty!" and found the strength to stand up and see what was happening. Part of a wall blocked my view so I couldn't see everything, but I could see them.

According to the clock opposite the cell, I've only been locked in for five minutes. And the processing took less than an hour. There shouldn't be any news on Laney yet. Unless… I couldn't even process *unless*.

"Misty!" Logan shouts, and fear squeezes my insides.

A gruff, male voice tries to settle my brothers. "You boys can't be here."

"Misty! Misty!" Logan repeats, his voice carrying through the air.

A moment later, Misty walks past the cell, her eyes narrowed, first at me, then my brothers. She asks, once behind the front desk, "What's going on here?"

Leo doesn't respond. He just pokes her shoulder. She steps back, surprised. Then Logan yells, "Whore!"

Two officers appear from nowhere and start to kick them out, but Leo says, "That's assaulting a member of the police, right? Shouldn't we be detained or something?" His voice breaks, his tone *desperate*. "Right, Misty?" And through the haze, through the fog, it all becomes clear. My head drops forward, smacks against the bars, and I do it again and again because I don't want them here and I don't want them to see me. Not now. Not like this.

"I got it," Misty tells the officers. She grabs my brothers by the arms and leads them to the cell where I let go of the bars and step back, waiting for them to slide open and for my brothers to join me. To me, she says, "I'm off for the rest of the night to be with Brian at the hospital. As soon as we know anything..." she trails off. The bars clank closed, echo off the walls, and I don't know how long I stand there, looking down at the floor, shame and fear continuing to build inside me. I look at my hands, at the blood, and without a word, I sit back down in the same spot, drowning in the same fear. Leo's the first to join me, sitting to my right. Logan's next, sitting to my left, and I finally manage to speak. "What are you guys doing here?"

"We're your brothers, Luke," Leo says. "We're here for *you*."

IN A SPRINT, every millisecond counts. In the holding cell, those milliseconds feel like eons. Every single time I close my eyes I see *those eyes, those tears*, and they haunt me.

I sit with my back against the wall, my knees up, my head between them and I cry silent tears and live in silent thoughts and then Logan says, "This is my fault."

I lift my gaze, look over at him, but he's staring ahead, his eyes glazed.

"I was outside drinking with Dumb Name, and we saw Lane and Cooper walk out. We hid in the fucking bushes like idiots so we could spy. We thought they were screwing around behind your back, and we wanted proof. But he was just *begging* her to take him back, and he kept apologizing. Something was seriously *wrong* with him. It was like he was possessed." He wipes his eyes on his forearm, his shoulders shaking. I try to breathe, but I can't.

"She told him she was done, that she wanted nothing to do with him and she started to go back in, but then he yelled *'Don't walk away from me!'*" Logan falls apart, his words as broken as himself. "And then he lifted the gun... Luke..." He faces me, sob after sob wrecking him. "I didn't know what to do and I got so scared and I just *ran away*. I didn't even check on her. I'm so fucking sorry."

I hold his face in my hands and lock my eyes on his. "This is *not* your fault."

He shakes his head, his tears falling. "I'll send the video to Misty. I'll do whatever I can to help."

"What video?"

"I told you," he says. "I wanted *proof.*"

FIVE HOURS and forty-six minutes after Misty left, she returns, along with my dad. My brothers and I stand, greet them at the bars. Dad says, "She's out of surgery."

"She's going to be okay, right?"

"Eventually."

Every muscle in my body seems to ease, and I grip the bars in desperation. "Can I get out now? Can I see her?"

I see the remorse in their eyes when they look away, just for a moment. Misty says, "The bail hearing is set for Monday, Lucas. I've requested that you stay here until then. That way you're close to me, close to *family.*"

I STAY in the stupid cell, alone, the eons ticking by one after the other. Dad returns to give me my emergency glasses I requested because contacts don't do well with tears, with pain and agony. I tell him not to come back, that I don't want to see him until the bail hearing.

When Monday morning comes, I change into a clean suit Dad brought me and breathe in fresh air for the first time in what feels like forever. I sit in the only courtroom in town, in front of the only judge in town, next to a lawyer I'd never met before. Dad has a lawyer for the business, but this one specializes in crime. Because that's what I am now. A *criminal.* All I want is for them to announce bail, for Dad to hopefully pay it, and for me to spend the rest of the day, the rest of *my life,* next to Laney.

Judge Nelson, a woman who should've retired years ago, reads a sheet of paper out loud explaining my assault charges, and I look over at Dad and Misty sitting behind me and for a second, just one, I'm scared for *me.* I didn't assault just anybody. I *wanted* to kill Cooper Kennedy, whose family has more than enough *Fuck You* money to get exactly what they want. I'm going to prison for a long time, too long to ask Laney to wait for me.

Judge Nelson sets bail and gives me the conditions of my release: *A restraining order has been granted from the Kennedys, meaning I can't be within a hundred yards of him.* Fine, I think, until I hear Dad murmuring to Misty behind me. Misty stands. "If I may, Your Honor."

Judge Nelson smiles at her. "Misty, I've known you since before you could walk." *Small towns.* "Why so formal?"

Misty clears her throat, squares her shoulders. "I'd like to request a temporary lift on the RO, limited to the hospital, with police supervision."

Judge Nelson's gray eyebrows bunch, and she switches her gaze from Misty to me and back again. She calls for a ten-minute recess and requests both myself and Misty to her "chambers." My head spins. I know nothing of what the fuck is happening, and I thought I was getting out. I need to get out. I need to see Laney.

Misty and I don't have time to discuss anything before we're sitting in leather chairs inside a room with Judge Nelson. It smells like old lady perfume, Band-Aids and hotel room Bibles.

"You want to tell me what's going on?" Judge Nelson asks, sitting down opposite us.

Misty doesn't skip a beat. "Cooper Kennedy is sitting in a hospital room four doors down from Lois Sanders."

And all of a sudden I go from knowing nothing to knowing *too much.*

Misty adds, "With the restraining order in place, Lucas—I mean Mr. Preston—can't visit her. I'm simply requesting—"

Judge Nelson cuts in. "You have a personal relationship with Miss Sanders, correct?"

"She's my boyfriend's daughter."

"And you think she deserves special privileges?"

"Your Honor." I don't recognize my own voice. "May I speak?"

Judge Nelson nods. "If it's quick. I have to be back in session soon."

My heart pounds, my breaths uneven. I push through. "Laney— I mean *Lois*—we've been best friends since we were eleven, and I've loved her every day since then. Right now…" A sob forces its way up my throat, out my mouth. "Right now, I'm lost. I have no idea what's going to happen to me. I just know that I need to see her. And if I'm feeling this, I can't even imagine how she's feeling. We've been side by side through everything, ma'am. And I understand that you have to do your job, that you have to abide by the laws set to protect, but no one was protecting her when Cooper decided to unload four bullets into her body."

Misty's hand lands on my shoulder and I hear her cries, louder than mine.

"You asked if we think Laney deserves special privileges as if there's a logical answer to that question. She fell in love with the wrong guy in the *wrong* way, and I let her down. I let him lead her away from me, and I was supposed to protect her. To save her." *To be her Wonderwall.* "And I need to see her so she knows she's loved, that she didn't deserve this, and selfishly, I need to tell her I'm sorry so she can forgive me. Because I *need* her forgiveness, ma'am. More than I need my next breath."

———

JUDGE NELSON CANCELS her sessions for the rest of the day, parking fines and petty disputes, and we ride to the hospital in a police cruiser while Dad follows in his car. The judge asks me about Laney, about the type of person she is, and about our relationship. I answer each one as best I can, but my mind is both numb and frantic, and there are too many words, words, words racing through my head, so many different ways to say I'm sorry.

MY STEPS FALTER and my gut twists when we enter the hospital, walk down the halls, and I see a police officer guarding Cooper's room as if he's the one who needs the protection. But Judge Nelson raises her hand, says, "He's with me." And the officer sits back down, reads his paper.

It takes fifteen steps to pass three rooms until I'm standing in front of Laney's door, lost. I look to Misty, look to Dad. "Go on," Dad says. "You need each other." He didn't say that I need her or that she needs me. We need *each other*. Like air in our lungs. Like life in our blood.

THERE ARE no words to describe the slaughtering of my heart when I see Laney in the bed, her right leg bandaged, elevated, tubes and machines hooked up to her body. "She's out," Brian says, sitting in the dark corner of the room. He looks like I feel and I force myself forward, step after step, until I'm standing next to her, looking down, and I've never missed *those eyes* as much as I miss them now, hidden behind her closed lids.

Dad pulls up a chair, sets it behind me as if he knows I'm struggling to stand, to *see*. I sit down, take her hand in mine.

Brian says, "I'm not sure if she's sleeping or if the pain meds..." He sighs. So tired. So broken. "Talk to her, Luke. She's been asking for you."

It's hard to pull words from your heart when there are four other people standing in the room, watching, waiting. "Hey, baby. It's Lucas." *Stupid.* "I'm sorry I haven't been able to come see you. I've been... don't worry where I've been. I just..." I drop my head on her hand and I forget the words, the need for her forgiveness, and I cry. You'd think that I'd be done with crying but seeing her, touching her, it's everything I wanted and needed, and I thought it would fix everything but it doesn't. Dad grasps my shoulder, his huge frame like a giant boulder when he squats down next to me. "It's okay," he says.

But it's not.

I'm crying harder, tears and snot and drool and bandages and hospitals and court dates and criminal charges and all I've ever wanted was coconuts, lime and *Laney*.

"It's not okay, Dad!" I shout, and he nods. He knows. "It's not okay. We were meant to have the rest of our lives, and it wasn't supposed to start like this. We were supposed to go to college together and get married and have kids and we're eighteen and this shouldn't be happening! I'm going to prison and she's never going to heal from this and what am I supposed to do, Dad? Tell me!" I plead. "Tell me what I'm supposed to do?"

"Lucas," he says, the same time Lane's hand twitches in mine and I stand quickly, look down at her, at *those eyes.*

"Luke," she whispers, her eyes fighting to stay open.

I wipe at my cheeks, try to hide my pain.

A single tear falls from her eyes, down her temple and into her hair. "I hurt, Luke."

I scan her body. No *crimson red. No blood everywhere.* "Where, baby? Where do you hurt?"

Her eyes drift shut again. "I hurt *everywhere.*"

CHAPTER THIRTY-SIX

LUCAS

LANEY FALLS ASLEEP.

Judge Nelson says she has some paperwork to get back to in her office. She also tells me she's "quite fond" of me. I tell her I "appreciate" her.

We leave.

I go home, pretend like I don't care that everyone is fussing over me.

Lucy offers *not* to cook dinner, and I tell her I appreciate her, too.

I do my one minute with Lachlan and he wraps his arms around my head, tells me he loves me, that he's glad I wasn't the one shot by the *bad man*.

I fall asleep in his bed and wake the next morning to a phone call from Judge Nelson. There are detectives asking questions, and she wants to meet me at her new "headquarters." I tell her I can't right now, that I need to see Laney. She says her new "headquarters" is Laney's room at the hospital. I tell her I appreciate her, again, and that I'll be there soon.

IT'S a media circus around the hospital. The Kennedys are rich and powerful and their son is in a hospital bed "fighting for his life." Fuck the media.

According to what Lucy's told me, the Kennedys have been very tight-lipped about it all. They refuse to speak, to answer questions, they just hope justice will be served. They want me locked up, and right now, that's their priority. They don't care about their son, about what might happen to him because he tried to fucking *kill someone*. Or that that someone actually *did* fight for her life. No. They care about fucking *justice*.

JUDGE NELSON'S waiting for Dad and me just outside the hospital doors. She says she lifted the restraining order on the condition that *she* be with me. I ask her why she's so invested in this. She says she's not invested in "this" so much as she's invested in "us"... *Laney and me*. She being the only judge in town, she'll be working both cases, Lane's case against Cooper and his case against me. I guess that's one good thing about small towns, everything is personal. And for the first time in days, I feel a win on my side. Because there are some things the Kennedys' *Fuck You* money can't buy, and Judge Nelson has them: common sense and common decency.

LANE'S AWAKE and half sitting up when I enter her room. She smiles weakly when she sees me and I can't help it, I smile back, race over to her.

"Hi," she whispers.

I rest my forehead against hers, unable to hold back my cries. "Are you okay?"

She grasps my wrist, chokes on a sob. "I've missed you."

"I've missed you, too, baby. And I love you. So much."

She pulls back, her tear-filled eyes ripping my heart in two. "What's going to happen to us?"

"Nothing," I assure. "I won't let anything happen to us."

"We're going to get through this, right?"

"Of course."

"I'm sorry, Luke. I shouldn't have left with him," she says, her cries hitching her words.

I kiss her lips, taste her tears. "Stop it. This isn't your fault. I love you. You love me. That's all that matters."

She chews on her lip and presses a button on the remote that moves the top half of the bed back down to laying position. Then she scoots over, just slightly, and pats the bed. "One minute?"

I don't care that there are other people in the room, the judge, my dad, her dad, our lawyers, two random detectives. Fuck, the media could be in here and it still wouldn't stop me from getting in the bed with her and cupping her face and kissing her eyes and her cheeks and her forehead and her nose and her lips and all the things I love about her.

"Lucas," she whispers, and I pull back. She pouts. "You went to jail?"

"No, baby." I shake my head. "I was in a holding cell. That's all."

"Are you going to jail?" She's so sad, so naive, so innocent. So Laney.

I don't answer. Instead, I close my eyes, rub my nose along hers.

"If you do," she says, struggling to breathe through her pain. "I'm going with you."

I kiss her again.

Tell her I've missed her. Again.

Tell her I love her. Again.

"I heard you," she says. "What you said in the ambulance, I heard it all. You were number four, Lucas Preston. I stopped counting at *four*."

I smile. "It's my new favorite number."

"Your favorite number to go with my favorite person."

"We're so lame," I tell her, my smile widening.

She laughs, reality shifts, and our reality is what she says next: "We're not lame. We're just in love." It's true. We are. And nothing and no one can take that love from us. Even the detective who clears his throat and introduces himself as Detective Keels and his partner as Detective Mayfield.

THE QUESTIONS START off easy and get harder from there until I'm sitting up in the bed, my hand linked with Lane's, and I replay the moment in my mind: *Was Cooper Kennedy in possession of the weapon when you began your assault?*

The truth is simple. "Yes."

"At what point was he no longer in possession?" Keels asks the questions, Mayfield takes the notes.

"Um… I guess when I lunged at him and brought him down."

"Do you know where the weapon landed?" I hate that he's calling it a weapon as if it's somehow less *deadly*. It's a fucking gun. I wish he'd just say it.

"Under a car."

293

"How far was the car, Lucas?"

I look at my dad. I look at my lawyer. "I can't be sure, sir."

Mayfield pauses on taking notes and looks up, speaks for the first time. "You run track, right?"

I nod. "Yes, sir."

Then he gets cocky, *obnoxious*. "So you have to have *some* idea of distance. Give me a ballpark, something to work with."

"I don't know. Like, ten, maybe fifteen feet."

Mayfield goes back to taking notes. Keels says, "So not within reaching distance?"

"I guess not."

"And you continued your assault on Mr. Kennedy even after the weapon had left his possession and was thrown *under* a car, out of reach. Correct?"

My heart thumps, my mind shuts down. "I—"

My lawyer sighs. "I guess self-defense is out of the question now."

Fuck.

Keels ends my questions there, for now, and moves on to Laney. Same standard questions with her.

What was her relationship with Cooper Kennedy?

How long have they known each other?

Were they intimate? (Like it fucking matters.)

And I start to wonder if maybe these fucking detectives are on the Kennedys' *Fuck You* payroll. Then they ask something that has Laney sitting up, joining me. *Where was she the first week of May?* She was in Charlotte, in a hotel. But she's taking too long to answer, and her eyes are everywhere at once. She won't make eye contact with Keels and she won't look at me, even when I squeeze her hand. I whisper, "You were in Charlotte, remember? In a hotel. You needed to get away for a while."

Her throat bobs with her swallow, but she still doesn't speak.

Mayfield flips his notepad, page after page, as if we have all the time in the fucking world. I wish they'd leave. I wish we could go back to fifteen minutes ago when *one minute* was the greatest thing in the world.

Mayfield finds what he's looking for among his notes. "So you weren't in the hospital… Carolinas Medical Center in Charlotte? Is that what you're saying?"

294

Her eyes go wide like they did when I asked her about her glasses, deer meet headlights, and nothing makes sense.

Mayfield continues, "It says here you were complaining about stomach pains. Two broken ribs, swelling around your jaw, large bruise on your back? That doesn't sound like stomach pains to me."

Brian sits higher. *Two* deer in headlights. "Lois. What is he saying?"

Lane shakes her head. "What do you want me to say?" she whispers.

Keels is blunt. "The truth, Miss Sanders." *Cunt.*

Lane's cry is quiet, almost silent. "I think you can guess, *detectives.*"

"We have to hear it from you."

"You want me to tell you that my boyfriend used me as a punching bag?"

Rage.

White. Hot. Rage.

"Which boyfriend?" Keels asks. "Cooper or Luc—"

"No!" she almost shouts. "Lucas would never... God, what is wrong with you two? Why are you even here when *he's* down the hall!" Her volume rises with each word. "You want the truth. Fine! I tried to break up with Cooper the previous week. We were in his dorm room, and he wouldn't let me leave. He locked me in there and said we could "talk it out" but we didn't talk. He yelled, hit, slapped, punched. And then he *fucked me* as if it was going to make everything okay."

I cover my mouth to stop the puke because it's right fucking there, like my anger, ready to explode.

"And it wasn't the first time this happened. It'd been going on for months, and I'm sorry," she cries, spit flying from her mouth, and she lets go of my hand and continues, "I'm sorry, Dad. I couldn't tell you." She looks at me. "I couldn't tell either of you because I thought he'd do something to hurt you and I couldn't..."

She cries into her hands.

Brian cries into his shirt.

And I'm too fucking angry to cry.

Keels looks at me, speaks to Laney. "If that happened, Ms. Sanders, then why is Cooper Kennedy's signature on the hospital bill?"

"It's not," she sobs. "It's not Cooper's. It's his mom's."

LUCAS

I'm on my feet before I can think, before the consequences come to me, and I march for the door with one thing on my mind: I'm going to finish Cooper fucking Kennedy. "Lucas!" Judge Nelson yells at the same time Dad grasps my arms, keeps me in place. The judge is in front of me now, her eyes red and raw. "Don't do this, Lucas. Don't make me question my *investments.*"

LOIS

"Your boyfriend's got quite the temper, doesn't he?" Keels asks, watching Luke storm out of the room.

I glare at him, eyes wide in shock. The Kennedys had requested detectives from a different precinct because they felt like Misty's connection would somehow sway the investigation. I didn't tell Lucas. I knew how he felt about the Kennedys. "You have no idea, do you?" I croak.

Keels crosses his arms, widens his stance like he's readying himself for a confrontation. But he's a blur. Everything is. I lost my glasses the moment I lost my breath somewhere in the parking lot of the hotel. He asks, "No idea about what, Miss Sanders?"

"Lucas isn't the threat here, sir. Luke's reaction is because he has a heart, not a temper. You heard everything I said, right?"

They don't respond.

"Because you're both looking at us like you don't know us, like you don't understand us. We're just kids, detectives. We didn't *plan* for this to happen. You think Luke's got a temper? Imagine if I were your mother or your wife, your sister"—I glance at Dad—"your *daughter.* And then try to fathom how you would react if you were Luke." I wipe my eyes, a memory searing my brain. "I got my first period when I was thirteen. By then it was just Dad and me. I didn't know what was happening or what to do, and we didn't have the supplies I needed. It was a Saturday; Dad was working overtime so I was all alone. I sat in my bathroom and I called my mom but she didn't answer, not that she'd do anything, but I was *that* desperate. I called Lucy, Luke's older sister, but she didn't answer, either. Then I called Luke. I was in tears by the time he picked up the phone. I was so nervous and scared and awkward. He thought something had happened to me, and he kept insisting he call 911. When I finally told him what was happening, he took charge as if

296

it was something he'd done a thousand times before. He raided his sister's bathroom and packed everything in his backpack and rode his bike over to my house. He sat on the other side of the bathroom door while I—you know—and he read the instructions out loud to me. He kept saying things like, '*This is normal, Lane. Nothing to worry about, Lane. It just means you're a woman, Lane...*'" I speak through the giant knot in my throat. "Lucas is still that same amazing boy he was back then, and up until Saturday night, he'd never laid a hand on anybody. He's the most caring, most gentle person I know. He tucks his little brother into bed every night. Without fail. No matter where we are or what's happening, 7 PM comes along and he's there for his youngest brother. He's there for all of them. It was those qualities in Luke I found in Cooper that made me fall for him in the first place."

The detectives are *listening* to me now, not just hearing me. Mayfield says, his voice weak, "Will you please tell us about your relationship with Cooper Kennedy. In detail?"

I nod slowly, fear of the memories squeezing my throat shut. I twist my hands, look over at Dad. "You can leave, Dad... if you want to."

"Oh, sweetheart." He sits on the bed next to me, his arm around me. "It won't be any harder for me to hear than it is for you to tell. You're braver than anyone I know."

I wipe my tears again and try to steady my emotions. I want to speak with conviction, with heart. And I do. I tell them about how Cooper and I met. How he'd call every day when he was on campus and we'd see each other every day when he was in town. I mention the jealousy Cooper felt for Luke, but how he restrained it. At least at the beginning. Then he started to do strange things like calling me in the middle of the night to make sure I was alone, that I wasn't with Luke. He'd call my work, make sure I was there when I said I would be. He didn't like me talking to guys. Any guys. And I'd never been in a serious relationship before so back then, I thought it was kind of flattering—the jealousy. He got me a car for my birthday, and I found out later that he installed a GPS tracking device in it. He did the same with my phone. When I realized, I was too scared to go home." I look over at Tom. "That's when you found me sitting in my car on your driveway and I wanted to say something, but I couldn't." I go back to the detectives, tell them how whenever I wasn't with Cooper, he stalked me from a distance. He knew where I was at all times. I tried to leave him during winter break. I said it was too much for me, and he promised he'd stop. New Year's Eve, I was alone in a room on a houseboat and I was sick and I was scared and I needed Luke, he'd always been there in the past. So I called his brother's phone because Cooper had blocked Luke's number, and I knew they'd be together. Cooper came down a few minutes after midnight and caught me talking to someone. It feels strange to say "caught me" as if I was doing something so terribly wrong. In truth, I was negligent with Cooper's wants, his needs, and those are the types of excuses I made throughout the entire relationship. I tell the detectives that New Year's was the first time Cooper hurt me physically. He pushed me against a wall, and I collapsed to the floor and my glasses went flying. When I went to reach for them, he stomped on my hand and then stomped on the glasses and he picked me up, his hands tight on my upper arms. He shook me and yelled and shook me some more until I puked all over him, all over myself. He made me clean it up while he went back to the party, to the loud music that hid the evidence of what he'd done to me. I had bruises on my upper arms, but I didn't tell anyone. I hid the truth, hid my shame, hid my guilt. Then I tell the detectives about how when school started again, things got worse. Cooper was under a lot of pressure. *Again with the excuses.* He had to maintain a certain GPA and his classes were killing him and his training was just as bad. His dad was *threatening* to kill him because his dad's a monster, another excuse, and he started taking amphetamines so he could stay awake, stay alert, but they just made him crazy, paranoid. He became manipulative and vindictive and destructive, and every weekend I spent with him felt like I was walking on eggshells. He'd always go for the places I could cover up: ribs, back, hips… and he knew I wouldn't tell. He used my weakness to his strength. I tell them about the time Cooper took me to a business dinner with his dad and some of his clients and Cooper's dad kept talking down to him, saying that he would amount to nothing and running track wouldn't earn him a degree and Cooper got so mad, so *livid*, and we got in his car and he pulled over in an abandoned parking lot and smashed my head against the window. It came out of nowhere. I screamed, and he covered my mouth and then he forced me to…

I stop there.

At the point where Dad releases me, and all I feel is shame.

Then I hear him cry and I look up, but it's not him, it's Tom. Swear, there's nothing sadder than watching a 6"4' man hunched in a seat, his head in his hands, shoulders bouncing, sobs slicing the air.

Mayfield asks, "He raped you?"

My eyebrows pinch, confusion swirling. "No. I mean, I was his girlfriend and I was scared, so I just let him..."

"Oh, Laney," Tom groans, rubbing his face. He looks up, his eyes locked on mine. "Why didn't you come to me, sweetheart? I understand if you were afraid to tell your dad or Lucas, but all these years you've been like a daughter to me. You could have told me."

I break down. *Shut* down. It hurts too much. Physically and emotionally. I grasp onto Dad, use his shirt to catch my cries. "Can we please stop now? I don't want to do this anymore." I look up at him, speak through my sobs. "Please, Dad, make it stop?"

LUCAS

I didn't kill Cooper.

Instead, I go outside and get some air, away from the bullshit media and the bullshit cameras and the bullshit reporters who have nothing better to do than wait around a hospital, digging for their next fucking angle. I go far away, more than a hundred yards, so I don't break my bullshit restraining order.

I find a bench under a tree. I sit. I think...

The glasses.

The clothes.

The blocking me from her phone.

The distance.

"We're still together. It's just hard... you know..."

"There's so much I want to tell you..."

He was controlling.

Unpredictable.

"I managed to escape—"

"I'm so tired, Lucas. Of everything."

"I'm finally free of him."

The darkness during sex.

"Be gentle with me, Lucas."

LUCAS

HOW DID I not see this?

How did I not save her?

"IS THIS SEAT TAKEN?"

I look up to see a familiar face. Mrs. Kennedy's standing in front of me, huge sunglasses covering her eyes. She clutches her purse as if I'm here to steal her fucking money, as if she's not the one who approached me. *Fuck you.* "No, ma'am. Seat's free."

She sits next to me, crosses her legs. "I didn't know kids still say ma'am."

I look straight ahead. "My mother taught me manners." She taught me a lot of things, like not to beat on women. *What the fuck have you been teaching your son?*

I'm sure she knows who I am, but she's faking it, and I'll play her fucking game and I'll win because I'm sick of fucking losing. My mom. My freedom. My perspective. My goddamn *mind.*

She pulls out a stick of gum from her purse and offers it to me.

"No, thank you."

We're not friends. We don't share gum. *What the hell does she want?*

"So polite," she mumbles.

"Like I said," I lean back on the bench. "My mother taught me manners."

"It's Katherine, right? Your mother?"

I hate this so much. I hate that my mom's name left the mouth of *his* mom. I start to leave, but she says, "Lucas?"

I sigh, sit back down. "With all due respect, Mrs. Kennedy, what do you want from me?"

"So you know who I am?"

"I saw you at the hospital the night your son tried to kill my best friend."

"I thought she was your girlfriend."

I face her. "She's *both.*"

She nods, smiles like she has a right to. "I met your mom once, at this charity event. She was dancing with your dad, and I remember looking at them and being so jealous. They loved each other very much."

"Love," I correct.

"Excuse me?"

300

"They *love* each other. You said *loved*. Love doesn't die just because one heart stops beating. When you love someone, you have the same heartbeat and it's still there, just not as strong. So no. There's no *loved*. Dad still *loves* her."

She stares at me a long moment, longer than I'm comfortable with. Then she looks away, tries to hide her emotions. "Like you love Lois?"

"Lois *is* my heart, ma'am."

She sighs, picks at imaginary lint on her *Fuck You* money dress. "You're lucky."

I'm lucky? My girlfriend's been shot multiples times and I may be going to prison. Fuck you, again, ma'am.

She adds, "I've never known a love like that. I met Lance in high school. He was a lot like Cooper. Popular and handsome and driven."

I don't care.

"The first time Lance laid a hand on me I was seventeen. I didn't have friends or family to run to, so when he said he was sorry and that it wouldn't happen again, I believed him. Through the rest of high school and college, it kept happening. Then I found out I was pregnant and I thought it would change things. We got married and had Cooper and for a while, it was perfect."

I still don't care.

"Cooper was four the first time Lance hit me in front of him. He ran away, up to his room, and locked himself in his closet. He was so scared, so petrified, and when he saw me and the damage his father had done, he started wailing. I should've protected him from it. I should've left Lance, but he was always there, a constant reminder that without him, I'd have nothing. Even if I left, he'd fight for custody of Cooper and I couldn't let that happen. I couldn't let him control our son. But without me realizing, he did it anyway. He wanted to mold Cooper into him, and he succeeded. He put so much pressure on that boy... and Cooper—he didn't know any better. That's what *love* was to him." She looks away, wipes her eyes, and continues, "I knew about Cooper's amphetamine addiction and I didn't do anything about it, and when Lois called me from the hospital, my worst fears came true. Lance had created an identical version of him."

"Did she tell you what happened... at the hospital?"

She doesn't answer me, instead, she says, "Cooper loved Lois so much and when she wanted to leave him, he lost his way. He wasn't himself that night, Lucas, you have to understand."

"No."

"*No?*" she asks.

"No. I don't '*have to understand.*' I've sat here and listened to what you've had to say, and it's not good enough and it's not going to change anything. He was still there, he pulled the trigger, *four times*, and she's lying in a hospital bed minus a spleen with two bullets still inside her and *you* want to see justice. You want *me* behind bars because I did something someone should've done to your husband a long time ago. If you came here to try and make peace with yourself, I hope it helped. But there's no peace for me, and there's definitely none for Lois."

She nods, removes her sunglasses so she can wipe her tears. I don't miss the scars, the darkness and swelling around her eyes, and for a moment, I feel for her.

Really.

Truly.

She asks, "Do you regret what you did?"

I think about the answer long and hard. "Every time I close my eyes, I see Laney. I see her lying on the ground in her blood-stained dress, and I didn't realize it at the time—I thought she was clutching her chest, clutching for breath, but she was holding on to this necklace my mother left her. I keep going back to that moment, and I try to come up with all these different scenarios. Try to think of other ways I could've handled it, and I *can't*. I just can't." I take a breath, look down at my hands, picture her blood on them. "I'm not sure if I'll ever regret what I did, but I regret hurting *you* in the process." I look up at her, meet her gaze. "I have five little brothers, Mrs. Kennedy. The youngest one's seven, and for some reason, he looks at me like I'm some kind of hero, and now it's up to my other brothers to try to explain why his hero is going to prison." I stand up, face her. "I'm sorry that you had to experience all that you've been through, ma'am. And if my mom were alive, she'd want me to open up my home to you, somewhere safe you can go if you get scared. And so the offer is there if you need it. But the excuses have to stop. For you, for Cooper, for *Lois*."

Then I head back to the hospital, make my way to Lane's room. I ignore the stupid flowers and stupid gifts and stupid police protection just outside Cooper's room and prepare myself to face-off with the detectives, but just before I open the door, my phone rings.

It's Chapel Hill.

UNC.

They've pulled my scholarship.

CHAPTER THIRTY-SEVEN

LUCAS

THERE'S this nightmare I have, only it doesn't just happen at night. It happens every time I close my eyes. I'm on my knees and she's in her periwinkle dress, limp in my arms. She offers me *those eyes* and that's when I get handcuffed, dragged away, and then I'm in a jail cell, bright orange jumpsuit, and in the middle of my cell is a giant hole in the ground, six feet deep, and in my dream, I always tell myself not to look because I know what's in there, *who*'s in there. Still, I look, and there's Lane, her arms crossed at her chest, and *those eyes* are closed and covered with crochet flowers.

"That's a little morbid, Luke," Laney said after I told her about the nightmare, the visions.

It's now been six days and twelve hours since the incident that's been dubbed *The Night the Town Turned Red, Blue and Black*. Three days since Cooper left his hospital room with a few broken ribs, a busted jaw and some bruising that won't be going away any time soon. But, at least he's not there, meaning I can see Laney whenever I want. It's also three days until my trial. My lawyers say I'm lucky I'm not being charged with attempted murder, but given the evidence (Logan's video) and the circumstances, Cooper with a gun (premeditated) and me with my anger, it would be easier for the Kennedys to get what they want on the assault and battery charges alone. The Kennedys had requested a different judge, someone who will see the *facts*, aka someone who accepts their *Fuck You* money. Their request was granted, so there are no doubts I'm going away. The question is for how long.

I WATCH Garray's car come up our driveway, then focus on Lachlan running around the front yard in his underwear, the sprinklers on, and I wish his laughter had the same effect as Laney's—that it shifted reality—just an inch. Because I don't want to be sitting on the porch steps looking at my baby brother and taking in the sight and sound of him, not knowing how long it'll be until I see this again, and I'm numb and I'm tired. So fucking tired.

Garray steps out of his car with a bunch of flowers and stops in front of me, assesses me. Without a word, he sits next to me, places the flowers between us. "I don't even know what to say," he mumbles.

"There's not a lot you *can* say."

Lachlan's standing in front of a jet of water, drinking it in.

"Lachy, don't do that, bud. The water's from the tank, it's not clean."

He spits out the water, laughs as he jumps through the maze of sprays.

"I heard about the trial coming up," he says. "I'll be there, Luke, not that it matters. And I spoke to Principal Jenkins; he assures me that you and Lois are going to graduate regardless."

Senior year.

Graduation.

It feels like a different life.

He asks, "How are Leo and Logan doing?"

I sigh. "Leo's locked himself in his room. He refuses to talk about it, refuses to see Lane. And Logan's going to therapy every day. It was tough on him."

"Yeah," Garray says. "They have that at school. The therapy. And now they're installing metal detectors at the doors and adding a security guard. It didn't even happen *at* the school."

I nod, but it makes me furious that the actions of Cooper Kennedy have set off a chain of events at a school where my brothers will have to attend. I drop my gaze, look down at the flowers. "Thanks for the flowers," I say.

He laughs once. Forced. "They're not for you. They're for Lois. I tried to see her, but they won't let anyone in the room that's not on the list."

I face him, eyes narrowed. "The list?"

"They have a list at the desk."

"Oh."

"You didn't know?"

I shrug.

Brian calls, says, "Can you get to the hospital? I need your help."

My heart pounds, and I look at Lachlan, look back at the house where Leo's in his room, refusing to deal with reality.

Garray nudges me, somehow knowing what's going on. "I'll watch him," he says. "Go."

I cover the phone. "Are you sure?"

"We'll have fun."

I tell Brian I'll be there soon and hang up. Then I tell Lachlan that Garray's going to hang with him for a while. Garray spins on his heels and starts chasing Lachlan around the yard, through the sprinklers, fully clothed.

"You have a dumb name," Lachlan cackles.

"Sure, *Latch-Lan*."

"It's not *Latch-Lan*. It's *Lock-Lan*, Dumb Name!" He laughs again, harder and louder, and Garray picks him up, throws him over his shoulders.

I get in my car, look up at the house and wave to Leo watching us from his window.

He doesn't wave back.

He never does.

IT TAKES six minutes and fourteen seconds to get from my house to the hospital, less than it took from the hotel in an ambulance, sirens and all. I rush through the doors, now clear of media (because who cares about the girl who was shot by the rich kid, right?) and go straight to her room. Brian's pacing, Lane's sitting on the edge of her bed, her bags packed next to her. Her arms are crossed, her gaze distant. I speak to Brian, "What happened?"

He says, "She's adamant on going home."

"But the nurses said—"

"I know, Luke. I can't get through to her. She's just been sitting there, *stubborn* as hell."

I crack a smile. "Like old times, huh?"

But he doesn't find it funny. "I need to go for a walk, clear my head."

He leaves, and I look at Lane again. She hasn't changed positions, hasn't stopped staring at the floor. I squat in front of her, take her hands in mine. "What's going on, babe?"

She doesn't look at me when she says, tone flat, "Do you know it costs us two grand a day just to be here? That doesn't even include the surgery or the medicine or the *fucking* rehab I'm going to need for my leg."

"I'm sure your dad's just relieved you're okay, Lane. All that stuff isn't important right now."

She shakes her head. "We can't afford to pay that, Luke. Not now. Not ever. And you..." Her eyes finally meet mine, so sad, so distant. "Why didn't you tell me about UNC pulling the scholarship?"

I sigh. "Because it's not important, either."

"It *is* important," she grinds out, her eyes filling with tears. Her jaw tenses, her breaths becoming harsher and harsher until...

Until she stands up, picks up a vase and throws it across the room. "It *is* fucking important, and I'm sick of you all treating me like this!"

I stand, shocked, look over at the shattered glass. "Lane!"

She shoves my chest, and I fall back a step. "I'm sick of you coming here every day and pretending like everything's going to be okay! You're going to *prison*, Luke. You're going to prison, and Dad has to take out *more* loans!" Another shove. I try to hold her, take her wrists, but she's too wild, too angry, and I let her push me, over and over, her cries getting louder and louder. "I keep going back, keep trying to work out what the hell happened to me! How the fuck did I get here?" She stops pushing. Starts limping around the room. "I've ruined everyone's life, Luke! Everyone's! And I want to go home. We can't afford for me to be here anymore!" She freezes, turns to me, her eyes on mine. "And you *need* to go to UNC! Even without the scholarship, you can still go, right? You can't stay for me! I won't let you!"

"Laney." I try to breathe through the pain. "I'm not going anywhere without you."

"Jesus Christ," a woman says, and my gaze snaps to the door, to Mrs. Kennedy standing there and *how the fuck long has she been here?* How much has she heard? She says, "Lois, you're bleeding."

308

I look back at Lane now sitting on the bed, looking down at her abdomen. The blood seeps through her blue hospital gown onto her hands. *Blood everywhere. Blood everywhere.*

"Lucas, call for a nurse," Mrs. Kennedy orders.

I find what little strength I have left, put one foot in front of the other, find a nurse in the hallway and take her back to Laney's room.

"What happened?" the nurse says, looking between Mrs. Kennedy and me and the broken vase on the floor, shattered, just like my heart. Whoever said the truth sets you free is a fucking liar. It cages you, keeps you locked in your head with no escape.

I don't speak. There's nothing I can say. Nothing I can do.

"Lois," says the nurse. "You've torn your stitches."

"Leave it," Lane snaps.

"We have to sew it back up and stop the bleeding."

"Just smack a Band-Aid on it so I can go home," Lane tells her. "It'll heal fine."

"Is she ready to go home?" Mrs. Kennedy asks, and *why* is she here?

The nurse shakes her head. "Not even close."

I stand by the door, my hands behind my back, look down at the floor.

"I didn't mean it," Lois cries.

"You didn't mean to break the vase?" the nurse asks. "It's okay, sweetheart. We'll clean up."

"No... Luke!"

I lift my gaze.

She's covering her mouth, muffling her cries. "I didn't mean it. I'm sorry."

"It's okay," I whisper. *It's not.*

She reaches for me, winces in pain. So I go to her, take her in my arms. She cries into my chest. I cry into her hair.

"I'm so sorry," she repeats, and I want to take her pain away. "I don't know why I said those things. I'm just trying to make sense of everything and I can't..."

"It's okay," I say, and this time I *mean* it.

"Can he stay?" she asks the nurse. "When you stitch me up?"

"If you're comfortable with him seeing your wounds, I don't see why not."

MRS. KENNEDY LEAVES while the nurse stitches her up again, changes her dressing. The physical scars that'll mar her body will be nothing compared to her emotional ones. Brian returns, his reaction the same as the nurses. "What the hell happened?"

"I lost it," Laney says, woozy from the anesthetic. "I'm sorry, Dad."

"It's okay," he tells her, but he's looking at me, his eyes worried.

A moment later, Lane's asleep, and I explain to Brian everything that happened as best as I can. "I think it was just building up and she needed to get it out and this was her way of doing that."

I motion to the door and he follows behind me. "Is it really costing two grand a day for her to be here?"

He rubs his sad, tired eyes. "That's just for the stay. I'm in over a hundred."

"*Grand?*"

"Welcome to adulthood, son."

"I have some money my mom left me," I offer.

He shakes his head, a man of pride. "I'm not taking your money, Lucas. I'll handle this the same way we've handled everything else."

We stand in silence a moment, a heavy thought hanging between us. It shouldn't be up to him to cover this. "*They* should be paying for this, financially and otherwise," I mumble.

He sighs. "You don't think I've thought about that? But doing that would mean forcing Laney through more hell with the Kennedys. She's experienced enough of that." He pauses a beat, looks away and avoids my gaze. "I failed her, Lucas. I was so wrapped up in my relationship with Misty, I never even saw this coming."

"I was with her," I admit. "I watched that entire relationship form and continue and break down, and I—"

"But I'm her father," he whispers.

"And I'm her best friend. I *let* her go with him that night." I grasp his shoulder, wait for him to look at me. "We're all going to walk away from this with regrets, but it's what we do with those that's going to change her life. And I think, right now, it's important to remember that at least she has the chance to live one."

310

I LEAVE him to stay with Lane, and I go in search of Mrs. Kennedy. I want to know why she's here, what the hell it is she wanted. I find her at the admin desk of the recovery ward, two folders in front of her. She says to the clerk, her voice low, "Are you able to make this one out as if their insurance covered it?"

The clerk nods, and I stop next to Mrs. Kennedy. "What are you doing?" I ask.

She flinches at the sound of my voice. "Nothing." *Liar.*

I look down at the open folders. Medical bills. One for Cooper Kennedy. The other for Lois Sanders. I don't even bother asking how she has access to the file because she is who she is. Instead, I ask, "How much did you hear in there?"

Her hand's gentle when she touches my arm, waiting for me to meet her gaze. "I heard *nothing.* Just like I'm doing *nothing.* You understand, Lucas?"

I swallow the lump in my throat, realization forming. "Yes, ma'am."

"Good." She releases me. "How's Lois? Or... it's Laney, right? That's what you call her?"

I nod.

She smiles. "Like Lois Lane?"

I nod again.

"That's a sweet name."

"My mom gave it to her."

Her grin widens. Then she reaches into her bag, pulls out a pamphlet. "I've done some research into some rehab facilities for *Laney.* The best one is forty-five minutes away, but I figured, you being you, you won't mind driving her."

I take the pamphlet from her, pretend like I'm skimming it as if I haven't done my own research. "Mrs. Kennedy, I appreciate this, but Brian—Mr. Sanders—he can't afford the best. He can barely afford mediocre."

"Oh, it's covered," she says, winks. "By *insurance.* Also, expect to be getting a call from your lawyers about us dropping the charges."

I stop breathing. "I'm sorry?"

She reaches up, cups my face in her hands, looks into my eyes. "I know evil, Lucas. I've stared it right in the eyes and wished for death. Evil people belong in prison. You're not evil. You're everything Lois said you were." She offers me one last smile before walking away.

311

When I sat in the holding cell, I started to question my mother's belief in *fate*. Instead, I wanted to believe in circumstance, in justice. But maybe Mom was right. Because right now, there's absolutely no logical reason why this is happening. "Mrs. Kennedy?" I call out, wait for her to stop and face me. I jog over to her. "Why are you doing this?"

She wipes at her eyes, lifts her chin. "Because I failed my son by not acting, not speaking up, not changing the course of his life." A single tear streaks down her cheek, and she wipes it with the back of her hand. "But it's not too late to change yours. Yours and Lois's. You're both amazing kids, and Lois is lucky to have you."

"I'm the lucky one."

"I knew you'd say that."

"I'm sorry, ma'am. About Cooper. About your husband. You really are a good person."

She drops her gaze, and when she looks back up, she's smiling. "Good is the enemy of great, Lucas. I want to be *great*."

MY LAWYERS CALLED a few minutes after Mrs. Kennedy left the hospital to confirm what she'd told me. The Kennedys had dropped the assault charges.

I wait for Lane to wake up before calling Dad and asking him to come to the hospital. I want them all here. Even Logan and Leo. *Especially* Leo.

"He won't want to," Dad says.

"Make him."

I hang up.

Laney says, "What's going on, Luke?"

"Wait. I want everyone here."

"Am I pregnant?" she jokes.

Brian's face pales. "Don't do that," he says, and I finally find something to laugh about.

LOGAN ENTERS THE ROOM, goes straight to Lane. Every other time he's come in, she's been asleep. "I'm sorry," is the first thing he says. "I should've stepped in—"

"Shut up," she cuts in. "I don't want to hear it. Not now. Not ever. You understand?"

"But—"

"Logan."

"Yeah?"

"Shut up."

"Okay." He chuckles. "You look really pretty, even in a hospital gown."

"Yeah. The pale blue really brings out the color in my eyes." She looks around the room. "Leo?" she asks me.

"I'm here," he says, stepping out from behind Dad, seeing her in the hospital for the first time. He raises a hand, refuses to look her in the eyes. "I miss you," he croaks.

Laney frowns, looks at me. "Can you give us a minute?"

We give them the minute, but the minute turns to fifteen and I'm sick of waiting. I go back in the room to see Laney holding Leo, his sobs catching in her gown. She raises a finger and I go back out, wait some more. Eventually, Leo appears, wiping at his eyes. "We're ready," he tells me.

LANEY SQUEALS when I tell her the news. "So we can be together? You're not going anywhere?" She hugs me tight, and I tell her to be careful—her stitches—but she doesn't seem to care. Her hug is replaced by Dad's, Brian's, and then my brothers. Leo holds me the longest, tells me he was scared, that he didn't know what he'd do without me, and the truth is, I was scared, too, of what I would do without *them*.

I call in another favor from the head chef at Pino's, and he's more than happy to oblige. Everyone knows about the shooting, about Lane, and he offers to make her meals every night she's in the hospital, on the house. I pick up the food, and Lane and I have dinner on her bed, the room light dimmed, and swear it, you couldn't wipe the goofy grins off our faces if you tried. "Are you sad about not beating Lord Voldemort's record?" she asks.

"Voldemort?"

"He-Who-Shall-Not-Be-Named."

I shrug. I haven't even thought about it. Haven't gone on a single run since prom. "Not really. It's petty compared."

"Yeah," she says. "Besides,"—she points to herself—"You got the grand prize right here."

She's crazy.

And I *love* Crazy Laney.

I GET HOME AT 6:59, get Lachlan ready for bed. I asked that I be the one to tell him, so he has no idea. I get into bed with him. "Guess what?"

"You're dumb and I'm not?"

"Well, yeah." I roll my eyes. "But… I'm also not going anywhere."

"No baddy jail?"

"Nope. You're stuck with me until you're thirty, kid."

He laughs uncontrollably, the sound contagious. He jumps on the bed, and I let him. I look around his room, see his shrine dedicated to me, see the trophies, the medals. And a calm washes through me, a vision of my future. I take one more look at the trophies, say goodbye to my old life. A life that never defined me like my family does. Like Laney does.

CHAPTER THIRTY-EIGHT

LUCAS

THE MINIVAN SMELLS like hot dogs and stale socks, and I smile in Dad's direction because he just said, "I'm proud of you for doing this, Luke." I should do more than just smile because I'm *lucky*. Really, I am. And everyone's told me so. Numerous times.

The day after Mrs. Kennedy paid Lane and me a visit at the hospital, two things happened. UNC called, offered me back my scholarship. I told them I'd think about it. The biggest thing, though, was that Lane's lawyers showed up at the hospital, along with Mrs. Kennedy, and they helped guide us toward a decision that would affect Laney's future, her life.

In the back of the van, the twins fight over an iPad, Lachlan licks the window, Logan listens to gangsta rap through his giant Beats headphones and Leo reads. Everything is back to normal. Only, it's not. Because I'm on the way to my graduation ceremony, while across town, Cooper Kennedy's pleading guilty, accepting a plea bargain that puts him away for eight to ten years. The back half to be spent in minimum security where his mom will do everything she can to help *heal* him. He wasn't a bad person, she told us, he's just really troubled. I wanted so badly not to believe her, but he's her son. And truth is, my mother would've done the same.

I SIT in a robe in the middle of a row of chairs, listening to Grace (the valedictorian) relay her speech about what a great four years high school has been, how high school is and will always be the greatest years of our lives, how excited we should all be about our future, how the rest of our lives start *now*. Next to me, Lois settles her head on my shoulder, excused from the alphabetized seating and name calling so I can help her up the steps and onto the stage. She didn't want to use her crutches.

Two days ago, she was released from the hospital under the doctor's advisement, not hers. That night, she and Brian also celebrated their freedom, away from the hospital, away from debt. Their "insurance" covered *everything*.

NAMES ARE CALLED, one after the other, and the families cheer and they clap, and when my and Laney's names are called, we slowly make our way up the steps, shake hands with Principal Jenkins. The cheers intensify, all for Laney, now known by the town as *The Girl Who Got Shot*.

AFTER THE CEREMONY, I help Brian move some bags from his trunk to the minivan. Laney's moving in with me. At least temporarily. She's set on life going back to normal, which means Brian going back to work. I'll be taking her to rehab, check-ups, taking care of her. I called Lucy, asked if we could have the cabin and they use the apartment, just for the summer, to save Lane from climbing the stairs. I also asked if she and Cam could help out with the boys so I can focus on Lane. Of course, she said yes. She's a Preston.

"I STRIPPED the sheets so we *should* be safe," I tell Lane, opening the cabin door for her. "And I filled the pantry, bought everything you like. I got some good recipes online, stuff even I can make. And I brought over all your craft stuff. I figure you can still use your hands so…" I drop her bag by the front door and pat down the couch for her.

"I love you, Lucas," she says, her smile heard in her words. "And I love that you've done all this for me."

"It's no problem."

"But you know what I'd *really* love?" She leans on her crutches, exhausted.

"Rest. Of course. I'll get the bed ready."

She laughs. "Luke."

"What?" I check over her. No *blood everywhere*. "What's wrong?"

"I want you to pick me up, carry me to the bedroom, and I want you to make out with me for, like, five hours straight."

I grin. "Yes, ma'am."

I RUN a finger between her bare breasts, around the dressing covering her wound, down to her panties, and back up again. We made out for a total of five minutes before she wanted me to take off my t-shirt, which of course I did. Then she asked me to take off hers, then her bra, then her pants, and then we made out for another minute more before she winced in pain and I told her we should stop. So now she's lying on the bed, her leg elevated, looking up at me while I smile down at her. "The doctor said we should wait a couple of weeks, make sure everything's healed before we start sexing again," she says.

"You *asked* him about it?"

She shakes her head lazily, worn out from the long, active day. "I think he could tell by the way we were around each other." Her words are slow, drawn out, and I can tell she's losing the fight to fake it.

"You should rest, babe. I'll go start dinner."

She nods, and less than two minutes later, she's asleep.

Once I've prepped dinner and it's in the oven, I go back in to check on her. She's sitting up in bed, and I watch from the doorway as she slowly puts her top back on. "You need any help with that?"

She shakes her head and looks up at me with *those eyes,* and I'm quick to go to her, to kneel at her feet, because I'm *that* guy.

"You need to stop doing that, Luke."

"I'm trying, babe." Honestly, I am. "But it's hard for me. You weren't there—I mean, obviously, you were, but..." I take her hands, look in her eyes. "I came so close to losing you once, to having my greatest fears come true, and I'm sorry that I'm fussing over you like this, and if the roles were reversed, I'd hate it, too. But, Lane, I fucking love you—"

She giggles, cutting me off. "You're so romantic." God, I miss her laugh.

I roll my eyes. "Sorry. I fucking love you, *babe.*"

"Much better."

317

LUCAS

"You ready for rehab tomorrow?" I ask.

She quirks an eyebrow. "You ready for your 4:45 run?"

"Why do I have to do that?" I whine. "It's summer."

"You ran every day last summer."

"But that's because I was on the track team."

"And you'll be on the track team at UNC. Did you call them yet? Tell them you're going?"

The oven timer goes off and I exhale, relieved. "I made a chicken and cheese pasta bake."

AT 4:45 the next morning, Lane's alarm goes off. Mine doesn't. She knew I wouldn't set it, so she set hers instead. *Sneaky Lane.*

"Have fun!" she shouts, and I roll over to my side and face her. "You're mean."

She smiles. "Old times, baby. I want old times."

I DON'T RECALL the last time I'd gone this long without running, and it's not fun. At all. I almost give up halfway through my standard route, but I push on because I know it's important to Lane. When I get back to the cabin, I shower, make breakfast. I take it to the bedroom on a tray and she sits up, puts on her new glasses. "You're the best boyfriend ever," she says, then looks down at the food: juice, yogurt, granola and dry toast. She looks up, nose scrunched.

"You have to eat healthier. No spleen means low immune system."

She frowns. *Those eyes.* "But I've been eating hospital food for weeks and this is…"

"This is mine."

"Thank God!"

I get her tray from the kitchen. Coffee, Pop Tarts and a Snickers bar.

She licks her lips, looks up at me. "I swear, as soon as I'm healed, you are totally getting a handy."

"I can give myself handies, Lane. This,"—I point to her tray of sugar—"totally earned me a blowy."

"You're *such* a dork."

318

"Will you at least let me shower with you?"

"You just had a shower."

"But not with you."

"Luke..." She drops her Pop Tart on the tray. "I have to shower without the dressing and—"

"And I've seen your wounds," I tell her.

"But not lately and they're all oozy and gross."

"Did you miss the part where I told you I love you?"

She sighs. Concedes. I win.

And just FYI, fooling around in a shower is fucking *rad*.

WHEN WE LEAVE for Laney's rehab, Dad and Lachlan (dressed in a police costume) are waiting outside the cabin. "What are you doing, Lachy?" I ask, holding the door open for Lane to hobble through.

Dad answers for him. "He wants to do a sweep of the property, make sure no baddies have been here."

"So cute," Lane says.

I leave the door open for him, tell him to go for it.

Dad says, "Thought we'd swap trucks for a while. Mine's got the bench seat in case Lane needs to have her leg elevated."

"So thoughtful," she says, going over to him. She tries to kiss his cheek, but he's too tall and Dad laughs, bends at the knees so she can give him what she wants.

"Good luck," he tells her. To me, he says, "Drive safe. Precious cargo."

THE REHAB FACILITY is more like a five-star hotel, and Laney doesn't stop looking around, touching everything she can reach. Alfie and Roger—the two male doctors in their mid-forties who are assigned to us are also the owners of the place, and they assure us that Laney will be a priority with them. Thank you, Kennedys' *Fuck You* money.

The entire appointment is them telling us about Laney's injuries, going through X-rays and other scans, and then telling us what their plan is. There are two bullets still inside Lane, one near her hip, one in her thigh. They were able to remove the one in her abdomen (goodbye spleen) and the one near her knee, but it's the aftermath of that last one which will need the most help. The bullet clipped her kneecap, tore through her ACL. "Do we work on it like we would any other ACL injury?" I ask.

"Yes and no," Alfie says. "It's going to take a lot longer to rebuild the muscles."

"Are you familiar with ACL injuries?" Roger asks me.

I tell them, "My buddy tore his last year. He runs long distance so he was out a while."

"You run track, too?" Alfie asks.

"I used to. In high school." *In another life.*

"You joining the team in college?" he asks.

I look over at the X-rays. "So a lot of wading in water initially, getting it used to subtle movement, right?"

"Right," Roger says. "Do you have access to a pool?"

"We have a lake," I tell them. "But the wounds are still healing, so I don't know about lake water. In the meantime, we can use the facilities here?"

"Doctor Lucas Preston," Laney announces, and the real doctors laugh. *Smartass Laney.*

IN THE CAR on the way home, Laney thanks me for asking all the right questions and knowing what to say. She admits it was all a little overwhelming for her. It was overwhelming for me, too, but while she's focused on life getting back to normal, I'm just as focused on fixing her.

"Are you looking forward to the tryouts this afternoon, Coach Lucas?" she asks.

"Yeah, it should be good," I tell her. "You want me to take you home, or you want to come watch?"

"I want to come. Leo's going to hang with me."

I watch her from the corner of my eye as she sends a text on her phone, a smile tugging on her lips. "I never really noticed how close you and Leo were."

She nods, her smile growing when a response comes through.

"Is that him you're messaging?"

"Yep."

"Did you guys... I mean not that it matters, but did you ever consider... you know?"

"Dating him?" she asks, all Casual Laney like.

"Yeah."

"Only to make you jealous. We had it all planned out, but then it got to the part where we had to kiss in front of you, and the thought alone was awkward enough so we vetoed that idea real quick."

"You had a *plan*?"

She nods, giggles. "I was so desperate for you to notice me standing on the sidelines, waiting for you."

"Funny," I say. "I always felt like you were the star player and I was up in the nose bleeds."

"You know what we are?" she asks, settling her hand on my leg.

I lift her hand, kiss her wrist. "We're idiots."

"The worst kind." She removes her seatbelt just long enough to sit in the middle. She rests her head on my shoulder, says, "Lachy's going to have a blast with all his friends and his big brothers coaching *his* team. It's going to be fun."

IT'S *NOT* FUN. Not at all.

Lachlan introduces me to his friends as his best friend. He introduces Cameron as his *bestest friend*. Traitor.

I'm quick to realize that coaching The Misfits will be nothing like I thought. It'll just be watching over a bunch of seven to eight-year-olds and making sure they don't fucking kill each other.

After three weeks of rehab and appointments and cooking and cleaning and taking care of Laney *without* sexing her, The Misfits are born, and the name doesn't do them justice.

"Quit eating crayons on the field, Bug Eyes!" Cameron yells, wearing the same uniform as the team—white and red and blue, the colors of the Preston Construction's logo.

"Stop peeing in your mitt!" Lincoln shouts.

"Yeah," says Liam. "Stop peeing in your mitt!"

The back of the twins' jerseys says: *Twin 1* and *Twin 2*. Cam's says: *Best Coach*. Mine says: *Bestest Coach*. Laney designed them. Clearly, *I* ordered them.

CHAPTER THIRTY-NINE

LUCAS

"Is that everything on the list?" Logan asks Laney, walking toward the checkout at the grocery store.

Lane sits in a wheelchair while I push her around. She hates the chair but the crutches are starting to bruise her armpits, and we both knew we'd be in the store a long time. She wanted to make The Misfits snacks for their game later in the afternoon, and when Laney makes anything, it has to be perfect and slightly over the top. I told her sliced oranges and water was the norm. She's baking them cookies.

"I think so," she says, her gaze shifting from the cart to her list, tick, tick, ticking off items.

"I can come back if you've forgotten anything," I say, because I know how important it is for her to do this. It's not as if she has a lot of anything else going on, and I can tell she's starting to go stir-crazy.

Logan starts loading the items from the cart while I get out Dad's company credit card—part of his sponsorship deal. That's when we hear two women ahead of us gossiping about *that Kennedy kid* and the *builder's daughter* and *The Night the Town Turned Red and Blue and Black*. I look down at Laney, but she's looking down at her hands. "That poor Kennedy kid," one of them says, "he must've been so lost to do something so horrible."

I clench my jaw, my fist. I start to speak, but Logan beats me to it. "That *poor Kennedy kid* tried to kill my brother's girlfriend, his best friend, our sister from another mister, lady!" he shouts. I *should* tell him to stop. I don't. He adds, "Now hurry up and buy your super-sized tampons and twelve-inch dildo and shove them up your ass!"

Swear, the look on her face is worth listening to her bullshit. She looks first at Logan, then to me. She ignores Lane sitting in the wheelchair, the aftermath of that *poor Kennedy kid*. "You Preston punks!" she scolds, aghast. I smile up at her, insist I pay for her groceries. Kill her with kindness and *her* guilt. Once her bags are packed and in her arms, Logan calls her a whore and Laney finds her voice. "Have a phenomenal *fuck you* day, bitches."

Logan cackles, high-fives her. I tell her she just earned a handy, and she high-fives me, too. And that's what life is like in our small town: *The poor Kennedy kid, the builder's daughter, and the Preston punks* — the topic of all gossip. But gossip is like dust, floating in the air, temporarily marring the things it lands on. It's not forever. It's not *us*.

———

"HEY," Cameron says, stepping beside me as I keep an eye on the game.

"First base is that way!" I yell, pointing to the base. "You're running to third! Come on, boys!"

"Yeah! Come on, boys!" Lachlan shouts, hitting the ground with a bat. "Remember, righty tighty, lefty loosey!"

"That doesn't even make sense," Lincoln tells him.

Cam shakes his head, lowers his voice. "It's true, though. Lucy's definitely not tight anymore."

"Dude!" I turn to him. "That's so wrong."

He shrugs. "So I was just walking past Bug Eyes and Freckle Face and Snot Eater's moms—"

"You *really* need to learn the kids' names, man."

He scoffs. "It's hard enough for me to remember all *your* names. I think I'm doing pretty well."

I go back to watching the "game."

He says, "They were talking about Kennedy's mom."

I ignore the twisting in my gut at the mention of his name. "What about her?"

"Apparently she's here."

I face him. "Where?"

He points to Lane sitting in the stands wearing the team jersey. She mentioned she felt left out so I ordered her one. The back of hers says: *Lucas Preston's*. Sitting next to her is a woman I hadn't seen since before Lane left the hospital.

"Snot Eater's mom said they've been sitting together, laughing and talking for half an hour. Is it her?" Cam asks.

"It's her," I confirm.

"What the hell is she doing here?"

"I have no idea."

The umpire calls the game, and Cam and I both whisper, "Thank fuck." Then we gather our shit, gather the kids who belong to us. He takes the gear and my brothers to the minivan while I make my way toward Lane. She stays seated, Mrs. Kennedy stands. "Hi, Lucas," she says, her voice soft. "Your team definitely has... potential."

"I don't know if potential is the right word," I tell her, but I'm looking at Lane who's looking down at her hands. "Mrs. Kennedy, you mind if I have a minute with my girl?"

"Sure," Mrs. Kennedy says. "I'll be down by the dugout."

I wait until she's no longer within hearing distance to sit next to Lane. "That was a little rude, Luke," she tells me.

"What is she doing here? Is she giving you a hard time?"

"No." She scoffs, shakes her head. "She's not like that."

"So what did she want?"

"She wanted to thank me. And *you*."

"For what?"

Laney faces me for the first time since I sat down. "For giving her the courage to leave her husband. She gave him the divorce papers a couple of weeks ago, and he signed off on it. He's leaving her the house and leaving town."

I nod slowly, look over at Mrs. Kennedy standing by the dugout, wringing her hands as she watches us. "I'm happy for her."

"Me too," Lane says, then taps on my arm. When I look back at her, she's frowning. "She doesn't have anyone, Luke. Her son's in—"

"I know where he is, Lane."

"And now her husband's gone and I'm her only real friend."

"You consider her a *friend*?"

Her gaze drops. "You know, when I spent that week in the hospital in Charlotte, she wasn't just there to pay the bill. She stayed by my side the entire time. She never left. Not once."

I sigh, take her hand in mine. "Babe, I *want* to like her. Really, I do. And I've *tried*," I tell her truthfully. "But she *knew* what was going on with you, and she should've told someone."

She shrugs, her eyes filling with tears. She's quiet for a long moment. Then: "I should've told someone, too, Luke. But you don't understand that *fear*." A sob escapes her, breaks my heart. "That fear chokes you. Silences you. And I want so badly to find a way to explain that to you, but I can't. And with her—I don't need to. She knows. She's lived in that fear for so long."

I grab her crutches, hand them to her. "Come on." Then I help her down a few steps and toward a waiting Mrs. Kennedy. I say, "I'm sorry for being rude earlier, Mrs. Kennedy."

She smiles. "Vivian, please."

"Vivian." It's strange—how knowing her name, saying it, separating it from the part that darkens her—changes the way I see her almost instantly. "We're having a cookout tonight—my family and Lane's. It won't be anything fancy, burgers and hot dogs, but I'd like it if you came."

She looks between Lane and me, unable to hide her uncertainty. "Thank you for the invitation, but I'm not sure that I'd be very welcome."

"You will be," Lane assures. "Luke's family doesn't just open up their home, they open up their hearts."

LOIS

I have the greatest boyfriend in the world, and I don't just say that because I've experienced both ends of the spectrum. I say it because it's true, because there aren't many guys around who are willing to sacrifice so much not just for me, but for his family. Who has a heart larger than the world, who spreads his love as if it's never-ending, and maybe with him, it is. "Go long," Luke shouts, football in his hand. The twins run farther away from him, shoving each other and laughing as they do.

"Luke's got a good arm," Misty says, joining the "grown-ups" and me at the table while Tom works on the grill close by. "He ever play?"

"He's played everything and been good, too," I tell her. "But when he started to get scouted by colleges for track, he cut out the rest and focused on that."

"Has he made a decision about UNC yet?"

I shake my head.

Tom says, "You know Luke. He does everything in his own time." It's true. He does.

"All these kids are yours?" Vivian asks Tom.

"All but that one," he says, pointing to Cameron sitting under a tree, Lucy in his arms. "I unofficially adopted him when he was fifteen. Eats all my food, takes up all my daughter's time."

"But they're married now," Dad says, doing his best not to make Vivian feel like an outsider. But it's hard for him. I can tell. He carries a lot more hate than Luke does, he's just a lot better at hiding it. "So now he's Lucy's problem."

Tom chuckles at Dad's comment, then levels his features. "I don't think I could've asked for a better boy for my only daughter. He's been her strength when I couldn't be."

Dad smiles, clinks his beer with Tom's. "I know that feeling."

I look over at Luke, now wrestling on the ground with Lachlan and the twins while Logan approaches, water pistol filled and aimed. Lachlan sees him, stands up, his arms crossed. He shouts, "No guns around Laney!" and swiftly takes it from Logan, throws it as far as his little arm can. My heart sinks and Logan looks over at me. "Sorry," he mouths. I shake my head. *It's fine.* And also really, *really* sweet. Luke's alarm goes off on his phone sitting on the table, and I call out to him. He approaches quickly, picking up Lachlan on the way. I show him his phone and he kisses my cheek, gives Lachlan to Misty. He runs to his truck and returns a few seconds later with his backpack. Then he sits next to me, his little notepad and all my pill bottles set out in front of him. I get a napkin, place it between us while he goes through his notes, sets out my meds. I don't take as many painkillers as I used to, but they made me groggy, unaware, and when Luke noticed, he made it his mission to take over. He places four pills, all different colors, on the napkin and slides it over to me along with a glass of water. "Wait," he says, checks his notes again, "Yeah, it's right. Go ahead."

I down the pills, notice Vivian watching me, sadness, sorrow and regret unmasked in her features. "The medication you need— it's all covered by insurance, right?"

327

I nod. "As long as we get them from the hospital pharmacy, it's covered."

"Is it a hassle for you to go there? Is there a different pharmacy that—"

"It's no problem," Luke cuts in, offers her a heart-stopping smile. "The service there is better anyway."

I squeeze Vivian's hand resting on the table. "Please don't worry," I say, my voice low, words only for her. "I'm doing well. I'm happy."

"Good, Lois." She holds back her tears. "That's all I want."

"And you?" I ask. "Are you happy?"

She looks around, takes in the joy that only the Preston family can bring. "I'm getting there."

LATER IN BED, Luke massages my injured leg. "So you and Vivian got pretty close, huh?"

"Yeah, we did."

"Even before Charlotte?" he asks. "It just seems like it was more than just a week spent in a hospital, but if you don't want to talk about it, I understand."

I watch him a moment, watch him focus on my leg and not much else, and I wonder how much to tell him, wonder which parts will be too much for him to handle. "We spent a lot of long nights cleaning each other up after..." *After the Kennedy men did their damage.*

Luke nods, his hands slowing, his throat bobbing with his swallow.

"But in Charlotte, it was different. We didn't have to whisper or tip toe around our feelings. They weren't there so we could be open about everything. I told her about you."

He looks up now, his eyes meeting mine.

"I pretty much spent the entire week telling her about you and me, how we met, your family. It was the only thing that could cheer me up, take my mind off everything that was happening."

"What did you tell her about me?"

"I told her that you were a man of strength and honor and sacrifice. I said that I'd been in love with you since we were eleven, since I saw you coming down your porch steps in your Superman t-shirt and your glasses. And I said that I made a mistake keeping my feelings for you a secret for so long." A smile tugs on my lips and I try to restrain it, but I can't. Because Luke's looking at me in a way I spent years *hoping* he would—as if the world begins and ends right where our hearts connect.

He stops massaging my legs, lies down beside me and kisses me once. "And what did she say to that?"

"She convinced me to go home, to not hold back my feelings anymore, to let you love me and to love you back. And now we do. We love hard, love fierce, and love *right*. And we're learning, Luke. Always learning."

CHAPTER FORTY

LOIS

I'M FINALLY off the crutches (yay)!

But I'm still doing rehab (boo)!

And I'm still limping around (bigger boo)!

The therapists at the rehab clinic say that it may always be the case, at least a slight limp, because of exactly where the bullet went through my knee. But my hip is better—I shouldn't feel any long-term damage from that. Also, I'm seeing a different type of therapist once a week. Well, Luke and I see her together. It kind of happened by accident. Logan and I were in the store, and a woman stopped him in front of the cereal aisle and asked him how he was doing, said she hadn't seen him in a while. Swear, I thought Logan was going through some weird *milf* phase, and I almost shouted "Pedophile Alert!" It turns out she was his therapist. At least, that's how he introduced Lily to me, his gaze lowered, cheeks red. He was embarrassed, I could tell. He told me later that after the shooting, he had seen her quite a bit. I didn't know that it had affected him as much as it did, and we spent most of the afternoon talking about it. "It helps to talk," he said. "Even if nothing *feels* resolved, getting it out there makes a huge difference."

I asked for her number, made an appointment to see her the following week. At first, it was to show that Logan had nothing to feel embarrassed about, but he was right, getting it out there helps so much. "I've been having these dreams," I told Lily in the first session, Luke next to me, holding my hand. "They aren't morbid like Luke's, but they're not really dreams, either. They're more like visions. Like flashbacks."

"Of the shooting?" she asked.

I shook my head. "Of the things he did to me before that."

Luke squeezed my hand tighter, not out of comfort, but from anger.

I told Lily, a sob caught in my throat, "I have trouble understanding how it is I let myself get into that situation. I've always thought of myself as a confident person, strong-willed and determined." I let the tears fall, and Luke put his arms around me, kissed my temple. "I don't know how I became so weak around him. How I let him do those things, how I let it—"

"It's not your fault," Luke cut in.

Lily raised her hand, smiled at him. "It's extremely important for Lois to get this out." And it was. It was exactly what Logan said. Talking helps. So I told her more about how I felt, not so much about the beatings or the shooting, but how I felt about *me*. Luke listened, and he learned. *Always learning.* And at the end, I said, "And I think it's important for Lucas to be here so he can hear it all, so he can deal with his feelings about what happened. I worry that he'll carry that anger, that fear, for longer than necessary. And I want us to help each other deal with those feelings."

Lily looked at Luke, then at me, back to him. He sighed. "I try hard not to show my anger to Lane—*Lois*— because I don't want her to think she's done anything wrong, but at the same time, my anger is justified. That asshole did *horrible* things to someone I love, multiple times, and I'm not going to apologize for the way he makes me feel."

It took three sessions for Lucas to understand that by me talking about it, it didn't mean that I blamed myself. I just wanted closure. For me. So I could move on and not second-guess everything I said, everything I did, especially when it came to our relationship— which, Lucas and I agreed—was the most important thing to both of us. "And sexing," Lucas quipped. Lily didn't find it as funny as I did, but... she didn't know him the way I do. No one does.

When we got home that night, he spent two hours showing me how *he* thought I *should* be treated. He was so careful with my body, so gentle with his touch, so open with his adoration both physically and emotionally. I cried when his lips skimmed my scars, when he whispered my name, when he told me he loved me, when he let me experience the pleasure of his mouth, of his fingers, of his determination to love me *right*. And when I was done, he lay beside me, kissed away my tears, and I thought of Dad's words all those years ago:

"You impress people with your mind. With your kind heart and humble attitude. And while you're a beautiful girl, your looks or the way you dress shouldn't be the reason people are impressed by you. And when you're older and boys start to notice you, I want you to remember that. Because if it's only your looks they're attracted to, then they're not the one for you, Lo. You can do better. You will *do better."*

I took Luke's face in my hands, kissed him until I could no longer breathe. "You're the one for me, Lucas Preston."

"ARE you sure you're going to be okay?" It's the third time he's asked in the past five minutes. Today's the first day he'll be working with his dad. It's also the first day classes start at UNC. He was able to defer a semester due to our circumstances (and also a little pull from Vivian), and it's the first time he's leaving me alone for more than an hour.

"I'll be fine."

"Are you sure?"

"Babe."

"I wouldn't go if Dad didn't need me."

"I want you to go. I want you to have more in your life than just sitting at home and taking care of me," I tell him, bagging his lunch at the kitchen counter of *our* apartment. As soon as I was able to climb the stairs without trouble, we moved back in, and I moved in—*officially.* Dad comes by every second day, like clockwork. I see him more now than I did when I lived at home.

Luke wraps his arms around my waist, kisses my neck. "But I like doing that."

I turn in his arms, look up at him. "And I love you for it."

"What are you doing today?"

"Hanging with Leo. He's taking Vivian and me to that craft store in Charlotte. She can't stop knitting now that she knows how to do it."

Luke's gaze narrows as he steps back, eyes me from head to toe. "Are you *trying* to make me jealous?"

I giggle. "No. But is it working?"

"Is this what you're wearing?"

I look down at my dress. Back up at him. "Yeah. Why?"

"It's a little too cute to be wasted on Leo, don't you think?"

God, he does crazy things to my heart... and other places, a little lower. I pull down the collar of his Preston Construction work shirt, kiss his collarbone, bite it gently.

He moans, cups my ass, squeezes it—not so gently—and I squirm under his touch.

"I know you want me, Lane. Just ask for it."

I do. "Shut up."

He shifts my dress to my hips, lifts me onto the counter, then raises an eyebrow. "So?"

I shake my head, press my lips tight, and he chuckles, nuzzles my neck, kisses me there, soft and slow.

I grasp his arms, try to stay upright. But then he lowers the strap of my dress and frees my breasts from my bra and his mouth is there and I go insane with want, with need, and my hands are on his belt, on his zipper, and I'm releasing him while he pushes my panties to the side, and the front door opens, and I squeal, and Luke says, "Fuck!" and Leo says, "Fuck," and Lachlan, eyes covered by Leo's hand, says, "Are they sexing?"

"Two minutes," I breathe out.

Lucas scoffs. "Twenty-eight minutes."

Without a word, Leo takes Lachlan, and they leave, close the door after them.

I laugh. "Twenty-eight minutes?"

"What?"

"So specific. Do you time yourself?"

"Shut up. And why is the front door unlocked? I told you to make sure—"

"You were out last when you went for your run!" I cut in.

"Was not."

"Was to!"

"Was not!"

"Was to!"

He rolls his eyes. "We're like an old married couple."

I smile.

"What?"

He knows what. "Nothing."

He stands higher, covers me up and adjusts my dress. I do the same for him. His pants—he doesn't wear dresses. He kisses me once. "Have a good day with Leo and Vivian."

"Have a good day at work." I hand him his lunch, and he kisses me again. "I'll miss you," I tell him, and I really will. I've gotten so used to him being around.

He heads for the door, and I start on cleaning the kitchen.

"Hey, Lane," he says, hand on the doorknob.

"Yeah?"

"I'll need a few years."

"For what?"

"For the whole married-couple thing."

My heart lodges in my throat, stops me from breathing.

"Wait for me, okay?"

I nod, unable to speak.

He smiles. "I love you, Lois Lane."

I GET HOME a half hour before Luke does, and when he enters *our* apartment covered in construction dust and dirt, I frown. "How was your day?"

"It was okay," he tells me. "I'm going to jump in the shower real quick."

He returns to the living room five minutes later, shirtless and in running shorts.

"You going for a run?"

He shakes his head, flops onto the floor between the couch and the coffee table, rolls his neck from side to side.

I sit behind him, massage his shoulders, and he moans in appreciation. "Tough day?" I ask, kissing his cheek.

"I don't think I realized how hard our dads work until today."

"Did you hate it?"

"As weird as it sounds, I really enjoyed it. I mean, I'd worked for him before, but it was different today. I was in the mix, you know? It's good, hard, honest work. And when you think about it, we're building a house for a family, and they're going to live and make memories in there. It'll mean so much to them. It's... *rewarding.*"

"So... you *like* working?"

He grasps one of my hands, stops me from working on his shoulders, and turns to me. "I actually wanted to talk to you about that."

"About what?"

"Well…" He moves to sit on the couch next to me and shifts my legs until they're on top of his. He massages my knee, says, "This project is going to be done in a couple of weeks. After that, they're building a new house from the bottom up, and I think I really want to be part of that. See it through to the end. Dad said he could use the extra hands, and I could work around your rehab and our therapy, and it's not like we couldn't use the money."

"I'll get a job."

"Babe." He laughs once, waits until I'm looking at him. "You're not listening to me."

"I am. But this isn't 1950, Luke. I'm not just here to make you lunch and send you off to work to provide for me."

He sighs, his gaze distant. "I don't see the problem with that, Lane. That's how things were with my mom and dad, and it worked for them. The point is I *want* to work. And I *want* to take care of you. I don't want you getting a job until you're fully healed, and even then you don't *have* to. You can go to community college, build up some credits, or not… I mean, you can do whatever you want. You can sit around and knit all day. I don't care. I just want you to do whatever is going to make you happy."

"And this job," I ask, loving him more with every second, "this job is going to make you happy?"

"I think so."

"What about UNC?"

"UNC is months away; we'll cross that bridge when we get to it."

336

CHAPTER FORTY-ONE

LOIS

WE DID CROSS THAT BRIDGE. Lucas deferred for another semester. He was in the middle of building a house, and he wanted to see it to the end, so he did. I got my old job back, working at the movie theater, day shifts only. It was pretty quiet during the day, so I spent most of the time flipping through course catalogs trying to find something that interested me. It's been six months, and I still don't know what to do with my life.

My injuries have fully healed, but like the docs said, I still have a slight limp. That's never going to change. Neither will my undying love for the boy sitting opposite me at the kitchen table, watching me, his eyes worried.

"Why didn't Vivian give it to me?" I ask, looking down at the envelope addressed to Lois Sanders from an inmate at North Carolina Department of Correction.

Lucas says, "She wanted me to decide whether or not to give it to you."

I look down at the letter, back at him. *Tell me what to do, Lucas.*

"Do you want a minute?"

"No!" I say quickly.

"Okay," he says, just as fast. Then he sighs. "You want to go down to the lake? Dad just got a couple of jet skis."

"Jet skis?"

"One of his clients is moving overseas, sold them to Dad real cheap." He starts bouncing in his seat. "They're all down there playing."

"And you want to play?"

He nods, his smile wide, the letter now forgotten. "*So* bad."

"Okay, let's go play."

"Good," he says, standing up. "I got you something." He takes my hand and leads me to the bedroom, where he points to a bag sitting in the middle of the bed.

I rush to see what's inside, and when I do, my heart drops. "Luke." I lift the bikini. "What is this?"

"It's what you're wearing today."

I shake my head. "I can't wear this."

"Why?"

"I'll scare everyone with my scars."

He shrugs. "Don't wear it for everyone, babe. Wear it for me." And I know it's not about the bikini, or the scars, or the fact that people will see them. It's about my confidence, about how he wants me to see myself the way he does. *The way you look at me, Lucas...*

He loves me, wants me, emotional and physical scars and all.

I put on the bikini.

He tells me I'm beautiful.

I believe him.

LUKE WAS RIGHT. Everyone is at the lake. His dad, my dad and Misty, all the kids. The only ones missing are Lucy and Cameron. Lachlan's the first one to notice the scars when we get to the lake. He covers his mouth, his eyes wide. Luke tells him it's rude to stare, and he runs off to Leo, whispers something in his ear. Luke says, motioning to an unused jet ski, "You want to go for a ride?"

I worry my lip.

"I won't let anything happen to you," he says, offering his hand. So I take it, follow him to the end of the dock where we had our first date, and he helps me on, gets on after me. I hold his waist tight as he starts the motor. "Do you know what you're doing?" I ask.

He says, "This ain't my first rodeo."

"When have you done this before?"

He turns to me, smirks, "Dude, I totally vacay in Malibu, like, every summer, *bruh*."

I laugh into his back, and a moment later we're moving, and I'm screaming and the wind and the noise and the speed and the bumps and the waves and the twists and the turns and "I think I'm going to puke!"

"Shit!" He slows the jet ski but it just makes it worse, and so I tell him to go faster. He does. "Close your eyes," he yells. So I do. And it's different like this. All I feel is the sun on my flesh and the wind in my face and Lucas's skin against mine. I rest my cheek on his back, hold him tighter. "You okay?" he shouts.

"Perfect." *Sensations are so much better in the dark.*

Luke gets us safely back to the dock where Logan's waiting for his turn. As soon as our feet hit the ground, Luke says, "You're, like, totally the worst passenger I've ever had, bruh."

I push him into the lake.

Logan asks, "Did you puke?"

"Almost."

Logan hops on the jet ski, waits for Luke to climb back on the dock before starting the engine. Luke says, "I don't like Mean Laney."

I reach up, swing my arm around his neck and pull his face to mine. I kiss his mouth, taste the lake water on his lips. Then I kiss down his neck, to his collarbone. "Don't get me hard in front of my brothers," he begs.

I push my breasts into his chest.

He moans. "Naughty Laney."

"Laney! Laney!" Lachlan calls, his little feet thudding up the dock toward me, Leo following behind him. Luke uses my body to shield his excitement. "Look!" Lachlan shouts, stopping in front of me. He points to a jagged line drawn on in purple marker, right down the middle of his abdomen. "I'm like you."

"Sorry," Leo says, "He wanted to."

I squat in front of Lachlan, run my finger across the line. "What's this?"

He smiles wide. "They cut my shpeen out! Like you!"

I pout. "Did it hurt?"

He nods, motions for me to come closer. Then he cups his hands around his mouth, whispers in my ear, "But I'm better now. *Like you.*"

AS THE SUN begins to set, Dad and Logan build a fire while Tom and Leo go back to the house to get food supplies. I lie across Lucas in a lounge chair, look up at the sky. "I hope we're having hot dogs," Lachlan says, and I glance over at him searching the ground for more sticks to join the eleventy-three he already has in his hands. "Are hot dogs really made of dogs?"

Luke chuckles beneath me. "You've been eating hot dogs all these years, and you think they're made of *actual* dog?"

Lachlan giggles. "Dogs are the shiznit, yo."

Luke shakes his head. "You need to quit hanging out with Logan."

"You work all the time and Leo's always studying, and the twins are... the twins, so Logan's all I got."

Logan shouts, "What's wrong with me?"

Misty joins in. "Pee in a cup lately?"

"Burn!" I yell, and Luke stifles his laugh on my arm.

Tom and Leo return with bags of groceries and a giant cooler. "Beers and wine for Laney and older. Soda for everyone else."

"Oh man!" Logan complains.

"I just want a cup, please and thank you," Lachlan says, standing in front of his father, hands out, neck craned.

"We got cans of soda."

"I want a cup."

"Why?"

"I want to pee in it."

"My bad," Misty says through a giggle. "Sorry."

WE EAT our food around the campfire, convince Lachlan that hot dogs are, in fact, made of cats. To which he responds, "Lucas! No! The pussy-whip!" And Tom and Lucas burst out laughing, and no one understands why. When we're done eating, the twins want to tell scary stories. Luke takes my hand, leads me back to the lounge chair a few yards away. "You've lived your own scary story," he says. "You don't need to hear theirs." And so we lie back down, his arms around me, and he looks at the stars. "That's my mom." He points to the sky. "Right there."

I kiss his cheek.

He asks, "You think she ever imagined that we'd be together?"

"She hoped," I tell him. "She told me so in the letter she left me."

Silence falls between us while I listen to Logan and Leo argue about the way the twins are telling their story. "It doesn't make sense!" Logan snaps.

"Just let them tell it!"

I lean up, smile down at Lucas. I keep my voice low, our conversation just for us. "Are you going to miss this when you finally go to UNC?"

He sits up, forcing me to do the same. Then he rubs the bridge of his nose, but he doesn't speak.

I whisper, "Every time I bring it up, you deflect. Why?"

"It's just not great timing. You know that as much as I do. Your leg is good, but it's not *great*. And we both know you won't keep up with the rehab exercises if I'm not around."

"So you're going to defer *again*? Because of me?"

He doesn't respond.

"It's a great excuse, but it's not the truth."

His eyes finally meet mine.

"I know you, Luke!" I keep my voice low, bite back my frustration. "God, it's like you don't even *want* to go."

His shoulders tense, and he looks away.

"Wait." I make him face me. "Is that it? Do you not *want* to?"

His eyes hold mine for a long time, searching. Finally, he sighs, says, "What do you want me to say? No. I don't want to go to college. I've never wanted to. It wasn't until you brought it up that I even thought about it."

My jaw drops, my head spins. "But... the scholarship. You worked so hard for it."

"My dad has seven kids, Lane," he whispers, glancing at his brothers. "I got the scholarship to help him out, but it doesn't mean anything to me. What the hell am I going to do there? Earn a hundred-thousand-dollar degree that means nothing in the real world? And running a decent time in a hundred-meter sprint isn't a career. At least not for me. I wanted to go for you. That was the *only* reason."

I shake my head, disbelief washing through me. "I'm so confused right now."

"Babe." He settles his hands on my waist, brings me closer to him. "I need you to *listen* to me."

I nod.

"If you want to go—if your heart's set on it, then that's what you'll do. And we'll do it together. I had money saved that Mom left me, and I've pretty much saved every cent I've earned since I've started working. I have enough for your first year and with Vivian's pull there, you can go."

"But that's *your* money." I look up, pray my tears won't fall, and continue to speak in hushed tones. "And what about us?"

"I need to stay here. I need to work so I can start saving for your second year—"

"I don't want us to be apart, Luke. Is that what you want?"

He sighs. "I've already spoken to one of Dad's business associates. The Warden Group just started a company in Raleigh,

341

and I can work there. It's a forty-minute drive if we stay at my apartment near campus. I'll work, you study. But, Lane, we'd have to kick the tenants out, we'd have to cover the mortgage and utilities, and that's all stuff I don't have to worry about here."

"But if you stay here, we won't be together." *I don't understand, Lucas.*

"I'll drive down every Friday night. I'll stay with you on campus all weekend, and I'll make up for the five nights of no sexing. I promise."

"You planned all of this without me?"

"I didn't want you to worry about it."

Behind me, our families laugh.

I drop my gaze, wipe my eyes.

"Hey," he whispers, lifts my chin with his finger. "All I want in this entire world is for you to be happy. And this whole college thing—it's not a decision we have to make right now. You've been through so much lately..." He hugs me tight, kisses the top of my head. "Take some time, take a break, a *breath*, just enjoy life for a while."

I pull back, look up at him. "If you didn't want to go to college, then what was your plan?"

He scoots back and spreads his legs. "Come here," he says, shifting my body so I'm sitting in front of him. We watch our families around the campfire, and he wraps his arms around me, pulls me closer to him. He says, "Even if I made it through college and got some random degree, I still would've ended up here, working with my old man, with yours. This is my family's legacy, Laney, and I'm the first son. It was never pushed on me to take over the business, but it's what I've always *wanted*." He kisses my shoulder. "I get to wear the Preston name every day, and I get to wear it with pride. I get to make people happy, give people a place to make moments and memories, and I get to do it all while being close to my family."

I exhale slowly, taking in everything he's saying, word for word, and I find myself smiling.

"Look around us," he says. So I do, I look at my dad, his girlfriend, look and listen to the joy that only the Prestons can bring. I look at the lake, at the house in the distance, at the perfect night sky. A stillness falls, at the same time a weight lifts. I turn in his arms, see the conflict in his eyes. "How do I give this up, Laney?"

"You don't," I whisper.

He shakes his head. "But I want us to work. More than anything."

"Lucas, *we* don't give this up."

He blinks. "What are you saying?"

I pull out of his hold and fish for the letter that's been burning a hole in my bag. Then I stand up, tug on his hand for him to do the same. "Come on," I say, leading him to the campfire. Conversation stops when I stand in the middle of the circle, Lucas next to me. I drop the letter in the fire, watch it burn, inch by inch.

"What was that?" Dad asks.

"The scars of my past."

EPILOGUE

One Year Later

LUCAS

THE BABY CRIES and Laney rocks him in her arms. "It's okay," she coos. "Uncle Leo will be back soon."

Okay, stop!

I just realized how this sounds.

Rewind.

Laney's little brother cries and she rocks him in her arms.

Much better.

Jesus, people, this isn't one of Lucy's romance novels with accidental pregnancies and almost-death drama.

Anyway...

Leo loads up Dad's truck with the last of his belongings and makes his way over to us. He strokes the baby's cheek. "I think I'll miss you the most, Little Preston."

Preston Brian Sanders was born two days after we celebrated Lachlan's ninth birthday. When Brian had come to us, asked us if we minded his son being named Preston, we all agreed that it would be an honor. Besides, it's not like any of us could call our kids Preston besides Lucy. Preston Gordon is fine. Preston Preston? *Nope.* One day, though, Laney will have to explain to her little brother why her last name is the same as his first name. That day is *not* today. And it won't be any day soon. I'm still a couple of years away from making *that* happen.

Leo goes through the line, one person at a time. First Brian and Misty, who congratulate him, wish him luck, tell him to stay out of trouble.

Then comes Cam and Lucy. After they had graduated a year ago, they moved back into the cabin. Dad recently made Cameron partner (after discussing it with me) and purchased office space above a store, as well as the store below it… a bookstore for Lucy. Her dream.

Cameron's four years at UNC earned him a degree in Architecture. My four years there, should it have happened, would've earned me nothing but wasted time.

Leo gets to Laney, and she hands the baby back to her dad, hugs Leo for way longer than I'm comfortable with. "I'll miss you," she says, and I can tell she's crying.

"I'll be back," Leo assures. "And NC State's only two and a half hours away. You can always come and visit. I expect you to." So yeah, Leo worked his ass off junior and senior year and got into NC State, and we couldn't be fucking prouder of him. He killed the odds, and now he's off to study criminology. Such a badass.

"I'm so proud of you," Laney sobs.

"It was all those reading sessions in the playground that got me here."

"Shut up," she cries, and I hold her, let her cry into my t-shirt because if I don't, she'll drown in a sea of her tears.

Leo shakes my hand. "Thanks for everything."

"I didn't do anything," I tell him. "This was all you."

He shrugs. "You were my role model, Lucas." He smirks. "My favorite big brother."

"I bet you say that to all your big brothers."

Next to me, Logan says, "Does this mean that if I get arrested, you can represent me?"

Leo shakes his head, hugs his little shit of a brother.

"Seriously, though?" Logan asks, pulling back. He dropped out of high school and now I'm his boss. It's rad. Dad wasn't surprised when Logan spoke to him about it. He said it was full-time school or full-time work, and if he worked, he had to get his GED. So Logan agreed. He's actually not *that* bad. In fact, he and Lane and I are all heading to Cambodia next month for three weeks to volunteer for Habitat for Humanity. Dad thought it was a great idea. So great he's now in contact with the NC division to volunteer some of his staff a couple of days a month. Actually, I should say *our* staff. Since Dad realized my dedication to the job, he gave me a promotion, a pay rise and a lot more responsibility at Preston, Gordon and Sons.

Leo moves onto the twins, too busy on their phones to comprehend what's happening. About a year ago, Linc and Liam uploaded a YouTube video about their feelings on bullying, and get this—it went fucking viral. Now they just post random videos on their channel doing all sorts of mayhem, and they get over a hundred thousand hits every time. They're earning a pretty penny as well as multiple marriage proposals daily. *Assholes.*

Lachlan… is still Lachlan. Only now he's started his own collection of medals and trophies for running track. The hundred-meter sprint is his specialty, of course. The little punk's already telling me he's going to break my high school record, and I want him to. But not as much as I want him to destroy he-who-shall-not-be -named's record. It'll be glorious watching a Preston erase that dick from the record books.

Laney rests her head on my now tear-stained chest, her hand on my stomach. We watch Dad and Leo get in the truck, wave a final goodbye before they're off.

"I need to get home to feed Preston," Misty says.

"Which one?" Cam asks, chuckling to himself. He's the only one of us *not* sick of that joke.

Lucy rolls her eyes. "Let's go, Dad-Joke," she says, taking his hand. They walk off toward their cabin while Brian and Misty get into Misty's car.

I look to my left, to my other brothers, but they're already gone. People around here disappear just as quickly as they appear. Then I look to my right, to my beautiful girlfriend who's now the official holder of a realtor license. She's had it about six months, helps Dad and me find properties to buy and flip, and she sells them. She loves her job, almost as much as I love her.

I sigh, happy and content with my life… until…

Until she fucking kicks my shin and points a finger in my face. "Are you cheating on me?"

"What?!"

"Are you?"

"No!" I rub my leg. "What the fuck, Lane?"

She crosses her arms, breathes through her nose. *Crazy Laney.* "Yesterday you left your lunch at home and I went to the site to bring it to you, and the guys said you hadn't been there in over a week!"

Shit.

"Where the hell have you been?" she screams.

"Laney, calm down!"

She does the opposite. "Oh, my God! Do you have a baby mamma?"

I shake my head, laugh loudly. "Babe. Don't ever say baby mamma again."

"Are you in love with her?" she yells.

"I don't know!" I yell back, trying so damn hard to keep it together. "Are you *insane*?"

"Where have you been, Lucas?"

I try to come up with a lie. Quickly. But I can't. So I cross my arms, lift my chin, revert to the age we first met. "I'm not telling!"

"You will so," she grinds out.

"Will not."

"Will so."

"Will not!"

And then she looks at me with *those eyes* filled with tears, and *those lips* now trembling, and she whimpers, and I feel like an asshole. "Baby, I'm not cheating on you."

"So why won't you tell me?"

I tell her the truth. "Because it was supposed to be a surprise."

She frowns. "That you have a baby with another woman?"

"Stop," I say through a chuckle, hugging her to me. "It's so silly that that's the first place you go when you think I'm keeping a secret. There's no other woman and there never will be. You know you're the one for me, Lois Lane." I rub her back, treat her like Lachlan, because right now, she's acting like him. I rear back, look in *those eyes*. "Wait for me by my truck, okay? I'm going to get the keys from the apartment. Just don't leave me. Please?"

She nods.

"Promise?"

She smiles. *I win.* "Promise."

I run up the stairs, quickly grab the keys, and run back out. Then I unlock the truck, help her into the seat. As soon as I'm behind the wheel, she starts on me again. "Are we going to meet the baby? Is it a boy or girl?" At least, this time, she's kidding. *I think.*

I start the engine, head toward the same place I've been going to for the past week without her knowledge.

"Where are we going?"

"Remember our first date? When you kept asking questions, and I told you to stop?"

348

"Yes."

"Stop."

We don't leave the property, but we go as far out as you can get. I park at a clearing on the edge of the lake that up until two weeks ago was covered in trees and bushes. Then I get out, open her door for her. "Are we still on your property?"

"Just," I tell her, helping her down. "I'm going to do that cute thing where I come in from behind and cover your eyes, okay?"

"Okay."

I remove her glasses, pocket them. Then I stand behind her, cover her eyes. They're still wet from her tears, but I ignore them, knowing it won't last long. I walk her through the yard, onto the concrete slab, tell her when to take a longer or higher step and when to duck. Then I let her go. "Open your eyes," I tell her, and she does.

I give back her glasses and she puts them on. "The lake?" she asks. "I've seen the lake before."

"No." I laugh. "Look down and around you."

She looks down at the concrete slab, then the beginning of the outer frame of a house. She turns to me, her eyebrows drawn. "You're building a house here?"

"I'm building *our* house here."

Her gasp is soft, *those eyes* wide. "*Our* house?"

I nod. "It's far enough away from the main house that we'll have our privacy, and I got a permit to build a driveway to the street so we don't need to come in through the main gates. It's three bedrooms, two baths, office and craft room—"

"Lucas," she cuts in, turning to me. "You're building me a *house*?"

I nod again.

Her mouth parts, but she doesn't speak. And *those eyes, those eyes* are staring at me, disbelief and shock and then glee and shock and then, "You're building me a house!" she repeats. "And there's a craft room?" She reaches for me and I take her in my arms. She whispers, "My heart... it's... I think I need to sit down." She's crying now, her tears of pain replaced with tears of joy.

I release her just long enough to grab the cooler from what will one day be the bathroom. I set it next to her, help her sit. She covers her mouth, her eyes locked on mine. She's shaking her head, laughing, crying, laughing some more. "I can't believe you're doing this."

I motion for her to move over so I can sit on the cooler with her. She melts into me, and I hold her close, look out at the lake.

"You're building me a house," she says. Again. She takes my hands. "With these two hands—you're building me a house. Why?"

I shrug, too overwhelmed by her reaction to speak.

"You *have* to take care of me, don't you?"

I look back at her, nod slowly, and I tell her, my voice cracking with emotion, "When I was growing up, I'd see the way Dad treated my mom and Lucy. It was so different to how he treated us boys. I didn't know what it meant then, but I do now. And I know it might sound sexist, and maybe it is, but when I watched Dad, it was like his sole purpose in life was to take care of his girls, and I feel the same way. I nearly lost you once, Laney. I'm not going through that again. I'm going to take care of you for the rest of our lives. No matter how short that might be."

She cups my face, rests her forehead on mine. "I love you so much."

You have no idea, Laney. "I love you, too."

"It's so beautiful out here," she says, and she has no idea that *she's* the beauty out here.

I rear back, kiss her hands. "I don't want to miss out on my brothers growing up, or my dad getting old, or Cameron and Lucy getting... whatever they're getting. My mom and dad envisioned the same thing—having us grow up close to each other. That's why they purchased such large land."

"It's perfect," she says, looking around us.

"The house is small, but we can always extend. I think it's a good place to start," I tell her. "Get married one day." I smile when she does. "Maybe have a kid or eight."

"Eight?" She laughs.

"You know I'm competitive."

"Oh God," she says, her smile wide when she looks out at the lake. Her hands shake as she covers her mouth. "I can't believe this."

I pick her up, settle her on my lap, absentmindedly massage her knee. Her arms wrap around my neck, her head resting on my shoulder. "So what do you think, Lois Lane?" I ask. "You picture yourself living here with me, growing up and growing old? Loving each other *right*?" I kiss her temple. "It may not be the stuff dreams are made of. It's a simple life… but a good life."

"No, Lucas," she says. "It's a *great* life."

THE END

ABOUT THE AUTHOR

Jay McLean is an international best-selling author and full-time reader, writer of New Adult Romance, and skilled procrastinator. When she's not doing any of those things, she can be found running after her two little boys, playing house and binge watching Netflix.

She writes what she loves to read, which are books that can make her laugh, make her hurt and make her feel.

Jay lives in the suburbs of Melbourne, Australia, in a forever half-done home where music is loud and laughter is louder.

For publishing rights (Foreign & Domestic) Film, or television, please contact her agent Erica Spellman-Silverm
an, at Trident Media Group.